The Edge of Madness

The Edge of Madness

MICHAEL DOBBS

ISIS
LARGE PRINT
Oxford

First published in Great Britain 2008
by
Simon & Schuster UK Ltd.

Published in Large Print 2009 by ISIS Publishing Ltd.,
7 Centremead, Osney Mead, Oxford OX2 0ES
by arrangement with
Simon & Schuster UK Ltd.
A CBS COMPANY

British Library Cataloguing in Publication Data
Dobbs, Michael, 1948–
   The edge of madness
   1. Information warfare - - Fiction.
   2. Nuclear power plants - - Accidents - - Russia
   (Federation) - - Fiction.
   3. China - - Foreign relations - - Fiction.
   4. Suspense fiction.
   5. Large type books.
   I. Title
   823.9'14–dc22

ISBN 978–0–7531–8396–0 (hb)
ISBN 978–0–7531–8397–7 (pb)

Printed and bound in Great Britain by
T. J. International Ltd., Padstow, Cornwall

To Helen and Katrina.
Beautiful nieces.

War *is* the continuation of politics by other means.

Chaos *is* the continuation of war, by even better means.

ACKNOWLEDGEMENTS

A couple of years ago my wife discovered an unexpected entry on her credit card statement. Apparently she had suddenly started gambling on the Internet. My heart gave a momentary flutter, but fortunately she was quickly able to establish that this enthusiastic yet sensationally unsuccessful gambler wasn't her. Someone had stolen her details and broken in to her account. And since the card was brand new and had only been used twice before its misappropriation, it was going to be pretty easy for the police to identify the culprit.

Or so we thought. But, alas, we were given many reasons why we couldn't point the finger of blame. Once you step into the cyber world, the police officer explained, nothing is as simple as it seems.

Shortly after that the media began reporting how individuals and organisations within many countries, and particularly within China, were targeting commercial concerns in the West, trying to steal their secrets and raid their vaults. "M15 ALERT ON CHINA'S CYBERSPACE SPY THREAT — 300 BUSINESS LEADERS TOLD OF ELECTRONIC ATTACK — CHINESE ARMY TARGETS BRITISH BUSINESS SECRETS", *The Times* front page roared. Fascinating and alarming stuff, but if they can do that with Barclays Bank and BT plc, I reasoned that they might be attempting to do much the same with United Kingdom plc. I began to ask questions, and was startled with what I found.

It's not just teenage computer geeks and criminal gangs that are involved. Cyber sabotage has spread to the very highest levels. A war is going on out there, being fought very quietly, but with huge intensity. And every one of us is in the firing line. The defence forces of many nations are involved, and none more so than the People's Republic of China. The potential for creating chaos and inflicting damage is enormous, and almost limitless. I was scarcely reassured when a senior politician told me he had listened in committee to much of "this cyber stuff", as he called it, only for him to regard it as no more than an attempt by various security agencies to grab bigger budgets. He rather reminded me of the Duke of Wellington, who confidently predicted that steam trains would never catch on because they would frighten the horses.

Anyway, it all seemed a pretty good starting point for a novel. So my thanks in the first place must go to Scott Borg, the Director and Chief Economist of the US Cyber Consequences Unit who is also a Senior Research Fellow at my old graduate school, the Fletcher School of Law & Diplomacy in Massachusetts. He, in turn, introduced me to Professor Brian Collins, another expert in the field of cyber warfare. I have merely dipped my toe into a vast sea on which these two wise men are master navigators, and I have also taken dramatic license with much of what they have told me, although in all truth it seems difficult to exaggerate the potential for cyber skulduggery. I can only hope that I have done Scott and Brian justice in what I have written.

Dr Chris Greef is another expert who has helped me on all sorts of technical detail. I hope he can forgive me for dragging him from his beloved garden on so many occasions and even interrupting his treks across England.

Old friends from previous books have once again come to my rescue. Jane Chalmers has guided me through the perils of air traffic control, as she did with *The Lords' Day*, and Justin Priestley has once again helped me with all those things that one of my kids calls "the bomby bits". As always, Daniel Caitlin-Brittan at the BBC has offered great encouragement, and he put me in contact with his colleague Robin Mortby. Between them they helped me illustrate the perils of Sammi Shah.

Former classmates of mine from the Fletcher School have played their part. Retired Rear Admiral James Stark of the US Navy has been very patient in answering my questions about the grounding of warships, although I hasten to add that his knowledge is entirely theoretical and he has never grounded any ship, least of all in Iranian waters, although in our school days I remember we sank a large number of beers. My Fletcher soul mate, Andrei Vandoros, has most generously lent me his broad shoulders on which to lean while I scurried to London in pursuit of my researches.

Other old friends and comrades have been equally generous. Gerry Malone has been there to answer my questions about matters Scottish, Tony Insall has guided me through the complexities of Chinese culture, while Tom and Svetlana Hickerson have done the same, and invaluably so, with my musings on Russia — although in all cases the personalities and politics described in this book are entirely my own invention. David Perry, a fellow parent at Chafyn Grove School in Salisbury, has helped me with matters aeronautical. I thank them all.

There are five more friends to whom I want to offer a special vote of gratitude. One is Dame Norma Major, who spent many years living at Chequers and as a result wrote a book about the house that is not only authoritative but simply beautiful. Her book never fails to spark ideas.

Linda Harrison Edwards is a wonderful American lady who bought for charity the name of one of the characters in my last book, *The Lords' Day*. She asked that I name a character after her delightful daughter, Blythe, and I took her name for the US President. I am delighted she has been able to make a return in the sequel.

As for Harry Jones, I rarely try to picture what he would do, think or say without reference to Ian Patterson or David Foster, who know more about him than I will ever be able to imagine.

And finally, as I write these words from the heart of the Wiltshire countryside, I want to thank Elizabeth Everill. A few years ago, she and her husband John not only sold us their house when they retired to Betty's native Scotland, but they have remained in touch, and she has been my inspiration for the legend of the Lady of Lorne. Rachel (my wife and editor-in-chief), the four boys and Bill the cat send her our warmest wishes.

Michael Dobbs
Wylye, July 2008
www.michaeldobbs.com

PROLOGUE

Arnie Edwards was no common or garden adulterer. He'd recently celebrated his silver wedding anniversary and was no longer in the prime of his manhood, but that left him with a sense of sexual urgency which screamed out for satisfaction. So much to do, so little time to do it, and Washington, DC was a town overflowing with opportunity. For a while, Arnie tried to take advantage of them all, wandering away from the kennel every chance he got. Bit of a selfish dog, was Arnie, and the excuses he made to himself were as prolific as they were predictable. His wife had other interests, was neglecting him, he couldn't remember the last time they'd spent an evening raking the embers. What did he expect when his wife was the President of the United States?

Screwing around by the First Laddie, as Arnie liked to refer to himself, required certain precautions. He couldn't bring the business home to the White House, he was unlikely to get away with booking a room at the Four Seasons under some assumed name, and there were always those wretched guys from the Secret Service hanging around. So when Arnie bumped into a clinically enhanced oil lobbyist from Texas named Gretchen who had her own apartment in the rabbit warren of the Watergate complex, the arrangement seemed ideal. He could pop round to her burrow almost any time. And he did.

Trouble was, her burrow quickly came to seem like home for Arnie in a way the White House could never be, and soon he began leaving his razor and toothbrush behind. He knew he was taking a risk, with his reputation, his marriage, even his complimentary tickets to the Redskins' games. Wouldn't do much for the institution of the presidency, either, but when you're lying between the thighs of a woman from Texas who's licking out your inner ear, you're no longer thinking with the right part of your anatomy. Responsibility? Nothing more than a strange word from a crossword puzzle. Six across, thirteen letters — or was it fourteen? By this time he couldn't even count, let alone reason.

The affair soon got to the point that Arnie was determined to continue with it, regardless. He came to that conclusion one evening after he had rolled over onto distressed sheets and felt as though he were twenty-three all over again. He could take it, no matter what the consequences.

Unfortunately for Arnie and many other people, he had no way of knowing that one of those consequences was going to help kick-start a global war.

There were to be no guns in this war, no missiles, no vapour trails stretching like accusing fingers across the skies, none of the obliterating explosions and sudden bursts of darkness you would expect. Not even a scream. There was nothing, save for the tentative striking of keys on a cheap keyboard. Yet make no mistake; this was warfare, it would bring the world to the edge of damnation. And the brilliance of the whole thing was that no one would realize it was happening.

Yet, like all weapons, the system required testing, and the first place they decided to test it was against the Russian nuclear plant at Sosnovy Bor. She was of the same era as Chernobyl, and her four RBMK-1000 reactors were almost identical in design. The grimy cooling towers of the Leningradskaya Atomnaya Electrostantsiya squatted on the shore of the Gulf of Finland, scowling in the direction of the ancient Russian capital of St Petersburg that lay only fifty miles to the east.

She was an old lady, so far as nuclear plants went, and like many old women she creaked and complained. Thirty years earlier there had been rumours of a partial meltdown of one of the cores, but in true *Sovetskii*-style that couldn't conceive of failure, let alone own up to it, the incident was swept aside. Much of the basic plant was all nuts and old bolts that wouldn't have seemed out of place in one of Sergei Eisenstein's black-and-white masterpieces, but after Chernobyl had blown the top off its reactor, the international community had poured millions of dollars into Soviet nuclear plants to ensure there would be no repeat, and Sosnovy Bor had received its fair share. They'd used the funds to upgrade the computers to take away the guesswork, double-banking all the vital equipment and fitting the latest cut-outs and fail-safes.

There was always the problem of the safety culture, of course, getting sodden-brained workmen to take responsibility for fluid spills and dripping pipes rather than wandering off to piss their salaries into the Gulf of Finland, but Rosenergoatom had got round that, not by simply duplicating the important systems but making them entirely separate. So Sosnovy Bor had one set of controls operated by computers, and another operated without computers, a belt-and-braces affair that provided two entirely different means of support and which was regularly tested to ensure both belt and braces remained in prime condition. Only one very small snag in all this: in order to test the safety system, the belt or the braces had to be taken off.

With hindsight it was a pity that they chose to unbuckle the belt in the middle of a harsh winter when the power demand from St Petersburg was at its height, but you don't put off an important maintenance schedule simply because of a little snow. So the control system that *wasn't* based on computers was taken out of service. Only for an hour.

But Sosnovy Bor had only a few minutes to live.

The computer systems had been hacked, been lobotomized, but no one in the plant knew it. So they took the first safety system out of operation. Immediately, the second began to misbehave, allowing temperatures in the reactor core to soar. The process was instantaneous and precipitous, and with extraordinary rapidity the temperatures rose above two thousand

4

eight hundred degrees Celsius. At this point the uranium-dioxide rods at the heart of the core started to melt, but there was no sign of this in the control room. The screens suggested the reactor was behaving itself, because the systems controlling the screens had been tampered with, too. The huge secondary array of lights and dials began to light up and flicker but there was always some small irregularity, an oil leak or an open door, and for a few crucial moments no one paid much attention.

That changed when the build-up of steam in the reactor core blew the pressure-release valves. The noise sent out a scream that made all who heard it freeze with terror. Other alarm systems began to sound. Operators began to shout, to panic. The plant's huge turbines began to shake and shudder. Pipes cracked, seals blew. Inside the reactor, the rising temperature meant that more of the water supposed to cool the reaction was turning to steam, which made the temperature rise still faster. It became a race to disaster.

How close Sosnovy Bor came to the point of overwhelming catastrophe, no one from Rosenergoatom was ever able to ascertain, even with hindsight, but it was at this point in the enveloping crisis that the hackers decided they'd overstayed their welcome and put the instrumentation back to normal. At last the terrified controllers could see precisely what was going on, yet even before they could react, the computers did it for them. At Chernobyl it had been too late, even for this, the melting rods in the reactor core had stuck together, preventing the circulation of water between them and so ensuring the core couldn't be cooled down. It blew the entire lid off, leaving the radiation-spewing inferno open to the air and turning Chernobyl into the destroyer of children. But at Sosnovy Bor, the gods were on their side and, with agonizing slowness, the operators watched the reactor-core temperature begin to slip back down. Russia could breathe again. For the moment.

There was no leakage of radiation beyond the reactor circuit, and none to the outside world, but the rods had melted and it was impossible to deal with them. They never reopened that burnt-out reactor Number Three at Sosnovy Bor, they just locked it up and threw away the key. Russia had survived a great terror, yet for some of those who thought about it there was a still greater terror lurking in the shadows. Despite all the analysis and examination and brutal inquisitions of those officials and operators who might have been responsible, the committee of investigation couldn't find out what had gone wrong. They were blind. Which meant, as they quickly came to realize, that they had no way of preventing it happening all over again.

Wu Xiaoling sat twisting the silken ends of the belt on her gown, overwhelmed with a sense of abuse and uncertainty. She was twenty-six years of age, slim yet profiled, exquisitely so, with remarkably round eyes for a Chinese girl. Something Occidental had swum in the family's gene pool during their days way back in Hong Kong that provided Xiaoling with the allure of someone special, different — not that different was a welcome characteristic in the new China, but that hadn't prevented her from becoming the most favoured mistress of the country's leader, Mao Yanming. Being so close to one so high gave her considerable privileges, but also placed upon her the most awesome responsibility for keeping Mao satisfied. And he was no easy man to satisfy. She had been summoned peremptorily to his private pavilion that was set next to the lake in Zhongnanhai, the protected quarter in Beijing beside the ancient Forbidden City that housed the country's government. As usual she had been met at a side gate to the compound by one of his personal guards who had led her directly to the pavilion, trying to shield her from enquiring eyes, but others knew, of course. Men are such fools; such things can never be kept secret. Even Mao's wife knew, Xiaoling had seen it in her eyes.

Mao had been waiting for her, but it had become immediately apparent that something was wrong. He had spent no time in small talk, had no little gift for her, but had screwed her roughly, brutally almost. Not that it had ever been Xiaoling's role to complain and in truth there was nothing he did that gave her any pleasure. He was a man of the provinces, not sophisticated, not even very clean. The road from his birthplace in Gansu had been long and dusty, and she was glad for the scent of honeysuckle and sweet camphor that filled these rooms and covered his trail. She had learned many ways of giving him pleasure, of distracting him from those avenues he sometimes liked to explore that gave her none, and she was skilled in easing away his cares with fingers whose touch was as light as an eagle's feathers. That was why he talked, and allowed her to steal his troubles from him, yet today he had uttered barely a word, except to give her instruction, and had taken her crudely, in a manner he knew she loathed. Afterwards she had cried quietly into her pillow while he made phone calls. Then he had returned, taking her again, hurting her, as though he were penalizing her and had seen through her wiles and little deceptions. It was as though he knew.

He had dressed and left, instructing her to remain in the outside sitting room, where she now sat tugging in distraction at her silken belt, staring at the ancient calligraphy scrolls hanging from the walls and the large all-too-modern photo-negative image of old Chairman Mao Zedong inside a heavy black-lacquered frame. The picture had two embellished red eyes. They seemed to be staring at her.

Then the door opened. Fu Zhang, one of Mao Yanming's closest personal colleagues, entered accompanied by a guard bearing a tray of tea, which was placed on a small formal table. Fu nodded a silent instruction and the guard left. Xiaoling disliked Fu, he was insidious, cold, a man who treated with contempt anyone who hadn't been with Mao as long as he had. That contempt increased ten-fold for women, for Xiaoling sensed that he saw no role in his life for the other sex. He was the sort who would prefer to sleep with goats, and probably did, yet now he invited her to join him at the table, where he was pouring tea, almost deferentially. Uncertain, hesitant, she exchanged the comfortable cushioned sofa for the hard, formal chair at the table. He invited her to drink. *Pu'er*, green tea, very old, as Mao liked it, with a hint of chrysanthemum.

"I have been asked to tell you that our leader has held you in very high regard," Fu said as she took a few tentative sips. It took her several moments to realize that he had used the past tense. Why? she wondered. She was still gnawing away at the question when, with a rising sense of panic, she realized she could not move. Not her hand, nor a finger. Her limbs were frozen. The tea. The rest of her senses were still active, almost enhanced, her thoughts and sudden doubts scrambling over each other inside her mind, the scent of honeysuckle now almost powerful enough to drown her. And through it all, insistently, she could smell her own fear as with the silken cord of her gown Fu began binding her to the chair, looping it under her arms, tying it behind her, ensuring that she would not slip. Then he ripped her gown wide open, exposing her.

She was screaming inside, but not a sound passed her lips. She could not resist him. For a moment she felt sure he was going to rape her, but no, he was a powder boy, he had no desire for what she had to offer. Then, from a small case withdrawn from his pocket, he produced a knife. A surgeon's knife, hardened, razor-sharp steel that glowed in the sun reflecting from the lake.

Within her mind she wriggled and thrashed, while in the chair she sat as passive as a rag doll.

"You should not have betrayed us," Fu said, his fat lips wriggling like serpents.

Then he started to carve.

"Ling Chi", they called it. The Death of a Thousand Cuts. Its literal meaning was to climb a mountain, very slowly. It was a form of execution practised in imperial China and not formally abolished until 1905, but even then it continued to be used. It involved cutting the flesh from the body in small pieces while the victim still lived, and was intended to be the highest form of degradation. That's why they had decided to use it on Xiaoling. Despite all their efforts they knew they could never completely erase the marks of her existence or cover up what she had done. She had betrayed Mao Yanming, poured humiliation upon him, caused him to lose face, but there would be no sniggering amongst those who knew or might hear of such things because they would remember nothing but the horror of what awaited those who crossed their leader. It was a lesson in terror they could never forget.

Wu Xiaoling felt no physical pain, but she saw her blood flowing thick and dark from the wounds on her arms, her thighs, and elsewhere. As her head dropped she wasn't even able to avert her eyes. She was forced to watch every moment.

In the few months since Sosnovy Bor was pulled back from the edge of oblivion, there had been other mysterious incidents. These didn't occur all at the same time or in the same corner of the world, but a pattern had begun to develop, one that was as yet so indistinct that almost no one recognized it for what it was. Instead of indulging in thoughts of conspiracy, most people put this plague of misfortunes down to incompetence. All the fault of the politicians. It was an easy explanation to accept.

On the north-east coast of America, in the midst of a summer heatwave that was stretching the resources of the electricity grid to its limit, a power line went down. Nothing unusual in that, the lines get struck by lightning all the time. There are always alternatives, other routes that are made to work that little bit harder, so long as care is taken not to overload them, otherwise they cut out, too ... But imagine you have the capability to model the entire grid system on a computer, to simulate it, or steal its software, to copy the codes that control the switching, to check out its weak points and to see what happens when you take out this line, or that line. If you could do that, then you would become its master. Just flick the right switch at the wrong time, and you could get the whole cotton-picking power system to fall apart like a house of cards.

And that's what happened. At a time when the system was under acute pressure from all that air conditioning and beer refrigeration, and with one line down from a summer lightning strike, another line suddenly dropped out. There was no apparent reason for this, no one ever found out why, but soon power lines were tripping all over the place and large swathes of the east coast were being plunged into darkness. There was no undue panic; hell, it had all happened before, everyone remembered the blackout of 2003. America had been promised it would never happen again, of course, those who were responsible for these things had sworn on a stack of Bibles, but it did. Promises were cheap, yet action costs money, lots of it, and time. When the day came that their time ran out, millions of Americans were left to sit in the dark and sweat.

There were other incidents. The Pentagon, with twelve thousand computer networks and five million computers, was used to hackers having a go at it, but the number of incidents increased sharply. NASA and the Departments of State, Commerce and Homeland Security all reported similar infiltration alerts. *Time* magazine, in a lead article entitled "Hack Attack", laid the blame at the feet of the ubiquitous Microsoft that supplied so many of the world's source codes. "We are placing our security eggs in one basket," it said, "and one day someone is going to come along and steal the lot." Yet it wasn't just in America. The banking system in Georgia was brought to a halt for three days, but not many people cared or even knew where Georgia was. And when the Parliamentary elections in Italy had to be held all over again because the new computer system that counted the votes deposited them in an impenetrable black hole, no one thought too much of the matter. It was, after all, Italy.

For all the misfortunes that struck others, none took the brunt more than Britain. Not all at once, of course, the game was spread over several months so that no one would guess the British were even in play. It kicked off when Egg, one of the country's largest Internet banks, made available its regular monthly statements online, yet when customers tried to access their personal and very private details, they were given someone else's. Intimate financial profiles were scattered around like seed in front of pigeons, and these included not just the Joneses, Smiths and Browns but also many prominent personalities, much to the amusement of many. As a result the *News of the World* was able to reveal that the Sports Minister was paying regular monthly sums to an entirely unsuitable female acquaintance, who promptly sold the details of the Minister's off-duty entertainments to the following week's edition. It included a colourful description of the Minister rehearsing his speech for the party conference while stark naked and complimenting himself on the size of his standing ovation. The Minister almost died of humiliation, a process his wife vowed publicly to complete, and much of the country was left crippled with laughter.

The railway system was also crippled. Three times in five days inter-city trains found themselves heading towards each other on the same stretch of line. None of these incidents ended in crashes, although there was one close call, but when the rail operators tried to rectify the faults the entire system went down. For four days not a single train moved anywhere in the country.

Ten days later, it was the turn of the national benefit system to screw up. Payments were still made, but none of them was for the right amount. Some gremlin had burrowed into the accounting software and moved the decimal point around. Pensioners from Cornwall to Carlisle muttered in disbelief, but the First Minister of Scotland had to be recalled from a conference in the Bahamas to cope with the riots that broke out in Glasgow. And south of the border, a highly dangerous sex attacker was released thirteen years before the end of his sentence when his name appeared on the list of prisoners granted early parole. The nation united in outrage.

Yet most people knew nothing of what was perhaps the most serious foul-up. On the London Stock Exchange, in the heart of the City of London, many of the trades began to be recorded twice, which exaggerated the movements in the market, making everything much more volatile. One expects the casino to play by the rules, but suddenly the punters were playing with a marked deck and if that news had got out they'd have stopped playing the game. Overnight one of Britain's most lucrative industries would have been destroyed. That's why the story was buried down the deepest institutional mineshaft. Better to lie, find a quick fix, move on. Even the Treasury agreed.

Throughout July, in different ways and in diverse places, the country was spun round like a child's top until it was left wobbling on the edge of chaos. And the game had only just begun.

Millions might have died in this game in Britain, but they didn't, that wasn't the plan, although the Minister for Sport came close when his wife threw a large bowl of cereal at him in their kitchen. He ducked just in time. Yet elsewhere there was a handful of fatalities, and most of those were in the United States as a result of the power failure. Two people were killed in a head-on collision in New Jersey that occurred when the lights suddenly disappeared on a stretch of the Palisades Parkway, and a man in Brooklyn succumbed to a heart attack after climbing seventeen flights of stairs because the elevator wouldn't work. A couple in upstate New York suffered carbon-monoxide poisoning after starting up their generator, and in Providence a family of immigrants was killed by a fire that started once the power had been restored. They'd been tampering with their ancient fuse box. Yet the electricity supply wasn't cut long enough for real damage to be inflicted.

The most important casualty, however, was a frail but remarkably spirited woman in her eighties named Abigail. She was feeling unwell and hadn't been on top form for some time, yet she was of a stubborn and independent nature and wasn't given to complaining. But the chest pains were insistent, and so was her doctor. Abigail was quickly transferred from her traditional New England clapboard home in Brookline to the cardiac unit of the nearby Massachusetts General Hospital in downtown Boston, where her doctor assured her she would be in the best possible hands. Despite her condition she remained feisty, issuing instructions, telling the doctors with a hidden smile that they weren't a patch on that cute Hugh Laurie, and above all insisting that they must not inform her daughter until all their test results had come in. No point in involving her unnecessarily, she told them, her daughter had other things to worry about. "I got the legal right to silence and I'm exercising it," she insisted.

Everything was done for the old lady's comfort. But still she died, one of the first casualties of war, from an overdose of insulin. When she was admitted she was diagnosed as having suffered a moderately serious heart attack, but the medical staff also discovered that she was acutely diabetic. It wasn't uncommon for a woman in her eighties and the treatment, even for a woman in Abigail's frail condition, was straightforward. Insulin. A regular measured dose pumping sufficient of the drug into her to stabilize her blood-sugar levels.

The dosage was critical. Too little and the blood-sugar level, already high following the stress of a heart attack, would soar. Too much and the blood-sugar level would fall, and since blood sugar is the body's basic fuel, life itself begins to fail. That's why they programmed the bedside computer to deliver just the right amount of insulin rather than leaving the process to the vagaries of human intervention. Life teeters on the brink for many frail old ladies, so she had little resistance when the infusion pump hit her with a massive overdose of insulin. Her blood-sugar level plummeted, and Abigail quickly started to sweat, her pulse racing as she fell into unconsciousness. The nurses on duty at the monitoring station scurried to respond, but it was too late. Within two minutes the patient was dead. They were left with little surprise, only a profound sense of disappointment — and a corpse. The wheel of life had turned one last time for Abigail, then stopped.

There were no recriminations. The medical staff had done all they could, had diagnosed the problem, devised the appropriate treatment, but in the end there was no coping with the vital organs of an elderly lady that had been placed under too much stress. They had no way of knowing that someone on the other side of the world had hacked into the hospital's systems, right up to the bedside of this particular patient, and temporarily boosted the dosage of insulin ten-fold. The nurses weren't negligent, they were simply deceived by readings on their monitor that had also been interfered with; they had no idea what was happening, even when it was too late. They ran a routine diagnostic check on the system, of course, in order to ensure that nothing had malfunctioned, but by that time, like the nuclear plant in Sosnovy Bor, everything was back in order.

Nearly three-quarters of those with diabetes die of heart attack or stroke. Abigail became one more statistic.

She hadn't been an intended target but was what you might term collateral damage. Incidental to the main affair. And it happened so quietly that no one realized she was a victim, she just lay there and died, right under the noses of all those doctors and nurses. The trouble was, they weren't paying attention to her, instead they were concentrating on their computers, just as happens all the time in so much of the world.

So she passed away and was gone, accompanied by nothing more than the routine electronic beeping of her killer. One of those things, if it hadn't been for the fact that Abigail was Arnie Edwards' mother-in-law, and her daughter the President of the United States.

CHAPTER
ONE

Tuesday lunchtime, late July. Central Beijing.

There wasn't much hint of elegance about most buildings in Beijing, the British ambassador thought as he fought his way through the dense traffic. Practical, brutal. A little like the Chinese themselves. Sweep away the old, throw up something new, most of which was hideous. There was another side to them, of course, the sort of China found in the Fragrant Hills on the outskirts of the city with its pavilions and ancient pagodas, where in autumn the foliage turned a deep red and in summer the air shimmered with the scent of pine, but here in the city so many of the old traditions had been lost, buried beneath concrete. Sir Wesley Lake glanced at his watch. He didn't wish to be late for his lunch appointment, which he was squeezing in before he left on a week's vacation — a trip to Eastern Ming Tombs a few hours' drive from the city, then on to the mountain resort at Chengde, where the imperial court used to withdraw during the summer to escape the heat. Lake liked to escape on his own, it had become something of a pleasing distraction since his wife had died four years earlier. He loved this country, despite its hard-nosed rulers, he had enough

Mandarin to get by and was accustomed to losing himself and his lingering pain in the colour and gentle chaos that he found outside the cities. Truth be told, he didn't want lunch, but he had been invited by a former Chinese ambassador to Benin and it had been difficult to suggest that his invitation was less compelling than a five-hour drive through the countryside. And it was to be at the Beijing Hotel, near Tiananmen Square, one of the less ruthlessly modern of the city's watering holes. It might have been worse.

He was met in the foyer by a minion in a buttoned hotel jacket. "Sir Wesley?" the man enquired, offering a bow of respect before leading the ambassador not to the dining room but to the elevator. He said nothing, and pressed the button for the top floor. The Englishman was surprised but also quietly delighted when he was led through into a carefully decorated suite filled with polished wood and silk trappings. Set in the window, in the sunshine, was a luncheon table prepared with flowers and cold meats. The man offered another reverential bow and departed.

The ambassador's delight slowly cooled when, after fifteen minutes, no one had appeared. His mood turned to astonishment and then anger when, ten minutes later, he discovered that the only exit from the suite was firmly locked, and no amount of banging and kicking on the door seemed to make any difference.

Tuesday evening. Heathrow Airport, London.

Five thousand miles and many time zones further east, the tyres of Air Force One scorched onto the tarmac of the runway as the presidential jet completed its landing. The American President had come to town. Blythe Elizabeth Harrison Edwards held a genuine affection for the British and their quaint pageantry and would normally have found her spirits lifting at this point, but a major problem had arisen that distracted her and dampened all her enthusiasm. It could be summed up in one word. Arnie.

It had been the day she had buried her mother, and she'd been sorting out what he should wear to the funeral. That's when she'd stumbled upon another woman's earring in her husband's pocket. Picked up from the floor at the last White House reception, he'd explained, yet despite all Arnie's dismissive logic, she trusted her instincts more than her husband. Then she'd found the number of his little tart plastered all over the White House call log. He couldn't even be bothered to cheat on her properly. And when, that evening, she had confronted him, he'd blamed her — her job, her absences, her distractions, and her lack of interest. John Kennedy had complained that he got a headache if he didn't have sex every two or three days, and Arnie said he felt the same. It was so brutally unfair, he'd wanted the White House as much as she had. Why was he punishing her, most of all on the day she had buried her mother? He'd told her that he wanted a divorce once they left the White House, that he'd only stuck with her for the sake of appearance. Her appearance. Made it sound as if he were doing her a favour. The prick. That's why he hadn't come on this trip to Britain, had stayed at home, looking after family business after Momma Harrison's death, so the official excuse had run. Truth was, Blythe couldn't bear to lay eyes on him, let alone to wake up beside him. Yet why did she feel guilty about that, too? As if it weren't bad enough that she hadn't seen her mother for a month or more before she died. Oh, God, she hurt.

He had promised to behave himself while she was away, so that they could talk like grown-ups when she got back, and even as Air Force One touched down she called him. But he was nowhere to be found. She didn't need the CIA to tell her where he was, but that was one number she wasn't going to call, not ever. As the Boeing rolled to a stop, Blythe gazed out of the window. It was a brilliant day but she could share in none of its joys. She'd been a fool, too soft, about Arnie, about everything, perhaps. Time to toughen up, girl, she scolded herself. For a fleeting moment she toyed with the idea of sending the Secret Service into the tart's apartment, along with television cameras, kicking down the door to catch him with his pants down, expose the wick-dipping little creep, but she knew that it was nothing more than a pathetic daydream because she would be the one to be exposed, as a failed woman, a failed wife. And they would say she wasn't up to being a president, either. Presidents aren't allowed a private life, not any more, they have no option but to wrap themselves in a blanket of heartlessness and get on with things. Can't ever break down in tears, no matter how much she wanted to. She shivered and pulled the blanket ever more tightly around her shoulders. She had no idea how much she was going to need that blanket before the week was out.

Tuesday afternoon. Seventh floor, the Beijing Hotel.

The well of outrage touches significant depths in most diplomats. Theirs is a profession guarded by centuries of custom and law, and the most fundamental rule in it all is that they remain personally inviolable and untouched. They're not supposed to find themselves locked up in a hotel room. It wasn't just his pride; Wesley Lake's foot hurt, too. He'd kicked the door so hard and so often that his shoe was threatening to burst at its seams. There had to be a better way.

The suite in which he was confined consisted of three main rooms, two bedrooms and a large central sitting room, along with two bathrooms and a small kitchen. As he explored he found one of the bathrooms had been equipped with an array of personal items such as toothbrush, hairbrush and razor, while the refrigerator in the kitchen was full of food. At the back of one of the shelves he discovered a dozen cans of beer. As he counted them, he realized this could turn into a long stay.

God, this was outrageous! You don't touch ambassadors, they have diplomatic immunity. You can shout at them, lie to them, deceive them, but you must never lay a finger on them. Those were the rules, except . . . Richard Sykes had been shot in Holland, and Chris Ewart-Biggs blown up in his car in Ireland. The rules hadn't saved them.

Damn.

He stared out of the window, which lacked a balcony or any means of escape, turning the possibilities over in his mind and finding that each grew more lurid than the last. It was as he wondered whether he could or should throw a piece of heavy furniture through the window to attract attention that the door behind him opened quietly.

"My apologies for keeping you waiting, Ambassador."

The man who entered with an apology and a bow of deference wasn't the former ambassador to Benin whom Lake had been expecting but a stranger — or was he? The Briton scoured his memory. Hadn't he seen this man somewhere before? He was on the small side, even for a Chinese, with a regulation haircut, impenetrable eyes, ordinary suit; everything about him was unexceptionable, except for the lips. These were surprisingly fleshy and expressive, and were now pinched in concentration. "Permit me to introduce myself. My name is Fu Zhang. I am the Vice-Minister of State Security."

Of course, that was why Lake both knew and did not know this man. The ambassador didn't deal with the State Security creeps who, like their counterparts all round the world, operated in the shadows. But he'd heard of Fu, one of Mao's closest associates, a man who came from the same small town in Gansu and had followed him all the way to Beijing, and who allegedly wielded far more influence than his secondary position in the ministry suggested.

"What the hell am I doing here, Fu? Why am I being held?" the ambassador barked, dispensing with the normal etiquettes. His face was flushed with anger.

The lips wriggled. "Held? Why, Sir Wesley, you are not being held, you are being protected. A thousand apologies for the inconvenience, but it appears that a threat has been made to your personal safety. We couldn't allow that, so we are providing you with shelter until the threat has passed."

The ambassador recognized the explanation for what it was — a cover story that both of them might find useful to paper over the cracks when it was all over. His spirit lifted; at least they didn't mean to throw him out the window. Not yet, at least. He decided against any attempt to give them ideas by hurling furniture at it himself.

"What threat?"

The lips smiled, but the eyes remained fixed and cold. "It appears that a young woman named Wu Xiaoling has been causing trouble. You know this person?"

The ambassador prayed he hadn't flinched. So they had unearthed Xiaoling. He understood what that implied and felt sick. He reached for a starched napkin from the table laid for lunch in order to wipe his lips.

"I'm not here to answer your damn-fool questions. I insist you let me leave!"

"In any event," Fu continued calmly, "your name has been linked with her, and it seems that anyone in an association with this troublesome woman is now at risk."

It was a threat, and Lake took it as such. "At risk? From whom?"

"We are still attempting to establish the full circumstances."

"But you say I am not being held."

"Sheltered."

"Then I thank you for your concern, but I'll look after myself, if you don't mind." With a snort of exasperation Lake crossed to the door and flung it open. Standing immediately outside were two armed policemen, their carbines pointing directly at his stomach. Further down the hall he sensed there were others of their kind. He turned on Fu in accusation. "You will allow me to leave!"

"I'm afraid that cannot be arranged, not yet, Ambassador — for your own safety, you understand. The Chinese authorities have a duty to ensure you are kept from harm. We cannot permit you to depart at this moment."

"Then which moment?"

"As soon as we have cleared up the mystery of Wu Xiaoling and ensured there is no longer any threat."

So that was it. They had nailed him for Wu Xiaoling and he knew the consequences of getting caught dirty-handed inside the Chinese leader's bedroom

26

would be immense. He tried to imagine what they would be doing to Xiaoling but his mind recoiled in horror, knowing that he, too, had entered a world in which there were no longer any rules to protect him. A small piece of elastic snapped inside the ambassador and he sank despairingly into an armchair. In his mind he was counting the cans of beer in the refrigerator once more, like the scratch marks on a prison wall that marked off the days, and he grew a little afraid. He was going to suffer. Somehow he knew that this man Fu would insist on it.

Thursday lunchtime. Berkeley Square, London.

Harry Jones stood in the rain. Lots of it. The sort of rain that sharks could swim in and that ripped airplanes from the sky. Welcome to summer in the city. The resulting flood that spread across London had taken on biblical proportions with rain choking the gutters and filling the streets with misery. People scurried for shelter, heads down, heedless of the traffic and each other, their umbrellas snagging in the manner of fighting cocks, gouging eyes, while Harry stood forlornly on the corner in the hope of engaging a taxi. He was heading for lunch with Gabriella, a wonderfully architectural American he'd bumped into the previous week who'd mentioned she was celebrating a lucrative divorce and wondered if Harry might care to assist. It had been a disgracefully unambiguous proposition and he liked that, everything up front. So unlike Mel, but

. . . Mel was — *had been* — another story. Harry was going through one of those phases in his life following his divorce when he could be disgraceful without consequence to anyone but himself, so he'd accepted Gabbi's proposition. She had proved to be inspirational as well as insistent, and Harry had discovered he liked her, both in and out of bed. They'd even talked tentatively about spending the weekend together before she flew back home, and lunch had been arranged to nail down the details. Harry couldn't deny it and didn't even try; he was excited.

But now he was late. The traffic was winding slow and snake-like, and appeared to have swallowed up every available taxi. From somewhere nearby the horns of buses bleated like lost sheep. Harry was a man used to being punctual — as one of his former commanding officers had remarked: "It seems there's scarcely a war anywhere in the world that can start until you've turned up, Jones" — and that, for twenty years of his life, had been pretty much the case. Sometimes, like now, he missed those times, yet through the midday gloom of the storm he could see salvation approaching in the form of a bright orange lamp. A free cab. He waved and began to collapse his umbrella as the taxi berthed itself near the kerb. The cabbie didn't risk lowering his window to ask the destination; gratefully, Harry clambered into the back. Yet no sooner had he sat down than the opposite door opened and another man heaved himself in. He had a heavy frame, a neck that swelled above his collar and an expression that

28

mimicked roots sucking at dried dirt. He didn't beat about the bush.

"Fuck off," the stranger snarled. "Get out of my cab."

"I think you're mistaken," Harry replied calmly.

The man bristled with indignation. His eyes were darting, his clothes expensive, the shoes hand-sewn and sodden. A trader from the City, Harry guessed, with a bee up his butt. "I got no time to argue with pricks like you," the man spat. "I hailed this cab. Now shove off."

"Let's ask the cabbie, shall we?" Harry suggested.

But the driver was having none of it. "What d'you think I am, from marriage guidance? Sort it out yerselves," he said, and slid the connecting window shut.

"Already sorted. This creep goes in five seconds or he ends up in the gutter," the stranger said, heat flushing into his cheeks.

Harry returned the stare. The man was younger than he was, perhaps late twenties, and was of impressive size, but Harry suspected that the once-solid frame had been softened by the temptations of City living. On the other hand, the overblown appearance might just be that he was wrapped in a raincoat. If it came to an inglorious wrestling match in such confined quarters, the other man had the advantage simply by dint of his weight.

"Five . . ." the man snarled, counting.

"Are you threatening me?" Harry demanded, incredulous.

"That's it. That's exactly it. Four . . ."

"Please. Look, I got in first. It's my cab."

"Three!" The stranger's knuckles grew white.

"Come on, you can't be serious. You're not really going to hit me," Harry suggested, determined to sound jovial.

"What part of 'fuck off' don't you understand? You some sort of retard? You got two seconds, then you're out the door, on your own or on your arse. Your choice."

Harry looked for help from the cabbie but the fellow had deliberately engaged his attention elsewhere, while the windows of the taxi were steamed up from the rain to the point of total opaqueness, depriving Harry of any chance of support from outside. He was on his own.

"One . . ." The man snapped, leaning back and looking for all the world as though he was preparing to strike. That was the moment when Harry raised his elbow, catching the other man beneath the nose. There wasn't a huge amount of force behind it since to use all his strength would have risked killing him, driving the nasal bones into the brain. And Harry had done that. Once. On a dark, swirling night in the bandit country of Armagh in 1988.

The IRA had been holding a hostage in an isolated farm just the other side of the border, and the mission of Harry's unit had been to spring him. On a night blowing so hard it threatened to rip trees out by their roots, Harry had got within fifty yards of the milking shed when he'd stumbled straight into one of the IRA bastards about to take a piss against a tree, cock in one hand, Armalite in the other. There had been an unseemly scramble — Harry couldn't use his own gun, it would alert those inside, and he had no time for his knife because the other man had the drop on him. That's when Harry had raised his elbow, hit him, just one time, and the gunman had fallen back into the mud and cow crap, quite dead. Harry had no regrets; they'd already used an electric drill on the hostage, straight through both kneecaps, and were about to do much, much worse. It had been another bit of dirty business in a despicable war which had few rules, but that was then and . . . well, this was the middle of Mayfair. Harry was no longer a soldier but a politician, a Member of Parliament, and it wasn't his job any longer to go round London adding to his body count. As he raised his arm, he took care to use just enough force to mash the cartilage of the nasal passages. It caused the man to scream with pain.

"Oh, dear, you seem to have banged your nose on the door. I feel sure it's broken," Harry said.

"You, you stinking . . ." But the burble of protest was cut short by the handkerchief that he was forced to clamp against his nose to staunch the flow of blood.

"I think you know where the door is," Harry added softly.

The taxi driver decided to become involved once more and began shouting at the wretch not to make a mess in his cab. Outnumbered, whimpering with rage and in considerable pain, the stranger stumbled back out into the rain, slamming the door shut.

The cabbie wasted no time in releasing the hand brake to lock the doors and prevent any further interruptions, revealing himself to be a man of instant loyalties. "Pushy bastard got what he deserved, you ask me. So where to, guv?"

Harry was just about to give instructions when his mobile phone began to vibrate. He plucked it from his pocket and listened intently for a few seconds.

"Can't it wait? I've got a lunch," he muttered with undisguised reluctance into the mouthpiece.

He said nothing more before the call ended. When it did, he sat back in the seat, his mind flooding with images of Gabbi and her manifold attractions. And that's how they would probably now stay, nothing but images. She was a girl from New York, lots of Latin blood, feisty, that's what made her such fun, and he was willing to take a large bet that she wasn't used to being stood up. Harry would call, do a little grovelling, try to firm up the weekend, but already he felt the moment slipping away. Anyway, she'd be back in New York by Wednesday, so not much point. But a pity. A very considerable pity, he decided.

The cabbie was staring at him insistently in the mirror. "Where's it to be, guv?" he demanded once more.

"Downing Street," Harry sighed. "The back door."

CHAPTER
TWO

Thursday afternoon. The Cabinet Room, 10 Downing Street, London.

Mark D'Arby carried many burdens. It wasn't just the responsibilities he held as Prime Minister, for those he had grown adept at dealing with. What had driven him on, and always a little further than any rival, were the ghosts of his childhood, and one ghost in particular, that of his grandfather. Frank D'Arby had started out as plain Mr Derby but by dint of audacity and a huge pot of luck had grown into Sir Frank, the sort of character who leaped out of boys' magazines, a war hero who didn't give a stuff about convention and who had lived into his nineties despite smoking forty Craven-A cork tips a day. He'd been a flier and had a good war, found himself promoted to air vice-marshal and lived in occupied luxury in Berlin after 1945, where he would fly around in Dakotas with stuffed armchairs for seats and chintz curtains on the window, often in the company of women who were frighteningly young. Grandpa made up his own rules as he went along. Arrogant, impatient, inspiring, unmissable. And often absent. It had made him an awful parent. Mark's father, the only child of Sir Frank's peripatetic marriage, sought solace in the ranks of the civil service, where he had remained buried in anonymity for most of his professional life. In disappointment, Sir Frank had turned his attentions to his grandson, Mark, who had grown up as shamed by his father's obscurity as he was inspired by the stories of his grandfather. Then, one day, shortly after his ninety-second birthday, the old man had gone out duck shooting and winged one, insisting on finding the bird to finish it off. He'd stumped back well after midnight, soaked and sore. Three weeks later he died of a chill, cursing with his last breath. After that the young Mark had dedicated himself to changing the world in the image of his beloved grandfather, yet at that time there'd been no handy wars to engage him so he had turned to the battleground of politics. Made a good start, climbed fast through the ranks, and when John Eaton had unexpectedly walked out of Downing Street, Mark D'Arby fought the campaign to succeed him in swashbuckling style. It matched the mood of the time. He had won a famous victory.

Yet as Harry Jones walked into the Cabinet Room he could detect little of that fighting spirit. D'Arby seemed drained, distracted, sitting in his chair, staring at the brown baize tablecloth, fiddling with his fountain pen although there were no papers in front of him. For a moment he seemed bent, older than his fifty-eight years, until he noticed Harry and sprang to his feet, the fire reignited in his face. "Harry, thanks for coming," he greeted, shaking Harry's hand vigorously, and for a little too long.

"No problem," Harry lied. "Sounded urgent."

"It is. Yes, it is." D'Arby appeared distracted once more, surprised to discover that he was still holding his pen. He threw it down on the table. "God, it's stifling in here. Let's go out in the garden."

"But it's pouring."

"Nevertheless . . ." The word hung between them, insistent, and the smile on the Prime Minister's face had grown stiff. Harry's mind suddenly began to spin in alarm. D'Arby clearly didn't want to talk inside, but why not? What could be so important, so serious, that it couldn't be discussed here, inside Downing Street? Harry was still trying to find first gear as D'Arby grabbed two umbrellas and led him through the doors at the far end of the room. It led them out onto a small patio.

"You see these red and white slabs?" D'Arby said, indicating the paving stones on which they were standing. "Hundreds of years old. And when those old lead flower troughs were made, America was still our colony, income tax hadn't been invented, and this country was still the finest nation on earth. Takes you back, this place. Gives you a sense of history." The flowers in the tubs nodded their heads in apparent agreement. "Come on." He led the way to the insubstantial shelter of the silver birch that stood at the side of the lawn. The rain beat down with the sound of a dull drum upon the umbrellas. He pulled out a cigarette, lit it, sucked deeply. Harry hadn't realized he smoked. The Prime Minister saw the curiosity in Harry's eye. "Condemned man's last wish," he said, trying to make a joke of it.

"You in the firing line?"

"Always." D'Arby's blue eyes fixed on Harry, as though searching for something he wasn't sure he would find. "Need your help again, Harry."

"Ah," The sigh of reluctance stretched out until it was lost in the rain.

Help wasn't a neat, tidy word when associated with Harry Jones. Two years earlier he'd found himself in the middle of a siege of Parliament in which the previous Prime Minister, the Queen, and almost every other powerful player in the land had been held hostage. That most of them had walked out alive had been largely down to Harry. The nation owed him, anything he wanted, and since that day he could have named his own price, but hadn't done so, had accepted nothing, apart from a George Cross, and had turned down D'Arby's offer of a Cabinet post. Harry distrusted systems, didn't want to be part of anyone else's team, valued his freedom — and not just for the latitude it gave him to date totally unsuitable women. So far as he was concerned, the Cabinet could wait, perhaps forever. "But I guess this isn't about making me the Minister for Floods and Biblical Disasters, is it, Mark?"

The Prime Minister leaned back against the trunk of the tree. He had a long, elegant face and silvered hair, usually accompanied by a roguish grin that cameras loved, but the creases that normally gave him an air of experience seemed to Harry's eye to have been carved more deeply, like a landscape that had been scoured by some recent flood. A grey pallor had settled over his complexion that Harry hoped was simply a trick of the light. D'Arby pulled once more at his cigarette. "You're a man of remarkable insight, my friend. So do a little Sherlock Holmes and tell me what you've already deduced."

"OK. You drag me here at a moment's notice, so it's urgent. And serious — you look like yesterday's breakfast. Something's happened. And it's too big, too important, for you to risk discussing it inside Downing Street. So we're out here, in the pouring bloody rain, which is ruining my bloody shoes and running down my bloody neck, presumably so that no one can hear us." Harry paused to allow the implication of what he'd said to sink in. "Christ," he whispered.

"Congratulations. Full marks. That's why I wanted you, Harry, you're good." D'Arby paused, unnecessarily buttoning his double-breasted jacket, making time to gather his words. "I know I can trust you. You have that wonderful ability to see things differently from others. Frustrates the hell out of me sometimes but ... right now I need you. This weekend. You got any plans?"

"Plenty."

"Cancel them. Pack an overnight bag. You're coming on a little trip with me. Until Sunday. But you must tell no one."

"What's this all about, Mark?" Harry demanded, frustrated, impatient, and, as he looked into the other man's eyes, suddenly a little frightened.

"I want you to help me stop a war."

Thursday evening. The Beijing Hotel.

Darkness had already fallen in Beijing. Outside the windows of the hotel, the lights danced across a city that refused to sleep, yet inside the suite on the seventh floor, time shambled along like a column of refugees. They had left Wesley Lake to stew, to worry, knowing that it would undermine his resistance. There had been no interruption for eight hours, apart from a man who had brought hot soup, but the ambassador had left it to steam on the table, untouched, determined not to be tempted into playing their game.

Then Fu returned. He was accompanied by another man who remained totally silent, standing guard by the door, a man who was surprisingly burly by Chinese standards. A thug, a muscle man, Lake concluded. Perhaps that was the intention, to plant fear, encourage it to grow.

"Sir Wesley, my apologies," Fu began. "This matter of the Wu woman. I cannot see how your safety can be secured until we get to the bottom of it." He stared directly at the ambassador but the Briton, who was standing by the window, gazing out at the world beyond, acted as if he had heard nothing, indeed as if he were still alone in the room.

"She was a traitor. She has been dealt with," Fu continued, as though delivering a weather report, delighted to see the tightening of the knuckles that Lake couldn't control. "Very serious allegations were made about her. I wonder if you might be able to help us clear them up."

38

Lake turned, just sufficiently to catch Fu's eye and let the man see the depths of his contempt for him.

"No, I thought not," Fu said, his lips puckered in disappointment.

That was when Fu hit him, a surprisingly sharp blow for a man of such small stature, directly in the solar plexus. The ambassador was a man in his early sixties, more accustomed to the ordeals of the cocktail circuit than long sessions in the gym, and his resistance to the blow was not what it might have been. Immediately his nerves went into spasm; he retched, couldn't breathe, clutched at the pain that was ripping him in two, and felt his breakfast rising. He stumbled towards the bathroom and collapsed on his knees before throwing up into the toilet bowl. He continued until he had nothing more to give.

There had been no warning, no small talk, no attempt to probe or wheedle information out of him. Such a blunt attack was unlike the Chinese, who rarely took the direct route between any two points. Even as his eyes streamed and his heart pounded, Lake tried to collect his scrambled thoughts. He came to one instant conclusion. Fu was in a hurry. Perhaps time wasn't on his side, either. And suddenly he was grabbed from behind by the guard from the door, and he felt a sharp jab in his arm. When at last the kaleidoscope of colours in his eyes had formed into a coherent shape, he found Fu beside him holding a syringe. It was already empty.

"Just a little encouragement, Sir Wesley," Fu was saying, "something that will jog your memory, and then will help you forget."

They dragged him back to an armchair, where he fell, but he no longer hurt. Already his limbs were numb and a greyness had fallen across his thoughts. He heard the name Wu Xiaoling, it seemed to be ringing in his mind, like church bells. He was drowning in confusion and he struggled to stay afloat, he didn't want to think of Xiaoling so instead he thought of his wife, tried to concentrate every fragment of his energy on her, and as she came to his mind he knew he had nothing more to fear, except disgrace. If he was about to be cast into Hell, let them get on with it, but he'd drag this little shrivel-dick Confucian with him every inch of the way. He gave a roar of defiance, which emerged as nothing more than a groan, and he remembered no more.

They worked on him for the greater part of two hours, prodding him, slapping him, pinching his cheeks, plying him with more serum, encouraging him with both kind words and threats, until at last Fu dragged a towel across his perspiring brow and slapped it across Lake's pallid face before hurling it into a corner in frustration.

"A little longer," the guard suggested.

But Fu shook his head. "There is no time left. No time!" he screamed. Then he stamped out of the room and slammed the door.

Thursday afternoon. Moscow.

The middle-aged man cursed, in the colourful manner drummed into him on the bare, brutal streets of post-war Leningrad. In those days the city was a frozen concrete wasteland that had been both playground and university to him, providing the sort of education that left scars, particularly on someone on the short side of average, but Sergei Illich Shunin had survived. Not everyone had; he'd lost both his sister and his eldest brother, and his father, too, after pneumonia had caught up with his scarred lungs. The young Shunin had grown up knowing that something more than the ordinary was expected of him, and he hadn't disappointed. He'd been born in a communal flat shared with two other families and an army of cockroaches, yet within fifty years he'd become the leader of the Russian Federation and had gone to live in a palace. Not bad, so far as it went. Inevitably such a rapid rise took its toll, it meant he was a man of few true friends, yet no one dared ignore him. Behind his back they called him "Malenkiy Napoleon", Little Bonaparte, and that pleased him. Others who had sat in his chair had done so much damage — that tapeworm Gorbachev, and that arse-nipping oaf Yeltsin who had viewed the world through the bottom of a bottle. They'd let the Chechens and every other separatist snake run loose so it was Shunin's job, his destiny, to nail them back inside their box and bury it so deep they'd wake up next to the Devil. Damnation to them all. One day Russia would be great again.

Yet right now, Sergei Illich Shunin felt overwhelmed by impotence. It wasn't just the weather, the crushing summer heat that had stretched on for weeks and was beginning to fry his brain and squeeze his asthmatic lungs, it seemed that God Almighty had taken up arms against Russia and was sending trials of apocalyptic proportions to test him. The poor harvest, the melting taiga, the industrial screw-ups, the Muslims and malcontents huddled in their camps just waiting for the chance to tear his country apart.

And that cursed nuclear plant. It had come back to haunt him. He'd pretended he'd dealt with the matter, put it behind him, fired the director, decimated the staff, but the spilling of so much blood had simply been for the sake of appearance. Deep down he had known it wasn't an answer. Then, two days ago, the nightmare had been revived. The British ambassador had delivered a hand-written letter from his Prime Minister, stating that it had been a deliberate act of sabotage. Cyber sabotage. How the hell did the bastard know? Know for sure? But he said he did. It had been one of the theories — guesses — put up by Shunin's own men, who had blabbed on about protocols and source codes and mysteries that came straight out of a child's fairy tale. Shunin had dismissed it all, he couldn't be dealing with make-believe, but it hadn't quelled the doubts inside and now this Briton was stirring it all up again. And he was suggesting that worse was to come. What could be worse than a nuclear meltdown? Shunin prayed he would never find out.

He crossed himself in the manner taught him by his mother, a good Orthodox Christian who had held to the faith even during the godless years of Communism. His hand moved slowly to the prescribed points about his body and came to rest over his heart. From the front seat of the vehicle his bodyguard watched every movement, yet beside him his son-in-law, Lavrenti, took no heed, his mind lost to the brain-scouring noises that were emanating from an electronic gadget jammed into his ears. It was some sort of multifunctional mobile phone. He was texting at the same time.

The presidential motorcade struggled to force its way through the groaning streets of the Russian capital in the direction of the air terminal at Sheremetyevo-1. Shunin's fingers drummed impatiently. He had no concerns about being late, of course, he wasn't taking a scheduled flight. His private Rossiya-1 Airbus was already fuelled, secured, thrice-checked by his own personal flight crew, and stocked with his fishing gear. Wasn't going to move without him. But he was an impatient man and fretted at the constant interruptions to their journey. Leningradsky Prospect was choked, not just with vehicles but with the interminable construction work, and the central-lane highway that was supposed to be reserved for official transport had become stuffed so tight it squeaked. The parts that weren't blocked by lumbering cement trucks and double-parked delivery vans had been overwhelmed by the number of new cars, private cars, cars owned by individuals, not the state. Even the thought of such things would have had Stalin banging on his box. When he spoke publicly of such things Shunin called it progress, but now the thirty-minute journey to Sheremetyevo-1 was likely to take more than an hour, even for the leader of all the Russias. The FSB were supposed to block off the streets for him, but what could they do when the streets were already blocked by others? He'd given them no notice, just announced that he was leaving in two hours, on a whim, so they supposed, but for the moment he was going nowhere, just like those ankle-tappers of the Moscow Dynamos whose stadium they were passing, a ramshackle concrete coffin covered in gaudy advertising hoardings where the hidden corners and stairwells stank of urine. Some things hadn't changed.

They slowed almost to a standstill. Somewhere up ahead a truck loaded with steel pipes was backing out from a construction site and had succeeded in stuffing up the entire Prospect. And Shunin's asthma was getting to him; he reached for his nebulizer and breathed in the comforting medicinal mist, but despite the relief he knew it was getting worse. The doctors had warned him, one day his lungs would get the better of him and he'd have to slow down, give up, or go just like his father. Shunin's response had been to get himself new doctors. Now he took a deep breath and turned on his son-in-law in irritation. "Lavrik," he said, using the diminutive, "I am a reasonable man. I don't mind you screwing my daughter, I don't even object when you skim a few per cent from the contractors on your architectural projects, but I swear on the Holy Mother

I'm not spending the next couple of days listening to you mash your brains to shit with that rubbish!"

The younger man looked up, bemused at the sudden onslaught. "It's just a toy. Something a friend gave me, Papasha."

"A contractor."

"A friend," the son-in-law insisted.

"It's gold-plated."

"So, a good friend."

"Throw it out."

Lavrenti laughed awkwardly.

"Throw it out," his father-in-law repeated. He was not a man used to repeating himself.

"Dammit, it's worth five thousand US."

"A trinket."

"And mine."

Shunin stared. He was a man of short stature with immensely broad shoulders, suggesting the sort of strength that in his younger days could have broken a horse with his bare hands. But the years, and the lungs, had got to him. In middle age his crinkled hair had grown thin and was now stretched desperately across his skull, giving the impression of a ploughed field, and he rarely smiled, for inside the Kremlin there was so little to smile about. A thick belt held his trousers round his wide waist, his shape was almost square, and when he walked he rolled from side to side, a man whose better days had been left behind at the roadside. Yet he was never a man to be underestimated, and anyone who did quickly found reason to regret their naivety. He had lost none of his legendary ability to switch from philosopher to huntsman in a single, wheezing breath, and although his neck might disappear into his collar the eyes were always sharp, cat-like, and gave the impression that they could see through people and leave them feeling unmasked. Now they were fixed on Lavrenti.

"Do as I say, Lavrik." The instruction was delivered in a whisper like a wind rustling through a graveyard. It was turning into yet another of his lessons in subservience.

"Come on, Papasha, just because we're stuck in this funeral procession, don't take it out on me." But Lavrenti found no trace of humour in the other man's expression. "Please, I need my phone," he murmured, but the plea froze to death in the space between them.

Shunin was like that. Took positions, stubborn, intransigent, but never pointless, always for a purpose. And so long as he was working over foreigners or Chechens the people loved him for it, they even sent each other postcards with his image on the front, showing him as a bulldog, a favourite pet guarding the home, but those who slept closer to him had reason to fear his moods.

And few slept closer than Lavrenti Konev. He was in his early thirties, one of the rising stars of this new Russia — how could he not be, so close to Shunin? But Russia had always been a place of suspicion and envy, and the new Russia had mixed into that potent gruel of mistrust the curdling power of money, mountains of it. The ancients of the Soviet era had rarely indulged in ostentatious wealth — oh, they had their dachas and their Zils, but none of it was personal property and most of it was poorly produced tat. Yet the days when the arrival of a refrigerator was cause for a street party were long since gone. Life had changed, and Lavrenti was part of that change. A media man.

He had come to Shunin's attention when his daughter, Katya, had brought him home at a time when Shunin had been under pressure from a political opponent, Kamenev. Within two weeks of Shunin meeting Lavrenti, a video of Kamenev had been aired on RTR, the state-run television channel, showing "a person resembling" Kamenev fumbling around with two much younger women. Exposing him to such ridicule was as good as putting him up in front of a firing squad; even before the world had finished laughing. Kamenev was gone, Lavrenti Konev was in, and ever since Shunin had allowed the younger man to run the media side of things. Lavrenti had become election mastermind, propagandist, chief censor and son-in-law, and had spread his wings into ever more lucrative enterprises. He'd masterminded the campaign that brought together a subtle mix of persuasion, corruption and intimidation which had persuaded the International Olympic Committee to award the winter games to the town of Sochi, a resort on the Black Sea where even in January the temperatures rarely touch freezing. Not an ideal location for snow and ice, some people thought, but an ideal spot to make a fortune from the property market. He learned quickly. While Shunin rode a white horse in public, more privately the son-in-law cleaned up the mess that was inevitably left behind. It had become a fruitful partnership.

Deep down, Shunin hoped that one day Lavrenti might do more, become more — perhaps and in time even his successor. Yet Lavrenti was his son-in-law and there were still areas of power that Shunin had shielded from him. Lavrenti had never been asked to get his hands dirty — really dirty, in the Russian way, Shunin had protected him from that. The hands that touched his daughter must be clean. Yet if Lavrenti were to grow, to follow in his footsteps, there must come a time when he would have to show his mettle, be tested. But in the meantime there could be only one master in any house, and Lavrenti needed to be reminded of it.

Already the guard had turned from his seat in front and was holding out a demanding hand.

"It's such a waste," Lavrenti objected. "Ridiculous. I need it."

"Not on this trip, you won't. And if that toy means so much to you, I'm sure you can always get your very good friend to give you another."

"For God's sake, this is pathetic."

"So is being bought for the price of a golden trinket."

"Nobody's bought me!" Lavrenti spat back, rising to the bait.

"Then prove it."

The younger man tried to hold Shunin's gaze, hoping for a reprieve, but none came. They rarely did.

"May Heaven piss on your picnic, Papasha," Lavrenti snapped in defiance before thrusting the phone at the guard, who released a lock and opened the door by a

48

fraction, just sufficient for the gadget to be dropped in the track of the vehicle's wheels. Half a ton of pressure beneath each wheel would do for most things; a mere gadget would have no chance, even if it was gold-plated. Lavrenti sank sullenly back into his seat, where he began chewing savagely at a fingernail, one of the disconcerting habits he'd picked up recently — and one of the reasons why Shunin watched, and wondered. There was so much for a leader to wonder about in this new world, even a son-in-law.

They had been stationary too long; the guard was growing anxious, muttering into his radio. Then, with a wave of his hand, he directed the driver to squeeze his way off the road and onto the pavement. The car rose up the kerb with a bump. Pedestrians looked on in bewilderment, their faces turning bright with panic before throwing themselves to one side as the convoy carved its way towards them, twisting around lampposts, at one point running over a hastily abandoned bicycle. A whiskery old man emerging from a shop doorway waved his rolled-up newspaper in protest, being either too blind to see, or too old to care what they might do to him. Then, with a nod of the bonnet, they had regained the roadway at a point beyond the cement truck and were speeding away. Before long they had left the city behind and were out into the greener suburbs of Khimki, yet even here they found disruption. Huge billboards were scattered along the roadside like pine cones on the forest floor, screaming the merits of everything from Starbucks to IKEA, while the open fields that had once protected the approaches to Moscow were disappearing beneath a sprawl of ugly shopping malls.

"Ah, the Wild West," Shunin quipped sardonically.

Everywhere was being ripped apart and once more they were forced to slow as they squeezed into a road tunnel being cut beneath a development that would soon be a new mega-mall. One day the road on which they were travelling would be an eight-lane express-way that would stretch all the way to Sheremetyevo, but for the moment it was just another construction site and soon the presidential cavalcade found itself on a diversion that reduced its speed to less than thirty. The FSB guard was once more glancing nervously around him as the police motorcycle outriders pulled over all other traffic in the tunnel to give the convoy free passage. Amongst those vehicles was an airport shuttle bus covered in so much summer dust that the sign announcing it was out of service was all but obliterated; it sat glowering in the tunnel as the motorcade approached, its exhaust belching dark, impatient smoke. The first vehicles of the convoy snaked past, waved on by the outriders, but as the rest began to follow the long yellow vehicle lurched forward, as though the clutch had slipped, and veered towards the path of the presidential limousine, forcing Shunin's driver to hit his brakes. Suddenly the air was filled with the sound of car horns and security sirens bouncing off the tunnel walls. From the front seat, the guard shouted in alarm.

The breath was still leaving the guard's lungs when the driver of the shuttle bus flicked a switch on his

50

dashboard. It wasn't a standard switch but one that had been specially installed and led via a wriggling length of wire to the luggage compartment beneath the seats. There it met a shaped armour-piercing charge in the form of an anti-tank shell, the sort of thing that slices through armour plate to a depth of seven or eight times its own diameter. And that was the moment the shell detonated.

CHAPTER
THREE

Thursday afternoon. Outside Moscow.

The presidential limousine had been supplied by a specialist subsidiary of BMW and was equipped with many kinds of protective armour. It was also fitted with electronic counter-measures that blocked radio signals in the vicinity and prevented any bomb being detonated by remote control. But the armour couldn't withstand a direct hit by a shaped charge, and even the finest ECM on earth was worthless in a suicide attack. As the blast wave from the explosion began to force its way down the tunnel, a jet of metal penetrated the limousine, creating an overpressure that instantly killed everyone inside. Even if one or more of the passengers had miraculously survived the initial blast, it would have served no purpose. When the fuel tanks ruptured, what was left of the BMW turned into a metal-melting inferno. Not even the fillings in their teeth survived.

Yet Shunin had. He'd not been in the presidential limousine, but instead had been riding alongside Lavrenti in one of the lead cars of the convoy. In recent years those who wished to see the President dead — and there were many — had grown bolder, particularly the Chechens, and there were several small armies of other separatists, too. Shunin's life was constantly at risk yet he was not a man to cower behind the thick walls of the Kremlin. He refused to hide, so those who were responsible for his security made a habit of trying to throw his pursuers off the scent, disseminating false information about his whereabouts and travel plans, switching his car or his plane at the last minute. In the garage beneath the Kremlin they had placed Shunin in one of the accompanying security vehicles, the one in which his son-in-law was travelling. And it had saved his life.

It had been a close call. Their black Mercedes SUV still caught the impact of the blast, hit from behind by the remorseless fist of expanding gases and debris that threatened to roll the vehicle over, yet although the tyres screeched and the driver screamed, it remained upright. The support vehicle was armoured, it absorbed the worst of the blow, and the SUV settled back on its wheels, its occupants shaken but unhurt. Soon it was surrounded by a posse of armed presidential guards, each more nervous than the rest, their eyes flooded with alarm and their hands filled with weapons.

"Are you hurt, *gospodin*, Mr President?" his bodyguard demanded.

Shunin's chest was heaving, he was short of breath, but there was no sign of panic. He reached for his nebulizer, sucked on it, his lungs slowly opening like a butterfly's wings stretching in the sun. He ran a hand across his head to rearrange the strands of hair that had fallen from grace, and only then did he turn to his bodyguard. "It seems it is not yet my time to die, Yuri Anatolyevich, not until the path to Hell is paved with the bones of ten thousand Chechens. We still have some way to go."

"Thank God!"

"Yes. We may both thank God." He touched the crucifix that hung beneath his shirt. "But not the man who told them of our plans. He will be begging to swap his life with a catamite from the slums of Africa when we find him." He stared intently at the guard, searching for any flicker of guilt. Yuri Anatolyevich had been at his side for many years, and yet the source who had supplied the bombers with the information must also be very close to him. No one was above suspicion. He turned to his son-in-law. "And you, Lavrik? Will I yet become a grandfather?"

Lavrenti's face was ashen but he nodded slowly. He had given no cry of alarm, there were no tears of relief or shaking. He sat silent, grim, but seemingly in control. A test passed.

And within seconds they were speeding away from the scene of his would-be assassination, the guard shouting into his radio and prodding a gun at the driver's ribs, just in case he needed encouragement. Now they travelled at very high speed, forcing other cars off the road as the SUV careened away from the scene until eventually Shunin ordered the driver to pull over. The bodyguard protested but Shunin was a man who made his own rules and, with Yuri Anatolyevich still mouthing protests, he heaved himself out of the car and gazed back towards the scene of the carnage. In the distance noxious, oil-stained smoke spilled from the mouth of the tunnel, billowing high into the humid summer air.

"You've beaten them, Papasha," Lavrenti muttered grimly.

"Perhaps. But in this game they only need to get lucky once."

"Please, Mr President, get back into the car," the guard interrupted, a bead of sweat sprouting on his brow. "We must get you to Zhukovsky." It was the military base about twenty-five miles from Moscow, a place of safety in times of trouble when even the Kremlin itself might not be safe. Shunin shook his head.

"No. We continue."

"But —"

"No stinking sewer rat from Chechnya's going to change my plans," Shunin snapped.

"Mr President," the bodyguard repeated, but this time more feebly, "the people — they will need to see that you are unhurt."

"The people can wait," Shunin insisted, "the fish won't. Come on, Lavrik, get back in the car."

The guard looked at the son-in-law in despair. It was one of those moods he knew he couldn't deflect. This was wrong, very wrong, Yuri Anatolyevich had standing orders for moments of crisis such as this, and carrying on with a fishing trip didn't feature in them. So he could disobey his commanding officer, or he could deny his President. Either way, he'd likely end up buried in the brown stuff. Yet Sergei Illich was a man after his own heart. Some twenty years earlier Shunin had been a senior KGB operative, head of section in East Berlin at the time the Wall was being pulled down, when a crowd had tried to storm the local KGB building and ransack its records. Shunin had stood on the steps, solid like a block of granite and armed with nothing more than eyes that could freeze a man's will, like a rabbit loses his mind in the headlights. The mob had seen him, and faltered.

"Your beloved West is over that way," Shunin had declared, pointing a thick finger in the direction of the Wall, "not behind these doors!"

And those East Germans, so conditioned to having their minds made up for them, had turned, and by deflecting them Shunin had saved an entire network of collaborators from being exposed. After that, his rise had been meteoric, and long ago Yuri Anatolyevich had decided he would happily die for this man, and yet, if that were his wish, how much better to go fishing with him. He came to attention, held open the car door, and, with an uncharacteristic screech of tyres, they set off once more.

Thursday afternoon. Behind Downing Street.

It had stopped raining. Harry's steps scrunched across the gravel of Horse Guards Parade as he left Downing Street the way he had arrived, anonymously, by the back door.

"Tell no one," the Prime Minister had instructed, "not even the birds."

56

"That we're about to go to war? What war, Mark?"

But D'Arby had shaken his head, wouldn't say.

"And why me?"

"Because you have background, Harry, and because you have balls. You've more experience in the tangled world of security than almost anyone in the country. I shall need to lean on that."

True enough. A career in the British army that had included active service not only in the First Gulf War but any number of other, less official wars. Harry had been at the sharp end, and had the scars to show for it. Fifteen years on, his military career had been exchanged for one in Parliament, where he'd become a Minister and a man on the move, one to watch, but Harry always had a stubborn streak that had never endeared him to his superiors. The army had tried to march the individuality out of him, the government had preferred to squeeze it out of him by giving him office, but neither had succeeded. He remained stubbornly his own man, yet it was precisely that bloody-mindedness that had saved the life of the Queen. After that, Harry Jones had been able to do whatever he liked — except, it seemed, spend the afternoon screwing a beautiful lawyer from New York.

"Mark, you've got an entire government machine at your disposal. And your Cabinet colleagues. You don't need me."

The Prime Minister had offered a bitter smile. "Who could I trust? Tricia Willcocks?"

Ah, dear Tricia. The most self-centred woman in government. A mouth full of spite and a dress full of ferrets. Harry had crossed swords with her and hadn't always emerged victorious. "A piranha in pantyhose, I grant you, but she happens to be your Foreign Secretary."

"Precisely. And may her travels be arduous and almost infinite," D'Arby sighed. The lack of trust was evidently mutual.

"Then what about the others? Defence? The Home Secretary?"

"I can't trust them, Harry, not completely, not as much as I need to. Defence would blab to his wife, while our esteemed Home Secretary would go bragging to his diary secretary. He's sleeping with her, you know. They'd talk, and someone would hear about it. I can't risk that. No, I've thought about this long and hard and I haven't found any sleep for three days, but the conclusion is still the same. You're the only man for the job."

"And what job is that, exactly?"

Still D'Arby wouldn't explain. "Not yet," he said, "not even in here."

They had returned from the garden to the Cabinet Room by this point, and D'Arby placed both hands on Harry's shoulders. "I must ask you to trust me, Harry. To be my guide, my support, and perhaps even my conscience."

The Prime Minister had smiled reassuringly, but up close Harry thought he could smell fear.

"And be prepared never to tell a soul about any of it," the Prime Minister had continued. "I must ask you to promise me that."

58

"You want me to swear an oath or something?"

"No. I want you to trust me, just as I trust you."

Trusted with everything but the truth, it seemed. "How do I prepare for this weekend? What do I bring?"

"Nothing more than a change of clothes, my friend. One night, two at the most."

Nights in which Harry wanted to be elsewhere, with others — no, just with Gabbi. He'd spent the last couple of years since his divorce screwing around, trying to forget, but for the first time he wanted something more. It seemed he wasn't going to get it.

Harry spilled in confusion onto Horse Guards, setting off on foot for his home in Mayfair, stretching out, trying to walk off his concerns. As he crossed the Mall, that broad tree-lined avenue that led up towards Buckingham Palace, he found it decked in flags. Blythe Harrison Edwards, the US President, had arrived for a state visit and the Union flag hung alongside the Stars and Stripes from the flagpoles, damply, like drying shirts. Instinctively his back stiffened, the shoulders went back.

"This isn't about me, Harry, you understand, it's for our country" — D'Arby's last words as Harry had left. Never had be been asked to serve as blindly as this.

Yet as he sprang out into the Mall, dodging the speeding cars, he remembered that wasn't quite the truth. Twenty years earlier he had been serving in Northern Ireland. An untidy war, on both sides. It had its rules, of course, and Harry like everyone else in the army was supposed to carry a Yellow Card spelling out the rules of engagement: what he could and couldn't do; whom he could kill and when the killing was supposed to stop. Queen's Regulations. But it hadn't always worked like that. Anyway, Harry was SAS, they had their own rules, the sort that were never written down on paper.

It had been a good night, up to that point. He'd nabbed a three-man IRA unit half asleep, scratching their crotches in their parked van, weapons neatly stacked behind, and he'd brought the guns back to HQ for the forensics boys to figure out when they'd last been fired and which poor bastard had been on the receiving end, but no one seemed interested in the bloody guns. There was a flap on, something big. And they wanted Harry. In a small back room, squeezed around a table and almost hidden behind a pall of cigarette smoke, he had discovered the Head of Military Intelligence, the Head of the Special Branch and his own commanding officer. When he walked in they all sprang to their feet, as though startled, caught in some guilty act.

"Hello, Harry. We've been waiting for you," his CO croaked in a voice dried hoarse by nicotine.

Then his CO took him to one side, another cigarette, this time outside in the car park, and in the dispassionate manner of a mathematician setting out a theorem he had explained how Harry might do a great service for his country. It wasn't an order, not even a request, for the CO took care to explain that it was a discussion that couldn't possibly be taking place. "Harry — you understand? And if anyone ever asks, I'll deny it to my dying day. No one must know." Then, like

Mark D'Arby, the CO asked Harry to trust him. "Just as I must trust you, with everything. My career. My honour. With my life."

Harry had left by the back door on that occasion, too.

And that had ended in murder.

Thursday afternoon.
The Balmoral Estate, Aberdeenshire.

The summer heat had grown oppressive, leaving Scotland simmering like a skillet on the stove. On the moors of Aberdeenshire, life had slowed to a crawl. Red deer hugged the shade of the pines, conserving their energies for the rutting season that still lay ahead, firewatchers in their towers found their eyes growing heavy, while even the plump grouse, in their prime and threatened with imminent annihilation as the days ticked by towards August, had grown lethargic. In every corner, life slowed down, yet Blythe Edwards found it impossible to relax. Give no clues, that's what the Prime Minister had told her. Be normal, act normal, play normal. But what, Blythe Edwards asked herself, was normal? D'Arby had taken her aside the previous evening during the state banquet at Buckingham Palace and had begun whispering in her ear, words that had tumbled into her already troubled mind and almost overwhelmed it. Troubles never came in single file. As the other guests had seen them talking they had been given a wide berth to allow them a little privacy. If only she could put such distance between herself and what he had told her. No sudden change of plan, he had urged with as much strength as he could muster, let no one take notice. So now, as everything threatened to fall to pieces about her, she sat beside a whispering river that nudged its way down from the heather hills above Balmoral as if she hadn't a care in the world.

Next to her sat her host, Elizabeth, Queen of all they surveyed and still a few places besides, while a little further away three generations of royalty stretched out along the bank. This was a place of cool, crystal water much favoured by trout, but today in the heat the fish had made way for family who had turned the rock pool into a swimming hole. This was the House of Windsor, at ease and al fresco, where guests could be entertained in what passed as privacy in royal circles. On such occasions the Queen might pour and a prince might throw a little meat upon the open barbecue, but they could never be alone. Everything had been prepared by others and set out on crisp cotton tablecloths, while retainers hovered discreetly in the shadows of the nearby fishing lodge, waiting for the call to serve. Protection officers stood a little further back, muttering into their sleeves.

The American President had been looking forward to this weekend at Balmoral Castle, the Queen's summer retreat. It had been in her schedule for more than a year and she liked Elizabeth, not just as a fellow head of state but as a woman, one with whom she had shared more than most. When Elizabeth had been held hostage in her own Parliament by Waziri gunmen, Blythe's own son had been there, too, right in the firing line. It had forged a strong personal bond between the two women, but what confronted her now, Blythe reflected, she would have to face on her own.

She was used to troubles, they went with the job, gave it purpose, excitement even. Politics was no place for those who wanted security and a soft life, with Friday nights spent stretching in front of the fire sorting through piles of letters from admirers. It was a tough, even harsh calling, but never had she sensed her chosen path might so suddenly disappear off a cliff. Her life was a mess. She was supposed to be the most powerful mortal on earth, yet here she sat, hiding behind dark glasses, holding a book whose pages hadn't turned for the best part of an hour. Her scrambled thoughts were distracted by the sound of splashing and childish laughter. She looked up, to discover Elizabeth staring at her, furrows of concern taped across her brow.

"You've been very brave," Elizabeth said at last. "The loss of your mother . . ."

"Thank you. I can't say it wasn't hard. I feel I've neglected her these past years."

"She understood. Trust me." Elizabeth offered a reassuring smile but she was leaning forward in her chair, her eyes probing, in concern, just as Abigail used to. With a start Blythe realized that the Queen was even older than her mother.

"And how's Arnold?" the Queen asked, her voice tentative, plumbing difficult waters. With a start Blythe realised that she knew.

"Arnie is . . ." she sighed. "Arnie."

"I've noticed you've barely mentioned him. I didn't wish to pry, but it would have been rude not to ask. I do so care about you, my dear. I think I know how difficult this must be."

Yes, of course she did. Blythe managed a tight nod of gratitude. There was no need for words of explanation; Elizabeth knew, but if a queen could tell, just by looking at her, how soon would it be before others picked up on her sordid family secret? Screw you, Arnie.

"And what with everything else," Elizabeth sighed.

Blythe arched an eyebrow.

"Oh, I don't know the details of what's going on this weekend," Elizabeth continued. "Mr D'Arby suggested it would be better that way, but I know that now, of all times, you might have been spared the burden of personal distractions."

"I'm not entirely sure myself what Mr D'Arby's mysteries are about."

"Whatever they are you'll deal with them magnificently, that I know. And Arnold can wait. Men can be so stupid. And often so unimportant."

Their gentle misandry was interrupted by a sudden commotion. Squeals of excitement echoed along the riverbank as royal grandchildren chased each other. Screaming with excitement, the youngest threw himself into the pool, hoping to find sanctuary from his pursuers, but when he emerged from the water he found himself staring into his monarch's terrifying eyes. In a moment, in a glance, the heat of July turned to winter. He had splashed her feet.

"Sorry, Grammy," he whimpered.

"You must always remember who you are," she said softly but in mild rebuke. "Otherwise I shall get your grandfather to read you a bedtime story."

"Oh, no, Grammy, I'd have nightmares for weeks!" the young culprit exclaimed, giggling, his spirits recovered, waving in gratitude before disappearing once more beneath the water.

Elizabeth turned to her guest. "It seems that perhaps husbands do have their uses, after all."

It was intended as tender humour, but Blythe's defences were so transparent that it barged straight through and hurt. Tears gathered behind the glasses, waiting to attack. Focus, Blythe, for God's sake focus! No time for this, not now with the world threatened by chaos. There were fires to fight, huge, earth-cracking fires, and it was going to take more than a few tears to put them out. But that was tomorrow. For now she picked up her book, cracked its spine, and pretended to carry on reading.

Late Thursday afternoon.
Sheremetyevo Airport, Russia.

Despite Shunin's reassurances, they weren't going fishing after all. As his car hit the outskirts of Sheremetyevo, he gave instructions to proceed not to the main public terminal but to a scruffier and older outlying terminal that was normally reserved for military traffic.

"What's going on, Papasha?" Lavrenti asked, confused.

Shunin gave him nothing but a cold, prohibitive stare. Yuri Anatolyevich, too, was agitated, but did as he was instructed, diverting the SUV through a military checkpoint where ambling guards were shocked to attention, their legs snapping like steel traps, cigarettes cast aside, eyes swivelling in anxiety. It was only a minute before the presidential vehicle was pulling up in a distant part of the airport, nestling beside a gangly four-engined plane dressed in dull military colours whose wings seemed to stretch awkwardly like those of a young crane. Lavrenti had been expecting Rossiya-1, the presidential jet, a luxurious Ilyushin airliner kitted out in soft leather and silk-lined walls with gold plate plastered everywhere, even in the shower, but this craft looked as if it would struggle to provide a cup of coffee or a place to wash his face. It had propellers. It was a Tupolev Tu-95, commonly known as a Bear, the workhorse of the Russian strategic air command, and it came with no guard of honour, no evident security, not even a maintenance crew. Standing alone at the bottom of the steps was Shunin's own personal pilot, who offered a crisp salute.

"Greetings, Boris Abramovitch. Is everything prepared?"

"Over a few broken bodies, Mr President."

"So long as they were broken quietly."

The pilot nodded.

A few steps behind, Shunin's guard was fidgeting in uncertainty as he stood beside the driver. "*Gospodin,*

Mr President — what are my instructions? Forgive me, but how am I to explain this?"

The question brought Shunin to a halt. He had his back to the guard. For a moment, he hung his head, as though considering his response. When at last he turned, his voice was quiet, little more than a dry wheeze. "You don't."

"*Gospodin?*"

"There has already been too much gossip about my travel plans."

Yuri Anatolyevich stiffened in alarm. He'd been with Shunin too long, he knew his moods, how quick they were to turn. He made no sound, offered no protest, but his eyes widened in accusation. He looked into his President's mirthless face and an absurd thought suddenly struck him. In all the time he had served Shunin he had never once seen him smile. Why? Why didn't the bastard ever smile? It was as if everything in his life came down to business, nothing was ever personal, no loyalty to anything, or to anyone but Russia.

Yuri Anatolyevich realized he was going to die, without understanding why and without ever truly knowing Shunin even after all those years. He could have lived to a hundred without figuring the man out, and he would very much like to have lived to a hundred, or at least to his next birthday, but Shunin was holding a pistol on him and . . . For the briefest of moments, Yuri Anatolyevich thought he saw a flicker on the other man's face. *He actually smiled!*

Two sharp retorts echoed across the tarmac, and they were gone, first the guard, then the driver. Two bodies crumpled on the tarmac, stains spreading across their chests.

"Holy Mother!" breathed Lavrenti. "What the hell did they do?"

"They died for the Fatherland," Shunin replied, touching the crucifix beneath his shirt before kissing the tips of his fingers. "Now get on board. We have no time to waste."

The son-in-law had no intention of arguing. With one last look at the welling blood, he did precisely as he was told.

CHAPTER
FOUR

Thursday evening. Buckinghamshire.

Harry drove himself to Chequers. There wasn't much traffic that time of the evening, it took him less than an hour. The storm front had passed but it was still stifling so he put the top down on his Audi coupé and let the air slap his cheeks, hoping it might blow away his concerns. The country roads of Buckinghamshire unwound before him through the Chiltern hills and he had to struggle to keep his speed down to sixty. He'd been taught to drive by his father on the roads that lead back into the hills from the coastline of the south of France. Their first lesson had been in a three-litre 1924 Bentley with a thundering leather strap around its bonnet — completely over the top, of course, but then his father was always that way. "Any idle bloody gendarme stops us, Harry, and they'll be wanting a ride rather than issuing a ticket," his father had told him. For additional insurance against the censure of the forces of law and order they'd also taken along his father's latest mistress with skirts that blew up around her waist. Mad bugger, his father. Now, with his old man's laughter ringing in his ears and the village of Speen disappearing in his rear-view mirror, Harry put his foot down.

Chequers was a sixteenth-century country house of red bricks and towering Tudor chimneys that a hundred years earlier had been presented to the nation as a country retreat for its Prime Ministers, a place for them to relax, although in recent years they rarely did. Harry had neither pass nor written invitation, but when he arrived at the police reception point at the edge of the estate he was halted only briefly before being waved through. As he drew up in the courtyard of the ancient house, D'Arby was waiting at the front door. The Audi came to a halt on the gravel and, as Harry levered himself from his seat, the Prime Minister advanced to take his hand. The scent of lavender clung to the evening air, fresh mown grass too; from somewhere nearby Harry could hear the gentle chugging of a motor mower. He stretched to retrieve his overnight case from the back seat.

"No, leave it, Harry. You're not staying."

"What? I've just driven all the way out . . ."

"I should have said *we're* not staying. You and I have more miles to cover tonight."

"Mark, I've got to say you're confusing me. And whatever help it is you want from me, I can't give it if I don't know what the hell I'm supposed to be doing."

"Come. Walk with me." D'Arby took his guest to the side of the house and through a wrought-iron gate until they came to a walled garden on the south side. It contained the most dazzling array of roses, long stems of colour that were reaching up to catch the light of the slowing sun. D'Arby led them to the middle point of the garden, through the spreading avenues of low box hedges, as though advancing to the centre of a bullseye. "You know, Harry, there might be satellites up there right now gazing down on us." He spread his arms and gave a hollow laugh.

"Seen. But not heard," Harry concluded.

"It's important right now that the world believes I'm tucked up here at Chequers."

For the moment Harry held back from asking why. The other man was in no hurry.

"You see this rose?" the Prime Minister said, taking a long stem between two fingers. "Floribunda 'Marcus D'Arby'. They named a bloody rose after me, Harry. Beautiful, isn't it?"

D'Arby cupped it in his hands and Harry bent to smell it.

"As you see it has no fragrance," D'Arby pronounced in disappointment. "All show, no substance. A politician's rose. And prone to early wilt, I'm afraid." He was mocking himself.

Harry straightened up. He hadn't smelt a damn thing, apart from a dash of whisky on D'Arby's breath. "I know bugger-all about roses."

"Really? But you're a man of so many talents," the Prime Minister said. Suddenly he crushed the rose in his fist and let the mash of petals fall to the ground. "OK, not roses, then. So tell me, Harry, what you know about that Boeing crash at Heathrow a few years ago — the 777 on its way back from China."

"The one that lost all its thrust just before landing?"

"That's right. A miracle that everyone on board walked away from it, but . . ."

"Something about the fuel-control systems, wasn't it? I seem to remember they thought it might be any number of things — bird strike, computer failure, pilot error, fuel contamination. But in the end they found some sort of glitch in the control systems."

"Yes. That's what they said."

"You're telling me —"

"They had to come up with something, Harry. We couldn't simply explain that the thing just dropped out of the sky for no reason."

"There's always a reason, Mark."

"Most surely, but we never found it. And I say 'we' because it ended up on my desk. There was nowhere else for it to go." He led them to an old lichen-covered bench where they sat facing out over the garden to the hills beyond before he picked up his story. "Yet those control systems were double- and even triple-banked. Fail-safe, or so it was thought. The boffins tore that plane apart, Harry, piece by piece, every nut, every bolt, every rivet, every bit of flap and fuel pipe in her." He cursed softly and slowly, and D'Arby didn't usually swear. He lit another of his cigarettes. "Then they stuck her all back together. They spent more than a year at it. And you know what? At the end of all their prodding and poking, they couldn't find a damn thing wrong with her."

In the distance, two armed policemen were on patrol, Heckler & Kochs in the crook of their arms and a dog at their heels.

"If it wasn't hardware that brought that plane down, it had to be a software screw-up. These things happen, of course." D'Arby blew smoke into the light air where it scattered and disappeared. "I remember once writing a speech for the party conference — typed it up myself. A fine piece of work it was, too. Spent bloody days on it. Something to be proud of, I thought. So then I pressed the save button and the whole thing simply vanished, like a wife's lover when he hears a key in the lock."

"No, like the lover, it doesn't vanish, it simply scatters," Harry countered. "You simply need to know where to look for it. You find it lurking in some corner — in the closet or behind a curtain, if you like. Some firms make a fortune out of retrieving lost data."

"Correct. Top-of-the-class stuff, Harry. And on the 777 we employed the best. Ran all the software, stood it on its head, turned it inside out, and you know what? It checked out perfectly. Which means . . ." He ground out his cigarette on the arm of the bench. "If someone did tamper with the software, they made such a good job of it they left not a trace."

"The perfect crime?"

"Far worse than that. These last couple of years, particularly these past few months, there've been any number of foul-ups in computer-controlled systems that no one can explain — not just in Britain, elsewhere too, but here more than anywhere. They don't simply crash, they start giving out the wrong signals, coughing up false information, and the world goes haywire. It's like being lost in a forest at the dead of night, stumbling through the dark with bear traps on every side. We've come this close to disaster" — he pinched his thumb and forefinger together — "and it's getting worse. The attacks are more frequent. We've managed to hide some of it, even allowed ourselves to be blamed for incompetence. Better that than the truth. Someone out there is hitting us, hitting us hard, and knows a damn sight more about some of our vital systems than we do."

"Not just hackers?"

"It's all been too consistent, too well coordinated. Anyway, hackers brag about their conquests; no one's claiming credit for this." D'Arby looked towards the embers of the sun, his eyes squinting into the distance. "And I believe it's about to get very much worse. Up to this point the bastards have been playing with us, flexing their muscles, trying out their skills and testing our defences. No outright disasters, not yet, but that's all about to change. You see, it's not just a perfect crime, Harry, it's the perfect war. It's about to start, and we are intended as its first victim." He shivered, despite the evening warmth.

"But who, Mark? Who's behind it?"

"China," he whispered, so softly that even the sparrows couldn't hear. "The yellow tide. And it's about to swamp us."

Thursday evening. Balmoral.

The route from the river back to Balmoral took them past the estate's cricket pitch, on which the local village team was playing. Shouts of triumph rose as another wicket tumbled, followed by polite applause for the victim. So very un-American, Blythe thought. Her mom would never have approved of the game, she'd been a baseball girl, through and through, a Red Sox fan, raw, unambiguous, who liked nothing better than when the benches emptied and the entire squad got stuck into the opposition. Showed team spirit, she said. Only last year, at a reception in the White House, she'd piled into the pompous figure of the baseball commissioner and told him to check out a proposed rule change with his father, if he had one. Damn, she missed her mother.

When they arrived back at Balmoral they tumbled in through the entrance hall with its jumble of fishing rods, hats and umbrellas stuffed into old barrels, just like any old country house, so it seemed, although the illusion didn't last long. Jeans and dungarees might be the order of the day, much as it was at Camp David, yet by evening things grew more formal. Dinner jackets and evening dress were required, and there were servants in a livery of long blue jackets and red waistcoats. This might be where the royal family put aside their crowns and codpieces and let their collective hair down, but evidently some traditions were worth clinging to. Perhaps those traditions included her bathroom, which was across the corridor from the rest of her suite and where the hot water seemed to be taking a detour via the village. She took a whisky while she waited.

An hour later, freshly bathed and dressed in something long and turquoise, she joined the throng as they assembled for dinner. Martinis in the drawing room first, stiff ones, mixed by an equerry. Franklin Roosevelt's favourite tipple and also, evidently, Elizabeth's. Blythe began to feel she might regret the whisky. As the Prince accompanied her into the dining room she passed a mirror, freckled with age inside an ornate Victorian frame. Her reflection stared back at her, somehow older than she had expected. Was that why Arnie had got his hooks into the tart? Was she past her best? *No, don't buckle, Blythe, don't stop believing!* The Harrisons were fighting folk — Indian-fighters in the old days — and she was the third member of her family to make it to the White House. It wasn't in their makeup to go down without a fight, but as the first of their Presidents, William Henry, had discovered when chasing Indians, you had to pick your battle, and right now she felt as though she were surrounded by hostiles and down to her last couple of bullets. She prayed she'd be able to save one for Arnie.

That got her thinking yet again about how the world would remember her. As the third Harrison? As the first woman President? Perhaps even as a great one? Or simply as a wife who had stumbled over her responsibilities, dragged down by sex and gossip and trapped in the same tar pit as the Clintons? Right now, she realized, the jury was out and her reputation was hanging not so much by a thread as from a pouting lobbyist's bra strap. She stopped and scolded herself. She was getting herself hopelessly distracted.

Once more it was Elizabeth who came to her rescue, appearing at her side. "Now, my dear, how are you?"

"Fine," Blythe replied, trying to recover her wits. "Thinking Chinese thoughts."

The Queen's eyes widened in surprise.

"Sun Tzu, the ancient Chinese strategist. He once said that if you wait long enough by the river, the bodies of your enemies will float past."

"Yes?"

"Heavens, we sat there all afternoon. No sign of Arnie."

There, a joke. A slip of humour. Perhaps she'd survive, after all.

"You know, you should take up fishing, like me," Elizabeth replied, smiling conspiratorially. "It will increase your chances."

Blythe couldn't resist a smile. "Thank you."

"I am old, my grandchildren think I'm practically pharaonic, but my memories are fresh. I still remember what it was like for me, all too vividly." Suddenly, unexpectedly, she took Blythe's arm, woman to woman. "I'll teach you to tie a trout fly," she continued, "it will help to pass the time down by the river, while you're waiting."

"Just so long as you don't teach me the rules of cricket."

"But they are so very simple. You must do what my own mother taught me. You wear a hat with a hideously large brim to hide your eyes, so you can nap. And make sure that whatever you are drinking is extremely well chilled."

The two women sat down and the others followed, twenty of them in all, an array of royals and presidential advisers. From a little further along the table, Warren Holt, Blythe's chief of staff, was nodding at her in relief. Dear and faithful Warren, who'd been with her from the start and who knew her every mood, and so knew how she'd been feeling. Now he glanced sceptically at the paintings on the wall — dark oils of wild-eyed stags with bloodied haunches being pursued by snarling dogs and Scotsmen. A little like an election campaign, she thought, not that the Windsors had to worry.

Opposite him sat another of her aides, who was cast from an entirely different mould. Marcus Washington was here almost under sufferance. He disliked small talk and had little interest in the nature of food; he survived on a diet of ideas and argument and seemed to have need for little else. He sat passively, resisting the offer of conversation from those around him, and when a freshly grilled trout was presented to him he set about it with a notable lack of interest. He didn't finish it, leaving the remains stranded on the side of his plate. Washington was her National Security Advisor, an academic, an intellectual (she was careful not to confuse the two), and a regular pain in the butt. Sometimes he treated her almost as a bus driver with whom he'd hitched a ride, a man who would decide for himself where and when he would get off, one who gave the impression of travelling with her not from any sense of loyalty but merely out of curiosity. Yet it was his sense of curiosity that made him so valuable; he took nothing for granted, probed deeper than the rest, and stripped every argument of emotion and irrelevance. Once, in the middle of a confrontation in the Oval Office, he'd told the Secretary of State for Defense that taking advice from him was like taking a suppository; it gave him an attack of the shits. His exact words. Not one who spent much time buffing backsides, was Marcus. And yet she couldn't throw him off the bus. He cut through tangled knots with a sharper mind and keener eye than anyone. She would need his talents, more than ever, in the next couple of days.

As the meal progressed, Blythe fell into distraction. They were fiddling while Rome was about to burn. When the fruit arrived, on plates that had been hand-painted by Landseer, she decided the time had come, the moment to make her move. The others continued with their meal, but she put aside her fork and spoon.

"Is everything all right?" Elizabeth enquired, as the room grew quiet.

"I'm not sure. A virus I've been carrying, a reaction to my mother's funeral, perhaps."

"Then you must rest."

"Would you mind?"

Immediately good, loyal Warren had jumped to his feet in concern.

"No, no, I'll be fine," she insisted. "If you'll all excuse me."

And the others rose to their feet, too, all except for the Queen. Blythe looked towards her hostess, who nodded. And it had started.

Elizabeth knew, of course, that the illness was feigned, was merely a pretence that would keep the most powerful politician on earth out of sight for the next couple of days without too many people asking questions. Not a word must get out, no suggestion made that she was anywhere other than tucked away and carefree in the Scottish countryside. The timing of this visit to Balmoral had been fortuitous, no one could have known that it would coincide with a moment of looming disaster, but you rode your luck when it trotted by, and Blythe hoped desperately that the luck might last. She had been told that war was about to break out. It didn't get more serious than that. Yet as she made her way to her room, she had no way of knowing that the war had already begun.

Early Friday morning. Beijing.

Something was stirring. Perhaps this wasn't evident to a casual observer but in the People's Republic of China, a land where Communism has held sway for more than sixty years and rigid custom for many lifetimes more, even a raised eyebrow or a sleeve tugged in impatience can betoken a change that might stir the entire world. And there were many raised eyebrows in Beijing that morning. During the night, a change had taken place that was far from subtle. First light — or what passed as light in that smog-crippled city — revealed that troops had taken up position outside many important buildings and at major traffic intersections. Not vast numbers of troops, for ostentation wasn't the Chinese way, but a guard of the People's Liberation Army had replaced the police who were normally on duty at the capitol's significant points, and larger contingents of troops could be spotted peering out from the side streets off the Avenue of Eternal Peace. They could be found outside many public buildings, and a couple of armoured personnel carriers were stationed as discreetly as these things could be in one corner of Tiananmen Square. Rumours began to circulate that a convoy of tanks was moving up on the railroad from Shanghai.

The troops didn't disrupt the normal life of Beijing — there seemed to be a conscious effort not to provoke alarm — but troops hadn't been deployed on the streets since the Tiananmen Square uprising twenty years earlier. No one needed to start casting joss sticks in the temple to know that the wind had shifted and was freshening sharply.

There was something else. These troops weren't from the regiments of the 38th Army, the local garrison, but from much further afield, some even mountain men from the Szechwan region in the south. Different dialects, different spices, different lifestyles, and that suggested different loyalties. These strange troops from distant parts even took up position outside the headquarters of the Beijing television service — it wasn't particularly their number that gave rise to comment, but simply the fact that they were there at all. Unmistakably, during the night, the military had placed its hand around the heart of China.

A new wind was most definitely stirring. The people of Beijing scurried on their way, heads low, wondering if this new wind might yet rise to gale force.

Thursday night.
Somewhere over the polar ice cap.

The Bear, with its four mighty turbo-prop engines that drove eight contra-rotating propellers, clawed its way through the thin air at more than three hundred miles an hour. It was a noisy craft and had never been intended for comfort; its strengths lay elsewhere. The first Bear had flown fifty years earlier, it had survived the test of time and Cold War, and its modern variant could fly for ten thousand miles, stay aloft all day and then all night, and was able to cause countless kinds of havoc with its twenty-ton payload of bombs and missiles. Yet it had been a while since those missiles had been launched in anger, and for the most part nowadays the Bear was used for reconnaissance, to test the reactions and the resolve of others, nudging up against their controlled airspace to see how quickly tomorrow's potential enemies might get off their arses and respond. So when the Bear took off and headed towards the polar ice cap before turning onto a flight path that would bring it close to British airspace, none of those watching these manoeuvres on the radars of various powers saw anything out of the ordinary. Neither had anyone noticed anything untoward when, moments earlier, Rossiya-1 had lifted off from

Sheremetyevo on its declared journey to Archangelsk. Everything was as expected.

They were flying at thirty-six thousand feet. Shunin had his eyes closed, pretending to sleep while trying to find what comfort he could in one of the flight engineer's chairs. An oxygen mask was beside him, just in case, as was a tumbler of Russkiy Standart thoughtfully provided by Boris Abramovitch and cooled to near freezing in some part of the bomb bay. The truth was that Shunin preferred bourbon to vodka but there were limits, even to a president's freedom. A man who had made his reputation standing up to America and browbeating his former Soviet neighbours couldn't allow himself to be accused of letting the Fatherland down. So many had, of course. They'd allowed Russia to become weak, left her flat on her back, waiting to be taken advantage of by Western businessmen, and now it was necessary to remind the world that Moscow had once been — and was again — a force to be reckoned with. The collapse of the Soviet Union had caused much crowing in Western capitals; in more recent times it had been both his patriotic duty and considerable personal pleasure to remind them that cock stew was one of Sergei Illich Shunin's favourite dishes.

His leg had gone to sleep. He shifted, aching. He understood that American bombers were more comfortable. How many years would it be, he wondered, before Russia caught up? How long before Ilyushin made an airliner with as much appeal as an Airbus, or Chaika a car that could last as long as a Volvo? And how much longer before Chechnya produced a man who wanted anything other than to slit Russian throats? Screw them. But he would sort it out, all of it, if God gave him time.

Thoughts of mortality had grown insistent in recent days, along with his shortness of breath. He was no fool, never that, he knew he wouldn't last forever. Someday they would get to him, and he would find himself on the wrong end of a bullet, just like Yuri Anatolyevich. He wouldn't deserve it, but neither had Yuri Anatolyevich, perhaps. And yet it was also possible that his death had been supreme justice, for there could be no more than six men who could have told the bombers of his plans and Yuri Anatolyevich was one of them. *Had been* one of them. One less suspect, one less thing for Shunin to worry about, and on that basis alone it had been a worthwhile death. A Russian death. Yet there were so many things for him to worry about.

What would happen after he had gone? Through half-closed eyes he examined his son-in-law once again. Lavrenti sat in his own chair on the other side of the cabin, lost in his own thoughts, drinking perhaps a little too much, occasionally drumming his fingers in impatience. Better in impatience than in thrall to that crap-encrusted music. Always in a hurry, was Lavrenti, which was why Shunin had to keep him pinned down, but it wasn't a grievous fault, the desire to get on. Shunin wanted a strong man to follow him, someone who could protect his legacy and everything he had achieved. Protect his family, too. Who better, perhaps, than Lavrenti? If only he could find better judgement, not just in music but in his friendships, and not get himself too deeply involved with rootless media men and cowboy contractors. He still had a lot to learn, but that was one of the reasons why Shunin had brought him along on this trip, to be taught. And to be tested.

The President stirred, glanced at his watch. It was time.

"Tell Boris Abramovitch I want to see him," he instructed Lavrenti, almost shouting to make himself heard above the noise of the engines. For once Lavrenti didn't ask questions, he hadn't spoken much at all since he'd seen his father-in-law kill those two men. He unbuckled his safety harness and did as he was told.

Soon, Boris Abramovitch Bulgakov appeared from the direction of the cockpit. He was a taciturn man of intense loyalties and few words, which made him excellent in general and ideal for this task. He was in command but not the pilot on this flight — it had been almost ten years since he had last flown a Bear in military service — so he had stood in for the co-pilot on this mission, taking the second seat, although no one on board questioned his authority.

"Boris Abramovitch, you've done well. But I have new instructions for you." The President handed across a sheet of paper. The pilot read it and couldn't disguise the astonishment in his eyes. He scratched himself, then read it once more, very carefully.

"But, Mr President, if I follow these instructions, no one back home will know . . ."

"Precisely."

"Forgive me, Mr President, but you must understand that there are dangers in what you propose."

"God has spared me once today. I'm gambling He's in no hurry to change His mind."

"You will need a tight belt. It will not be a comfortable flight."

"Then I'd better leave nothing to spill," Shunin replied, draining his glass. And nothing to chance, either, he muttered, reflecting that Boris Abramovitch, too, was one of those six — no, make that five — suspects.

CHAPTER
FIVE

Thursday night. Buckinghamshire.

Darkness was falling as Harry and Mark D'Arby drove away from Chequers in what amounted to disguise — a dusty six-year-old Range Rover with a parking dent on its front wing and the interior infused with the dull smell of cigarette ash. The air con didn't work and they had to lower the windows to allow the inside to cool down as they drove through the avenue of beech. It was a private vehicle, borrowed from God knew where, not one that came from the official pool, and it lacked armour, communications gear, sat nav, had none of the usual Special Branch presence and didn't even have a tracker device — which was part of the point, so D'Arby had half-explained in his mysterious you'll-have-to-guess-the-rest manner. Harry was driving, the Prime Minister slumped in the seat beside him, apparently slumbering, hidden beneath a hat as Harry was waved through the checkpoint at the gates. The policemen were relaxed, they were looking for madmen sneaking in, not escaping. The two men pressed on into the enfolding gloom and were soon lost to sight.

"So where are we headed, Mark?" Harry asked as, under D'Arby's direction, he drove through the darkening Buckinghamshire countryside.

"Scotland."

"What? You're kidding. That must be the best part of four hundred bloody miles! At this time of night?"

"Why do you think I asked you?" D'Arby replied, a grim smile flickering in the headlights of an approaching car. "Need you to share the driving. And you can hardly expect me to get out and pay for the petrol."

"I think you'll find it's diesel."

"Then my point is made." Suddenly D'Arby realized that he hadn't filled up a car in more than three years, hadn't cooked a meal, bought a train ticket, spent a lazy half-hour lingering over the sports page, and as for sex, well . . . Perhaps that was one of the reasons why he was more than a little envious of Harry and his freedom. "And it's four hundred and seventy-six miles, to be precise."

"Couldn't we fly? Use a chopper?"

"And leave our footprint all over the map?" The Prime Minister shook his head. "The technology's available nowadays to track not just planes and helicopters but every car on the road. Surveillance isn't something you leave behind in the High Street, it covers every part of the world and in astonishing detail. That's why we're using this shitheap of a car — no one will suspect it's us. And that's why I made you leave your mobile phone behind. You know they can track those bloody things to within three feet, even when they're switched off?"

"Is that what the Chinese are doing?"

"Possibly. Can't know for certain, and can't take the chance. Right now we're targets, Harry, and that's why we must hide."

Harry slipped through the gears as they navigated past yet another of the interminable roundabouts on the A41. He cast a glance at his companion; in the light of the street lamps his face looked stiff, drained, like a wax mask.

"Where the hell were you in the Sixties, Harry?" D'Arby started up again. "Oh, forgive me, bloody stupid question. You were scarcely born even when they finished. But I'm a full-blown child of that era, that's me. They always say it leaves a mark."

"Too much flower power and free sex."

"In all honesty I was still a little too young for all that. Tried to make up for it later, of course."

"Some of us still are."

"So I hear."

"Tell me you're not going to lecture me about my sex life, Mark."

"No, not tonight. Not this trip," D'Arby replied, his voice wistful. "Instead I'm going to give you a little lecture about Mr Mao Yanming."

"The One-Eyed Bandit of Beijing."

"The very same. He was a child of the Sixties, too, you know. One of Mao Zedong's little red warriors during those years of madness they called the Great Proletarian Cultural Revolution."

It had been one of those seminal moments in history that left scars on everyone. A decade of madness, great only in the extent of its destruction, proletarian only insofar as its miseries were shared by almost all, there was nothing in any respect cultural about its savagery and if it was a revolution it was of the most exceptional kind, since it had been started by the man who was already in charge. A total dictator and a revolutionary to his core, Mao Zedong had imposed policies that even at the time many people thought were signs of insanity. In the pursuit of perpetual renewal he had decided not so much to shake up the country as to kick it to pieces by questioning everything and everyone, and for that task he had set loose millions of young people known as his Red Guards. Armed with little more than printed copies of Chairman Mao's rambling thoughts and their overwhelming numbers, they'd ransacked the country, bringing industry to a halt, ritually humiliating and often executing anyone in authority, marching the country back towards the Stone Age. "Let a hundred flowers bloom, let a hundred schools of thought contend," Mao had preached, but the flowers had been pulled up by their roots and the schools had soon been destroyed. It had turned into nothing but an excuse for the humiliation of an entire generation of Chinese leaders. Academics were dragged from classrooms, accused of thought crimes, beaten by mobs, and sent to the countryside to work in the paddy fields, where many of them sank without trace. Generals were tried in front of their troops and banished. Senior politicians around Mao disappeared; some committed suicide, while Lin Biao, his heir apparent and publicly proclaimed "closest comrade in arms", was killed when his plane mysteriously fell out of the sky while he was trying to flee to the Soviet Union. The Cultural Revolution was an inferno, sparked by one old man and fanned into uncontrollable life by millions upon millions of teenagers. In the West the youth of that time smoked dope, practised desperately unsafe sex, and clung to the thoughts of maharishis and John Lennon, while in the East they washed in blood as they chanted the name of Mao Zedong.

Now there was a new Mao. Yanming. It was clearly an adopted name. Yan conveyed the meaning of someone strict or stern, Ming that of something brilliant or explicit. In other words, one tough Chinese cookie. He was a man who had changed his name, and now wanted to change his country.

"We know so little about the man, Harry. I've never met him, very few Western leaders have. He's an ardent nationalist, dynamic, radical, brutal. Truth is, we know next to nothing about him until he emerges as a Red Guard from the mess of the Cultural Revolution. For his sins he gets himself banished to the desert with orders to make it bloom. Almost starves to death, loses an eye, and gains a streak of single-minded bloody ruthlessness. Ten years later he reappears and starts going through the system like a bad oyster. Then, as world energy prices soar, so does the cost of basic foods and suddenly the Beijing economic miracle begins to lose its gloss. Very privately, because that's how things always happen in China, the government begins to panic. A billion Chinese start asking why five per cent of their fellow countrymen are living in the lap of luxury while they're coughing up their guts after working eighty-hour weeks in the inundation of filth that passes as their local factory. So the Politburo pick on Mao to take over — partly because he's a bit of an outsider, largely perhaps because they need someone new to shoulder the blame. But he grabs the whole thing by the balls and announces that he hates bloody foreigners. Gives the country something new to talk about."

Harry was listening attentively as they pulled onto the M40 motorway and swung out into the fast lane. At last he was beginning to understand what was hounding Mark D'Arby so pitilessly.

"The old guard's terrified it's all going to get flushed down the pan like the Soviet Union," the Prime Minister continued, "while the new industrialists are worried they'll return home to find five hundred coolies living in their spare room. So they've given Mao unprecedented leeway. And he's intent on using it. China First."

"Wave the flag, piss over the garden fence, and hope the masses don't notice they're choking to death on recycled plastic."

"Something like that. But he's different, he means it. This guy is for real."

"So what does he want?"

"Revenge. On the Russians for putting the screw on him over energy prices, and on the Americans for being cultural syphilis and the only reason Beijing hasn't yet got back Taiwan. That's his ambition."

"China reunited? That'd be a feather in his cap."

"The biggest from China's point of view. Mao brings Taiwan back in from the cold and he becomes the most feted leader his country has ever had, a name they'll remember right up there alongside Confucius and chilli prawns. Not an insignificant inducement."

"You think he means that?"

"Not only does he mean it, he may now have the tools to do it."

"The perfect war," Harry whispered, remembering their earlier conversation.

"To be precise — cyber war."

For a moment, Harry said nothing. He flicked the lever to engage the cruise control and settled back in the middle lane while a thousand thoughts rushed past him. Cyber warfare. The concept was simple, its ramifications endless. The use of computers to disable, deceive, or destroy your enemy. To cause chaos in their control systems, to make them malfunction, to do things they shouldn't, to mess around and foul up your enemy so badly that they lose their will to fight. The theory was simple: anything that had a computer chip could be attacked, and nowadays everything had a computer chip — everything from a microwave oven to a nuclear deterrent, from a remote control that ran a television to the systems that manage the world's financial markets, not forgetting missile guidance, heart pacemakers, air-traffic control, burglar alarms, sewage pumps, power generators, food factories, transport grids, dishwashers, traffic lights and car engines. Even the central-locking system on this Range Rover. Didn't have to knock it out, just confuse it, tell it to do the wrong thing at the wrong time and it would mess up, perhaps catastrophically, all by itself. Just like the systems on the 777.

It reminded Harry of something else Mao Zedong had said, something Harry had learned at Staff College. "To achieve victory we must make the enemy blind and deaf, and drive his commanders to distraction by creating confusion in their minds." Perhaps the old pimple-faced bastard hadn't been completely raving after all. From the darkness beside him, Harry could hear the strain in D'Arby's voice. The British Empire had come and gone, the Soviet Union had collapsed, the American dream lay submerged in Prozac, yet the Han endured, as if knowing that their time would come. And, with Mao Yanming, perhaps now it had.

"His ambition's simple," D'Arby continued. "He wants to make China great once more. Repay all the historic insults, put an end to the kow-towing. No more exploitation, no more pillage, no more watching Chinese babies being bounced off the end of foreign bayonets."

"It's been a while since those days."

"Grandmothers still remember. And the Chinese have a collective memory that makes the *Encyclopædia Britannica* look like a comic strip. The Opium Wars, the Boxer rebellion, the imperialist invasions, the era of Unequal Treaties, the rape of Manchuria, the foreign settlements, the enforced leasing of Hong Kong — and Taiwan, of course. They remember it all as though it were yesterday. Mao wants to wipe the slate clean."

"Settle scores."

94

"He'd call it restoring face. But he has a problem. For all its mass, China doesn't have enough muscle. The People's Liberation Army is still light-years behind the competition, some of it's still riding bikes, so Mao knows he's got to find an answer on the cheap,' and that appears to be precisely what his boys have done. Cracked the cyber-warfare codes. Now they can worm their way inside our systems, mess with them, and apparently get out without leaving a trace. That's what they've been up to, trying out their new box of tricks on targets all round the world, Harry. Russian nuclear plants, American power supplies, all sorts of things . . . The list is endless."

Harry tapped the brake pedal, knocking out the cruise control. Suddenly he didn't trust it any more, wanted to be back in charge. He put his foot down, sped away. If only life could be as simple as a Range Rover. Beside him, D'Arby's breath was coming in short, shallow bursts. When he spoke again, he seemed diminished.

"And you know what really terrifies me, Harry? What's got me throwing up every night?"

"Right now I don't care even to imagine."

"That Chinese bastard has made this country his number-one target."

Early Friday morning. Beijing.

Fu strode away from Mao's office in his own peculiar manner. He had a bobbing gait, a little like a wading

95

bird, his body leaning forward while his feet seemed to be searching for a secure foothold. The step summed up the man. Nothing was taken for granted. He was a private individual who preferred shadows to sunlight. Not for him the interminable speeches that others made from the podium of the State Council. He didn't care to explain, certainly not to others, and sometimes not even to himself. Introspection, he found, was a worm that ate away at a man's courage.

As he walked into the cleansing morning air beside the lake at Zhongnanhai and towards his car, a large sedan passed. In its rear seat, squashed uncomfortably together, sat three of the most senior commanders of the People's Liberation Army, dressed in their full military regalia; strutting peacocks all, Fu thought. Their eyes met his yet there was no greeting, nothing but coldness. The PLA's world was one of military codes and inflexible structures, a world in which minds were always turned back on the last war, not towards the next one. These men had no time for subversives such as Fu, and the mistrust they felt was reciprocated in full.

Ducks scampered for the safety of the water as Fu approached along the bank. He smiled inside. The generals would be scampering, too, when they found out what was afoot. Not long now: the country had arrived at the crossroads that separated the past from its future. It was time to decide. Modern China was a great nation, and one that carried great burdens united only by the pollution and muck that engulfed them all. It must move on, but to where? It was no longer

Communist in anything but name, on that point there was agreement, if on little else. Mao knew which direction to take, of course, but so many were too blind to see it, were reluctant to follow. There were doubters, there were whisperers, there were malcontents and traitors, and that was what made Fu so necessary, like a surgeon who dealt with discontent and cut out the gangrene. Yes, that's what he was, a surgeon.

Wu Xiaoling had been part of that malady, a whisperer, a traitor. Yet how much had she whispered, how much had she told? And just how much had Mao told her? Fu hadn't dared ask, but women had such wiles, could extract so much, infer even more. Fu rejoiced in the fact he had no time for them, it made him feel almost pure.

It was possible that Wu had told too much, had revealed their plans, so Mao had insisted that those plans be brought forward. But we aren't ready, Fu had argued. Neither are our enemies, Mao had replied, and we must give them no opportunity to prepare. It must be now! The generals wouldn't care for it, when they were told, but once the plan succeeded they'd be scrambling over each other's backs to grab a slice of the credit. It was about to start, the great adventure, the moment when China would stand tall once more, their enemies crushed like ripe fruit and their skins left for the birds.

Fu swatted at the mosquitoes hovering around his face. There was no time to waste. As the sullen-faced generals disappeared inside the compound, Fu quickened his pace. More ducks scattered in alarm, seeking the cover of the bulrushes. He smiled as he watched them. In just a few hours, there would be nowhere left for anyone to hide.

Late Thursday night. Moray, North-east Scotland.

"Mayday. Mayday. Mayday."

The air-traffic controller at RAF Kinloss on the north-east coast of Scotland sat up sharply. It was going to be one of those nights. The station commander was on the prowl, breathing down everyone's necks, making one of his unannounced checks, and now this. There'd been an unidentified aircraft nudging into restricted airspace somewhere to the north and a couple of the new Eurofighter Typhoons from the Quick Reaction Alert force had already been scrambled, but the emergency signal dumped the matter directly into her lap. She tugged nervously at the sleeve of her blouse.

"Mayday. Mayday. Mayday," the voice repeated. The voice had a dull, dough-like accent.

"Aircraft calling Kinloss, your Mayday acknowledged. Squawk seven-seven-zero-zero, pass details when ready." 7700 was the international distress shout that would alert everyone to the pilot's difficulties.

"RAF Kinloss, decline Squawk. Keep situation between ourselves, please. This is Russian military. We are Bear. We have major loss of hydraulics. Request straight-in landing."

The announcement caused her to catch her breath. This wasn't some idiot in a Cessna who'd got himself lost in cloud but a big, ugly Russian Bear. Old enmities die hard and the officers' mess at Kinross was still full of bits that had fallen or been blown from some ancient Soviet warplane, and now she had the latest version, the whole thing. It was a chance for her to shine — and in front of the station commander. Even an experienced controller with the rank of flight lieutenant was allowed to enjoy a moment in the spotlight. She sipped at her tea; the meniscus gave an expectant shiver. "Roger, Mayday Russian Bear. This is RAF Kinloss. Pass your message."

A silence, as though he were teasing, until: "Kinloss, this is Russian Bear. I say again. Major loss of hydraulics. We are one hundred sixty miles — I repeat, one-six-zero miles — north-east of your position. Descending."

"Mayday. Stand by."

The station commander was hovering, trying not to interfere but inevitably drawn like a moth to this Russian flame. The controller didn't need his advice — had she ever taken advice from any man on this station that hadn't by the morning seemed limp and ridiculous? — but there was no harm in acknowledging the group captain's presence. She turned and raised an eyebrow.

He bounced on his toes, as he did when concentrating, hands clasped behind his back. "What do you think, Flight Lieutenant? Shall we make it a bit of an exercise? Hold off on the D&D boys and see if we can handle it ourselves?"

She took his point. Distress & Diversion, along with a variety of other support services, would normally be brought in to assist with Maydays, but in a full-scale emergency — with the country under attack, for instance — they might not be available. In these circumstances Kinloss would be on its own, so she was being given a chance to try it out, to stretch her wings, and she enjoyed that. When she came back on air, her voice had lost its tight, formal edge and reached out with greater confidence. "Russian Bear, you are cleared. Straight in Runway Two Six. Report ready to copy weather."

The voice repeated the instructions, still dull and as heavy as an uncooked pudding, very Russian.

"Surface wind two-five-zero," the controller said. "Twenty-three knots. Visibility six miles. Cloud broken two thousand five hundred feet. QNH on one-zero-one-seven."

The voice copied the information.

"Russian Bear, this is Kinloss. Do you request radar assistance?"

"Kinloss, Russian Bear. No. Thank you. We know where you are. And we see you have sent two of your flying traffic policemen to show us the way. We will be with you soon."

"Russian Bear, this is Kinloss. Glad to hear it. We'll put the kettle on for you."

"Kinloss, Russian Bear. Thank you. Just a few thousand feet of runway, that is all we need. But tea would be very good, too."

The controller turned to her station commander. Funny that he'd been here, just at this touchy moment, she thought. "English breakfast with a nip of vodka it is, sir."

He glanced at his watch. "Then you'd better hurry, they'll be here in twenty minutes."

"I'll alert the ground emergency services, of course, just in case, sir."

"And I suggest you tuck our Russian friends away quietly in one of the hangars. They'll want to lick their wounds and repair their hydraulics in private."

"We let them do just that, sir?"

"This is a diplomatic situation, not a military one, Flight Lieutenant. We give them whatever assistance they need, then get rid of them."

"Yes, sir," she replied, an edge of deflation creeping into her voice. No medals, then. No souvenirs for the mess.

"You did well, Jayne."

"Thank you, sir." She brightened, utterly unaware of the part she'd taken in a dance of shadows. The station commander's presence was no coincidence, his orders had come straight from the air marshal in Whitehall. No discussion, no explanation, in fact he had almost as little idea of what was going on as the flight lieutenant, but station commanders tucked up here on the Moray Firth had to be adaptable. During World War Two one of his predecessors had found food supplies so hard to come by that he'd dropped a bomb into Burghead Bay to stun the fish. Nobody had asked too many questions, they'd just got on with it. Now he had been asked to give sanctuary to the crew of a Russian bomber until Sunday — and that's precisely how long he'd been told they would need to fix their problem. Sunday. The air marshal was a most gifted man but even he couldn't know how long it would take to fix a Russian leak, which meant that hydraulics weren't the problem at all. What the real problem was, the station commander hadn't any idea, and neither, perhaps, had the air marshal. Oh, and the station commander was also asked to lend the Russian crew his private car. That's what had kept him bouncing on his toes the entire evening.

He was still wrestling with his thoughts when the Bear landed, its four huge engines trailing smoke. Once it had taxied safely to a halt the emergency services were stood down as the follow-me vehicle led the lumbering bomber to its haven in a hangar that would normally house one of the RAF's Nimrod MR2 reconnaissance planes. The Bear and all those on board would be secluded there, for as long as they needed.

It was only once he had seen the Russian bomber safely tucked away that the station commander returned to his quarters. He glanced at his watch; he was five minutes behind schedule, but that wasn't bad, given the circumstances. He picked up a secure phone, dialled a number, and as soon as it was answered said only one word.

"Bingo."

That was the agreed signal, a word opaque enough to confuse anyone trying to listen in. That was odd, too, it was as though Whitehall no longer trusted their own secure communications. He glanced down at the blotter on his desk. "Beware of Russians bearing leaks," he had scribbled. He sighed and scratched his balding head, more confused than ever. Damn world had grown so complicated. Difficult to know whose side you were on. How he missed the Cold War.

CHAPTER
SIX

Late Thursday night. Balmoral.

The Russians were coming, and so were the Americans, but not without a little difficulty. That difficulty was named Warren Holt. He was caring, boundlessly loyal, prissily Yankee, and hated being left out. And he was knocking at Blythe's door.

"You OK?" he asked as his head appeared round her bedroom door. There were few physical secrets between them, he'd seen her in sickness and in health, in curlers and in nightdress, in tears, in tantrum and in triumph, even in the bath, if the phone call was urgent enough. In fact, they'd held few secrets of any kind from each other, up to now.

"I need you, Warren."

He stepped inside the bedroom, and his eyes flared in surprise as he saw her standing over a small suitcase. "You're packing?"

"I'm going away. A day or so. I want you to cover for me."

"But you can't."

"I am."

He made a noise as though he was being strangled. "For heaven's sake . . . Where?"

"That I can't tell you."

"Then why? I don't understand." He was both anxious and a little angry. "You can't just disappear. It's ridiculous."

Slowly, she closed the lid of her suitcase and zipped it up. "Nevertheless, I've got to. And that's why I need your help."

"Come on, get serious."

She gave him a stare of rebuke that told him she was already so.

"Madam President," he declared, growing a little pompous and stepping further into the room, "you're perhaps not well. You know you simply can *not* do this. Go off on your own."

"I'm not sick, that's just pretence. And I'm not going on my own."

"Then . . ."

"With Marcus."

He stepped back, flabbergasted and deeply hurt, the eyes flooded with confusion. A private weekend? With *that* man? Was she on the rebound? Surely it couldn't be . . . "Are you somehow trying to punish me because I didn't tell you about Arnie?"

So, he had known about Arnie and his little pneumatic distraction, and kept it from her. Damn him. She was angry now, too.

They had a fine row, raised voices, home truths, the lot, standing toe to toe, and he gave back as good as he got because he was in pain, called her hormonal and absurd, which was half true, and gave voice to his suspicions about an affair with Marcus Washington, which made her burst into scornful laughter, and even while she was shouting back at him she could see the claws of confusion scratching at his face and wondered what she had done to deserve so forthright and faithful a friend as Warren.

"You're not going, not without security, not without the nuclear codes!" he stormed, pounding his fists in exasperation.

She took his hand, slowly unwrapped his fingers, one by one, and held them, not like a president but as an old and very dear friend. "Warren, I'm not able to tell you what I am about to do, only that it may turn out to be the most important thing I've ever done in my life. I have to disappear, until Sunday, and you're the only one I can trust with that secret, as I trust you with my life. Always have."

"You're worrying the heck out of me, Blythe," he said, his anger seeping away through her fingers.

"I want you to explain to the others that I'm unwell. And I'm going to give you an envelope which you will open only in an emergency. Inside you will find a telephone number and an address, that will be the only way to contact me for the next two days. You're to use it only in the most extreme of circumstances."

"Define that."

"War. Or some similar crisis. Nothing less. In all other matters, for the next forty-eight hours, you'll have to be the President of the United States, acting in my name."

"From a bedroom in Balmoral?"

She held his eyes, and nodded.

"They'll lynch us from the White House flagpole if ever they find out."

"Which is why that must never happen — and why you are the only one I can ask to do this."

"What do I tell Arnie if he calls?"

"He won't. And I guess you understand why." She had grown distant once more.

He flushed with guilt.

"How long have you known?" she asked.

"Too long. I was waiting for the right time to tell you, but . . . Heck, there never was a right time."

"Don't ever do that to me again, Warren, not ever, do you hear?" She was presidential once more, her eyes flecked with resentment, and he retreated.

"I apologize." His shoulders sagged in defeat.

"Not that in Arnie's case there will ever be an 'again', not so far as I am concerned." She sighed. "Time to move on."

"Is it as easy as that?"

"No. But I have to try."

"I wish I could help."

"You can. Right now."

"But . . . what about the nuclear codes?" he asked once again, back on the job. "And your personal security?"

"We can't avoid taking a few risks," she said. "Call me, and I can be back inside the hour." She waved away his protests. "Oh, I know that's not enough, not how it should be, but it's the best I can do. And as for my own security, that'll have to rely on the fact that no one, apart from you, will know I've gone. Hell, there's

107

more danger of my being shot by a prince out on the estate."

"It's not the hunting season yet."

"It is where I'm going."

"Blythe, you're scaring me."

"One other thing. I want you to rustle up the Vice-President, the Secretaries of State and Defence, the Joint Chiefs and the members of the National Security Council — all the usual suspects. But don't go through their offices, I want you to get hold of them personally. Invite them to a drink with me at the White House for as soon as I get back. Just in case."

"Of what?"

"Make it sound casual," she continued, ignoring his question. "Don't get them clucking around like old hens."

"Jesus H. Christ, that sounds like a War Cabinet."

Her silence was intense.

"You're meeting with a whole tribe of Congressmen Monday evening. Rearranged from your mother's funeral. I'll have to put them off again."

"Not Monday, Warren. Sunday. The moment I step off the plane."

His lips were working with so many unasked questions. "You know you can trust me," he said.

"And I do."

"But not as much as Marcus Washington, apparently."

"You're missing the point."

"I surely am."

108

It was at that moment he made up his mind. He stood looking at her, examining her for any sign of fever or distraction, anything to explain what she was doing. Then he stiffened. "I'd better go. They're expecting me downstairs with a report on your condition."

"Tell them it's fragile, not fatal."

He turned at the door, reluctant to leave. "Will you tell me about it, when it's all over?"

"If I can."

It wasn't the answer he wanted. He slammed the door on his way out.

Midnight, Thursday. M6 motorway.

They were making good time. Harry had been driving almost three hours and they were approaching Stoke. The rhythm of the wheels on the roadway had a hypnotic effect; beside him, D'Arby had been drifting into bouts of silence — or was it sleep? — before suddenly snapping back from whatever world he'd been visiting in order to start once more on his tale. They were making progress on that front, too.

"But what I don't understand is why us?" Harry pressed as D'Arby stirred once more. "What the hell's driving Mao to take it out on Britain?"

For some while there was no answer, until Harry thought the other man might have fallen asleep once more in the darkness. Eventually, D'Arby shifted in his seat.

"Why us?" he whispered. "Well, pick any number of reasons. Because of all the many countries that over the last couple of centuries have humiliated and hacked away at China, we are as guilty as any. Because of the Opium Wars, because we got millions of Chinese addicted to the stuff as a deliberate act of policy, because we stole Hong Kong, because we sent gunboats and General Gordon to blast the balls off them, because we surrounded Beijing and looted their Summer Palace. And because everywhere we went we placed less value on a Chinese life than we did on our pet dogs. Because . . ."

"I think I get your point."

"The Chinese have never forgotten, never forgiven. You remember Charlton Heston saving those brave imperialists from the Boxers in — what was the ridiculous film called? — *Fifty-Five Days in Peking?* For some reason they didn't make the sequel, the one that came after the siege was lifted when European troops went on a rampage and raped and massacred fifty thousand Chinese civilians. That was part of our story, too. Not a pretty one."

"I suspect you're going to tell me that's the bit the Chinese teach in their schools."

"But there's an even more powerful reason, the simplest reason of all. It's because they can. They can bring us to our knees within days, and no one else'll lift a finger to stop them, unless I can persuade them otherwise."

A police car with its blue lights flashing raced past them. Harry checked his speed, it wasn't the time for them to be pulled over and questioned, with names and details being flashed across the police radio. It went against the grain but he eased back, just a touch.

"We have friends, allies even," Harry pressed, not certain that he'd got to the nub of the matter.

"Hah! You mean our friends in Europe?" D'Arby couldn't hide his scorn. "They might send an auctioneer or two to help prepare for the biggest fire sale in history. United Kingdom plc, on the block, and everyone with a dollar or a euro in his pocket on the last flight out of Heathrow."

He took out a cigarette but Harry told him not to. "Don't be in such a hurry to kill yourself, Mark. Wait until we stop."

D'Arby sighed and crumpled the cigarette, letting it fall to the floor. "And there's Taiwan, too, that other offshore island. A lot like us. We're the dry run."

"OK, next it's Taiwan. So what the hell we doing on the road to Scotland?"

D'Arby smiled grimly. "We're going to meet an old friend of yours. And perhaps someone who might just become a new one, although I have my doubts. We're going to spend the weekend with the two most powerful people in the world, Blythe Edwards and Sergei Shunin."

Harry spluttered in astonishment, struggling to keep the car on line.

D'Arby chuckled drily, enjoying his moment of surprise. "But not a whisper, Harry, there mustn't be. That's vital. Our security lies in absolute silence. So no telephones, no messages, no tracker devices, no satellite links. Trust no one except those directly involved. We're all taking this risk, Harry, because the stakes are so high. The Chinese want nothing less than to obliterate us. We have the weekend to stop them."

"And we're going to do it with a beaten-up Range Rover about to run out of diesel." He flicked on the indicator and began to pull over towards a service area looming in the distance.

"Two presidents and a prime minister, Harry. Think about it. It's happened before. Together, we can achieve almost anything. Otherwise we'll be picked off one by one."

"As your nominated bag carrier I'm delighted your bag is so modest."

"No, Harry," D'Arby protested, "I told you, you're the only man for the job. I want you to back me up, to use your connections with Blythe Edwards, help me break down the barriers with Shunin. You're his type of man, I'm sure. I told you, there's no other man I'd rather have with me right now."

Somehow Harry didn't quite see it, couldn't get the sceptical buzz out of his mind, but there was no time for further questions. They were pulling up beside the fuel pump.

"Use cash," D'Arby instructed. "Don't want our credit cards leaving a trail all the way up north, do we?" But his wallet remained in his pocket.

"Sandwich? Soft drink? Something for the weekend, sir?" Soldier's humour.

"I'll take a leak. But not here. Somewhere a little darker where we can't be recognized."

"Don't know about you, Mark, I'm usually recognized by my face, not any other part of my anatomy."

"Harry, from what I hear, that's no longer true."

Harry filled up the tank, feeling very slightly used — even abused. He paid for the fuel from his own deep pocket and walked back to the car, expecting D'Arby to take some of the strain of driving, but discovered him soundly asleep. With a sigh and a pinch of his own cheeks, Harry turned the key and began driving once more.

As he turned out of the service area back onto the motorway, squinting through tired eyes and chastising himself for not picking up a coffee, he thought about what D'Arby had said. Russia, America and Britain ganging up against the common enemy. Yes, D'Arby was right, it had happened once before. They'd called it World War Two.

Friday morning. A road leading out of Beijing.

Fly! Fly! Fu Zhang urged his driver onwards. No time to waste, for enemies were lurking everywhere, even in Mao Yanming's own bedroom. They had dealt with her, but she was not alone, there would be others, always there were others. Even as Wu Xiaoling lay beside Mao, her poisonous heart had been elsewhere, with the British. Now it was their turn to suffer.

The timing was propitious, Mao had argued. The first day of the first weekend of the eighth month — the month when the red-faced British were always caught off their guard, snoring in the sun. And after that it would be the turn of others, those who stood in Mao's way, who conspired against him closer to home. Even in Beijing. The capital was a long way from Gansu, where Mao and Fu had first begun their journey together, days when their formal schooling had been ripped to rats' tails by the abomination of the Cultural Revolution, when they had spent three years of their young lives counting the grains of sand in the Manchurian desert for the purposes of their "re-education". Yes, Beijing was an exceedingly long way from Gansu, and even though it was the capital it could never be their home. It was a place of suspicions and disloyalties, Wu Xiaoling had proved that. So Mao had sent him on his way, to cast his spells in what Mao called his Room of Many Miracles. Mao had instructed him to tell no one, trust no one. Consider nothing safe unless it is locked up here, he had said, tapping his temple with his index finger, but Fu knew that even inside someone's head, secrets could still be unpicked, given time and the right tools. They'd been in too much of a hurry with Wu, too keen to take their retribution and perhaps a little anxious not to allow her to drag Mao himself into her shame, and they had needed more time with the ambassador — the man was proving stubborn. But they had no more time, not if Wu had talked too much and told the British of their plans, and not if those home-grown barbarians in the People's Liberation Army had found out about them, either. So fly! Fly! There wasn't a moment to lose!

114

Early hours, Friday. The Scottish border.

Almost five. The sky to the east was beginning to lose its mystery, softening at its edges. They'd crossed into Scotland but to Harry the border had been just another road sign trying to drag his wearied eyes from the unwinding highway. During his time with the SAS at Hereford he'd been trained for moments like this, when the body simply wants to give way, so desperate to sleep that the pain of staying awake is far, far worse than a kick in the balls. He'd been taught to cope, of course, but that had been twenty years ago. An hour earlier he'd been forced to pull over, afraid that he was losing it, and while D'Arby continued to snore obliviously Harry had catnapped for ten minutes — no longer, not enough for him to fall deeply asleep, just a short break to dampen the fire in his eyes, as he'd learned on sentry duty, but the long turns of this anonymous night had sapped his strength and were once again squatting on top of his eyelids, trying to force them to close. This had become, as so often in his life, a battle with himself.

Beside him, D'Arby stirred, then started, sitting up abruptly as though some inner alarm had pierced him into consciousness. "What time is it?" he demanded, still befuddled, trying to focus.

"Near five."

"Bugger — stop! We need a telephone. God, a public telephone, Harry." He began gesticulating in anxiety.

"But I thought you said —"

"A land line. A risk we have to take."

115

They pulled off the motorway but it took them the best part of a quarter of an hour before they found one of the old red metal boxes, stuck at the edge of a small farming community. Public phones were yet another of the endangered species in D'Arby's Britain, and this example appeared to be on the very edge of extinction. It was unkempt, the glass dirty and cracked, the light inside flickering intermittently. While Harry relieved himself in the bushes and washed his face in the cool air, the Prime Minister stood fumbling with coins and punching in a number. His conversation drifted through the broken pane.

"What do you have for me?" D'Arby snapped, not bothering with introductions.

Away back in London, in an office within the Privy Council building very close to Downing Street, the duty clerk began his report. He was a retired diplomat, from the spooky end of the business, who filled some of his spare time and supplemented his pension with turns as a night-watchman guarding government business. He had the experience to know what was important, and the maturity not to flap and wake everyone up in the middle of the night without proper cause, yet this night, although he had a cot available, he hadn't slept a wink. He began his report in the calm, matter-of-fact manner, while in a muddy lane somewhere near the Scottish border the Prime Minister began to show increasing exasperation, chewing at his lower lip and slowly screwing his knuckle into the wall of the telephone box.

116

"What — nothing?" D'Arby growled, but as he listened, the bark grew subdued. "Then try them again, right now. Insist! Badger the bastards! I'll call you back in five minutes."

He replaced the phone but didn't move. He stood in the box, like a prisoner in the dock awaiting sentence, staring at the wall, breathing heavily, the bulb flickering above his silvered head. He called back in four, too impatient to wait longer. He said nothing, just listened. As Harry watched him, he thought he saw the Prime Minister flinch.

Then he swore. Again, and again, and yet again, and with every curse he smashed the receiver of the telephone against the wall until he was exhausted, leaving the mutilated receiver swinging pathetically from its gibbet. It took him a while to recover. Eventually D'Arby lifted his head and braced himself, taking a deep breath before he turned and left the telephone box. Harry could see the turmoil in his eyes.

"Been trying to get hold of the Chinese government," the Prime Minister said, struggling to regain his calm. "Suggested I might fly there to talk to Mao himself, face to face, man-to-man stuff, you know what I mean. Hoping he might see the human side. I thought it might be a way out of this mess. Asked for an answer by five — noon their time, just about now . . ." He flapped his hand as though trying to fend off despair, then sucked in a lungful of cool night air, trying to restore his spirits, but it sounded like a sob. "Anyway, duty clerk's been waiting all night — heard nothing — so I got him to call the Chinese ambassador on his direct line."

117

D'Arby clearly had no appetite for finishing his story. The lips moved, but for a moment the words failed him. Then: "There was no reply, Harry. He wouldn't even pick up the phone."

"Then I think we have their answer, Mark."

Stiffly, reluctantly, D'Arby nodded in agreement. "But there's more. Our ambassador."

"Wes Lake?"

"He's gone missing."

"Missing? But he can't. Ambassadors don't simply go miss —"

"He went off on a short break a few days ago. Apparently he never made it. His car's been found at the railway station, his gear still inside, his mobile phone, too. He could be anywhere." He paused. "Or nowhere."

"He's a good man, Wes Lake. Wouldn't do anything silly."

"Perhaps he had no choice. He's a Briton, right now that's enough to get him into a tubful of trouble." D'Arby began ransacking his pockets in search of a cigarette. "Harry, they won't talk to us, they've probably taken our ambassador. I wasn't expecting this, not so bloody quickly."

"What do you propose to do?"

"A century ago I'd have sent a gunboat up the Yangtze to pound the crap out of them!" he spat in exasperation. He was completely out of cigarettes.

"And now?"

"We drive, Harry, we drive."

Midday, Friday. On the road to Shanjing.

On the far side of the world, another car was hurtling in search of the future. Fu Zhang had been travelling several hours, his destination Shanjing, which lay two hundred miles from the capital on the old Silk Road south. As they drove they had passed several troop convoys heading in the opposite direction. Fu wrinkled his nose, he didn't trust soldiers.

Power grows out of the barrel of a gun, Mao Zedong had once said, and the People's Liberation Army had been clinging to that concept ever since, pouring their energies and enormous budgets into bits of rusting metal. They didn't want to accept that it was all changing. Now there was another Mao in charge, and another proposition. *Power grows out of fear*. It was the new way. Some of the old generals had grumbled and tugged their whiskers, but most of them would rediscover their loyalty when they realized they'd become the defence force of the most powerful nation on earth! Why, by next week the muttonheads would be rejoicing and claiming it was all their idea. And if they didn't — well, Fu had a list, and a solution. There was no need for worry, Mao Yanming was the most far-sighted leader their country had ever had, and he, Fu Zhang, was his most loyal lieutenant. What could go wrong?

The road to Shanjing was new, some of it still under construction, yet at the roadside there was so much that remained of the old China. Women working knee-deep in the fields alongside the oxen. Toothless old men

119

sitting forlorn and useless on the doorstep of some half-finished hovel. Ribby mongrels wandering the street. A child no more than eight years of age seated in the sun, perched on an upturned beer crate, his eyes beseeching, trying to dismember an old computer for salvage, his grandmother beside him, her emaciated hand holding out tiger balm and other potions for sale. In every corner the wind whipped up dust from building sites and over-tilled fields, swirling it around in vicious spirals of grime.

But it was all about to change, everything was about to change. Mao Yanming would see to that, with a little help from his friend Fu.

Fu had taken tea with Mao that morning, and they had embraced, and talked, and plotted but now all that tea was getting to him. He'd tried to hold out until his arrival in Shanjing but the road was long and his bladder ageing, until eventually he could take it no more and with unseemly haste he ordered the driver to stop so that he could relieve himself behind a roadside bush. He jumped out, hurried a little distance to find cover, and immediately felt better. As his bladder began to relax, he found his worries floating away.

As he was pissing another long line of military vehicles crawled past, filled with young conscripts with their bright eyes and straight backs. The young men of China. Mao's men. Fu's men! With his free hand he waved them encouragement.

When they saw Fu Zhang, they pointed. They began to cry out, in the manner of disrespectful oafs, ridiculing him, mocking his manhood, throwing back

120

his advances and taunting him with laughter. Fu boiled with indignation but they jeeered all the more. They left him standing beside the road to Shanjing, a middle-aged man with his penis in his hand, and with murder on his mind.

CHAPTER
SEVEN

Early Friday morning. Western Scotland.

It was one of the most rugged and beautiful parts of Britain. Argyll was in western Scotland, squeezed between the craggy Highlands and the sea, where crude elemental forces had torn the coastline into ragged ribbons of bare granite. Here, where the rock gave way to the ocean, nature had formed a natural amphitheatre and in the middle of that mystical spot stood the old keep tower of Castle Lorne.

Lorne was the ancestral home of a branch of the MacDougall clan. At one time the castle had protected a community that spread around it, but of that settlement there was no longer any trace, apart from the ruins of an old thick-walled chapel on the cliff top above the bay. Yet there was no denying the strength of Castle Lorne's setting, standing on a rocky islet that protruded into the firth and that was reached by a narrow causeway that stretched out from a shallow sand-shingle beach. Judging by the seaweed and damp lichen clinging to its sides, this causeway kept its head above the waterline for only part of the day. It was less a castle than a fortified tower, yet it was formidable and slightly forbidding, its square walls stout and old, too old for anyone any longer to be sure, overlooking a timeless coastline that was emerging from its blanket of morning mist. It was deemed to be a million miles from anywhere, which, Harry assumed, was the point of being here.

"You remember Alan MacDougall?" D'Arby enquired as they approached along a road that wriggled down from the surrounding hills.

Harry shook his head. After more than eight hours of driving through the night he wasn't up to memories, let alone conversation.

"Member of Parliament — before your time. Fine man. Lost his seat in one of those passing political squalls that cross this part of the world. Retired here to restore his ancestral home. Put the roof back together, filled in all the cannonball holes, managed to get power and phone lines put in. Should never have been allowed, of course, but his cousin was the chairman of the telephone company and there was another MacDougall high up in electrics, so he not only got his power line but even got it buried. Nothing to disturb the view."

"The good old days," Harry remarked, tired, sarcastic.

"They weren't so bad. I'd have them back at the drop of a hat right now."

"Is he our host?"

"Alan? No. He died. Broke his neck in a climbing accident a few years ago. His widow, Flora, kept the place on — should have opened it up for tourism or sold it to some ridiculous Arab oil man, but wanted to spend her days here with Alan's memory."

"You knew him well?"

"Saved my skin once." He snorted as though allowing a bad memory to escape. "You aren't the only one to have a lively social life, Harry, and there was a young woman who became an important part of mine — too important. I was a rising star, and she was just the sort to drag it back down. Alan was a Whip, heard rumours, took me to one side and told me I was making a bloody fool of myself. He was the only one of my friends who had the guts to tell me the truth. So I got rid of her, and when she started dribbling little titbits to the newspapers, he gave me an alibi. Nothing was ever printed, my marriage survived, and I clambered all the way up the greasy pole to . . . to this." He turned to look Harry in the eye. "You see, no secrets. I trust you, Harry."

They had reached the end of the short causeway and Harry pulled onto a small parking area of crushed rock. From the corner of his eye he caught sight of some sort of ancient royal crest above a heavy doorway; it wasn't like any crest he could remember, but this was Scotland, almost foreign parts. As he switched off the engine, his forehead came to rest on the steering wheel. "Next time, Mark, we take the train."

"Thanks, I won't forget this, Harry." D'Arby stretched to grasp Harry's arm in appreciation. "But there's not a railway station for miles. That's the beauty of the place, don't you see?"

"I can't even see my bloody feet, Mark."

"Don't worry. You've got a little while to rest before the others get here. Sleep, if you can. You may need it."

124

Moments later an elderly round-faced woman was at the door to greet them. Flora MacDougall was so much part of this place, her hair silver like the mist, her cheeks burnished from the regular rubbing of the sea breeze, and a soft, rolling accent that mimicked the waves of the firth. She cast one look at the dark pits around Harry's eyes and with remarkable energy for a woman of her age and girth led a charge up the creaking wooden stairs until she stopped on the second floor and held open the door to a bedroom. He stumbled after her, didn't bother unpacking, simply threw himself upon an old wooden bed. Seconds later he had drifted away.

While he slept, the rest of them arrived in their own stages of sleeplessness. The American President hadn't slept properly since she had learned of her mother's death and her husband's infidelity, while her National Security Advisor, Marcus Washington, was an ascetic type who had little time for the joys of dreams, and Lavrenti Konev hadn't been able to relax since he'd seen his father-in-law gun down two innocent men. Only Shunin himself seemed relatively rested. The cots on the Bear had been rudimentary and offered no protection from the pounding of the huge turbo-prop engines, and the seat in the commanding officer's vintage two-seater Triumph Spitfire had been about as comfortable as a dentist's chair, yet somehow he had managed to snatch a little rest. Evidently his conscience wasn't bothering him. It never did.

Late Friday morning. Castle Lorne.

Harry stumbled from a deep sleep to discover a distant banging in his ears. He stretched in order to re-establish contact with the various parts of his body, and discovered his bed awash with sunlight that was pouring through the window. The bedroom was a low-ceilinged affair, although the floors he had passed on his climb to his room had been considerably more magisterial; he seemed to remember that there were five floors in all. The room was practical, with floral wallpaper and a small cast-iron fireplace that was still in working order. Beside it stood a young boy, around the age of nine, with an outpouring of red hair that resembled a volcano, and a pale face that carried an earnest expression.

"Hello. I'm Nipper," he declared, "and that was the gong for lunch. My grandmother says the others are gathering and would you be caring to join them, please." There was something awkward about his voice, but Harry couldn't place it. He rubbed his eyes, trying to force more of the sunshine into his brain, and opened them again to see the boy turn for the door.

"What's your name?" Harry called after him, but the child took no notice and didn't tarry, bouncing through the door and leaving Harry to stumble from the bed and wonder whether he should shave and keep them waiting longer or simply appear in scruff order.

He joined them, shaved and alert, ten minutes later. He barely had a moment to take in the subdued magnificence of the hall, which was clearly the central room of the castle with a huge hearth and soaring chimney-breast. Every inch of wall space bustled with pieces of recovered Gaelic heritage — broadswords, dirks, pistolettis and sections of old armour sprouted like thistles across fields of distinctive red MacDougall tartan, and there were heavy oil paintings and rich wall hangings, too, yet for the moment Harry's attentions were demanded elsewhere.

"A little late, I'm afraid," Harry said.

"No apologies necessary," D'Arby replied, waving away the expression of regret. "I explained that I had taken outrageous advantage of you and that you needed a little beauty sleep."

"Mr Jones, I thought you were standing me up again, second time this trip!" a voice called out. Blythe Edwards frowned and crossed her arms. "First you don't accept the invitation to the state banquet at the palace, and now this."

Harry smiled, seeing through her mock irritation. "I'd lost my penguin suit," he replied, inventing an excuse. He didn't care to explain that he'd come to the conclusion that an evening spent with Gabbi without any rules had been a far more enticing prospect than standing around all evening in a stiff collar.

"In which case I forgive you — as always," she said, laughing gently as she advanced upon him with outstretched arms. The most powerful individual on earth stood on her toes to kiss his cheek.

"How's William-Henry?" Harry asked.

"Sends his warmest. Training hard to be the best lawyer they ever kicked through Harvard. Says that jug of beer still has your name on it, next time you're through."

"I'll get back in training. He may have a fine brain but he's also got hollow legs." He smiled. "And Arnie?"

"I don't think you've ever met Sergei Illich Shunin, have you," she responded, steering both Harry and the conversation a little too obviously towards fresh pastures. Shunin was even shorter than Blythe and three times her width, an aspect which no amount of tailoring could hide.

"Mr President, it's my pleasure," Harry offered.

Shunin gave a nod, but didn't extend his hand. His eyes offered little warmth, suggesting a measure of unease at the show of familiarity between the others, as though this somehow left him outnumbered.

"And his son-in-law, Lavrenti Ivanovich Konev," D'Arby intervened, taking up his role as chief organizer once more.

More nods, and this time a handshake, a small sign of independence from the younger man.

"Any relation to the marshal?" Harry enquired. A Konev had been one of the finest if most brutal of Soviet military leaders during the Second World War.

"My great-grandfather," the other man replied in very presentable English, more fluent than that of his father-in-law. He'd spent time at an international lycée in Switzerland, while Shunin had nothing more than the stiff, formal English he'd picked up while training in the officer corps of the KGB. The old Konev, the great Russian hero, had been no more than a peasant with little education, but Harry noticed that the great-grandson wore a French-cut shirt and a Rolex on his wrist.

"You appear to know your Russian military history, Mr Jones," Shunin interjected.

Too damned well, from Harry's point of view. He'd not only studied them but fought against them, clandestinely, in Afghanistan. Not actually shot any of them, the Soviets were already turning tail and heading out of the country by then, but he'd been sent in to advise some of the mujahedin how to do the job for themselves and lob a few Milan missiles at the retreating Soviet tanks. Yet in the extraordinary confusion that had become Afghanistan, Harry had found himself rescuing a Russian officer from the clutches of mountain tribesmen, and risking his life to do it; he wasn't the kind who was able to watch a man being slowly sawn to pieces with kitchen knives, no matter what he might have done. War makes for strange bedfellows, he thought, but no stranger than diplomacy. He was still pinching himself that these people were gathered together in one room and he was there as . . . As what? He wasn't yet entirely sure.

"And Blythe's National Security Advisor, Marcus Washington," D'Arby said, leading him further on.

"Mr Washington," Harry greeted, wondering if the other man would suggest a more familiar form of greeting, but the other simply shook hands in a distracted fashion. He was a remarkable-looking fellow, tall and gangly, with a perpetual frown like a bloodhound on a bad morning, and a cranium that was completely shaven and seemingly polished, with a profusion of lumps and bumps around it that suggested powerful internal forces were attempting to break through. An intellectual's head and a phrenologist's paradise — and, what was more, an American dream, for Washington was a deep shade of black, the great-grandson of slaves, which served to make his appearance all the more dramatic. His eyes were bright, prominent, constantly questioning, always on the move, and his overall appearance matched his reputation as a man laden with intellect and light on passing emotion. His furrowed brow lent him an air of permanent scepticism.

"Ah, but I've left the most important until last," D'Arby said, leading Harry towards the woman he remembered from the early hours. "Our hostess, Mrs Flora MacDougall. You met, but briefly."

The woman smiled and offered a hand that was strong and clearly used to work. "And this wee man's my grandson," she said, indicating the child. "Here for his summer holiday." She turned and faced the boy. "Greet the gentleman properly, now."

The child smiled and extended his own small hand.

"And your name?" Harry enquired, but the boy merely smiled.

"His christening name was Iain, but he doesnae bother much with his name," his grandmother responded. "My late husband explained to him that he would always be a MacDougall, man and nipper. That was the morning he died. Ever since, the child has taken it upon himself to be known simply as Nipper."

"His parents?" Harry enquired.

"My son and his wife are away for a few days in Edinburgh." She wrinkled her nose as if she didn't entirely approve of the place. "It's a matter of convenience, given these rather exceptional circumstances. There's just me and Nipper, we'll be taking care of you all," she continued. "But we don't do things á la carte here, just as it comes. So you'll know where to bring your complaints."

"I doubt we'll have much cause," Harry replied, eyeing the table that was piled with a buffet of cold meats and salad. The table itself was made of rough-hewn oak planks four inches thick, stained with age and use, perhaps timbers from an old wreck. The place reeked of family tradition.

"Then Nipper and I will be leaving you all to your business," she said, turning, making a final check of the arrangements before she departed.

"Shall we start?" D'Arby suggested, indicating that Blythe should take the middle place on one side and Shunin the other. Before he had been given any indication of where he might sit, Washington claimed the place on his President's right. Somehow Harry picked up that it was the seat D'Arby had allocated to himself, but the Prime Minister voiced no objection, sitting instead on Blythe's other side, but to Harry it seemed an inauspicious beginning. He found himself a place, along with Konev, on either side of the Russian leader.

Dishes of cold meats and smoked fish were passed around, along with a mountainous salad. Washington looked at the fare mournfully, picking over it like a startled crane before passing over every scrap of meat and settling for some elements of the salad. D'Arby, trying to reassert his authority, made a point of acting as host, extolling the virtues of each dish, but Shunin seemed to treat him as little more than a waiter. The Russian began eating without waiting for anyone else, forking the food into his mouth with wolf-like tenacity.

"So, security — what do we do here for security? I haven't seen much. In fact, I haven't seen any," he asked pointedly, twisting a slice of rare roast beef around his fork.

"Walls three feet thick. A stout front door that's withstood everything from battering ram and cannonball to marauding horde," D'Arby responded.

The Russian stopped eating, looking up from his plate with a cynical eye.

"Our security lies —" D'Arby paused, trying to hide the irritation in his voice — "in the fact that no one knows we are here. That's at the heart of it all."

"Security based on nothing?" Shunin snapped.

"If no one knows we are here we have total safety. You've got nothing more to worry about than a vexatious seagull or two, Mr President." D'Arby was trying to make light of the matter, but he had slipped into a formal means of address. The atmosphere was stiff, not yielding to his charms.

"Then what are the rules of engagement?" Shunin continued in his dull middle-European accent that took the passion out of words, making it difficult to tell if he were merely impenetrable or indeed had a fine sense of irony.

132

D'Arby laughed, hoping for the latter. "No rules, Mr President. We need to be as free and as open as we can. And no written record, I suggest." He stared intently across the table to where the American National Security Advisor, his plate already pushed aside, was scribbling in a notebook. "I hope that's in order with you, Mr Washington?"

The American stopped to consider the proposition as if he were sucking a candy bar. "I always used a little axiom when I taught at Princeton," he mused. "A statesman never forgets the need to win every battle twice — once at the time it's fought, and yet again when the historians start writing about it. So contemporary jottings, scribbles, whatever they may be, have an extraordinary value. They're much more reliable than the official record."

"I'll leave others to judge how much of a statesman I am. There will be no written record of any kind," D'Arby responded quietly, his lips drawn thin and unamused.

"Then what's posterity going to rely on?"

"The results."

"I think we owe it to others." Washington returned D'Arby's stare. "But I see you object."

"Let's concentrate on the matter in hand, not worry about what people might say later, shall we?"

"But we ought to be thinking about history," Washington countered, tapping his chin with his pen. "And whichever way we look at it —" he glanced around the table — "this is already a rather unusual piece of history."

"Nevertheless," D'Arby persisted.

Washington sat still, debating with himself. He made a point of not looking to his President for instruction, he was insistent on making up his own mind. Then, very slowly, almost insolently, he put his pen away.

What the hell's going on here? Harry began to wonder. They hadn't got beyond a couple of lettuce leaves and already the boat was rocking. If they were here to forge an alliance, they'd made a pretty miserable start. They hadn't even got the fire going.

Late Friday afternoon.
The coastal resort of Beidaihe, China.

The coastal resort at Beidaihe, three hours east of Beijing and overlooking the Gulf of Bo Hai, couldn't claim to be the most spectacular in the world, but the sea was clean, the beach shelved gently into cool waters, the resort town itself was sleepy and laid back, and the sea food was superb. A little to the north the might of the Great Wall swept down from the hills to meet the shore. The beach at Beidaihe was scarcely breathtaking but it provided a welcome retreat from the cloying heat of the Chinese capital, and it was here that the Chinese leaders were accustomed to spending their summers, in villas set back amongst the groves of pine trees that clung to the beach.

Mao Yanming's villa was no different from the rest, relatively modest, its privacy protected by a high wall and a police guard, its cool white marble floors leading to a veranda that overlooked a garden of little more than an acre. Around the garden ran a whispering stream that bubbled forth from a small granite outcrop. This was unusual in the dry countryside around Beidaihe and made the villa a prized location. Its lawns were the colour of deepest jade, the pool glistened with flashes of ancient carp, and fruits of deep orange filled the branches of the *shizi* trees. Wind chimes announced the arrival of every cooling breeze.

This place was Lao Wang's idea of heaven. If her next existence could give her this much happiness she would want for nothing, and now was a moment of particular joy, for she expected the arrival of her beloved boy, her *xiao* Yanming. Lao Wang was in her eighties, of the old school, from the days before the revolution when women like her were allowed to dote on young children rather than be dragged off to work in the fields or foundries. She had been the closest friend of Yanming's mother, and when the unfortunate woman had died of a broken heart brought on by her husband's brutality, Lao Wang had gladly become the child's *ayi*, or nanny, filling the gap that had suddenly and so cruelly emerged in his life. Both she and the boy hated the father. For years they were forced to endure his drunken tyrannies and unpredictable tempers, and when at the height of the Cultural Revolution Yanming had denounced his father for a multitude of ideological sins, the father had been dragged away by Red Guards and was never seen again. That had been a moment of profound celebration for Wang, for it gave her undisputed ownership of Yanming. Some had spread vile rumours that the boy had personally executed his father with a lump of rock, but Wang didn't listen to scuttlebutt, she had more than enough to do caring for Yanming, and it had grown to be the loyalty of a lifetime. As Yanming had clambered and dragged himself up his mountain, she had travelled with him; she knew how he liked his food, his flowers, how cold he wanted his beer, how to fold back the linen on his bed in just the right manner. She saw much less of him now, of course, for he was too burdened with affairs, but his time in the summer at Beidaihe made up for all the lonely months of absence. And Lao Wang was queen of this place. She was no longer sprightly enough to carry the burden of hard physical work but she retained a voice more than strong enough to order others in her meticulous, pernickety way. "No! No! Do you want to choke Mao Yanming with the dust you have left?" or "Are you in the pay of some foreign power? Are you deliberately trying to poison our beloved Mao Yanming?" or "You should be hacked down, just as you have hacked down Mao Yanming's favourite flower!" As they prepared for the leader's arrival, her voice would ring out across the marble floors and make life a misery for all.

She knew they hated her but she was from the old world and no one had sacrificed as much for the boy as she — why, hadn't she forsaken marriage, a husband, children of her own? Yet why did she need such things when she had Yanming? She wove her life around him.

And any moment he would be here. He was already late, which made her ever more nervous, and her voice redoubled with instruction and denunciation of the staff. She fussed and she bustled, waiting only for the commotion that would announce that her beloved charge was outside.

So when the telephone rang to tell her that he wasn't coming after all, it was as though the thread of her existence had been snapped. Her misery was total. The staff didn't try to hide the malicious glint of pleasure that filled their eyes, she could sense their sniggers, even if her old ears were too dull to hear. Her time, her moment, was gone. She couldn't understand it, what had detained him, was it illness, or some political indisposition? But she had received neither explanation nor apology. She felt insulted, humiliated. From near at hand, within the kitchen, she heard laughter loud enough even for her muffed ears to catch. They were mocking her. It was more than the old woman could withstand. Lao Wang let forth a wail of misery so prolonged, so heartfelt and shrill, that it not only drowned every other noise in the house but might have been heard as far away as Beijing. The wheel of fortune had moved on and passed right over her old toes. This wasn't *right*. Something was desperately amiss, she could feel it in her old bones. Her world was being torn apart, and her motherly instincts told her that nothing would ever be the same.

CHAPTER
EIGHT

Friday lunchtime. Castle Lorne.

D'Arby pushed his plate away, clearing the deck. "Cyber warfare is a monster," he began. "No bombs, no explosions, nothing, really. You don't even know it's happening, until it's too late. But it will revolutionize the nature of war as fundamentally as did gunpowder. I seem to remember that the Chinese invented that, too. But unlike gunpowder it doesn't attack its targets and leave them in ruins, it destroys them from the inside. His voice was soft, almost hushed, but filled with emotion; his audience listened attentively. "Capture the computer systems that control our modern world and our societies will soon be paralysed. This new Chinese game is a little like acupuncture, or one of their martial arts. Find the right pressure point, squeeze, and your enemy is rendered powerless." His fingers grasped at an imaginary opponent. "Unable to defend themselves, unable soon even to feed themselves. And that is precisely what Mao is planning. Not a declaration of war, not any statement of outright hostility, and certainly not a conventional military attack, but a series of incidents that will result in a catastrophic undermining of morale in our countries."

"You mean public opinion?" Shunin asked in a disinterested tone that refused to engage with the Englishman's sombre mood. He shrugged. "I like public opinion. I have an entire collection of it mounted on the walls of my hunting lodge."

"It's more than that," D'Arby continued, ignoring the provocation. "It's no longer a matter of who has the bigger bombs but who has the most sharp-witted hackers, who has the ability to know more about the opponent's system than sometimes he does himself, enough not only to mess up those systems but also his will to fight. I suppose it's a little like marriage, Mr President," D'Arby added, deciding to return Shunin's joust.

The Russian was married to a former Aeroflot stewardess who reputedly was familiar with every excuse in the book and kept this most awesome man on a tight domestic rein, the price for having provided him with two daughters on whom he doted. Yet Shunin was a man who had never loved, not to the bottom of his soul, anything apart from his country. He'd married for companionship and convenience, and his wife had earned his respect, but not always, in those early days, the respect of others. Once, in the early days of their marriage and his service in the KGB, he'd overheard one of his colleagues describe his wife as "cabin screw". Years later that colleague had become one of his first sacrifices, poisoned by a radioactive isotope mixed into the man's meal during a mission to New Delhi, years before Alexander Litvinenko had been murdered by similar means. No one had raised an eyebrow, it had

139

been diagnosed simply as a bad case of curry. Oh, but it had felt good. *Khuy*, very good! Another victim, another speck of suffering on his country's history that Shunin had discovered was no speck at all on his conscience.

D'Arby was still speaking, painting a lurid picture of the future. "By the time you realize you're under attack, it's too late. Your transport system chokes, your economy disappears down a black hole, your food supplies dry up, and your country begins to fall to pieces. It's almost like history comes to an end. We'll be back in the Middle Ages."

They had listened attentively to him, but at this point Washington began shaking his head. "No, not that, not that at all. The Middle Ages . . ." He chewed distractedly on the end of a carrot stick as though trying to dredge up sufficiently simple words that they might understand. "The Middle Ages," he pronounced, "had a degree of certainty and order about them — you know, the feudal system. Everyone knew what was expected of them, how they should live, what they should do, even who they should marry. What you describe is not that, but quite the opposite. It's an age of no order at all, it's not feudal, simply brutal."

"Let's not dicker about words, Marcus, I think the Prime Minister's point has merit," Blythe Edwards intervened, for the first time. "We rely totally on computers to the point that we've forgotten the art of thinking without them. We all know that." Her tone was gently scolding, but if it were rebuke, it bounced off Washington.

140

"You'll forgive my historical inexactitudes," D'Arby retorted, intent on pursuing his argument and buggered if he was going to be lectured by some sort of irradiated rabbit, "but the point I was trying to make is that if we get caught in the crossfire of a cyber war, we're already history." He offered a thin smile. "No matter how many notes we take."

"Some of this cyber stuff is certainly worrying," Blythe responded. "Chinese industrial espionage is truly massive. We've graded it as the single greatest risk to American technological security. But you're proposing something in an altogether different league, that they intend to use this not for industrial purposes but as a military weapon."

"Let's not beat about the bush, Blythe, every single one of us is looking at these options," D'Arby responded. "Correct, Mr President?" He looked towards Shunin. Some years earlier the entire Estonian banking and parliamentary systems had been closed for several weeks as a result of a cyber attack, believed to have been launched from within Russia. Shunin offered nothing in reply but a gentle shrug.

"But you're suggesting the Chinese are about to use this in an unprecedented fashion," she continued. "Can you be more specific? It all seems a little vague — how can you be certain?"

"We can't, not of the details. The whole point of cyber warfare is largely psychological — you outwit your opponents, undermine their will and their ability to respond. Take a moment to think about what would happen if your power supplies could be switched on and off by others — as they already have been."

"That's not proven," she persisted.

"Can you take the risk? Premature babies left without incubators, the elderly without heating, kids without schools, fathers without work, mothers without food. That's what you're threatened with. And the beauty of this mind game is that you know who'll get the blame? Not Mao — because, as you say, you couldn't prove a thing. Even if we tried to say this was all his fault we'd get laughed out of the saloon. We'd be back in the desert all over again searching for weapons of mass destruction."

She winced. That thorn would still be sticking in their backsides on Judgement Day.

"Remember the Millennium Bug? We were swept with panic over Y2K, the fear that our computer systems would go down because they couldn't handle the change of date. Billions were spent trying to prevent that happening, flights were cancelled, emergency workers were kept on alert, leave was cancelled in parts of our armed forces. You all know that our governments were secretly rocking with fear of a catastrophe — that's even part of the reason why Boris Yeltsin suddenly decided to retire days beforehand, isn't it?" D'Arby demanded, turning to Shunin. "Many people thought he'd just had a bottle too many, but he was no fool, he knew his health wasn't up to dealing with such a catastrophe if it happened."

Across the table, Shunin didn't respond, but neither did he rush to deny it.

142

"And the Millennium Bug was nothing compared to what we face today. Mao's men have made some sort of collective breakthrough — you all know how hackers have been pounding your most sensitive sites, but my information is that they're no longer knocking on the door but creeping in through the back window so we don't even know they're there."

"But you don't know that for certain," the American President continued to insist.

D'Arby nodded, as though accepting the point, but immediately returned fire. "There's only one thing you can know for certain, Blythe, and that's this. Forgive me for putting it bluntly. If New York City or Los Angeles or Chicago is knocked out, the one person who can be blamed, who is *certain* to be blamed — is you."

She flinched. He was being unnecessarily violent, but it was all too believable. She had watched the presidency of George W. Bush buried beneath the blame for the war in Iraq, she'd even participated in the interment. The rules of the game were clear; those who lived in the White House had nowhere to hide.

It was at this point that Washington re-emerged from his salad. "But from what I've seen, the main target isn't America, or even Russia. It's you here in Britain. As for the rest of us — well, frankly I don't think he'd dare."

D'Arby smiled, a genuinely insincere gesture. "You know, Mr Washington, I never taught at Princeton, but I seem to remember precisely that argument being used in one of my history books when I was at school. What was it now?" He touched his forehead, as though in confusion. "Yes, it's coming back to me. I think it was called *The Road to Pearl Harbor.*"

Washington sniffed in disdain.

"Why on earth would Mao spend his time focusing on a small, faraway island like Britain?" the Prime Minister scoffed. "We're merely the trial run, nothing more than the appetizer before he starts on the main course. You all know what he wants." He glared around the table. "World domination. And he won't find that in Piccadilly Circus!"

Harry sucked his cheek. It wasn't quite the story D'Arby had relayed to him in the car. What words had the Prime Minister used? Something about that yellow bastard having made Britain his number-one target? But perhaps it didn't matter so much, he reflected, D'Arby was in the middle of the game of his life — perhaps even a game for his life — and all negotiation requires a little flexibility.

The wind that filled D'Arby's sails was restless and consuming. He turned his sights on Shunin. "And what will happen when the cyber attacks hit Russia? How long will it be before the factory lights go out and you're back to the days of bread lines in the street? It could even be worse than that. Gorbachev lost you the Soviet Empire. Next time you might lose Russia herself."

Shunin's hands were in his lap, out of sight beneath the table, but beside him Harry could clearly hear a knuckle crack. The Russian wasn't used to taking insults, least of all comparisons with Gorbachev, a man whom he regarded as being on a similar level of

144

evolution as a slug. And Shunin knew precisely what the Englishman was implying. If the government in Moscow were seen to weaken, let alone lose control, then every separatist dog in the country would be baying for the moon. The race to destruction would be on. He wouldn't survive, and D'Arby was suggesting that perhaps Russia herself wouldn't survive. That was possible. Give a Chechen an excuse, and he'd grab not only your balls but your immortal soul.

"We can all speculate, Prime Minister, but how do you know all this?" the Russian snapped, angry, echoing the American President's query.

"Because we've all had too many episodes of computer systems that have failed or gone haywire that no one can explain. And in your case, because of Sosnovy Bor."

"You cannot prove a thing!" Shunin exploded, pounding his fist on the table, rattling the silver.

"Then why are you here?" D'Arby fired back. "I wrote you a letter and you came running! Why did you do that if you didn't believe it's true?"

The Russian didn't respond but sat staring at D'Arby, drawing short, wheezing breaths, his broad nostrils flaring. Then his chair scraped backwards on the flagstones. The others watched as the Russian rose, very slowly. For a moment it looked as though he might be walking out on them, and certainly it was a little piece of theatre designed to remind them that he could do precisely that, but instead of leaving he moved to the end of the room where a decanter of whisky had been left on the vast Gothic sideboard alongside a number of cut crystal glasses. Slowly he poured, two fingers, then a little more. The rest watched as the peaty liquid washed into the tumbler. He took a sip as he turned and moved towards the smoke-streaked fireplace. "Speculate as much as you want about Russia, but your country *is* a target, Prime Minister, without question, otherwise why did you invite us here?" He threw D'Arby's taunt back at him, but his voice was measured, under control. "Be so kind as to explain this to me. Why should I risk Russia — for *you*?" He took another, longer draught. "No, I tell you, this is fantasy. Nothing but fantasy. Perhaps better that I leave."

"Even better that you stay, otherwise your journey would have been wasted."

"I came out of curiosity. Yes, I am a curious man, I wanted to know what you had in mind. But this —" the Russian shrugged, affecting disinterest — "is not enough."

D'Arby smiled, like a theatregoer offering approval of a performance. He stretched for one of the bottles of wine that stood on the table, so far untouched, and carefully spilled a measure into his glass. Two could play at that game. He raised his glass in salute to the Russian President, but he didn't drink. When he spoke, his voice had lost its stridency and was like that of an old friend. "You are here, Sergei Illich, because you are a wise man. Wise enough to be afraid — afraid that what I am saying is true, for you know that the Chinese have more reason to hate the Russians than any other country. All those wars

146

and border confrontations, all the land that over the centuries Russia has grabbed from China. And all the oil and gas that now is plundered from beneath that same ground and is sent back to China at exorbitant cost. Russia has never been happy unless it had its neighbours by the neck. Now Mao wants to repay the compliment." At last he took a mouthful of wine, savoured it. "Oh, and by the way. Your missile systems. The ones you've got aimed at China — and at us."

"Our defensive systems," Shunin replied doggedly.

"Computer controlled. With each computer controlled by a chip."

The Russian said nothing, it wasn't necessary.

"And where do so many of those chips come from? Where are they produced? Whose miniaturized and siliconized and transistorized little bits of magic lie at the very heart of your *defensive* systems?" D'Arby's tone was almost mocking and demanded a response, but none came. They all knew the answer to the question he'd posed.

China.

The moment had been handed back to Shunin. D'Arby had challenged him to show how serious he was, about leaving, about staying. The Russian drained his glass and replaced it on the sideboard. He didn't refill it. When he turned his face was as ever impassive, never smiling, the eyes direct and locked onto the Englishman. The head nodded, only slightly. "OK, I am still curious."

Friday afternoon. Beijing.

Sammi Shah, the BBC foreign correspondent, had grown to loathe Beijing. The initial enthusiasm that had persuaded him to accept the posting had quickly been swept aside by the noise, the cloying pollution, the multitude, the unremitting battering of the senses that was Beijing. It was like standing under a waterfall, waiting for the moment he would be swept away. But most of all he hated the obtuseness of the place, the fixed Oriental eyes, the scorn of a sustained smile, the scream contained within a prolonged silence. Nothing could be taken at face value and he couldn't crack the code, no matter how hard he tried. The Chinese were inscrutable, and unscrewable. He'd tried that a few times, too, without much to show for it. This was a land of endless subtleties, too many for an up-front guy like Sammi.

Yet that didn't stop him realizing that something was going down. The pond had an unmistakable ripple. Soldiers who had spent the day secluded in side alleys were, by late afternoon, to be found standing on street corners, their Type 95 assault rifles replacing the pistols of the traffic cops. An official news conference about crop harvests was cancelled at short notice, as was a concert at the Olympic Stadium that was supposed to attract tens of thousands. No explanation was given for any of this, but nothing happened in China without a reason. Even the doves in the Forbidden City seemed unable to settle. And Sammi Shah had picked up enough of the subtleties of the place to know that a ripple on the pond might be caused by a raindrop, yet it could also be a sign that the earth was about to crack.

He tried his contacts at the British Embassy: the information officer, the defence attaché, the second secretary, who was responsible for the spooky stuff, even the ambassador. Sammi had all their numbers. He couldn't get hold of any of them. It was at this point he began to suspect that something serious was amiss. Telephones rang inside the embassy, yet no one picked them up, and every one of the mobile-phone numbers he tried left him with nothing but a recorded message telling him that the service was not available. Perplexed, intrigued, Sammi decided to see for himself.

That was when he found the answer. The embassy was located on Guang Hua Road, an area where many diplomatic buildings congregated, and outside every one of those embassies he passed he discovered that the normal complement of Chinese guards had been doubled. As he nosed around, he stumbled across a couple of parked buses with still more guards inside. The British embassy was a modest affair, a two-storey pink-stucco structure with the lion and unicorn emblem above the portico, built during the parsimonious times of the 1950s and rebuilt after it had been ransacked by Red Guards during the Cultural Revolution. When Sammi arrived he found visitors being pushed back behind the solid green railings, and when he tried to ask why he got nothing but the bark of command to join them. Whatever was going on had no clear shape and was all blurred edges, but something was up and it seemed enough to merit a short report and to cover his daily expenses. So he found his spot in the roadway directly outside the embassy and set up his equipment — by himself, he hadn't been able to get hold of his producer, wayward bugger, but that made no difference. The gear was simple but immensely powerful — a battery-powered laptop with a flip-up lid that acted as its antenna, plugged into a small video camera and connected to the Inmarsat satellite network that would link him direct to the BBC in London. All he had to do was stand in front of it and talk, and that's exactly what Sammi did. As he found his spot, tugged at his shirt, and looked down the lens, he was still debating how he would finish his report. He didn't realize the decision had already been taken for him. He never saw the officer, gun in hand, approaching him from behind.

Friday afternoon. Shanjing.

At first glance the Sunrise Toy Manufactory on the outskirts of Shanjing appeared an innocuous facility. It was a trading warehouse, so the large sign above the perimeter fence suggested, but no one was fooled. The security was too tight for a simple toy shop, and there was no sign of the usual trucks and entrepreneurial bustle. Casual visitors were discouraged. When the proprietor of a soup kitchen attempted to set up stall near the main entrance, he was rapidly persuaded to change his mind by the barrel of a QSZ-92 semiautomatic pistol that was pointed in the general

150

direction of his half-digested breakfast. Any further seed of curiosity that might have been sown amongst the locals was smothered when they saw that many of the visitors to the warehouse arrived in long-wheelbase Hongqi limousines, the ones with darkened windows. That smelt of something official. So it was simpler and far safer for the neighbours to avert their eyes and get on with their own lives. It was the Chinese way.

When Fu Zhang arrived the director was waiting to greet him and immediately offered tea, which Fu declined. He found himself being treated with courtesy but also considerable caution; it wasn't usual for State Security to dip their fingers into this pie and Fu had never been seen at the Sunrise Manufactory before. His arrival had been heralded by instructions from the highest quarters in Beijing and already dark rumours were swirling in every corner of the director's office. Soon he found himself being ushered with an unmistakeable edge of reluctance into the heart of the complex — Mao's so-called Room of Many Miracles. Not that those he found gathered there were a pious bunch. The room was about the size of a school gymnasium, high ceiling, no windows, lots of air conditioning, along with the constant low humming of computer drives. It was a little like a cinema with one wall covered in a huge screen made up of a series of smaller high-definition screens butted tight up against each other. Instead of rows of seats there were individual workstations with their own hi-def screens for around three dozen people, all of whom were young and mostly male.

Fu Zhang didn't feel at home. He was a fastidious man used to order and a proper way of doing things, and while the room itself was remarkably clean and lacking in any sign of clutter, those who worked here were not. Many of them dressed bizarrely in styles so outlandish or unkempt that not so many years ago they'd have been thrown in jail for deviation. Some of them weren't even wearing socks. The director, Li Changchun, was deferential enough, indeed he seemed a little frightened, which gratified Fu, but most of the young staff seemed to ignore him, almost making a point of it. They drifted around, joking to their colleagues as they passed, indulging in horseplay or holding out their hands and "high-fiving" in the Western manner. But perhaps it was only to be expected; most of them had been educated abroad, their sense of responsibility turned to mush by Coca-Cola. And to Fu, ageing and recently mocked, these people were guilty of the most heinous crime of all; they were young, scarcely old enough for a barber's rash, even the director was no more than thirty. They reminded him of those wretched soldiers. They also reminded Fu that he had been young, once, a long time ago. Too long.

Yet Fu Zhang needed these people. This was a day when the world would spin a little faster and these were the people who would do the pushing. That didn't mean he had to like them. In his view, miracles shouldn't come dressed in jeans and unironed T-shirts, and as though to goad him, in a far corner two of the miracle-workers burst into raucous laughter.

152

"Do they think this is a time for amusement?" he snapped at Li.

"They are young, Minister, and nervous. That's why they laugh, to expel the devils of anxiety."

"This is a war room!" he screamed, sending spittle flying. He realized that he was nervous, too.

His hostility seemed to shock the director and, like a silken sheet rippling in the breeze, the rest of the room gradually came to calm.

"We are ready. We require only your instruction," the director said softly.

Fu pulled a handkerchief from his pocket and hawked into it, letting the soiled tissue fall to the ground. The director was still looking at him, impassive, youthful, insolent.

"So what are you waiting for?" Fu Zhang barked, on edge. "Begin!"

CHAPTER
NINE

Friday afternoon. Castle Lorne.

Flora MacDougall stood at the counter in her kitchen casting her eye over the marbled cuts of venison she was preparing for the evening. She took things at her own pace, for she was no longer young, yet she was secretly delighted to be entertaining so many guests. She was never happier than when the old place was brought to life. The clans in this part of the world had lived on the edge of disaster for as long as memory could trace — they had been followers of William Wallace, the Bruce and the Bonnie Prince, and they had taken their share of the suffering that went with such loyalties, but the death of her husband Alan was a blow that the redoubtable Flora had found almost unbearable. The two of them had spent much of their young married life in the colonial service, travelling to some of the most impractical yet darkly exotic parts of the world, after which Alan had given a large chunk of his life to Westminster. But in the end, as they'd always intended, they came back to the place where it had all started, in Lorne. Then, and all too soon, she was left alone.

Yet she was an intensely practical woman, never maudlin, and retained a passion for her heritage as boundless as the ocean that lay beyond the end of the firth. Nipper was part of that heritage, and he was a survivor, too. He'd been out walking with her husband the day they'd both fallen. No one knew exactly what had happened, but the boy had been found unconscious at the foot of a cliff, with her husband dead beneath him. Nipper could remember nothing of the accident, but in her mind Flora imagined the child slipping, clinging to the cliff edge, and Alan stretching to reach for him, swapping his life for the boy's. But the accident had done damage to Nipper, shaken his brain so badly that it had left him epileptic. It wasn't enough that he'd lost his granddad, he'd lost part of himself, too, and yet with his freckled face and rolling lilt of an accent he was still a MacDougall, and no time was more precious to Flora than the weeks in the summer when he came to stay.

He was with her now, in the kitchen, helping prepare the vegetables. She had switched on the small television that stood on the dresser in the corner, the volume turned down low and tuned to one of the news channels, for she still retained a fascination for those distant places she knew from her early married days with Alan. She wasn't paying much heed, her attention was focused on the venison, so it was some time before she became aware of what the newsreader was discussing. When she had finished watching she put aside her kitchen knife and wiped her hands with great care on an old cloth.

"What is it, Granny?" Nipper asked, as ever alert.

She turned to face him, a furrow on her old brow. "You know, laddie, I made a solemn promise that we'd no' be disturbing them," she said, "but there are times in life when you have to be making up the rules for yourself. And I've a strong sense that maybe this is one of them."

Early Friday evening. Shanjing.

In the Room of Many Miracles the tension was running high.

"What are you waiting for?" Fu Zhang demanded. "I instructed you — begin!"

Li Changchun fidgeted. "Of course, Minister. But may I ask —" the young director stumbled as he reached for the appropriate phrase — "whether this most awesome order should not be given in writing? It is historic. Our children and our children's children should know what has been done here."

Fu's nostrils dilated in disgust. Posterity go hang, it was clear what the director wanted. His arse covering. The instructions had changed, the timing been brought forward, their carefully prepared system was being rattled, leaving the director ill at ease. "If you succeed they will chant songs to your memory," Fu replied. "There is no need for paper." The whole point of this facility was that not a soul should know what was going on here, not even the cleaners who were specially chosen for their dulling age and stupidity, yet this half-wit wanted to write it all down.

156

"I do not wish in any way to contradict you, Minister —"

"Then don't!" Fu snapped, letting forth a snort of irritation.

Li Changchun paused, considering whether he should pursue the matter one more time. He lived in a world of logic where matters were always pursued to their limits, often to extremes, but he also enjoyed his elevated position and the material benefits that accompanied it. Those who sat in high seats sometimes had a long way to fall, and Fu was just the type that might give him a push. Anyway, if this failed he'd soon be scraping camel dung from the distant wastelands of Xinjiang, no matter how many pieces of paper he had to show for it. Reluctantly, he gave a nod. "As you wish, Minister." He turned to his workstation.

"You know what to do," Fu muttered, impatient.

The director produced a computer fob that was dangling from a rope around his neck. He examined it with the reverence he might have reserved for an ancestral bone, inserting it carefully into a lock on his computer console. He twisted it gently. It told the computer who he was, and that he was authorized. Li composed himself, made a fractional adjustment to the position of his keyboard, then tapped out a short code. Immediately the aspect of the room underwent a change. The long video wall flickered into life.

Friday afternoon. Castle Lorne.

Blythe Edwards popped a sweetener into her coffee. "Fair enough, Mark," she said, giving the muddy liquid a stir before casting aside her spoon, "I take your point about Russia, but why on earth should Mao try to give the United States a kicking?"

D'Arby held up his hand, spreading his fingers. "How many reasons do you want?" he asked, beginning to count off the digits. "You're right up there at the top of Mao's list. Because of Taiwan, because of your old trade boycotts, because of all your whingeing about the Dalai Lama and Darfur and human rights. And he won't have forgotten about the Korean War, either, although he was nothing but a baby at the time." He had now come to his thumb. "But, in truth, he only needs one reason."

"Which is?"

D'Arby's expression suggested that the question was redundant, the answer all too obvious. "Because you are the United States. The superpower. The international hate figure. For an entire generation the malcontents around the globe have needed no other target but you. Whatever the problem, you are its cause. And wherever crowds gather and flags are burnt, there you'll find the Stars and Stripes in the ashes."

"There has to be more to it than that," she countered.

"China has both motive and means."

"But you don't have a body! Heavens, this isn't some old episode of *Miss Marple* where we rely on instinct," she returned, paying him back for his earlier abrasiveness. "You've got nothing more than a theory. I'm not sure what it is you want, Mark, what you're expecting out of me and Sergei, but whatever it is has to be based on something more solid than coincidence and ancient squabbles."

As D'Arby considered her words, his head dropped in sorrow. "Sadly, I do have a body. An exceedingly brave young woman who was very close to Mao." He paused, battling with his feelings, wondering how much he should tell them. "Her family was from Hong Kong. British connections. We found those connections extraordinarily useful . . . when she found her way into Mao's bed."

"You mean his mistress was your spy?" Blythe exclaimed in astonishment. "Jesus, we had no one anywhere near as close as that."

"She told us so much of Mao's thoughts and plans. Apparently he liked to talk. It was his form of foreplay, got him excited, telling her what he was going to do to the rest of the world. That's why I know the Chinese were behind the boiling reactors and the mysterious blackouts, and all those tiny glitches in our systems that screwed up our pensions and sent crates of toilet rolls instead of mortars to war zones. And *that* is why I know he intends to attack us all, very soon."

"You use the past tense when you talk about the girl," Shunin interjected. "What happened?"

"Somehow Mao found out. I suppose it was inevitable that someday he would. Sadly, that day came a few weeks ago. What precisely happened to her?" He shook his head and shrugged. "You know Mao, you know what we're dealing with, you've all done your own psychological profiles on the man. He's out of the same stable as Genghis Khan. I hate to think what has happened to her, but she disappeared. Completely. That's why I can't be more precise about when he plans to attack. Except that it will be before the summer is out."

"He may have changed his mind, even been forced to change his mind," Washington suggested.

"Are we willing to take that chance?"

From his chair in the middle of the table, Shunin began to chuckle.

"Something amuses you, Mr President?" D'Arby enquired.

"We scour the heavens for electronic tittletattle and spend billions on the latest eavesdropping devices, while you make do with — how do you say in English? — a tuppenny tart. I like your style, Prime Minister." Somehow even his compliments came basted in sarcasm.

"Intelligence doesn't come simply from machines, Mr President."

Shunin continued to chuckle, without humour, shaking his head.

"Would you wait, mocking, until you are on your knees?" D'Arby suddenly exploded. "Until your people are pounding on the door of the Kremlin with their children starving in their arms? Until the world around you has been reduced to darkness, until all the rules by which you live have been torn up and even the snow turns yellow? He is planning this — that I know! He's planning it now, and if we don't fight him together he'll pick us off one by one." He turned breathlessly to Blythe Edwards, firing on all sides like a gunslinger in a saloon. "And what will you do, Madam President, when Mao turns to you and says he's going to take back Taiwan? How will you respond — how will you be able to respond when you've lost control of your own country?" Then back once more at Shunin. "And when, Mr President, Mao says he wants to renegotiate those oil and gas contracts, how will you respond? What will you do when he says that he wants to renegotiate all those unequal treaties you forced down China's throat in order to steal vast tracts of his land? Oh, you might threaten him, say you'll retaliate, but you won't even be certain that when you push the bloody button your missiles will work!"

"I'd never go to war on the word of a Chinese tart," Shunin bit back sharply.

"A tart who paid for her words with her life!"

A silence descended upon the table, stretching so long it began to be painful. No one knew what to say next; perhaps too much had been said already. That was when Flora MacDougall reappeared.

"Flora, I asked that we not be disturbed," D'Arby snapped, his tone too blunt for politeness.

"I'm sorry, Prime Minister — my apologies to you all," she offered, her voice calm and sweet, addressing the others, "but there's something I thought you might be needing to see. It's been showing on the news this last half an hour or more. If you'll allow me?"

The Prime Minister nodded stiffly, in the manner of a man on a scaffold giving the sign to his executioner. Flora crossed to an ancient carved elm cupboard and opened its doors to reveal a television hidden inside. She switched it on, then stood back. It took only moments for the news item to appear.

It showed Sammi Shah, standing before the pink-fronted British embassy. As the picture juddered slightly across the satellite link, he announced that strange events were taking place in Beijing. Troops had begun to appear on the streets. Communications had been interrupted and many official meetings had been cancelled. The British and several other embassies had been cordoned off. Something out of the ordinary was happening in the Chinese capital, Sammi told the world.

He was in the process of explaining that the usual government contacts were unavailable for comment when, from behind his shoulder, an officer of the People's Liberation Army appeared and grabbed his shoulder. Sammi resisted, pushed back, determined to continue with his broadcast. Two more soldiers joined the officer and a hand came out to cover the lens, but not before those sitting around the table were all able to see Sammi, the BBC's man in Beijing, being clubbed to the ground and beaten senseless with rifle butts.

"Oh, my God," whispered D'Arby, his voice hoarse with fear. "It's already started."

CHAPTER
TEN

Friday mid-afternoon. Castle Lorne.

They sat motionless, buried in their own thoughts. D'Arby hung his head in despair. "Not so soon, not so *soon*," they heard him whisper.

"The reporter mentioned other embassies," Blythe Edwards said, her voice grim.

"We need to find these things out," Shunin added. "There is a telephone here?"

"Most certainly," Flora replied.

"Then, if I may, Mrs MacDougall, I would like to use it to call my embassy," he said, for the first time deploying impeccable manners.

"We can't," D'Arby said, looking up.

"But we must," Shunin countered.

The American President nodded her support. "We have to know what's going on."

"Think about it. Just think!" D'Arby demanded, growing animated. "You know the Chinese. They've got the capacity to scan the skies for key words that will alert them to any significant calls. One false word — just one — and it will give them our location." He wasn't looking directly at anyone but focusing his attention on a silver napkin ring that he was twirling between his fingers. "Look, you know what they can do, because that's what we've all been doing, too. We've got listening stations around the globe and up in space, ransacking private communications for incriminating language. That's how you Americans have been able to wrap up so many al-Qa'eda cells," he said to Blythe, "and you to dig out so many Chechens," he continued, turning to the Russian. "We all listen out for our enemies. And we have to assume that Mao's men are listening out for us."

"Even so," Blythe responded, "we have to take the risk. We can't do this blind."

"No, you don't understand," D'Arby said, looking up at last. "You can't telephone. Not from here."

"But why not?"

"Because . . ." He paused, seemingly unwilling to finish his explanation. As he fumbled with his thoughts the napkin ring, too, escaped from his clutches and began to roll across the wooden tabletop. They all watched, hypnotized, as it slowly moved towards the edge and, with what seemed like its last breath, fell to the floor where it rattled around noisily on its rim until it finally fell silent.

The ensuing silence was broken by D'Arby, his voice subdued. "Because," he said, "I've had the line cut."

A chorus of protest began pouring forth from all sides.

"It was the right thing to do at the time," he insisted, awkward but defiant. He glared at his accusers. "Security in silence, that's what we all agreed."

An argument erupted and was about to grow bitter when a new voice could be heard. It was Flora

164

MacDougall. "You might have done the courtesy of telling me, Prime Minister. I would have understood." She was very formal, her sense of personal violation clear. This was her home, one the MacDougalls had defended for six hundred years, often with their lives. It brought the others to a halt.

D'Arby screwed up his face, and his courage. "Flora, I apologize."

"You didn't trust us. Any of us," Shunin accused.

"I felt we shouldn't take the risk of being discovered by accident and kick-starting the whole thing."

"But it's already started!" the Russian snapped.

"I wasn't to know."

"You brought us here to solve the problems of the world," Shunin said, acid in his voice, "yet we can't even order pizza."

The colour drained from D'Arby's face, and with it his control of the moment. He had called this summit, made the arrangements, set its goalposts, but the game was no longer his. Instinctively, the Russian reached to snatch the advantage. "Where may we find a phone, Mrs MacDougall?"

"We passed through a small place a short while before we got here," Lavrenti chipped in, "a few miles back along the coast road."

"That'll be Sullapool," Flora said, still sniffing in disdain.

"It has phones?" Shunin asked.

"And a church, if you'll be needing it."

"Lavrik, you will go, find one of those phones. See what the hell's going on."

"It's still a risk," D'Arby said, trying to make up the ground he had forfeited.

"I fear, Prime Minister, that the world has suddenly begun to overflow with risk," Shunin replied dully.

"Then we must be careful. Use public phones. Ambiguous language," Blythe added.

Konev rose to do his master's bidding.

"Marcus, you go, too," Blythe instructed.

His face grew petulant, offended at being given an order. "If I must. I'll call Warren."

"No, that's too direct. Just in case they're listening."

"The embassy, then?"

"Call Ed Schumacher at CNN in London. He'll know what's going on an hour before it happens, and long before anyone at the embassy on a summer weekend."

"Suppose I'd better drive," Harry offered. It was the first time he had spoken during the entire lunch.

"Ah, Mr Jones," Shunin replied, "I'd wondered why you were here." There was no apparent humour in the remark. D'Arby was down, so now his lieutenant could be lashed.

The alliance hadn't even made it through lunchtime.

Friday mid-afternoon. Sullapool.

The road to Sullapool was narrow, winding, steep and uncomfortably hot. There was no breeze to disturb the heather that cloaked the hills, no relief from the humidity that seemed to bear down on this part of the coast. Harry's head still felt as though it were stuffed with polystyrene bubbles; the last thing he needed was to spend more time in the front seat of the old Range Rover, whose gearbox complained on the gradients and whose windows squeaked in protest as they were wound down. Yet slowly, the sea air began to revive him.

The journey had started inauspiciously. Washington had almost raced to claim the rear seat; he'd grown fed up with watching Shunin take control and would be damned before he would allow the son-in-law to do the same. He'd been made to feel like a messenger boy, running errands while the grown-ups relaxed and reflected on what had transpired. He knew the President herself couldn't be found wandering around the town and there was no other choice but for him to go, yet even so he felt affronted. He was being treated like an errand boy, and something deep in his background made him resent it. He slumped in the rear seat and sulked while Konev climbed up in front beside Harry.

The ribbon of road before them was rumpled. The ground at this point rose steeply from the firth, and for a while the road clung to the sides of the hills before making a dash to a notch in the brow. At this highest point on the road they passed a small, dilapidated stone shelter, which Harry thought might in earlier days have served as a lookout for the farmers and fishermen who by night would have turned their hand to a little lucrative smuggling. The spot gave a fine view across the firth to the islands beyond, where the sea shimmered in the heat, disturbed only by battalions of seagulls, squabbling as they hunted for food. Beyond the shelter the road tumbled precariously towards the small town they could see some five miles in the distance. There was no sign of life along the road itself.

"God, this is bleak," Washington muttered from the back seat.

He should try it in the middle of winter, Harry thought. He had. It had been twenty years since the SAS troop he'd been leading had been dropped a little further up the coast at dusk one short January day. Their mission was to test the defences of the country's main nuclear submarine base at Faslane that lay sixty tortuous miles to the south. They'd marched through these hills for three snow-driven days and as many frostbitten nights before they'd reached the base, only to find that an army of peaceniks had arrived before them and Faslane was buttoned up as tight as a nun's knickers. So instead of trying to go over or under the wire, they'd walked through the front gate early one morning disguised as a painting and decorating crew. Once inside they'd nabbed the base commander in his home while he was concentrating on his kippers. His wife had still been in her nightdress and curlers. Mission accomplished. Oh, but there had been hell to pay. Apparently Harry hadn't played by the rules — yes, apparently there were rules about how you were supposed to break into the place, so a week later Harry had taken his troop back to these hills and done it all over again.

"Bleak? It has its own beauty," Harry said, responding to the American's jibe. "People become very attached to it. The clans in this part have been slaughtering each other for centuries over its control."

"Why would they bother?"

"Perhaps for no more than the privilege of being able to be the first to spit upon the English."

"Pointless savagery."

"Oh, no, you'll find the true savages in Glasgow. The East End, around Rugby Street. You need a police escort to get in, although why anyone would bother I've never figured out."

Washington realized Harry was sending him up, and fell back to irritated silence. This man knew how to sulk, Harry thought.

Shafts of evening sun were squeezing between the clouds gathering to the west as they came to the outskirts of Sullapool. It was a community of no more than a few hundred souls who teased a modest living from hill farming and the sea. On its outskirts lay the ruins of an abandoned slate quarry. The houses were small, neat, almost entirely single-storey affairs that appeared to be ducking their heads beneath a levelling winter wind. Most had whitewashed walls and postage-stamp gardens. The town was scattered across a spit of land that projected into the firth from the surrounding hills, with a small but stout harbour at its far end where several fishing boats were tied up. This was where Mrs MacDougall had said they would find one public telephone; another was located outside the old church.

"Here we are," Harry said as he drew up beside the church. The street was empty, not a soul in sight. "You'll be bothered by nothing but the midges."

Washington, still insisting on pre-eminence in the pecking order, moved quickly to claim squatter's rights in the red phone box, closing the door against them. It appeared warped, he had to force it closed with his foot. Seconds later, he was wrenching it open once more. He stuck his head out. "I haven't used one of these things before," he said peevishly.

So many degrees, so many accolades, so many bumps on that burnished skull of his, yet still he couldn't work out how to get a dial tone. "A system built only for savages, of course," Harry quipped as he showed the American what to do, building a little tower of coins beside the receiver in case he should need them. He made sure Washington had his dial tone, then left the rest to him.

He backed out of the phone box, made a point of closing the door carefully, then retreated to the car to give the American space to make his call. That's when Harry noticed the Russian was missing.

Harry swore, coarsely and with passion. Konev was nowhere to be seen. The street was narrow, in one direction leading up towards the old slate quarry and in the other down to the harbour. Paths and alleyways led off in all directions. The bloody man could be anywhere. Harry swore again, but it didn't make him feel any better. There was little point in trying to chase after the Russian, he had no clue which direction to take, and it would mean abandoning the American, who was locked in the depths of his telephone conversation, his head lowered and his shoulders hunched. Anyway, Konev had presumably disappeared by choice and Harry wasn't his jailer, although right now he felt like applying for the post. He stood in the middle of what felt like nowhere, wondering, as Shunin had, what the hell he was doing here.

It was some time and several coins later before Washington finished his call. He emerged from the phone box, his brow creased in agricultural furrows beneath his shining pate.

"Lavrenti's gone," Harry said.

"Eaten by locals?"

"We've got to find him."

"We have to get back," the American corrected.

"Not without the Russian."

Washington shrugged in indifference. "He wanders off, that's his funeral. You may have picked up on the fact that there are considerably more important things at stake here than a clown from the Kremlin. I need to get back."

"Then you walk."

Washington's eyes grew bright, like pebbles in the surf, washed with impatience. "What sort of security are you?"

"Crap, evidently."

"How many times can you Brits screw up? Losing your empire is one thing but losing your telephone, then losing your guests, that's an entirely different order of incompetence. When are you going to realize

171

that this isn't your show any longer, never was? Just get me back to the castle so the grown-ups can get on with it."

"We stay."

They stood their ground, neither giving quarter. Raucous seagulls circled overhead and squabble over perching rights on the roof of the Range Rover. The two men were still contesting the issue when the Russian reappeared, walking back up the hill from the direction of the harbour, flapping away at the accompanying midges.

"Where have you been, Mr Konev?" Harry asked, trying to shake the irritation out of his voice.

The Russian affected to look puzzled by the question, shrugging his shoulders. "Is there a problem?"

"I wouldn't want you to get into any difficulty."

"No difficulty. I just went down to the harbour to use the other phone. Thank you for your concern, but we Russians don't need babysitters, Mr Jones."

Lavrenti offered him a smile. Harry looked into the Russian's eyes, saw them dancing in agitation. It reminded him of a calculating machine working out the odds. He knew the man was lying.

Late Friday evening.
The Room of Many Miracles, Shanjing.

The room was filled with remorseless concentration — heads bowed, keys tapping, faces lit by the glow of the

172

screens, voices that earlier had been loud and youthful now fallen to whispers as energies were focused on the task in front of them. Fu Zhang was sweating, little pearls of perspiration strung beneath his hairline. "Why is nothing happening?" he asked.

"The deadlines have been brought forward, Minister. We were given no warning. We need a little more time."

"How much time?" Fu snapped.

"This is not something that can be over in a minute, or even a day," Li Changchun persisted. He sighed; he didn't care for this man with lips like wriggling worms who had descended from Beijing to turn their plans upside down. It was the blind leading the quietly brilliant. And Fu didn't show respect. Computer programmers were often gifted souls but, simply because they seemed at times to have pulled their clothing straight from the bottom of a dirty laundry basket, they were regarded by the likes of Fu as alien life forms.

Yet despite appearances, many of them were supremely talented. It was their kind who had built the cyber highways and online architecture that defined the Twenty-first Century, but that didn't stop them being treated like slaves from ancient Egypt, forced to toil over their master's pyramid. So, in the manner of all slaves, they were constantly in search of shortcuts, ways of lightening their load — like creating a trapdoor through which they could come and go whenever they pleased. Just as with the pharaohs' tombs, these digital pyramids were intended to be impregnable, but they never were. There was always a way in or out. It meant the modern slave could often complete his work not under the eye of his master but from the comfort of his own bedroom simply by hacking into his own programs — and while he was at it he could also brighten up his spare time by borrowing a few hundred gigabytes of computer space to store games or a little pornography. It was strictly against the rules of the game, but the programmers were always better players than the bosses. The programmer's view of life was often as simple as his clothes were crumpled and his programs were complicated. You build it, it's yours.

The cyber world was a world full of trapdoors. If you knew where to look for them, they allowed anyone access, and if you didn't know, you might well be able to buy the details off those who did in a surreptitious online trade. Then you could raid the pharaoh's tomb, run off with a few gold goblets tucked under your tunic or leave rude messages daubed all over the walls. Or you might just leave a logic bomb, primed and waiting to explode. A logic bomb is a chunk of malicious computer code, bad software — malware — that, once triggered, can inflict the most extraordinary damage. It might give instructions for the next pyramid to be built as a rectangle, or in the wrong location, with the wrong name above the door or with no door at all. Or it might allow the pyramid to be built to apparent perfection and then, many months later, and for no apparent reason, for the whole bloody thing to be blown to smithereens. Like the fate that had nearly overtaken Sosnovy Bor.

174

"We have established trapdoors into all these systems, Minister," Li was saying, "but we must take care to keep them open."

"And you can do that?"

"So long as the other side don't know the trapdoor is there."

"And if they do?"

"Then we will have to hurry to finish our work before it is closed. Or find a different means of entry. There is only one golden rule, Minister. Adapt."

Yes, Fu muttered to himself, it was like any other aspect of life. Adapt. Or be crushed.

Li Changchun understood the punishment for failure would be terrible. Fu didn't say as much, he didn't need to. The director already knew. When he'd been offered the job in charge of this establishment, one of the vice-ministers had entertained him to lunch. Li Changchun had asked what his new responsibilities might be. The vice-minister had put aside his chopsticks and poured more beer.

"Consider this as a military appointment," he had said, weighing his words, "with the difference that you don't report to those stubborn recidivists in the People's Liberation Army. Technically you will be a unit of the Ministry for Innovation and Enterprise, but in truth your orders will come direct from the leader's office. Your commanding officer will be Mao Yanming himself. Yet as with any military operation, in a time of war, the general staff may need to find a special means of encouraging the troops." He had paused, offered a cold smile. "At some point they may require that someone be taken out into the courtyard, put up against the wall, and shot. And, as director, that is your job," the vice-minister had said. "You must either find the body. Or be the body." Then he had laughed, as if he hadn't meant it at all.

Now that war had begun. There would be a need for bodies. Yet, as he glanced around him, Li saw no problems. The operation was underway, his units advancing stealthily on all fronts. He wasn't one to believe in the inevitability of success, he'd spent too long struggling with mangled lines of computer code to take things for granted, but he was young, loved life, and wanted to get rid of this pompous and self-preening politician. The minister was drawing closer, under the pretext of looking ever more carefully at the computer screen, pretending that he understood. Li could smell stale garlic and he had this awful sense that the man was about to make a lunge for his thigh.

Fu Zhang stared, and wiped his flushed face. He found himself looking at what appeared to be a control-room monitor from some sort of facility. The details were offered up with astonishing clarity but at first he was confused. The script on the screens was in English. Fu Zhang's understanding of the alphabet was miserable, but slowly he spelled the words out.

Sizewell B. Britain's newest nuclear reactor.

His heart was pounding with excitement. The moment had come. No more holding back. Time to open the door to a new world — no, to kick it off its hinges so that it would never again close!

With a nod, Fu Zhang gave the signal for the new miracle to begin.

CHAPTER
ELEVEN

Late Friday afternoon. Castle Lorne.

Harry had waited in Sullapool only long enough to make his own telephone call — to the duty clerk in Whitehall, as instructed by D'Arby — before heading back. The drive had seemed twice as long and far more tortuous than the journey out. Both the American and Russian sat in silence, Washington oozing with sullen resentment while Konev appeared lost in thoughts of his own.

As soon as they returned they disappeared to report to their masters. Harry had precious little to offer. There was still no trace of Wesley Lake, and Sammi Shah had disappeared, too, although whether under his own steam or under armed guard was not clear. The Chinese ambassador in London had also gone, recalled to Beijing for what were described as "new instructions". That meant that the ambassador's deputy had to be summoned to the Foreign and Commonwealth Office to receive a formal complaint about the scenes outside the British embassy in Beijing, but since the Foreign Secretary himself was away on holiday, the ritual rebuke had to be delivered by one of his junior ministers. It rendered the whole exercise pretty pointless, like puppies growling at each other.

Harry had also attempted to have Flora's phone reconnected, but even invoking prime-ministerial authority hadn't been sufficient to get the job done, not after close of play on the first weekend in August. No one was answering their phones, so Flora's would be left unanswered, too. The only solution would have been to sound trumpets of alarm in all directions, but that wasn't at all what D'Arby had in mind. Harry had been given all kinds of assurances by the telephone company that everything would return to normal on Monday. Somehow he doubted it.

He found D'Arby in his bedroom. The Prime Minister listened without comment to Harry's report, thanked him, then turned back to staring out of the window, doing his Greta Garbo impersonation, wanting to be alone. Harry had no desire to talk either, his eyes were still on fire and his head seemed filled with cooking fat, but as he made his way up to his own room, hoping desperately to snatch some sleep, he almost collided with Nipper on the stairs. The boy had the sort of earnest stare that only those who haven't yet become teenagers can manufacture.

"Hello, Mr Jones. You're important, aren't you?"

It was a boyish question delivered with such certainty that any degree of disappointment would most certainly bring the roof crashing in upon him. Harry had experienced many forms of cross-examination in his time, even at the point of a bayonet, and as a politician he knew many ways of rewrapping the truth, but a child's wide eyes were an interrogation technique he found totally unable to resist.

"No, Nipper, not at all."

"Granny says you are, all of you. Important." Nipper hesitated. "But none of you are any more important than me, she says."

Harry laughed. "She's right."

Nipper sucked his lower lip in thought. As a Highlander he'd been brought up to take the obligations of hospitality most seriously. "Would you like to see my collection of model planes? I've made most of them all by myself."

Harry was ready to drop, his mind focused on nothing but satisfying the pressing demands of sleep, but the child's enthusiasm burst upon him like a fountain of colour in a world that in most other directions had turned to shades of grey. He straightened his back. "I'd love to," he said.

Nipper led him up another two flights of stairs, to the very top of the castle. The boy's room had a low ceiling and sturdy walls decorated with brightly coloured posters of Scottish heroes — a cartoon of Rob Roy, a film poster of Mel Gibson made up as William Wallace, and there was even one of Superman in a tartan cape. The duvet cover was the blue-and-white saltire of the Scottish flag, pillows to match, and on the table beside the bed was placed a football covered in the signatures of the Scottish national team. As if to confirm the point, on one wall was pasted a map of the world that had Scotland at its centre. There were books, too, Robert Louis Stevenson and John Buchan and many other adventures that started in, finished at, or passed through these lands.

"You let foreigners like me into your room?" Harry enquired, staring into Nipper's face and smiling.

"Only if you swear an oath to defend Castle Lorne against all aggressors, whether they be English or infidel. But particularly the English."

"I swear."

"No! You've got to swear on the dirk," Nipper protested, leading him to a small glass and mahogany case that stood on his chest of drawers. In it was a small dagger, around six inches in length. Age had dulled its blade but not its charm, and it had semi-precious stones set into the curved hilt. A woman's blade. Nipper lifted the lid of his case with care. "It belonged to my great-great-something granny," he whispered, his voice hushed in reverence. "We call her the Lady of Lorne. Her dirk is magic, you see — my Grandda' told me. And so long as it's here, in the castle, it means the MacDougalls will be here, too."

Harry received a nod from the boy and reached out, placing his fingers on the hilt. "I so swear."

"Then you are welcome."

The formalities done, Nipper whirled round the room to show off his collection of airplanes. They seemed to occupy every spare corner, on bookshelves, the top of the cupboard, even suspended by fishing wire from hooks in the ceiling. By the open window, swinging on their wire in the draught, a highly painted Spitfire engaged in a dogfight with a stealth bomber. One of the larger exhibits was a model of a Tiger Moth made completely out of matchsticks.

181

"That's my favourite," Nipper announced, his eyes bright with enthusiasm. "Grandda' made it for me. He used to fly one."

"Would you like to learn to fly, Nipper?"

"I'm going to! Although Granny says I can't because I've got a silly sickness. It came after my fall. It's called epilepsy."

A mist of sadness settled on Harry. That made it impossible, of course, for Nipper to fly, not with such a disability. They'd never let him off the ground, not on his own. But Nipper seemed to pick up on Harry's doubts. He drew close, whispering, like a conspirator. "But Granny also said that Grandda' couldn't smoke his pipe. And you know what, Mr Jones? He did! Every time we went for one of our walks."

On the wall directly above the matchstick model hung a black-and-white photograph of a young clansman in full ceremonial dress with his right hand resting on the hilt of a claymore. Grandda', Harry supposed. And above the bed Harry noticed what might have been that self-same claymore, fixed firmly to the wall. Suspended from its tip by another piece of fishing wire was a space shuttle.

As Nipper was showing off his collection of models, Flora appeared at the door. "There you are, Nipper, I wondered where you were hiding. Time has this awful habit of flying, too, you know, and I'll be needing your advice in the kitchen."

"I was just showing Mr Jones my room, Granny," he replied, brimming with good humour. "It's all right, he's sworn the oath."

182

"Then we'd better make sure there's some dinner ready for Mr Jones. It wouldn't do to let your new recruit go hungry."

"OK," Nipper said, skipping happily towards the door. He stopped at the threshold and looked back at Harry. His boy-serious face had returned. "I will learn to fly, you know." With that, he ran down the stairs.

Early Friday evening. Castle Lorne.

They had gathered in the library for drinks before dinner. Harry loved libraries, their smell of knowledge, their passion, the air of peace, yet the library on the third floor was unlike any he had known. Almost one entire length of wall was taken up by a series of mullioned windows that offered the most spectacular views across the water to the purple-green archipelago of the Inner Hebrides, to Jura and Islay and Mull. There was gold in these islands, he knew, liquid gold that made up the most stunning selection of malt whiskies. He felt sure Flora would have a cache.

The library was on the seaward side of the castle and below him Harry could see nothing but swirling waves and spray-soaked rocks that cast back the reflection of the evening sun. Gulls competed in a show of aerial acrobatics while two dark-feathered cormorants scythed low across the water, racing each other back to their evening roosts. For a while Harry was content to lose himself in the view, trying to identify the different species of birds, until he realized he wasn't alone.

183

Blythe Edwards was tucked away in one corner, perched on the arm of a cracked leather chair, staring idly at an old globe, looking uncomfortable and out of place.

"Evening, Madam President."

"Don't give me that 'Madam President' crap, Harry Jones," she replied, offering her cheek for him to kiss.

"You're looking . . ." Harry hesitated. Suddenly he saw that she looked drained, her eyes rimmed with pain or fatigue, almost as if she'd been crying. "Wonderful," he added, a fraction too late.

"Not you, too, Harry. I need someone to tell me the truth."

"OK. You look as if you need a good night's sleep. In fact, several of them."

"That's better. Or at least more accurate," she replied, trying to rustle up a smile of appreciation.

Their moment was broken when Nipper appeared at their side bouncing from foot to foot before he came stiffly to attention like a guard on parade. "May I offer you a drink, Madam President?" he enquired in a formal little voice.

"Yes, that would be very good," she replied.

Nipper took it as encouragement. "And will you come and see my planes later?" he added enthusiastically.

"I can recommend them. They're quite a collection," Harry said.

"I'd love to," she replied, relaxing, squatting once more on the arm of the chair so that the boy could more easily see her face. "You know, Nipper, I have a son — he's a little older than you, but when he was your age he collected toy soldiers. Whole armies of them. He used to lay them out on the dining table and shoot them with a gun that fired matchsticks."

"Were they English soldiers?"

"Some of them, probably."

"And is your son a soldier?"

"No, wants to be a lawyer." She could see a flash of disappointment cross the boy's face. "But Mr Jones here was once a soldier. He saved my son's life."

"Really?" Nipper jumped on his toes with eagerness to know more, but a thousand questions seemed to crowd in on him and his frown returned. "So can you fly, Mr Jones?"

"No, I'm afraid not."

"That's a pity, because I would have liked you to teach me. Still, would you like a drink?" It was clear that Harry hadn't come up to par in Nipper's judgement, but the boy was still willing to forgive. He took his instructions, then danced away to the other side of the room to fetch two glasses of wine.

"Kids," Harry laughed.

"Husbands," Blythe responded dully.

"Ah."

"Sorry, Harry, I didn't mean to . . ."

He could see her struggling. "No, I'm the one who's sorry, Blythe."

"It's just the telephone thing. Brought it all back. I went through the White House call log, you see, found everything there. He's seeing someone else, and by the looks of it she's not the first. Arnie's a son-of-a-bitch jack-rabbit who's been burrowing under every fence in town."

Yeah, he knew what that was like. Mel had been built along those lines, too.

"Mixing your metaphors, Blythe."

"What?"

"Son-of-a-bitch? Jack-rabbit?"

She found herself forced to smile. Harry rubbed the top of her elbow, to let her know she wasn't alone.

Her news came as no great surprise. He remembered a weekend when he'd been invited to Camp David, the President's country retreat tucked away in the Catoctin mountains of Maryland. Arnie and he had enjoyed a game of tennis, doing the male-bonding bit, and Arnie had thrown around a whole lot of male barrack-room banter — too much for Harry's taste, when Arnie's wife was only a few yards away marinating steaks and fixing salad for the family's evening barbecue. Arnie knew that Harry felt awkward. "Look, Harry, my old friend, they say there's a time and a place for everything. Trouble is, I'm supposed to know my place, too. Walk three paces behind, smile, don't fart in front of the press, swallow all their bullshit, smile some more . . . Gets to me at times, right here, I swear." And he had grabbed his own balls, then spent the rest of the evening getting just a little too drunk. Not a good drinker, was Arnie, and apparently not much of a husband, either.

"Is it serious?" Harry asked.

"Terminal. As soon as I leave office, Arnie wants off."

186

God, he knew about that, too. "You'll get over it. You know you will. I did."

"Only one problem with that, Harry. I don't want it over," she whispered.

He had no words for that. Instead of offering up platitudes, he took her in his arms and held her until she could breathe once more and had dried her brimming eyes on his shoulder.

"One day, Mr Jones," she said, raising her head, "I'm going to give you a presidential citation for that."

"You already gave me one, remember?"

"Getting to be a habit." A smile returned to her lips, then her eyes flickered over his shoulder. Shunin had appeared at the door. The Russian took a charge from his nebulizer, gave a polite nod in their direction and then, less than politely, went directly to the table where Nipper was still pouring the glasses of wine.

"An interesting man, our President Shunin," Harry said.

"I'm not sure I trust my opinion of any man right this moment," she replied. "You're all from some weird and distant planet. A place to which, frankly, I'd like most of you to return."

"I suppose that's why you've brought Mr Washington along," he countered, "to make that point for you."

"Fair enough. I suppose, next to Marcus, our Mr Shunin is positively overflowing with social graces."

"Why do you put up with Washington?"

"Because of his brutal honesty. You don't get much of that in the White House, Harry. Too much equivocation, too many subtleties. There's nothing subtle about Marcus Washington. He has a mind like a razor — cuts through all the excuses, gets right to the heart of the matter quicker than anyone I know — and can perform transplant surgery on it while most other members of my Cabinet are still scratching round trying to find out which end of their bodies their backsides are pinned to. Not a comfortable man, but politics isn't a comfortable business."

"A great intellect doesn't necessarily make a man right."

"Nor necessarily make him wrong, Harry."

"I stand rebuked. And if he's a friend of yours . . ."

"No, never a friend, not like you, Harry. But a relevant man, that's Marcus Washington." Nipper at last delivered their two glasses of wine, holding them in stiff, extended arms, desperate not to spill them.

"Thank you, young man," the President said.

Nipper bent towards them conspiratorially. "Mr Shunin over there has asked for a whisky. Do you think I should give him an ordinary one or one of Granny's specials?"

"Just whatever's on the table, I suggest," Blythe whispered in return.

"Save the specials for later," Harry added, bending low. "For us."

Nipper nodded in his most serious manner and stepped back across the room to the Russian.

"Kids," Harry said once more.

"Bloody men!" she exclaimed, raising her glass to thank him for rescuing her. "Time to stop being a sentimental slush-bowl, Mr Jones. Let's get to business." She turned to smile at Shunin. He accepted her summons and walked towards them, an enormous whisky in his hand.

"This is like being on the bridge of a ship," he exclaimed solemnly, indicating the view through the windows. "But not the *Titanic*, I hope." He raised his glass to them and drank.

"To those in peril on the sea," Harry said, returning the toast, praying there was a Russian sense of humour buried in there somewhere.

Soon Washington and Konev made their appearances; only D'Arby was missing. Strange, Harry thought, for the host to keep others waiting, but almost everything D'Arby had done since they'd arrived puzzled him. As he thought about it, a nail of concern began driving itself into his skull, but even as Harry puzzled about him the Prime Minister was there, amongst them, taking a glass of wine, apologizing for his late arrival. "I've been scanning the news channels," he explained.

"Perhaps we should all report what we have discovered," Shunin suggested.

No, thought Harry, it wasn't so much a suggestion. With that heavy Eastern European delivery of his, with its detached and relentless pace that was reminiscent of an artillery barrage, it came across as more of an instruction. And they obeyed. The six of them gathered before the library window, suspended halfway between jagged rocks and the doorstep of heaven, and told what they knew.

The reports they shared were like the patterns of a kaleidoscope, a picture that could be seen from so many aspects, yet one that still came from the same puzzling source. More troops had appeared in Beijing, guarding every major approach road and rail link as well as pitching up outside many more embassies. And it wasn't only the Chinese ambassador in London who had been recalled; most of the ambassadors from major Western capitals were on their way home to Beijing, although no one would say why. Konev told them that Russian units stationed along the border with China were reporting an unusually high number of Chinese air patrols along much of its length, while there had been an eruption of coded military and diplomatic radio traffic across the country that was more intense than anyone could remember. The Chinese authorities were talking — screaming — at each other, even though they were maintaining a steadfast silence to the rest of the world. Meanwhile in New York, the Beijing Opera Company had failed to appear for the start of their nationwide tour. They simply hadn't got on the plane. When the reins in China were jerked, everyone felt it, even the divas.

It was clear that Sammi Shah's beating hadn't been an accident. The Chinese juggernaut was on the move, ready to squash anyone who stood in its way, although in what direction it was headed no one could say for sure. Except D'Arby. He sat by the window, a little apart from the rest of them, rolling his glass in both hands. He didn't say a word, didn't have to. Even the surf pounding on the rocks below seemed to be saying, "I told you so."

"I congratulate you, Mr Prime Minister," Shunin muttered.

"Not necessary, Mr President. We need ideas, not applause. What do you suggest?"

The Russian considered the question, chewing a mouthful of whisky. "Dinner," he finally responded, draining the rest of his glass. "Let us build our strength while we decide what sort of message we should deliver to Khan Mao and his Golden Horde."

For the briefest moment D'Arby closed his eyes and offered a silent prayer of thanks, then rose to his feet. He was about to lead the way, yet Shunin was already ahead of him, striding out of the room, intent on getting on with business. He didn't need the Englishman's permission for dinner, or for anything else, come to that.

As his footsteps echoed from the far side of the door, it was clear to everyone that it wasn't only the world outside these walls that was changing. A change of pace had overtaken them, too, and a change of direction. Up to that point they'd been sitting back, uncertain, unconvinced, except for D'Arby, but now they were heading off on the front foot, behind Shunin, who was leading them not just off to dinner but all the way to the Forbidden City, if that were to be necessary. And Harry, for one, didn't care for this. He didn't know Shunin, couldn't trust him, not a Russian. Snow on his boots, ice in his heart. And bloody rude.

The group descended the broad staircase, constructed from ancient oak with huge thistles carved deep into the newel posts. The treads creaked comfortably in greeting as they made their way, and from somewhere down below came the compelling aroma of their dinner, but Harry was distracted. He tugged at D'Arby's sleeve, holding him back from the others.

"What's going on, Mark? I feel as if you've been playing with us all."

For a moment the Prime Minister seemed ready to protest his ignorance, but one glance into Harry's eyes told him that it would be pointless. He stopped, allowing the others to continue until they were too far away to hear. "I see you haven't figured out the game."

"The game?"

"We're in a hole, Harry, one that's too deep for me. The game is to get out of it but there's no easy or clean way to do that, not on our own. We need these people, need them desperately, but they are the ones who will have to take charge, make it their own. They won't follow us. It's been years since we British have been in charge of anything on the international scene, even a game of cricket, so we let them take the lead, while we follow behind."

"To where, Mark?"

"To wherever it takes us." The words came very slowly.

"I'm not sure I understand."

"Look, Harry, if they think it's their game they'll play it to the hilt, no half-measures, take their fair share of the blame for the consequences. If that means I've got to act the chinless Englishman who gets dragged behind the big guys, it's a small price to pay. By the time this game is finished, I've a suspicion we'll be needing some very big guys to hide behind."

D'Arby could see the understanding beginning to coalesce in Harry's eyes. "Come on," he urged, brightening, "we can't afford to miss Flora's feast." He bounded off down the stairs, trying to catch the others.

Below him, Nipper was striking the gong, demanding his presence for dinner, yet his Prime Minister's words were still ringing like alarm bells in his ears. "*Wherever it takes us.*" Suddenly Harry discovered he had lost his appetite.

Late Friday evening. Northern Persian Gulf.

The Room of Many Miracles was by no means a unique operation. It was responsible for a vital coordinating function, but the seeds of cyber war were scattered far and wide, in institutions and facilities located in many different theatres. What happened next originated in one of these other locations.

It was a standard watch for those on board the USS *Reuben James* — or, at least, as standard as any watch could be in the controversial waters of this part of the world, where the territorial waters of Iraq bump up against those of Iran. Always a hot spot, made worse by ongoing disputes about boundaries and navigation rights and the wretchedly shallow waters, but those factors weren't a problem for the *Reuben James*, which

193

had an IBMS (integrated bridge-management system) that formed the frigate's eyes and brought together all the navigational information pumped out by its radars, the gyro, and the GPS gear. That didn't mean to say that ships didn't have to take care, for in this part of the world the coastline was flat, so the radar systems gave off an indistinct picture, which meant that all the more reliance was placed on the GPS. Still, that gave the ship's position to within a metre, so there couldn't be a problem — and you didn't want a problem in these waters, not with Iranian gunboats buzzing around like horse flies.

The *Reuben James* had a crew of more than two hundred officers and men and was four hundred and fifty feet in length — not the biggest US vessel, but it packed a ferocious punch with its missiles, 76mm cannon, helicopters, torpedoes and other armaments. A proud example of American naval might. Until it gave a sudden lurch which threw many of those on board off their feet and even sent the officer of the deck sprawling on the bridge, chipping a tooth. By the time he regained his feet, the ship had come to a halt and was beginning to list. The USS *Reuben James* had run aground. Alarms began to beep, ring and wail, hornets swarming around his head. The officer gazed in horror at the IBMS display, trying to see what could have gone wrong, for it showed the nearest sandbank more than two miles away. He felt sick, this was the end of his career, but he was a professional, he knew the drill. He turned to the boatswain's mate, but had to spit into his hand before he could find his voice. "Boatswain," —

the voice dried, he hawked again — "sound general quarters."

Immediately another alarm began to penetrate throughout the ship.

Mechanically, his hand reached for the intercom. "All hands man your battle stations! This is not a drill. I repeat: this is not a drill!"

And not a dream.

He was about to summon the captain to the bridge when the door burst open and his commanding officer was there, face flushed with horror. "This could not happen. *Not happen!*" he shouted.

The officer of the deck found himself unable to do anything but point feebly at the displays. The computers of the IBMS still showed the ship clearly in the main channel, miles from any trouble, not stuck on a sandbank that was inside waters belonging to the Islamic Republic of Iran.

CHAPTER
TWELVE

Dinner, Friday. Castle Lorne.

The dining hall had been impressive at lunch but now, set for dinner, it was magnificent. As the light of the day began to fade, its theme was taken up by candles that flickered from the walls, picking out every stone and granite muscle. The oils in their gilded frames appeared like windows into an earlier, more heroic world, one that was inhabited by derring-do clansmen and wild-eyed stags. The hall was large but its atmosphere was intimate and its table brimming with surprise. Flora and Nipper served the fare, all of it fresh and none that had come far. Succulent scallops, shrimp, white crab and prawns nearly as large as the lobsters. A little mayonnaise, a pot of melted butter and a fresh, uncomplicated wine from somewhere along the Loire, although Shunin chose to stick with the whisky. The atmosphere was intense, almost timeless, and the silver sparkled in the candlelight, just as it would have done three hundred years before when Scotland had its own kings.

"I'll be leaving you all to your dinner, then," Flora said when she had made one final check that all their requirements were satisfied. "I'll be sending Nipper up from time to time to see to your wants, while I'm away to the kitchen to take care of your venison."

For a little while after she left they engaged in small talk, but Shunin was desperately poor at the game and none of their hearts were in it. The seafood was delicious, but D'Arby could only toy with it. Soon he was cleaning his hands in a finger bowl, wiping them with elaborate, almost over-zealous care before bringing the others back to their point. "So, Mr President," he said, turning to the Russian, "you suggested we talk to Mao."

"Did I?"

"Send him a message. That's what you said."

"One he can't ignore," Shunin muttered, biting messily into the soft flesh of a lobster.

"What did you have in mind?" Blythe Edwards asked.

"One with a clear point, Madam President. Preferably driven home with an ice pick."

"You mean an ultimatum?" Washington asked, examining a prawn. He hadn't bothered with the lobster; it seemed too messy, and too much like hard work.

Wearily, Shunin raised his eyes from his plate. "And give him the chance to tell us how we can dance our way to Hell? What would be the point?"

"We must try to reason with him," Blythe insisted.

"But Mao is not a reasonable man." Shunin sucked his fingers before wiping them on his napkin. "You want a solution? Then you must get rid of him."

"Get rid . . .? But even if we could, what sort of message would that be?"

"A most effective one," Shunin said.

She shook her head, not in contradiction but in confusion. "I'm not sure I can accept that. There are rules, laws. We mustn't forget the hand of history is on our shoulders."

"Nor must we forget that Mao's hand is at our throats," Shunin added drily.

"So what are you suggesting, Papasha?" Konev asked.

"I repeat," Shunin replied, in a manner that suggested he wasn't used to repeating himself, "there is only one way to persuade Mao, and that's to get rid of him." He picked at a sliver of lobster flesh he had found attached to his thumb. "Permanently."

Suddenly D'Arby, who had been uncharacteristically quiet, began to splutter in disbelief. "Assassination? That's comic-book stuff, Mr President. That sort of thing just doesn't happen, not in civilized countries."

"Depends on your definition of civilized," Washington interjected. "The Chinese claim thousands of years of civilization, and every one of them has been marked by butchery."

Much like the Russians, Harry thought, although they couldn't claim their version of civilization went back anything like so far. And what had the British and Americans between them achieved in Iraq, apart from leaving the Iraqi leader dangling crook-necked on the end of a rope? Sometimes the definition of civilization seemed to have indistinct and very grubby edges.

198

"Prime Minister," Shunin said, "you have brought me to this place, and to this point. I didn't seek it, but you insisted. You can't now pretend to be elsewhere."

"But you're talking . . . butchery," D'Arby protested.

"Not butchery," Washington corrected, joining in. "A little judicious carving. *Let's carve him as a dish fit for the gods.* Shakespeare. He was British, I seem to remember."

"We need more than an ancient cliché to justify what you're suggesting," D'Arby bit back, rustling in discontent, yet Harry had the suspicion that this was all part of D'Arby's game, egging the arrogant American on. Now the Prime Minister was looking at Blythe, wanting to test her opinion. Harry sensed from her frown that she was still undecided.

"Where's the law in all this?" she asked softly.

"The law?" Shunin shrugged. "The law of survival. What more is needed?"

"But assassination. Deliberate assassination," she continued. "That can never be a legitimate weapon."

The Russian's dark eyes danced in mockery. "Forgive me, Madam President, but how many times did you Americans try to kill Castro? And wasn't it you who sent bombers after Gaddafi? There was Saddam, of course. And Diem in South Vietnam, butchered in the back of a van, even though he was your ally. Not to mention Allende and all those Africans."

All before her time, of course, but it would have been a feeble excuse to offer. She didn't bother, settling back in silence.

"Think about it as a pre-emptive strike. A judicial assassination," Konev suggested. "One blow and we can wash our hands of the swine."

"You'll never be able to do that." It was a new voice. Harry's. They all looked at him in some surprise.

"Ah, Mr Jones. I'm glad you could join us," Shunin said. "And what is it, precisely, we will not be able to do?"

"Wash your hands and be clean."

"You are something of an expert in this field?"

Harry used no words; his stare said it all.

He had killed, of course, that was part of Harry's job, as a soldier. And not always from an anonymous distance. Sometimes you had to look the poor heathen in the eyes. Like Michael Burnside. Yes, he'd even known the poor bastard's name.

That time in Northern Ireland, the time of the great flap. Late 80s. The dirty war at its height. His commanding officer told him the story. Burnside was a civvy clerk at headquarters, loyal, likeable, trusted, the man who inputted all the most sensitive security data into the computer system — data like the names and backgrounds of every single one of the informers on their list. And something had turned the data clerk — they didn't find out until later that he'd discovered a British soldier screwing his wife, and those Northern Irish Prods weren't the forgiving type. Burnside couldn't forgive, and neither could he forget. It tortured him, and he had wanted to fight back, to hurt them as much as he had been hurt. So he had agreed to switch sides, provide the IRA with the details of everyone on that security list — not make a copy, nothing that anyone could find in his pocket and lock him up for, but stored in his mind. He was a man who enjoyed memory games, so he had sat patiently and memorized the entire list, every single man, woman and teenage snitch the British had. A hundred lives, all about to be lost because of one undersexed misfit.

In telling him all this, Harry's commanding officer knew what he was asking him to do. Not that he said so in as many words, everything was deeply deniable, but the British army was in a hole and Harry was just the sort of man who might dig them out.

Mavericks make up their own mind, and sometimes they make their own law, too. For Harry it wasn't so much a matter of right against wrong, because he had enough understanding of what the British had been up to in Northern Ireland to know they had no exclusive claim on virtue. But he knew just how many names were on that list, how many families were wrapped up in it, how many lives would be destroyed if the list was exposed. So many lives, matched against one.

He went to the address of the clerk, a terraced house in the Shankill area of west Belfast. Harry knew the wife had left and there were no children. That made it easier. He followed Burnside across a patch of waste ground to the pub, where he watched the man, sitting alone, morose, no eye contact with others, ignoring their casual greetings, trying to disappear beneath the varnish of his booth before finishing his drink and rising to make his solitary way home once more. A pathetic figure, the sort of guy Harry imagined was never happier than when filling his evenings with a pub quiz, using that blotting-paper mind of his to show others that he wasn't just as wimp. And yet this no one was someone, someone who had a right to his life, as dull as it might be. And yet, and yet others had a right to their lives, too, and, in Northern Ireland, life and death was sometimes a zero-sum game.

Harry intercepted him on the waste ground. Burnside stopped as soon as he saw Harry on the path ahead.

"Hello, Michael," Harry said.

"What do you want?" Burnside demanded, but Harry was close enough to see that in his eyes he already knew. There was no room for untidy ends, not on the Shankill.

"I'm sorry, Michael."

And Harry shot him twice. Head shots. No suffering.

It had seemed the right thing to do, even the righteous thing to do, to save so many. Yet it had cost Harry a part of his soul.

And now D'Arby and the rest were staring at him in the candlelight.

"You do this," Harry said softly, "and you will wake up feeling a little dirty, every day. You'll spend the rest of your life trying to wash it off your hands, Mr Konev, but no matter how hard you scrub, you won't succeed."

"Are you suggesting it would be wrong?" Shunin asked.

There was a silence, interrupted only by the sputtering of a candle.

"It's not my decision to take, Mr President."

The twist of contempt had barely begun to flare in the Russian's eye before Harry extinguished it.

"But I'll not use that as a reason to duck your question. If getting rid of Mao could save my country, I'd do it myself."

"Ah, a patriot," Shunin observed quietly.

"A soldier, Mr President. I was once a soldier. It was as a soldier that I met my first Russian."

"Where?"

"Afghanistan."

They were like two medieval knights sizing each other up, and for the first time Shunin allowed himself to show a little emotion. No one came back from Afghanistan without having first struggled to the other side of Hell. He offered a slight nod of the head. Harry took it as a warning that Shunin would never again underestimate him.

"Now, perhaps, I understand why your Prime Minister brought you, Mr Jones." He moved the tips of his fingers together. "Did he live, your Russian?"

"He was alive when I left him."

"Then may his good fortune follow us all."

"With the exception of Mao," D'Arby added, taking his cue to bring an end to their personal joust.

"In any event, I don't think we need to worry too much about getting our hands dirty, do we?" Shunin growled. "It seems that Mao has a substantial lead on us in that department."

The Russian had the moment, and he used it. "So, Madam President, Mr Prime Minister — the proposal is that we rid ourselves of this menace." He left the thought to hover between them. "Does either of you disagree?"

No one moved. Even the candles froze.

"Do you believe there can be any other solution?" he added quietly.

Silence.

Then Blythe began slowly shaking her head, she hadn't yet caught up with the rest of them. It was Washington who, in his own idiosyncratic style, came to his President's rescue.

"Pointless," the American said drily. "Even if you could find a means of getting to him, it would be a waste of time."

"What on earth are you talking about?" D'Arby snapped, not bothering to disguise his irritation.

"Oh, I have no ethical problem with the elimination of Mao, not at all," he responded, pronouncing the name as if the Chinese leader were salad dressing. "Justice requires he come to a sticky end. But let's think it through. The problem with China isn't one man, it's the entire system. We get rid of Mao, but nothing will change. The system will go marching on, millions and millions of little yellow worker ants ready to take over the world. Take just one of them out? Totally pointless."

It was as though a hand grenade had been tossed into the room and was slowly rolling across the table. They sat transfixed by his words.

"What are you implying, Marcus?" Blythe demanded softly.

204

"We go the whole hog."

"Are you being deliberately contrary?" D'Arby snapped.

Washington's expression glowed with contempt.

It was Nipper who broke the moment, bouncing into the room, his arrival announcing that Flora was on her way and their dinner was ready to change course. Blythe looked at her plate; it had scarcely been touched and she had no appetite. She put her napkin to one side. "If you don't mind," she said, "I'll pass on the rest of dinner. I'd like to reflect on things for a while. We can pick the discussion up in the morning."

D'Arby sprang to his feet, helping draw back her chair, and the others rose in their places. Shunin was last, his movements as always considered, almost defiant. From the doorway Flora set her jaw in discontent as she saw her carefully planned meal being cast into disarray. As Blythe departed, Shunin helped himself to another drink, Konev sat silent, his face taut and grim, while Washington leaned against the mantle, staring into the hearth and quarrelling with the ashes.

When Harry looked at D'Arby, he expected to find the expression of a man who had been pushed too far. Instead he thought he saw the flicker of a smile. This was still his game. And in that instant, Harry knew he could no longer trust him.

The early hours of Saturday morning. Shanjing.

"We must stop," Li Changchun announced, his voice frail with fatigue.

"Never!" Fu insisted.

"Minister, we must rest."

"But we have almost finished."

"Almost finished, yes. So now it becomes even more important that the task be completed accurately, not by those who are so exhausted that they cannot tell the difference between computer code and a child's puzzle."

"This is not a time for faint hearts."

"Nor for mistakes," the director insisted stubbornly.

Fu's lips wobbled in indecision. He had not a glimmer of understanding of what these people did, only that he needed them, and he could see how whipped they all were. One had collapsed over her desk. "So when?" he demanded.

"In a few hours. After we have slept."

"And then?"

"We finish the task. Go on to the next." The director thought he had the measure of this most unwelcome visitor. "You, of course, will have the honour of pressing the final button, Minister."

They were about to destroy a nation, one that had been unconquered for a thousand years and had ruled the greatest empire the world had ever known. Fu Zhang was not a patient man but it was said that the journey of a thousand miles is taken one step at a time, and this was to be the first and most glorious step of them all. A few hours more could make no difference. The rest might even make the experience more memorable. The wretched Li was right, there was nothing to be gained by hurrying and tripping. With a lingering sense of reluctance, Fu rose from his chair.

CHAPTER
THIRTEEN

Bedtime, Friday. Castle Lorne.

Blythe Edwards lay in her bath, an old-fashioned roll top, surrounded by sweet-scented candles with a tumbler of whisky at her side, hoping the hot water would seep away the many miseries that had wormed their way inside. First it had been Arnie, now Mao, men who seemed determined to bring low all the things she stood for. Bastards.

She loved her country and had promised to serve it, no matter what the personal cost, and she'd always accepted that would require sacrifice, but until this evening she'd had no idea how difficult it would be, trying to run the world while at the same time dragging a ruined marriage behind her. That hadn't been in the game plan. It undermined her sense of self-worth, knocked away the foundations. She was beginning to fear she couldn't do it all on her own. She felt so lonely.

No, she felt far worse than that. She felt humiliated. It was absurd, she was the most powerful woman on the planet, yet she couldn't even keep hold of one miserable excuse for a man. When the rest of the world found that out, the jackals would have a field day, and no matter how she tried to tell herself otherwise, it mattered what they thought. She was a politician, after all. And a woman.

She had screwed up big time. Her life stank, this whole Mao thing stank. And it was all going to get worse. She took a gulp of whisky, chewing it before swallowing, trying to find comfort, but it didn't work. She wasn't right for the job, as a president, or as a wife. A trickle of perspiration made an unsteady path down her temple. Her face was flushed. She was on the point of tears.

She wasn't up for this, but was anyone? Yes, she thought, some were up for it, seemed almost enthusiastic. Wanted to go to war. Yet what had Sun Tzu written? *Know your enemy.* Sound advice. But she didn't know this enemy, it was all confusion. Truth was, right now she didn't even know herself.

She lay back in her bath, miserable, as the steam mingled with her tears and trickled them away.

Late Friday night. Castle Lorne.

Nearly eleven. Harry lay awake in bed. Despite the rigours of the last couple of days, he couldn't sleep, Michael Burnside wouldn't let him. The clerk sat in the chair on the opposite side of the room, staring. As always, he said nothing, it was Harry who did all the talking, contriving a one-handed debate about the rights and wrongs of what he had done. It was simple; he had murdered an unarmed man. Except Burnside hadn't been unarmed, he'd had information, and information could be the most devastating of weapons in the wrong hands. And it hadn't been murder, either; it had been — what was the phrase Washington had used? A judicial assassination. *Except* it hadn't been judicial, merely necessary. Harry wouldn't even offer the excuse that he'd been obeying orders, because his CO had taken care to ensure that not even a whisper of an order was given. He didn't need to. Unwritten codes, unspoken appeals, that was how soldiers fought the dirty war. OK, so Harry had done no wrong, his action had saved dozens of lives, and the entire army command structure would back him to the hilt, in private. Except — *why were there always so many exceptions, Michael?* — if the matter ever became public, his commanders would say not a word, and the only word that others would use then would be murder. *But you won't say anything, will you, Michael? You can't. Because I killed you.* And so it went on, with Harry's conscience scurrying around in the darker recesses of his soul, looking for a place to hide.

The house was silent. Everyone had long since retreated to their rooms and Harry's head was buried in his pillow when he thought he heard the creak of a footstep on the stair. A couple of seconds later he was sure of it. Someone was out there, and not in search of a glass of water, for then they would have switched on the light, but there was none showing beneath his door.

Harry went to his window, which gave him a view across the forecourt to the causeway beyond. The moon was new and the cloud cover thick, but in the fragments of light Harry saw a figure gliding past, heading for the causeway. A man, by the size, he thought, but couldn't be sure. And not on a night-time stroll, judging by the cautious yet determined step.

Harry hesitated. What to do — to follow? Or to ignore and forget? Yet from the far side of the room the eyes of Michael Burnside reminded Harry that he wasn't a man of hesitations, he was a maverick, one who got on with things in his own style. So he dressed quickly and crept down the stairs.

There was a side door leading from the kitchen; Harry found it left on the latch. The night walker was clearly intending to return, and wanting to do so as surreptitiously as he had left — yes, *he*, Harry was sure of that now, from the manner of his walk. Harry set off in pursuit, his shoes crunching on the gravel, feeling for every step on ground he could not see.

When he reached the causeway he sensed, as much as saw, that it was under water. High tide. He swore, took off his shoes and socks, and stuck a tentative foot into the sea. It was surprisingly warm, always was up here. Gulf Stream. And only a few inches deep. He hitched up his trouser legs and plunged on. He'd have to hurry, the man had a ten-minute start. And the bloody midges were at him. He'd never understand those mad Gaelic buggers who wore kilts.

At the point where the road forked, several hundred yards beyond the causeway, Harry stood still and listened, sharpening his ears to the sounds of the night; sheep, faint rodent rustles, a distant fox, the call of an owl, the complaint of a disturbed grouse, the high-pitched scream of a dying rabbit, the hush of breeze brushing across dry heather and the rumble of waves from the nearby shore. But no footsteps. Yet Harry knew one branch of the road staggered along the coastline to Sullapool while the other, so far as he could remember, led nowhere for a considerable distance through the hills. He chose the little fishing port.

He climbed through the darkness, maintaining a steady pace. He'd gone a good couple of miles before, up ahead, he made out the silhouette of the brow of the hills set against the palest of moon-milk skies, and the notch that showed where the road cut through and dipped down towards Sullapool. He remembered the half-ruined shelter they had passed earlier in the day, and that was where he saw a momentary flicker of light. A match, followed by the glow of one — no, two — cigarettes. So a rendezvous. He was still several hundred yards away but the cigarettes stood out with the intensity of stars; they drew him on, and soon he began to detect the low rumble of voices that carried on the gentle night breeze. He was still too far away to make out what was being said when whatever business was being transacted came to its end; one cigarette was cast down to the roadway and ground out — thank heavens not tossed into the summer heather — while the remaining cigarette, still glowing, began dancing in his direction.

In his bowels Harry knew that someone from the castle was ploughing a very untidy furrow and he was anxious to discover who, but equally he had no desire to be discovered himself, not until he had collected a few answers. So he retreated, intent on getting back to

212

the castle before the other man, and before the midges sucked him dry.

He was moving faster than the smoking stranger and reached the causeway well ahead. The tide had turned, no need to remove his shoes this time. The side door from the kitchen was still on the latch, just as he had left it. He stepped inside, knowing that this would be the way the other man must come, and concealed himself behind the large pantry.

He didn't have long to wait. A couple of minutes later he heard the scrunch of gravel on the pathway outside the door; the man must have got a move on these last few hundred yards, for Harry could have sworn he'd had a good five minutes on him. Now, in the darkness of the kitchen, Harry's breathing came like the roar of bellows. He straightened his leg; the knee cracked with the sound of a rifle shot. Surely he would be discovered?

Once again, as he had done repeatedly since he had started tailing the man, Harry debated with himself who it might be. D'Arby, perhaps, the man who had set up this unwholesome enterprise and was playing so many games? Or was it Washington, the arrogant oddball who played no one's game but his own? Or Konev? No, it had to be D'Arby, he decided, for he was the only man on home turf, but in heaven's name why?

His mind still bubbled in confusion as the door opened on its well-oiled hinges. A figure stepped in, yet in the darkness Harry could see nothing but a vague shape. And it had stopped in the centre of the kitchen, casting around, searching for something. Harry, fearing he had been undone, was preparing to throw himself at the figure and at least gain the advantage of surprise when the man made a step forward. Harry felt him reach out. A second later the door of the refrigerator was tugged open, filling the kitchen with a pale glow.

Harry struggled to restrain the gasp of surprise forcing its way past his lips. What he saw was the worst, most dangerous of all the outcomes he had envisaged. Standing exposed in the thin light cast by the refrigerator, searching for a beer, was the unmistakable form of Sergei Illich Shunin.

Dawn, Saturday. Castle Lorne.

Harry tried to get back to sleep after his excursion through the night, but his mind wouldn't let him rest. So, as he so often did, he decided to block out the mental agitation with a little physical exercise. He was in the habit of taking his running shoes with him when he travelled, and not long after first light he laced them up and slipped out of the castle. He was surprised to discover, at the end of the causeway, undertaking some serious stretching exercises and swatting at the early midges, the gangling form of Marcus Washington.

"You couldn't sleep either?" Harry said in greeting.

"On the contrary, I slept excellently. Five and a half hours. Never more."

"You care for a little company on your run?" Harry offered, struggling against his instincts to be cordial.

214

Washington's face carried an expression that suggested Harry had just asked for a substantial loan, but in the circumstances even the haughty American would find it churlish to refuse. "Mrs MacDougall tells me there's a circuit along the cliffs. Does that suit you?"

"I'll try to keep up."

And so they set off. The American was clearly a practised runner, his muscles were already warm, and his lanky gait coped comfortably with the succession of steep rises and gullies they encountered. And, as always, the American had a point to make: he was better than Harry.

"You like Scotland?" Harry ventured, as they settled into their strides beneath the early morning sun.

"I've always avoided it, until now."

"Avoided?"

"Plantation people. Slave traders. I can't help wondering if it was from here, along these stretches of water, that they set sail."

It was a comment deliberately designed to make Harry feel unsettled. "That's entirely possible," he acknowledged, "although the Scots have never had it easy themselves. During the clearances the crofters in these parts starved in their thousands, and that was long after the slave trade had been abolished."

"It's not the same," Washington replied, keeping his breathing regular, his sentences short, and his strides long. Harry was attempting to stay abreast of him, to share the trail along with the argument, but the black American seemed intent on pushing ahead with both, stretching to get to any corner or crest first, instinctively wanting to leave Harry in his wake. It was developing into a race.

"So, you really think hitting the Chinese is necessary?" Harry asked, deciding they should change the subject. He was puffing a little, yawning, still only half awake.

"You doubt it?"

"I'm *questioning* it."

"The Chinese are the imperialists of this century, just as the Europeans were of the last. They are racist, exploitative and exclusionary, most of all towards the black man."

"You feel that personally?"

"How could I not? The colour of my skin is part of who I am. It's the same with the Chinese, of course, except their skin and my skin speak different languages." Just like you and me, he seemed to be saying. "You find me arrogant?"

"Since you ask, I understand why people might come to that conclusion."

"For a black American it's a defence mechanism, the result of generations of abuse. But for the Chinese, their arrogance is a religion. They regard themselves not just as equal but as fundamentally superior. It's the same sense of racial superiority that crammed millions into slave ships and sent millions more to the gas chambers — apart from the fact that their arrogance is here, it's now. That's why we have to deal with it."

If arrogance is a defence mechanism, Harry thought, this guy's an entire factory. A startled rabbit charged across their path, scuttling for cover in the gorse.

216

"The Chinese constitute the greatest threat of our age, Mr Jones. And right now, we have an opportunity to change the way our world is spinning. We've got to grab it. Grab it — or go down. That's the choice."

A man in a hurry, was Mr Washington, Harry told himself. One hell of a hurry. They were approaching a gulley that crossed their path. The American, who was a good few inches taller than Harry, simply stretched his legs and crossed it with ease, but Harry found it more of a challenge. He was on less favourable ground and was forced to check his stride. He fell behind, and had to put on a spurt in order to catch up with the other man, who showed no inclination to slow down and wait.

"As you say, Mr Washington, it's the way the whole world spins, and the whole world will be sticking their fingers into this one," he puffed when at last he had caught up to the American's shoulder. "And if we lift a finger against the Chinese, let alone a huge fist, they're going to say it's a throwback to the old days. All that Anglo imperial stuff."

"White man's mischief? But that's why I'm here, can't you see?"

The man's self-belief came through in every panted breath. He was pushing hard, trying to leave Harry and his antiquated world far behind. Harry dug in to stay in touch. It had become a contest not just of physical ability but of race, of skin, of outlook, two men who were dragging their birthrights behind them as they raced across the cliff top. They were neck and neck when they passed the ruins of the old chapel on the cliff top and Castle Lorne came back into sight. Their pace quickened. Ahead lay a narrow cutting through which the track passed, only wide enough for one man at a time; whoever reached it first would have a decisive advantage on the run down to the causeway. Harry edged ahead. He could sense, could smell the American's alarm, the horse eyes, the tightening of the stride. Harry was stretching out, barely a few feet from the narrowest point, when he felt his heel being clipped. He stumbled and was sent flying into the heather. He thought he heard a cry of delight as Washington passed him. Furious, Harry picked himself up and threw himself in pursuit, but the American's long legs had the advantage on the slope down to the causeway. He reached it a step ahead.

Washington was gasping, bent double, sucking in deep lungfuls of air. "You must have hit a rabbit hole," he exclaimed.

"You're probably right," Harry replied. "I'll remember to avoid it on the second lap."

Slowly Washington raised himself from his crouch, his eyes wide with confusion. "What?"

"That could only have been around four miles. I normally do eight. You up for it?"

"You're . . ." Washington was about to suggest that the other man was indulging in a joke, but as he straightened himself, still panting, he noticed that Harry's breathing was alarmingly regular.

"Come on," Harry urged, "it'll make room for breakfast."

"I'm afraid I have work to do. Otherwise . . ."

218

"Sure. I'll see you later, then." And Harry took to his heels once more. Sometimes, men like Washington just had to be put in their place.

Early Saturday morning.
Sizewell, on the Suffolk coast.

The golf-ball dome of Sizewell's second reactor could be seen for many miles along the long stretch of Suffolk's heritage coast, near the small fishing village that bore the same name. It was Britain's newest nuclear power station, facing out across the North Sea, with its riches of fishing grounds and oilrigs and its control of the navigation routes that gave access to London and many of the other major ports of northern Europe. As was appropriate with a nuclear reactor in such an extraordinarily sensitive area, Sizewell B was fitted with the latest security systems. Safety, as the power company proclaimed, not afraid to grasp the cliché, was their number-one priority.

So when the reactor desk engineer, sitting before his array of screens, keyboards and buttons in the control room, noticed that the pressure inside the reactor core was slowly creeping up, he decided to investigate. Nothing would be left to chance. Irrespective of the corporate clichés, he took pride in his work, and his family lived only a bicycle ride from the plant. He wanted to know what was going on.

But the engineer could find nothing wrong, apart from the gentle tickle of pressure. None of the other safety systems was registering any fault or problem, it was a bit of a mystery. So he picked up his blue phone and instructed other engineers to take a look around the plant itself, checking the hardware, the nuts, bolts, rivets and turbines from which Sizewell was constructed, to make sure everything was operating as it should be. He wasn't going to accept the word of the instruments in the control room, it was always better to find out what was going down on the other side of the door. But it seemed everything was in order.

Except, that is, for the slow drift upwards of the pressure in the reactor core.

Perplexed, but conscientious, he discussed it with his colleagues in the control room. No one had an explanation, so they decided to call in the duty physicist. He'd be able to figure out what was going on. He lived, as regulations required, no more than an hour away, but there was a problem. On a hot August holiday weekend near the coast, with tourists hauling their trailers and caravans and clogging every approach road, that hour was going to stretch well beyond its sixty minutes.

Sizewell B didn't have sixty minutes. Its core was already melting, because five thousand miles away, in Shanjing, the morning shift had assembled and that final button had been pushed.

CHAPTER
FOURTEEN

Saturday morning. Castle Lorne.

Breakfast. Even condemned men are allowed it. The meal was served next to the kitchen in an informal room that the family used for recreation. When Harry arrived, D'Arby had already set anchor to a wicker chair drawn up in front of the television in a far corner. A single slice of toast was on a plate beside him, but he had done no more than nibble, his attentions fixed to the screen. It was tuned to the news. Shunin sat apart, at a low table by the windows with a view over the rocks. He was playing chess, by himself, clearly not wishing to be disturbed. And at a sideboard laden with everything required for a self-service breakfast, Blythe Edwards was hovering over a selection of cereal, porridge, grilled bacon and kippers.

"Sleep well?" Harry enquired.

"A little." She stretched out to squeeze his hand.

"What's that for?"

"Nothing. Nothing in particular. Just for caring." She couldn't manage a smile, but there was steel behind her eyes. "We've got a busy day, I guess, deciding what to do with the world. So why do I find it so difficult to make up my mind what to eat for breakfast?"

"Take the kippers. They'll be from Loch Fyne, not far from here. The best in the world."

"And there's another man telling me what to do." Ouch, she was on edge, and rushed to apologize. "I'm sorry, Harry, I didn't mean it like that."

"I still suggest the kippers." He smiled.

Almost without their noticing, Shunin had joined them at the sideboard. He picked up a fork and began prodding the contents of each dish in turn, a Cossack picking over the battlefield. Harry looked closely at him. The eyes were rimmed with a reddish crust of sleeplessness, and there were midge bites, angry, incriminating, on his cheek and the back of his hand.

"Did you enjoy your game of chess, Mr President?" Harry asked.

"Yes. I won. I always win, Mr Jones," he replied, before wandering off with a laden plate.

"That man plays with himself too much," Harry muttered.

Then, as if on cue, Marcus Washington walked in. He offered a brief greeting to Blythe but seemed reluctant to accept Harry's persistent suggestion that he join them; instead he wandered off, muttering something about macrobiotic yogurt.

Suddenly their breakfast plans were interrupted by a low moan from the far end of the room. D'Arby was scrabbling for the remote control, switching up the volume, waving for their attention. It was the latest CNN report from Beijing. More troops on the streets. A clampdown on the Internet. Many foreign websites blocked. An eerie silence from the government quarter in Zhongnanhai.

It was as though China was drawing itself in, like a tiger waiting to pounce. Blythe pushed her plate away, her food untouched. D'Arby sat silently shaking his head. From his seat by the window, Shunin knocked over his white king and stomped out of the room.

They had agreed to resume their business at ten, but Shunin thrashed the gong some minutes early, loud enough to shake even the ancient mortar. As they began to assemble around the dining table once more, Lavrenti stumbled down to join them, bleary eyed.

"Sorry. Overslept," he muttered, his eyes dancing in apology around the room.

"Shut up and sit down," Shunin snapped, in a humourless manner that seemed to have the same affect on Lavrenti as a cold shower. As he was bidden, he found his place and sat silently.

"Mr Washington, I believe you had the floor," Shunin observed, laying claim to command of the bridge.

"My point is this," Washington began, "the Chinese threat is like a weed. Hack off its head and it just sprouts up again all over the place, ever stronger. So there's no point in taking out Mao without taking out their cyber-war facilities, too. We have to disarm them, otherwise we may as well be pulling the tail of a hungry bear." He sat back and began a distracted examination of the pictures hanging on the wall.

"And that's it?" D'Arby muttered.

"What more do you need, Prime Minister?" Washington replied, his voice buttered in condescension.

D'Arby spread his hands, clutching for something that was clearly eluding him. "A little elaboration, perhaps. Some deeper justification for what it is I think you're proposing."

"What part of it don't you understand? If you could explain that to me, I'll be happy to *elaborate*. Draw a few diagrams. Beginning with the bear's backside."

Blythe interrupted the spat. "Marcus, let's take the animosity out of this, shall we?"

"Forgive me, Madam President, but I don't see how we can. Animosity is the name of the game we're playing right now, in its most extreme and absolute form."

He glared defiantly at D'Arby, who pushed his chair back from the table and rose to pour himself a cup of coffee, anything to put distance between himself and the obnoxious academic. It was Harry who picked up the gauntlet.

"You said we should be 'taking out' their facilities. Can you be more specific?"

"Taking out," Washington repeated. "As in obliterating. Destroying. Blitzing the barnacles off them. Most of these cyber-warfare ops are soft targets, in university campuses, civilian research complexes, that sort of thing. We're not talking hardened nuclear-missile sites here, this isn't Strangelove territory. And of course we have to use our own cyber resources to attack them, cyber on cyber, but frankly that's entirely unknown territory. So we have to add a little muscle to the mix."

Blythe interjected, her voice as full of soft uncertainties as her adviser's was of confidence. She turned to Shunin. "And what about you, Mr President? What are your thoughts?"

The Russian rested his forehead on the tips of his fingers, as though trying to complete some electrical circuit to stimulate his troubled mind. He thought of Chernobyl, and of Sosnovy Bor that had come within moments, within a few blobs of misplaced molten metal, of total destruction. Had that happened, it would have destroyed St Petersburg, his birthplace, the most magnificent city in all the Russias. And it would have destroyed him. That's why they'd chosen Sosnovy Bor, because of him, of that he was sure. For Shunin, this had become very personal.

His head came up. "A question first. For Mr D'Arby. Your little Oriental tart has put you at an advantage. Tell me, in your view, in *her* view, was Chernobyl down to them?"

Chernobyl. The bringer of death. It had promised eternal light yet it had cast his world into darkness. Of all the psychological burdens born by the leaders of Russia, that was perhaps the greatest.

D'Arby knew he had his moment. He was standing beside the great fireplace, cup in hand, and while they waited he put it slowly to one side. Then, as they all stared, he shook his head. "No, Mr President. It was too early for that. I believe that Chernobyl was nothing more than an accident — a Russian accident. But it gave the Chinese a template. Chernobyl was their inspiration."

"In what way?"

"What Chernobyl did wasn't simply to inflict colossal physical damage, like a missile strike. It went much further. It inflicted dread. It's a name known throughout the world, and although not one per cent actually understands what went on there, everyone fears it. It's the perfect psyops — scaring your enemy into submission. It's the very uncertainty of something like Chernobyl that rips at the entrails, and that's what the Chinese are so very good at, sticking pins in the right points. It's psychological acupuncture. In the days of the early Han dynasties they'd set off rockets and beat drums to frighten the wits out of the barbarians without a sword being raised in anger. Now, a thousand years later, they want to do the same. Quite simply, they want to drown us in despair."

Yet, even as they listened to his analysis, the Chinese were making a few other plans, too.

Saturday mid-morning.
The Sizewell B reactor, Suffolk.

Ninety minutes after he had been summoned the duty physicist still hadn't made it to the nuclear plant. Police were trying to clear an accident on the road up ahead, he couldn't turn round, and no amount of increasingly animated mobile-phone discussions with the control

226

room got him any nearer to the answer of what was going on within the reactor.

The instruments were indicating that the pressure in the core was still gently, tantalizingly, rising, but the rest of the system seemed in good order. Temperatures were stable, the cooling system was functioning as it should. The system was designed to adjust the flow of coolant to the core so that the reactor remained at the right temperature, hot enough to create the steam required to drive the turbines, yet cool enough to keep the process under control.

What no one could know was that the instrumentation had been, to use a basic engineering term, stuffed. It had been persuaded that it was delivering too much coolant to the core, so it had begun to cut back. That was causing the temperature inside the reactor to rise but this instrumentation, too, had been compromised.

It wasn't like Chernobyl, where the water had been turned to steam in such quantities that it created pressure so huge that it had blown the top off the reactor. What was happening at Sizewell B was more like the nightmare that had struck Three Mile Island in Pennsylvania a few years before Chernobyl. Not enough water was getting to the fuel rods to cool them. The rods themselves were beginning to melt. As they turned to liquid, they began to form a puddle at the bottom of the reactor vessel. It was double-skinned, made of steel, but even hardened steel was no match for temperatures that were beginning to resemble those found a stone's throw from the sun.

Saturday mid-morning. Castle Lorne.

D'Arby was still holding forth, pacing up and down in front of the fireplace, a teacher before his class.

"You see, the People's Liberation Army are still light-years behind us. They could never beat us in a straight fight. Our bombs and missiles are so good they can reach their targets with pinpoint accuracy — we see it all, even the horror on the face of the truck driver in that fraction of a moment before he gets it right between the eyes. The Chinese are trying to do the job more subtly — and more cheaply. Instead of blowing that truck driver to bits, they want to scare the crap out of him, cutting off his fuel supplies, sending his truck on the wrong road, loading it with the wrong cargo . . . He ends up not knowing what the hell he's doing or where he's going. And for that single truck driver you can read an entire Western country — you, me, any of us. It's all about psychological rather than physical advantage, ying instead of yang or whatever the correct terminology is. Everything straight from Sun Tzu."

"Hacker wars," Washington declared. "Their recent literature is full of it."

"Winning without fighting," Shunin muttered.

"So, what conclusion do you draw from this, Mr President?" Blythe repeated, pushing him once more.

"I conclude," the Russian responded, "that Mr Washington's point has significant merit. If you're going tiger-hunting, you'd better carry a damned big stick. Or perhaps you would prefer to wait until the tiger has you in its jaws and your country is little more than breakfast, Madam President?"

She returned his cold stare. "Mr Shunin, I live in a democracy. It means I have to tread carefully."

"I understand democracy. I have millions of democrats in Russia."

"Not all of them in gulags, I trust."

He lunged forward in his chair, filled with passion. "If we don't show them we mean business straight from the start, get it over and done with, then we lose control. We'll be playing into the hands of every Islamist, terrorist and rebel, all the stinking parasites that have wormed their way into our systems. Show any hesitation, any doubt, the slightest sign of weakness, and they'll crawl out of their sewers and get on with the job of ripping our countries apart!" His hands were clenched, his fists like clubs. "But open your minds. By God, this isn't just a crisis, it's also an opportunity. To get rid of those soul-sucking bastards once and for all. While we're cleaning out the Chinese stables, we can clean out our own, too. You get re-elected, I get on with sorting out Russia. Why, in five years' time we could be looking back and wondering why we ever hesitated."

They all understood what he was suggesting. His price for getting involved with the Chinese was a free hand to deal with those little local difficulties that had proved such a distraction. China, Chechnya — it was all much the same to him. They were threats that required squashing, and he wanted no chorus of complaint from squeamish Western souls.

His performance was interrupted by the arrival of Nipper to check the supply of tea and coffee, but Lavrenti had other ideas. As D'Arby helped himself to more coffee and offered some to Blythe, Lavrenti Konev wandered over to the sideboard and poured a large whisky. Harry glanced at his watch. It was a little early, even for a Russian.

When they were all resettled, it was D'Arby who spoke first. He grew reflective, his voice softer, and all the more penetrating for it. "Let me say a few words, if you'll allow me, about how I see our position. We have come here as leaders from our different backgrounds, bringing with us our often rival loyalties and competing ambitions. And leadership can be a harsh calling, it rarely leaves us easy options. We seek not crowns or personal enrichment, we do what we do for one reason above all else. That reason is the love of our homeland. And in her service we are little more than slaves. Our first duty is not to ourselves nor to those things we wish to be remembered by, but to our country. Sometimes that means we are required to do things we find distasteful, painful — yes, even occasionally unprincipled, because we all know that this imperfect world of ours is built of confusing colours. Those who seek a straight path to the gates of glory are either saints or more often sad failures. None of us sought this challenge which now faces us but we cannot shrink from it, no matter how much we would wish it otherwise. For my part, I can only say that I will do what I believe is right, not for my own peace of mind but for my people, whatever that takes." He picked out the words one by one. "*Whatever* that takes."

It was a powerful performance. Shunin was nodding, Blythe Edwards shifting in discomfort. They were on the edge of a momentous decision, one that would change the nature of their world, whatever they decided.

"Whatever that takes," Blythe repeated, trying out D'Arby's words for size. "Which in this case means —"

Yet before she could finish her thought there came the most extraordinary sound as Shunin pushed a tray from the table and cast it to the floor. Everyone jumped, their concentration shattered.

"Clumsy of me," Shunin confessed as Nipper bounded across the room to retrieve the tray. "Young man," he continued, "why not take the dirty cups to the kitchen before I knock them all over? We'll call you if we need anything else."

As a smiling Nipper disappeared through the door with the crockery, Shunin tapped his ear and pointed after the boy. "You can't be too careful who's listening. Not when you're about to go to war."

Lunchtime, Saturday. Castle Lorne.

Blythe Edwards called a pause to their discussions. She wanted time to think. D'Arby protested, in a gentle but persistent fashion, suggesting that their time was too short and they should continue with the matter over lunch, but she insisted. "Lunch can wait, Mark, the next hundred years won't be so patient." She retired to her room, instructing Washington to remain at hand in his own room. Away from the others. To isolate the infection, perhaps.

Lavrenti Konev also disappeared. He had remained remarkably silent during their discussions, almost morose, drawn in upon himself and no sooner had he made it to the top of the stairs than Shunin decided to follow. Harry, too, made his excuses to D'Arby. He needed fresh air more than food, he would stretch his legs along the cliff.

Harry was sitting on his bed, changing into stouter shoes, when he heard the raised voices escaping from Konev's room a little further down the passage. The exchange quickly grew to a quarrel of extraordinary ferocity. Konev and his father-in-law were having the sort of fight that would leave scars. It was in Russian and Harry couldn't understand a word, but venom needed little translation. Shunin seemed to be on the point of losing his self-control while Konev was struggling to force his own views into the torrent of fluent Slavic curses.

Then it grew physical. Something was thrown, a brush, a shoe, perhaps; it hit the bedroom door and clattered onto the floor. Harry, unable to resist his curiosity, took up position by his own door. He heard what sounded like a drawer being emptied and luggage tossed around, as though the room was being ransacked. Konev was protesting, but to no effect. There came ripping, as though clothing was being torn, then an abrupt silence, filled with exquisite menace, followed by a single word, a name — Katya. After that came the distinctive sound of violence, of a punch — no, more likely a full slap, landing across a cheek, one so sharp that it must have inflicted intense pain.

A few seconds later Shunin emerged onto the landing. His face was flushed, a dark spot of fury glowed on his brow; he was wheezing, and his arms hung heavy and leaden by his side. And his hand, the one that bore his presidential ring, was covered in blood.

CHAPTER
FIFTEEN

Saturday lunchtime. Castle Lorne.

Harry bumped into Nipper in the hallway by the front door.

"Are you going out, Mr Jones?"

"For a walk."

"Can I come?"

"Will you be allowed? It's lunchtime."

"Luncheon," he declared grandly, "has been cancelled."

"So has the *Mr Jones* thing. If we're to be fellow travellers we'd also better be friends, so you must call me Harry. A deal?"

Nipper nodded enthusiastically. So they set off across the causeway, but they didn't follow the road, instead taking a path that emerged faintly from the heather. It led them up towards the cliffs, weaving it's way through the gorse and scrub that hugged the coastline. They didn't talk as they climbed — or, in Nipper's case, skipped. Harry stretched his legs and fell into the long, even paces that he could maintain for many miles when he'd had to. He'd once done that across the Iraqi desert. Three nights. With a bullet in his back and a friend's body across his shoulders. The other soldier died after the second night, but still Harry had carried him. Harry was stubborn that way. They'd been on a mission that nobody was permitted to talk about, one that had been undertaken before the war started. He had known those desk generals at the Ministry of Defence would never tell the wife what had happened; left up to them, she'd get neither the truth nor her husband's body. Thanks to Harry, she got both.

Now, along with Nipper, he came to a crevasse in the cliff top, not much more than a yard wide; Harry stood ready to jump, holding out his hand to give Nipper his support, but Nipper wanted to do it himself.

"Don't worry, I've done it a million-zillion times before," the boy exclaimed as he stood on the edge, yet despite his determination he looked a trifle apprehensive. Harry remembered the story of Nipper's fall. The boy was still protesting when a razorbill, startled from its nesting place, burst from the crevasse directly beneath his feet in a flurry of feathers. Nipper screamed in alarm, then slipped. He toppled backwards.

It was nothing short of a miracle that Harry was able to catch the boy's flailing hand and heave him back to safety. Nipper stood shaking, gulping for air, yet when at last he looked up his face was filled not with childish fear but with determination. Then, with one bound, the boy skipped across the crevasse.

A little further on they stopped to rest in the thick heather at a point overlooking the castle. From here they could see how the granite cliffs swept in an arc like an audience before a stage on which stood the towering figure of Castle Lorne. The ruined chapel looked down from its perch amongst the gods while a thousand gulls beat their wings in applause. This was an enchanting spot, and Harry knew why Flora MacDougall wanted to spend the rest of her days here.

"Mr Jones," Nipper began, "do you live in Heathen?"

"In where?"

"Heathen," the boy repeated, his face set in earnest. "Where the Heathens come from."

Harry bit his lip, desperate to control his desire to be engulfed with laughter. "Why do you ask, Nipper?"

"Granny said you are all Heathens. She was upset because you'd walked out on her lunch. But I don't know where Heathen is."

Now Harry could resist no longer and the laughter burst forth. He tousled the boy's brilliant mop of hair. "A little part of me is English, Nipper, and that might make me a Heathen in your grandmother's eyes. And I'm sorry for her lunch. One day, if I'm allowed, I'd like to come back. We can do everything properly then."

"I'd like that, too. When I get my pilot's licence I can fly you here myself."

Suddenly the laughter had blown away with the wind and Harry's heart ached for the disappointment that was waiting for the child. "Heathen," Harry said, "isn't a place, it's a description. Of those who don't believe in God. But I think your granny was using the word in a looser sense to describe those who don't believe in her cooking, and if it comes to that, I'm no Heathen."

"You missed her lunch."

"I just needed to let the sea wind blow the cobwebs away so that I could do a little thinking."

"It almost blew me away, too."

"I think your granny will be unhappy that I brought you here. You've had bad experiences with these rocks, I believe."

Nipper's brow formed a perfect single furrow. "No, Mr Jones, she wouldn't be cross. Granny's very clear about it. She says that living in fear isn't living at all."

"She is a very wise woman, your granny."

"When my Grandda' died, I was unwell for a little while. But as soon as I got better she took me back to the place where we had fallen. We threw some flowers off the cliff, then we sat down and had a little picnic. Grandda's favourite, Marmite sandwiches. She hates Marmite but still she ate them, and she cried. I asked her why she was so unhappy, but she says she wasn't unhappy, she was simply giving thanks for having met Grandda', and for having me. That's when she told me I must never be afraid."

"And that's why you had to jump across the rocks."

As they sat there, the wind picked up and began to ripple through the heather.

"We should go back, Nipper."

"But I thought you came up here to think. Have you done your thinking?"

"Somehow I think you and your granny have done it for me."

When Harry and Nipper returned to the castle they found D'Arby sitting in the sunshine by the causeway. He was perched atop a weather-beaten stone block that might once have been used by guests to mount their horses.

"Ah, the travellers return!" he greeted as they approached. "I've been waiting for you, Harry. A word?"

Taking his cue, Nipper held out a hand and solemnly shook Harry's, thanking him for his company. Then the boy scampered back inside, his arms out wide, pretending to be an airplane. D'Arby, too, extended an arm, placing it round Harry's shoulders and leading him away from the castle until they were entirely on their own. They sat themselves on a rock close by the shore.

"We've come to that time, Harry. The next couple of hours will decide all, and I need your help."

"In what way, Mark? I feel I've done nothing since I've been here."

"You have been waiting for the moment. Now it's here." D'Arby bent to scoop up a handful of pebbles and began casting the stones, one by one, into the waters of the blue firth. For a while he seemed to have lost his train of thought. "It's moving much as I'd expected," he said eventually. "Shunin's up for it. Stands to reason. Whatever else he may be he's a patriot, a devoted Russian, and no fool. He knows how fragile his country is. He was part of the nineties when old women stood in the streets of Moscow, begging in the snow for a stranger to buy their only coat because they hadn't eaten in three days. Once the Chinese start playing their games, he'd be only a snowstorm away from disaster. All the Muslim areas, the Tatars, the Ingush, the Humpty Dumpties, they'll go, but Chechnya will be first, and at that point the Russian

238

dream is over. Our Mr Shunin knows very clearly what's at stake."

"You think you can trust him?"

"Trust him? Trust that bastard? Good God, no! But I think I *know* him, Harry, I think I've known how he'll react."

"It seems Shunin hasn't been the only one playing chess."

"The man's an animal, Harry. Put him in a tight corner and the only thing he knows is to fight. And Washington is a notorious hawk. Wind him up and watch him go. Totally reliable. But Blythe . . ." He sighed and threw the rest of the pebbles into the water, grown tired of his game. "Frankly, she's been a disappointment. So slow to see the point, to make up her mind."

"She's had distractions. Personal problems."

"Ah, I see." He squinted into the sun. "I knew you'd understand her better than any of us, Harry. I've seen the two of you together here. I knew I'd made the right choice in bringing you."

"How?"

"She trusts you — as do I. Help me to bring her back into play."

"What do you expect me to do?"

The Prime Minister took Harry's arm and squeezed it. "Whatever it takes," he said, slowly repeating the words he had used earlier.

"Give her a little time, Mark —"

"But we have no time! We're about to get hung out to dry! Brought to our knees! Made to beg!" His shoe kicked out in frustration at the pebbles that lay at his feet, sending them scattering. "Blythe is our only chance." he cried, raising his arms to the gods, imploring their intervention, but then his shoulders sagged and his hands fell to his side. "Without her, Shunin won't come with us, not on his own. He'll be on the first plane to Beijing hoping he can scratch out some sort of deal, while we shall be left entirely alone. Everything — *everything* — depends on us staying together, and right now that's down to Blythe. We have to persuade her — *you* have to persuade her!"

"And how do you suggest I do that?"

The arms were waving once more, this time in frustration. Harry was supposed to know, not be asking damn fool questions. "Reason with her. Plead with her. Tell her she owes it to you for saving her son — and she does, Harry, you pulled her fingers out of the wringer on that. And if guilt doesn't work, appeal to her sense of history. Tell her she'll be right up there with George Washington. Flatter her. Promise her anything. Whatever it takes . . ."

Now, with a clarity so sharp it was painful, Harry knew why he had been brought along. Being the keeper of D'Arby's conscience had nothing to do with it; in fact, the man appeared to have no conscience at all. Harry was a donkey, a beast of a burden intended to carry Blythe along the chosen path, whether she wanted the ride or not. He sat looking out towards the islands, his loyalties in turmoil. He felt used by D'Arby. He let forth a long sigh.

"Why so glum, Harry?"

240

"It's just that I'd been planning to spend the weekend with a ridiculously entertaining woman from Manhattan named Gabbi. So far, your alternative isn't coming up to scratch."

D'Arby gave a dry chuckle. "Come on, old friend," he encouraged, placing his arm round Harry's shoulder. "Your country needs you. And we don't have much time," he said glancing at his watch as he led the way back inside.

Saturday, 2.17 p.m. British Summer Time; 5.17 p.m. Persian Gulf.

A barge, ugly, smeared with grime and rust, nudged up against the USS *Reuben James* as it unloaded the fuel and water, anything to lighten the load. While they waited, the warship's crew offered up their own private prayers that the high tide would re-float them and send them far away from this bug-infested place. They knew they might be attacked at any moment, stuck out there in the open, but they scarcely needed the Iranians to finish them off; the humiliation alone was going to be enough to kill them.

They had gathered a mighty audience. Patrol boats of the Islamic Republic of Iran were swarming in the sea around the *Reuben James*, while along the smudge of coastline on the horizon, military units massed in their support. Above the scene, helicopters of the US 5th Fleet hovered in close attendance, and many thousands of feet higher their warplanes kept a vigilant eye on everything that moved. Almost lost amongst the crowd was a commercial tug, sent from Kuwait, just in case the high tide didn't do its job. It was turning into quite a party. And as they rubbed shoulders, the Persian Gulf teetered on the brink.

The day seemed endless beneath the withering sun. Nerves were frayed. When, many hours earlier, the commander of the frigate had first reported his difficulties, a rescue plan had been put into immediate effect. At first light the commander of the US 5th Fleet, from his flagship in Bahrain, had sent a senior officer to the stricken frigate in order to take over its command — the ship's own senior officer could no longer be trusted, not after parking on a sandbank. The nuclear-powered USS *Ronald Reagan*, one of the US Navy's newest aircraft carriers, had also been ordered to the area. It was as long as the Empire State Building was high and carried an awesome inventory of armaments, and although it hadn't yet reached the scene its mere suggestion cast a long shadow.

The Iranian patrol boats had arrived shortly after dawn. They were small and not heavily armed but they posed a direct threat to the safety of the *Reuben James*, and in any other circumstances the Americans would simply have blown them from the water. Yet there was one glaring problem with such a response. The patrol boats were on home territory. Instinct suggested the Iranians should be swatted like flies, but caution dictated that instead the Americans wait and see. So the *Reuben James*' new captain gave orders that the patrol boats should not be attacked unless they showed

242

hostile intent or came within four hundred yards of his ship. This was radioed to the boats but the *Reuben James* had no way of knowing whether it was using the right frequency or whether the Iranians even understood English, so to back up this message three helicopters were sent to mark the perimeter, squatting menacingly above waters that began to boil in the downdraughts. For the moment both sides waited, pistols at the ready, with no one entirely sure who was the sheriff and who the bad guy.

There was more immediate justice to be dispensed. The new captain of the *Reuben James* was on the point of having his predecessor relieved of all duties and flown from the ship — the standard consequence for such a godawful screw-up — when strange faults in the navigation systems were discovered. At first the mess seemed like a straightforward case of catastrophic incompetence, but when the computer history of the navigation system was examined, it suggested something more sinister had taken place. Four thousand tons of warship can't jump more than two miles in a nanosecond, but that's what the computer logs showed. They had to be wrong, so . . . Sabotage. And that meant the Iranians — didn't it?

These were dangerous seas, no stranger to confrontation. A few years earlier a large detachment of British Royal Marines in pursuit of smugglers had been arrested by the Iranians and held captive. It hadn't been the first such incident. Tehran had crowed, the British had been humiliated, yet in the end the Britons had all been safely released. Twenty years earlier it had been a different story. The US had shot down Iran Air Flight 655 after mistaking the civilian Airbus for an attacking warplane. All two hundred and ninety passengers on board had died, including sixty-six children. No apology had ever been forthcoming from the Americans.

Memories die slowly in the desert, and the Iranians had not forgotten. So was the *Reuben James* to be the means of their revenge? As the day drew on and temperatures rose, fingers grew tighter on every trigger. And in the Persian Gulf, there were so many triggers.

Saturday, 2.22p.m. Castle Lorne.

Harry headed up the stairs to his room, taking them two at a time, so swiftly that the old oak boards didn't even have time to squeak. He was hurrying not simply to change his shoes — the gong had already been sounded to summon them all — but also to leave behind what the Prime Minister had said. He was seeing Mark D'Arby in a new and far less attractive light.

He had just reached the neck of the stairs when he came to an abrupt halt. Ahead of him, in the hallway, he saw Shunin. The Russian was coming out of Harry's room, quietly closing the door behind him.

The Russian hadn't seen him and Harry was about to retreat, not wanting to let the other man know he'd been spotted, when Shunin set off in the opposite direction towards the back staircase. As he passed his son-in-law's room he paused. For a moment he seemed to be debating whether to go in. Then he stiffened and hurried on, disappearing from sight.

You get around, don't you? Harry whispered to himself. What was the bastard up to? Harry scurried to his room, seeking answers, and his first impression was that nothing had changed — perhaps the Russian had simply lost his way, grown confused in a strange house, wandered in innocently? But even as he offered up the excuse, he knew it was bollocks. Innocence and Sergei Illich Shunin were such improbable bedfellows. He scanned the room, everything seemed as he'd left it, except . . . Weren't the pillows disturbed? Hadn't the contents of his drawer been lifted and left rumpled, and those clothes hanging in the cupboard pushed just a little further along the rail? Harry was an orderly man, not anal but simply disciplined from the days when you either assembled the components of your assault rifle in the dark in precisely the right order or ran the risk of a bullet from the bad guys. And, damn it, his things had been moved, he was sure of it. Then in the bathroom he discovered his wash bag sitting on the wrong side of the sink — OK, so maybe he was a little anal, he admitted, but there were worse things. Worse things, too, than finding your wash bag had been tampered with, but what the hell was the Russian President up to? Nothing good, that was for sure.

Saturday, 2.30p.m. Castle Lorne.

Someone had decided they should pick up their business in the library — perhaps it was Flora, to enable her to make preparations for the evening meal in the dining hall. As Harry walked in, it was as though he had been presented with a picture that would tell the whole story of what was to come. Washington was huddled with Shunin, seated in two of the deep armchairs. The American was animated, clutching the cracked leather arms and levering himself forward in his eagerness to draw closer to the Russian. Shunin sat back, listening with intent. They didn't appear to notice Harry as he came in, or perhaps they simply didn't bother. Meanwhile, D'Arby was checking the news channel once more, leaving Blythe to gaze out of the window, a little apart from the rest. She was fiddling with her wedding ring, twisting it, pulling it over the knuckle. When Harry crossed to join her, she shot him a look that might have cut a lesser man in two.

"Sorry," she muttered in immediate apology. She took a deep restorative breath. "I spent lunchtime with a coat hanger pretending the pillow was Arnie. I beat the crap out of him. Feathers everywhere." She jammed the wedding ring back tight on her finger. "Mrs MacDougall will be as mad as hell."

"She's a woman. And she's a Scot. Her only complaint will be that you let him off lightly."

She managed a guilty smile.

"When Mel and I split, I almost ran out of coat hangers."

246

"Is that why you started leaving your coat slung across the backs of chairs all over town? Because you'd run out of coat hangers?"

Ouch. She was blazing away in all directions. It seemed she wasn't in the mood to be friends with anyone at the moment — at least, not with anyone in trousers. "No," Harry responded, determined not to rise to the bait, "I simply went out and bought more coat hangers. They're the easy things to replace."

They began to settle themselves in an informal group, sitting by the library's vast window, as outside the gulls plunged and soared in the air currents rushing past the face of the castle. As Harry crossed the room to join the group, he began to realise what a bizarre bunch they made. He wondered whether any of them were fit for the decisions they were about to take. Not that summits had ever been the orderly occasions people might expect. In Harry's experience such gatherings were often carried out in varying states of exhaustion or inebriation, or both. George Bush Sr. had been plain unlucky when he'd thrown up in the lap of the Japanese Prime Minister, that had been a genuine case of food poisoning, but Brezhnev had been drugged up to the eyeballs while Yeltsin had been so drunk in Ireland he couldn't even get off his plane. At least, fast asleep, he couldn't do too much harm.

"No Lavrenti?" Harry asked.

"He is not well," Shunin replied gruffly. "He had an accident. Slipped in the bathroom. He —" Shunin waved his hand across his face — "has a headache."

247

"I bet he has," Harry whispered, to no one but himself.

They were interrupted by Mrs MacDougall, who had come to ensure that all their needs were satisfied. Her face was still clouded by the damage that had been done to her carefully planned lunch. "Are there any requirements?" she asked in the manner of a seaside landlady kept up by rowdy guests.

"I wouldn't mind a vodka, if you have one," the Russian replied.

"This is a family home, not a distillery, Mr Shunin," she replied tartly. "Now, if there's nothing else you require . . ." She glared at them. They lowered their eyes, like guilty schoolchildren, even Shunin. "Then dinner will be served at seven o'clock — sharp!" And with that, she bustled away.

"She reminds me of my mother," Shunin said in quiet appreciation as the door closed on them.

"Now you understand why Hadrian built his wall," D'Arby added.

They enjoyed their joke, even Shunin. It was a small but welcome distraction from what lay ahead, a way to relieve the tension as they settled back and began to prepare for war.

But war had already overtaken them.

The duty physicist was still several minutes away, clinging to the back of a commandeered police motorcycle, already too late to prevent catastrophe. The pressure in the reactor core was continuing to rise, and now the instruments that recorded the rate of flow of the coolant were beginning to act up. The engineers still couldn't work it out, but at the heart of the reactor core, beyond the limits of their understanding, the melting fuel rods were beginning to create blockages inside the cooling system. The reactor was out of control. The slow, localized, almost imperceptible meander towards disaster was about to turn into a sprint.

Yet the instrumentation in the control room still suggested that everything was in order, almost. The engineers were puzzled more than panicked, right up to the point when monitors positioned near the pipes that carried the coolant began to go haywire, blasting out a warning. Radiation was finding its way *outside* the reactor core, and the levels were rising. It was a sign that the fuel was failing — melting. And as it did so it threatened to spew radiation over the surrounding countryside, not by blowing its lid as Chernobyl had done but through a creeping, invisible tide of nuclear pollution on a scale Britain had never known.

The desk engineer gasped, his thoughts overwhelmed by the sudden outpouring of alarms. He cast a bewildered look at his screens, then turned to his supervisor. As their eyes met, the moment seemed endless as their unspoken fears tripped over each other, although the report of the Royal Commission of Enquiry later revealed that they had hesitated for no longer than a couple of seconds.

The minds of the men in the control room were racing. They knew the potential consequences. Sizewell stood on the coast. Any leak of radiation would find its way straight to the sea. Millions of residents along the east coast of England would have to be evacuated. The swirling currents and tides would disperse the radioactivity over a huge area, throughout the fishing grounds of the North Sea, right up to the oil and gas fields that kept the British economy afloat. The tides would even push this atomic storm into the Thames Estuary until it had reached the heart of London itself.

Catastrophe.

Then they began to think about the consequences for themselves, and for their families, of standing in the middle of the greatest radioactive puddle in history. It was at that point that the supervisor screamed, and the desk engineer thumped the large red button in front of him. It tripped the reactor, which immediately began to shut itself down. It flooded the core with coolant, yet the neat geometry that should have allowed the coolant to pour freely between the fuel rods had long since disappeared. A large number of rods were no longer in place but slopping around in a radioactive sludge at the bottom of the reactor. That sludge was still heating up and eating its way through the steel casing, towards the world outside.

CHAPTER
SIXTEEN

Saturday, 3.12p.m. Castle Lorne.

The wind had freshened, it seemed a storm might be brewing. "So, run something past me. How would this attack of yours work?" Blythe Edwards asked.

It was a question that, like the blustery currents outside, seemed to imply a new course. It indicated she was at least willing to consider the idea of an attack, but they also noticed her use of the conditional. She was still sitting on the fence, but pulses raced faster.

Washington took up the challenge, rubbing his forehead with the palm of his hand as though attempting to polish it still further. "This is what we do," he began, indicating that there were no qualms on his part. "We act on this thing together. Everything together. Attack and Explain, our two guiding rules." He cast around, making sure they were paying attention. "So, we all have some idea where the Chinese cyber facilities are located — no, I know it's not a comprehensive inventory, Madam President," he added quickly, warding off Blythe's half-formed question, "but if we pool our information we're going to be able to build a pretty accurate picture. Join up a large number of the dots. Now, as I've already said, these will be mostly soft targets, not buried underground or burrowed into mountains but located on university campuses and in research institutes and the like. We know how it is in our own countries. Most of these facilities have been built with kids, by kids, for kids. In military terms it's no more of a challenge than kicking over a playpen."

In Russia, Shunin reflected, they'd begun to go quite a lot further than that, and he suspected the Americans had, too, as the world started to catch on to the lurid potential of cyber-struggle, but the point was fair enough. By comparison with the rest of the military game, cyber remained something of a cottage industry.

"OK. So if we pool this information, we know what to target. And if we also pool our strike capabilities, we're in business. We use nothing too big — certainly nothing they might mistake as nuclear. First thing, we hit them with every bit of kit in our cyber armoury, try to blind them in the headlights, but we've got to expect that they're going to be ready for that. We can't rely on a cyber attack working all by itself. So simultaneously we hit them physically, too. We use precision-guided munitions, JDAM bombs, that sort of thing, but since many of the Chinese facilities will be a considerable way inland we'll have to rely extensively on cruise missiles. These attacks will also have to be at night to lessen the extent of any collateral damage."

"You mean casualties," Blythe said.

"Correct. Make sure the university campuses and office complexes aren't flooded with people."

He made himself sound almost like a humanitarian, Harry thought.

252

"And these attacks will be launched from where?" Blythe pressed.

"Good question. We'd have trouble with the natives if we used our bases in Taiwan and South Korea without warning, and we can't afford to consult them because they'd only go and squawk to their cousins in China. Mainly, I think, we'll rely on the navy, use missiles based on carriers and submarines. Tomahawks. And it would be a great opportunity to try out our newest bit of kit, the Joint Strike Fighter, we have some in our Pacific Fleet. Coordinate everything with our Russian friends, of course, share out the targets. Try and get the job done in a first strike. The Chinese air defences aren't up to much, but we wouldn't want to go back in after they'd been alerted."

Shunin nodded thoughtfully and in agreement.

"No warning," Washington continued. "Total surprise."

"Surely we have to give them at least a chance to back down," Blythe interrupted. "An ultimatum. Twelve hours, even. Something to cover our backs with neutrals."

Washington turned to the Russian. "How long did it take for Sosnovy Bor to go critical, Mr President?"

"Not even twelve minutes," Shunin replied dully.

"Give them any sort of warning and we hand the Chinese an opportunity to scramble all our satellite-guidance systems, maybe even the warheads," Washington continued. "The missiles might not even get there."

"But we have no idea whether the Chinese have that capability," Blythe persisted.

"Precisely, Madam President. We don't know. So we don't take that chance."

And now, thought Harry, we are planning a war based on fear — fear of the unknown. Something like that had started World War One. But now D'Arby was intent on having his say.

"I want to make it clear that the British will be part of this, and right behind you. We may not have much left in terms of military capability in the Far East, but whatever we can do, it will be done."

"Your most important form of support, Prime Minister, comes in the next phase, I think," Washington replied. "The propaganda war. The information offensive. I've already drawn up a few chapter headings." He spread sheets of hand-written notes across the low table in front of them.

"There's also the little matter of explaining it to ourselves, to our own people," a voice added quietly. It was Harry. Blythe nodded in agreement.

"Together!" D'Arby burst in. "That's what makes it all work, Harry. I go to the Cabinet and say that the United States and Russia are in this with us, that we're as one, a band of brothers, and not one of them will dare stand against such a tide. It's the tide of history, Harry. Hell, which side are they gonna take? Western civilization or the Oriental plague?"

"Seize the moment!" Washington applauded enthusiastically. The tide was already flowing.

Yet immediately it swept up against Blythe Edwards. She was unwilling to be moved so easily. "If we hit them without warning, we give them every reason for striking back."

"So what would you have us do, Madam President," Shunin said, "wait until St Petersburg has melted into a radioactive haze?"

"It'll work," Washington insisted. "These cyber facilities — they're a little like a jigsaw puzzle. Lots of small, independent pieces that mean nothing until they're brought together. We kick the jigsaw to bits, scatter the pieces, take half of them away, and it'll take time for them to be put back in shape. Time that we must use. To boost our cyber defence. Embargo their markets. Kick out their students. Cut off their contacts. Sure, we make soothing noises, too, offer them the hand of peace, but until they take it we blow every single one of their god-damned satellites out of the sky. Have them looking at stardust for the next twenty years, if that's what it takes."

"It's feasible. If we do it together," Shunin said.

"You'd agree to that, Sergei? Pool your cyber resources with ours?" Blythe asked.

His eyes stared at her across the rim of his glass, but they were no longer little chunks of permafrost. They had grown animated, had caught some new light and now sparkled. "You scratch my back, Madam President, and I'll be more than happy to scratch yours."

Christ, thought Harry. Here they were plotting World War Three and the Russian was hitting on the President of the United States. He felt sure Franklin Roosevelt had never had that effect on Joe Stalin.

Saturday, 3.43p.m. Balmoral Castle.

The shafts of responsibility for the disastrous situation of the *Reuben James* were flying around the world. As soon as he had become aware of the magnitude of the situation, the commander of the US 5th Fleet had alerted the Chairman of the Joint Chiefs of Staff. He in turn had summoned his colleagues on the JCS and alerted the Secretary of Defense. Members of the National Security Council had also been informed, although not instructed to gather. It was an August weekend, many were out of town, and the decisions that were required to salvage the situation weren't going to hang around for their holiday plans.

It was also a great pity, given the fraught circumstances, that both the President and her National Security Advisor were abroad. Still, it was always possible to keep them in the loop through the White House, no matter where they were. Several large fortunes had been spent over the years on the most sophisticated communications systems in the world to make sure that was so.

The crisis had caught up with Warren Holt shortly after lunch. Since then, his telephone had scarcely stopped ringing, and with every call his mood had grown more desperate. He now knew it had been madness on his part to let the President disappear, and the consequences for indulging her folly would be terrible. He had lied, to everyone, said she was unwell and in bed yet he had assured them that she was following every detail. It had started with a small deceit that with every successive conversation had turned into a far greater lie. God, it was like Watergate.

He had to stop it. Perhaps there was still time. She'd said she wasn't to be contacted for anything short of war, but this mess in the Persian Gulf might yet be as good as. She had also said he would have to decide. And so he did. He took her envelope from his breast pocket where it had stayed since the moment she had given it to him. His hands were trembling. The paper was thick, heavily woven, with a royal crest on it. He opened the envelope and extracted its single sheet of paper.

Then he dialled.

Dialled again.

And again.

Nothing. Just a recorded message to tell him the number was temporarily out of service, and that he should try again later.

The phone slipped from his sweat-streaked fingers and started swinging giddily from the end of its wire. It reminded him of a body on a gibbet. Stiffly he bent to retrieve it. It wasn't just his hands, his knees were unsteady, too. It took two attempts before he was able to replace the phone in its cradle. Warren Holt felt ashamed. He knew he was about to panic.

Saturday, 4.10p.m. British Summer Time; 11.10p.m. in the Room of Many Miracles, Shanjing.

"We have finished our first task, Minister."

Fu Zhang leaned back in his chair and let forth an almost post-coital sigh. Then he remained silent, staring at the screens he did not understand, wrapped in this moment of triumph. It was some while before he was able to rouse himself. "What is next?"

Li Changchun tapped a few keys and a different set of views began dancing on the screens in front of them. "The London Flood Barrier," he announced. "It protects their capital. We will cripple the barrier, but this will not be discovered until a high tide coincides with a storm surge. At that point the control systems will go haywire. The barrier will stay down, even as the Thames starts rising."

"Do they not have an override? A manual system? Surely they cannot be so foolish."

"Oh, yes, but that requires power. And when the next high tide meets up with a storm surge . . ." Li shrugged his shoulders. "They will discover a major electrical malfunction. Their emergency generators will begin to vibrate until they disintegrate in a cloud of smoke and metal splinters."

"You can do that?"

"*You* will do it, Minister. Once again you will have the privilege of taking the final step!"

Fu Zhang's lips were working as hard as a whore's. "And what will be the consequence?"

"Very simple, Minister. London will drown."

"How can you be sure?"

"Most of the important parts of the capital lie on a flood plain. Hundreds of years ago, when the river flooded, they rowed boats through their Parliament

258

building at Westminster. And fifty years ago, before the barrier was built, the tide rose nearly forty feet and hundreds perished. Yet they have learned nothing. They have continued building more and more of their vital facilities in the same area, thinking they are safe. The barrier for them is their Great Wall, the only thing that lies between the City of London and complete disaster."

"But — will they know the cause? Will they be able to tell it was us?"

Li smiled. "We have taken temporary ownership of the computer system that runs the tax affairs of the government of Nigeria. That, in turn, has routed instructions through the command and control facilities of the Plesetsk space centre."

"Russia?"

"And that is what the British will find when they climb out of the mud and start looking. The British will suspect the Russians, the Russians will blame the Africans, and they will all grow dizzy. It will be like looking for grains of sugar in a bowl of porridge. They may have their suspicions but they will never find their proof."

"They have grown old, addled, accustomed only to fighting battles on television. They will not fight with wet socks!" Fu Zhang chortled. "Li Changchun, I will not forget what you have done."

"But, Minister, we have only just begun."

"More? There is more?"

Li indicated a group of his colleagues who were gathered before a series of screens on the far side of the room. "The largest computer system in Britain is the one which controls their health service. The medical records of every person in the country have been captured on one central system. The expense and effort have been vast. All their most intimate details have been gathered together." Li's face lit with pleasure. "They have built us the finest playground in the world."

Fu Zhang started applauding.

"The system contains private, painful details they would not share with their closest friends, and certainly not their families, Minister. Did you know, for instance, that the British Foreign Secretary's wife is being treated for a sexually transmitted disease? And that she is unable to identify for certain the lover who gave it to her?"

"No, I did not!"

"And neither, we suspect, does the Foreign Secretary. Not yet, at least."

Fu Zhang's enthusiasm left him short of breath. "Think of it — sixty million secrets, scattered to the wind," he panted. "Sixty million people with every reason to resent and mistrust their government. Sixty million revolutionaries!"

"As Sun Tzu said, Minister, it is not always necessary to drop bombs in order to win wars."

Saturday, 4.28p.m. Castle Lorne.

"People will die. I want to know how many?" the American President said.

"Very few. An infinitesimally small part of the Chinese population," her security advisor replied. He was standing, looking out of the window. Dark clouds were writhing on the horizon; a storm was brewing to the west and headed their way.

"Five hundred? Five thousand?" she persisted.

"You can't put numbers on it, Madam President." His tone was dismissive.

"Many fewer than between us we have killed in Afghanistan," Shunin added.

Washington turned from the window. "Madam President, this is the most significant moment of your presidency. One way or another it's what you're going to be remembered for. Please don't let it be dictated by cheap newspaper headlines."

"And what do you mean by that?"

"It's omelettes and eggs. Some things have got to get broken. That's what war is all about. Hitting them. Hurting them. But only enough to knock them to the ground. This isn't Vietnam or Iraq, this is sweet and sharp. Just how wars ought to be fought."

Harry, the soldier, winced.

"Ten, twenty thousand." Shunin wheezed, scrabbling for his nebulizer. "To the Chinese, that's no more than a flea bite to a camel."

"I thought we were talking five," Blythe retorted sharply.

"The Chinese themselves execute almost that number each year," Shunin replied. "They drag them off to some football stadium or stretch of waste ground and put a bullet in the back of their neck. So let's not shed tears for the crocodile."

"We are not like the Chinese, Sergei. That's the whole point. We put a different value on things."

"Which is exactly why we must do this," Washington said. "Because we put value on human life. Particularly on American lives. That's our job."

"My job above all," she snapped, stung by his tone.

"But we're not talking troops on the ground," he countered in impatience, as if she were a freshman student who hadn't grasped the point. "No American casualties, just in and out with a few missiles, and then a media onslaught on world opinion, hand in hand with our Russian friends. Do it right and the two of you will probably end up with a Nobel Peace Prize."

"And what if they retaliate? Use their own missiles?"

"They wouldn't dare," he said, spreading his hands in exasperation. "That's why they're going cyber. We've got so many more missiles than they have. And ours work."

"I need to think," Blythe insisted.

Washington slapped his thigh, his voice rising. "George Washington didn't need to think, Madam President. He didn't hesitate. He just rowed across the Delaware and . . ." And beat the crap out of the British. Perhaps the comparison wasn't entirely apt. He let the words fade away, leaving a trail of heat.

"Marcus, I think you and I are going to need a little talk about respect after this."

"We get this wrong and there ain't gonna be no '*after this*'!" he exclaimed, his voice adopting the defiant drawl of a Southern slave.

Her eyes flamed with fury at his insolence. "I believe you owe me an apology."

But he remained mute, sullen. The two of them had jumped into a fetid swamp that sucked them back through three hundred years of American history layered with injustice, slavery, sexism and guilt. She was the most powerful woman her country had ever had, he one of its most prominent blacks, and neither had made it this far by giving way.

Their confrontation faded as they became aware that the others had been drawn to the television screen. It had been left on by D'Arby, who seemed to be addicted to it, with the volume muted. Now the pictures were demanding their attention. The Prime Minister hurried to turn the sound back on.

The screen showed amateurish and jerky pictures of a US warship, sitting in the sun and stranded, according to the commentary, on an Iranian sandbank. Small patrol boats were circling the ship, their Iranian revolutionary flags streaming in the wind. The lens of the camera, which was clearly located on one of these boats, foreshortened the perspective to make it seem as though Iranian hornets were buzzing tight in upon the flank of the hapless American vessel. The images panned in to show the warship, its superstructure, its armaments, its flag. The caption on the screen revealed its name. The USS *Reuben James*.

The Iranians were accusing the Americans of an act of deliberate aggression that had been foiled solely by the vigilance of the Iranian coastal defence forces, the commentary said. The Americans, in turn, were blaming catastrophic computer failure in the navigation systems and were seeking Iranian understanding.

"This can't be coincidence," D'Arby whispered. Blythe gave a moan of despair.

As they continued to watch, the Iranian craft kept circling, mocking, tormenting, their banners flying in triumph. Then the tug, low, squat and ugly, came into view. Hawsers were cast to secure it to the frigate. They were going to attempt to drag the *Reuben James* backwards off the sandbank, like a beached whale, all in front of the cameras. The American humiliation was complete. Even if the incident could be restricted to nothing more than a war of words, it was clear that the Iranians had already achieved a spectacular victory.

CHAPTER
SEVENTEEN

Saturday, 5.32p.m. Castle Lorne.

They had taken a break, discouraged by the scenes of the *Reuben James* and exhausted by their own bickering. For a few moments Blythe Edwards had debated whether she should return immediately to deal with the crisis, but was persuaded to stay by the knowledge that their other crisis was still more pressing. Yet whatever it was they decided, they knew it had to be decided that night. Time had become their enemy, too.

Harry was resting on his bed, trying to clear his thoughts, when he heard a knock at the door. It was D'Arby. The Prime Minister smiled as he entered, but in a manner that didn't reach his eyes.

"We're running out of options, Harry."

"What can I do about it, Mark?" Harry replied wearily.

"Nail Blythe."

"What?"

"Bring her alongside, Harry. You may be the only one who can."

Harry swung his legs over the side of his bed, but didn't get up. He felt wounded by what D'Arby had suggested. He was a man who relied on his instincts, they'd kept him alive more than once, yet right now the tingling feelings swirling in his gut were pulling him in different directions. D'Arby was a long-standing colleague and friend — *political* friend, at least — and there was no doubting that this was one of the most perplexing and dangerous moments that either of them had ever faced. It was a time for leadership and D'Arby, his Prime Minister, was calling on his loyalty. Yet D'Arby was also using him, using everyone — nothing wrong in that, except it felt like a snake wriggling up his trouser leg. And there was still so much about this business he didn't understand. Throughout his life Harry had done the loyalty thing and done it very well, yet right now he didn't want to turn out for D'Arby's team any longer.

"Do your own dirty work, Mark."

"What?" The Prime Minister's face was tired, grey with fatigue.

"You brought me along to be your conscience, so you said. But you don't want a conscience, you want a pimp."

"Harry, no. I didn't mean it like that. Look, this Chinese thing, it's sweeping aside all the niceties. But right now it's the only thing that matters. We have to fight it, beat it, no matter what it costs."

"Do we? Do we really, Mark?"

"But of course . . ."

"On my mother's grave I wish I could be as certain about anything as you seem to be about everything."

"Harry, my friend, the evidence is irrefutable."

266

The Prime Minister took a step forward to bring them closer, but as he did so Harry's gut gave another turn. "The only evidence I have for any of this comes from you, Mark."

D'Arby sighed. It was a sound like a wind in autumn. "Your point being?"

"I don't think I trust you any more." Harry could scarcely believe he was hearing the words, least of all that they were his, but that instinct kept screaming at him. Don't stay here, this is not a safe place to be!

"You think I'm lying about the Chinese?" D'Arby said.

"I've begun to doubt your judgement, Mark. I'm feeling manipulated, just like you've been manipulating everyone else. You've goaded Washington, incited Shunin. Now you want me to do a snow job on Blythe."

"Harry, this is the only chance we have. We bring them all together in the next couple of hours or Britain goes under. We leave here without an agreement and we're dead men walking, all of us. You seriously want that on your conscience?"

"I don't want World War Three on my conscience."

"I never thought you'd be one to run from a fight. But you can't be neutral in this one, Harry, there's no place in this for priests and hand-wringers. You're either with us —"

"Us?"

"The country, Harry, with your country. Your poor fucking country." Despite the coarseness he spoke slowly, softly, and he was staring at Harry, assessing him dispassionately, like a surgeon. "Last time I looked I was the country's Prime Minister. And in this you're either with us or . . . Or you're not. It's simple, really."

"It doesn't seem simple to me."

"I've always admired you, Harry — envied you, your strength of character, your independence. So rare in the sport we play at Westminster. I should have realized you wouldn't be like the others. My mistake. A pity. For both of us."

"Are you threatening me?"

"Oh, I thought I was flattering you. But . . ." D'Arby wiped the corner of his mouth, his pale blue eyes bored into Harry. "Whatever it takes, Harry. Whatever it takes."

"You brought me here to watch your back. Now it seems I'll have to watch mine."

"We all dig our own graves," the Prime Minister whispered, before walking out the door.

Saturday, 5.53p.m. Castle Lorne.

Harry needed fresh air. The castle, with its deceits and conspiracies, was growing claustrophobic, so he set out through the strengthening breeze towards the ruins of the chapel on the cliff. He wasn't a religious man, he questioned too many things, sometimes to destruction, even at times himself, yet he respected those who were able to embrace firm beliefs, so long as they weren't trying to put a bullet in his back.

The pathway up the cliff was well trodden and as he approached the chapel he could see why. A small graveyard lay close by its entrance, family graves, and Alan MacDougall's the most recent, with fresh flowers leaning against a simple dark granite headstone. The chapel itself was small, no larger than a cottage, the glass of its narrow windows long ago carried off by sea-borne storms and its roof a patchwork quilt of old, failing slates. A weathered wooden door pierced by deep cracks hung from a single hinge, yet the walls still stood thick and firm in the afternoon sun.

As he stepped inside, Harry blinked in the sudden darkness. The chapel was completely bare, its artefacts and furniture long since gone, but despite the signs of decay the uneven stone floor was clean, with no sign of debris blown by the wind or dragged in by birds. Someone still cleaned in here, still cared. The atmosphere was dark and intense, yet on the bare stone wall, near where the altar would have stood, the sun was piercing through the battered roof forming a crucifix of light that stretched from the floor almost up to the rafters. A sign, for those who believed in such things. Around the walls ran a narrow stone ledge, worn with age and on which, in the times before pews, those who had come here would have seated themselves. And on that uneven ledge, in the chapel's gloomiest corner, his knees pulled up beneath his chin, sat Lavrenti Konev.

"I'm sorry. Didn't mean to barge in on you," Harry said.

Konev shook his head, as if the interruption was of no consequence. "I came here to think," he replied quietly from the shadows. And to drink. Beside him stood a bottle of Flora's finest. It had already suffered considerable damage, and he took another substantial swig.

As Harry's eyes adjusted to the gloom he noticed a vivid fresh wound on the Russian's cheek. The eye above it was closed. "Are you OK?" he asked in concern.

Slowly, and for the first time, Konev turned his face towards Harry, his fingers tracing the path of the wound. "A small misunderstanding," he whispered.

"With a door, I'm told."

"Something like that. Yes, it must have been a door. How stupid of me." His words were slurred, his tone ironic. He gave a short, humourless laugh. "So what of our little enterprise, Mr Jones? What do you think about the fact that we're going to make war on the rest of the world?"

"It might be easier to understand if we weren't so busy making war on each other."

Konev nodded awkwardly. "I fear we shall find rivers filled with much pain in which we shall all drown." He paused. "That's what I told him. That's what I said to Papasha."

"War has unpredictable consequences."

"Families, too. They have consequences," he mumbled. "But there are some things we know all too clearly, Mr Jones. Papasha has already spelled them out. He will use this war to make all argument and all

270

opposition disappear. The landscape around him will be flattened in every direction and Russia will bleed, just as Russia has always bled."

There was an unmistakable edge to his words, Harry felt. It was as though every mention of Shunin, and of Russia, was being carved into Konev's flesh with a blade.

"Mr Washington was wrong, you know," the young Russian continued. "It's not the system we have to fear, it's the people who control it, who bend and twist everything to their own purpose. Get rid of those individuals and you have no system. And then, please God, you would have no war." He looked up with his one good eye, which seemed empty, like a lump of coal in the snow. It reminded Harry of a wounded soldier, on morphine, senses dulled to kill the pain. "Getting rid of one man can make all the difference," Konev continued, mumbling past thick lips.

"You mean Mao?"

Konev wrinkled his drunken brow as though testing out a new thought. "Perhaps." He sighed. "We all have to die. You. Me. No choice in that, Mr Jones. And sooner than we would like. Papasha will make sure of it. Didn't you know? He kills everyone." He began to laugh until, suddenly, it seemed as though the joke was sticking in his throat and choking him. He struggled for a few moments, heaving, then he reached for the bottle once more before closing his eye and drifting off into another world.

Saturday, 8.18p.m. Castle Lorne.

The venison that Flora MacDougall served them for dinner was as close to perfection as ever Harry had tasted, yet it would prove scarcely more successful than her lunch. The mood of the company was as dark and forbidding as the skies gathering outside. Their conversation was desultory; they'd gone over the details of what was proposed to the point where there was little purpose in pursuing them further. All that was required now was a decision. And that required Blythe Edwards.

Yet she hesitated. She had learned from the mistakes of others that war, so hastily gathered, was yet so difficult to put aside. There were many other reasons for caution, too, although somehow as the day had dragged on they seemed to fall out of focus and grow elusive. She was finding her isolation difficult to deal with. The others had come to their conclusion, had been able to see things more clearly than she. Where was the weakness in it all, was it in their argument, or simply in her? She had to consider that possibility, that she was the one who was missing the point. Was she being blinded by emotion, distracted by the loss of both her mother and her marriage?

The images of the *Reuben James* had affected her deeply. The gunboats circling the frigate weren't jeering simply at the ship but at her nation, mocking the entire American dream, a dream that was threatened from so many quarters. Any sign of hesitation and that trickle of derision might grow into a flood that would sweep her and all she stood for to one side. She was a Harrison, and she couldn't allow herself to be accused of allowing the dream to die, least of all without a fight. On the other hand, she wasn't ever going to let herself be buried in the same bottomless pit as George W.

It was while she was lost in her world of indecision, toying with the food on her plate, that the lights went out. Every single one. The power had been cut. There was no panic, there were candles aplenty on the table, and soon Mrs MacDougall was fussing around in the manner of a farmyard hen to bring them more. She assured them this was not an uncommon occurrence, nothing more than another sign of government incompetence — "There's no underestimating the uselessness of those ne'er-do-wells in Edinburgh," she said, "on account of their being half-English." D'Arby roared with amusement, although he wasn't entirely sure whether she was joking. Yet, as they returned to their venison, the same thought began to insinuate itself into all their minds. Was this mere coincidence?

When, after a few minutes, the lights came back on they all prayed quietly in relief.

"You know, for a moment there, I thought it might have been the Chinese," Blythe suggested, giving shape to their doubts, "that we had been discovered and somehow they'd managed to focus in on us — just us. Turned the switches off."

"Not possible," Shunin answered gruffly, seeking reassurance in his glass.

"But I'm afraid it is," D'Arby countered. No sooner had he spoken them he bit his lip as though regretting his words. He gazed round the table; he saw they were all waiting for his explanation, and his expression grew mournful. The silence became acute before he broke it, addressing himself directly to the American President who was sitting beside him. "I hadn't wanted to tell you, Blythe, not yet — it didn't seem relevant — and you've had enough pain to deal with. In all honesty, I never knew when the right moment would come, so I . . ." His words faltered. "Please forgive me."

"For what, Mark?" She sounded more curious than alarmed, but even as she posed the question the balance was shifting.

He stared at her for some while, then he whispered. "Your mother."

"My . . . mother?" Her lips twitched in pain.

"Your mother was a diabetic, I believe."

She nodded awkwardly. "They discovered that in the hospital."

"Where her life was sustained by insulin. Regular doses. Delivered by something called an infusion pump. It sat at her bedside."

"What are you suggesting, Mark?"

"The infusion pump was controlled by a computer."

The words pierced her like a knife. She screamed silently, as presidents must. "No, please. You can't be telling me . . ." She couldn't finish the thought. She didn't need to.

"I'm so very sorry, Blythe. What can I say? It was an unimaginably despicable act. But it seems the Chinese have the capacity to fine-tune their cyber systems to an extraordinary degree."

274

"They chose my mother?" The words had to fight their way past her trembling lips. "But why her?"

He held her eyes, but hesitated before he replied, very slowly, as though in pain himself. "Because she was your mother. What other explanation could there be?"

She could hold back on her emotions no longer. They burst forth in a moan of despair that was ripped from a place very deep within her and that left the candles guttering in protest.

"My heart reaches out to you, Blythe, but the truth is, I didn't want to tell you," D'Arby continued, overflowing with guilt. "I was too shocked. In all honesty I ran from the responsibility, but there was also another point."

He paused, gathering his composure. "I didn't want what we have to do here today to be about personal animosities. We have to be as clear-headed as Solomon and I didn't think anyone should be asked to come to judgement with such terrible distractions. That was probably a mistake on my part. I apologize."

"You didn't kill her, Mark."

"I feel wretched."

"Not your fault."

"But, given the circumstances, I hope you will understand that I couldn't keep it from you any longer."

"I'm grateful." She struggled, not just with the words but with every part of herself. Tears were escaping down her cheeks, strings of pearls caught in the light.

"If they can do such things — are *willing* to do such things — then none of us can feel safe," Shunin said.

Washington clenched his fists. "What warped sense of civilization declares war — deliberate war — upon a frail and innocent old lady?"

D'Arby reached to squeeze her hand. She squeezed it back until the nails bit into his flesh.

"It's been so hard carrying this secret with me," D'Arby whispered, "but now you can understand why I had to bring you all here. And yet, even now, we have to reach a conclusion. I'm sorry to be persistent, but . . . What are we to do?"

They waited on her. She would be the one to decide. When Blythe spoke again, her voice was tight, fighting for control. "But what is there left to decide?" she said quietly. "I think we all know what has to be done. This disease must be burned out." Then she let go of D'Arby's hand; he found blood on it.

She rose. There was a general scraping of chairs on the old floor. "Gentlemen, please forgive me. I need to be alone for a little while. But we know what must be done."

D'Arby walked her to the door. "I feel as if I've let you down so very badly, Blythe."

She smiled, an expression of exquisite sadness. "No, Mark. I thought I was the one to blame. I've been beating up on myself for not being with her when she died, wondering what else I might have done. Now, at least, I know her passing wasn't my fault. I need feel no guilt. Neither should you."

With bowed head she found her way from the room. No one spoke until they had heard her light footsteps fade up the stairs.

As they resumed their seats, D'Arby glanced across at Harry, holding his eye, as though claiming victory.

"I need another drink," Shunin announced, heading towards the decanter. "Anybody else?"

"Yes, I'll join you," D'Arby declared, "although whether to celebrate or drown the pain, I scarcely know."

But Harry did.

"You going to join us, Mr Jones?" Shunin asked as he splashed whisky into crystal tumblers.

"If you don't mind, I'll pass. I promised to say goodnight to Nipper, if you'll excuse me."

D'Arby looked at him across the room, his expression almost contemptuous. "Take just as long as you want, Harry. I think we can manage without you."

CHAPTER
EIGHTEEN

Saturday, 9.03p.m. Castle Lorne.

"Hello, I thought you'd forgotten," Nipper exclaimed in delight as Harry's head appeared round his door.

"A promise is a promise, Nipper."

After his long climb to the room at the top of the castle, Harry found the boy in bed, wrapped up within the folds of his saltire, his grandmother sitting in a chair beside him. He was reading a story to her while his bedside lamp cast its light across a timeless fragment of childhood made up of pillows and stories and hot cocoa — the sort of thing that had never been part of Harry's life. His father had always been in too much of a rush for that. There had been many other things offered in compensation, of course, like foreign holidays and fast cars and still faster women, even for Harry as a sixteen-year-old, but never any cocoa or bedtime stories. Now, for Harry, they seemed beyond price.

"Is it OK, Mrs MacDougall?" He asked.

"Of course it is," Nipper shouted, too impatient to wait for his grandmother's blessing. "I'll read you a story, too."

"Away wi' you, young man, it's the end of the day, and Mr Jones here has much to be getting on with."

"But Harry is my friend," the child protested in a slow persistent voice. "And Daddy's away."

"You'll be straining your eyes," she insisted.

"Then Harry can read to me." Nipper turned his attention back to his guest. "Do you read stories to your children, Harry?"

"I don't have any, Nipper. One day, perhaps."

"Then I'll let you practise on me if you'd like."

"Enough, Nipper," Mrs MacDougall objected, reaching out to take his hand and grab back his attention, "no more prying into Mr Jones's personal life." But Nipper's face was a picture of expectation and turned directly upon Harry.

"Perhaps, instead of me reading you a story, you should tell one to me," Harry suggested. "That's the way it was always done in the past, not from books but from memory, around the campfire when the day was done. You must have a favourite."

"It's about the Lady of Lorne," Nipper replied, accepting the challenge. "But it's a very sad tale."

"Then I'd guess it has something to do with the English," Harry sighed.

"Oh, you know it already?"

His grandmother couldn't restrain a chuckle. "If you'll not take offence, Mr Jones, I'll be leaving the two of you to it. I have preparations in the kitchen to attend to." She bent to accept a kiss from Nipper. "You tell him just the one story, mind, Nipper, no more, and then it's lights out." She left them, smiling.

Nipper gave several bounces of approval, already brimming with his adventure, while Harry accepted his invitation to perch on the end of his bed in the half-light.

"In ancient times, in the days before the Bruce, there was a terrible battle," the boy began. "The Lord of Lorne was slain and his only son taken prisoner." The language was a little archaic, clearly handed down on evenings before the hearth until Nipper could recite it by heart. "The English arrived at the gates of the castle, but the Lady of Lorne had barred the door and refused them entry. She said no Englishman would ever enter the castle while she was alive. So they dragged her son before the door and told her that if she failed to surrender the castle and all that lay within it, including herself, her son would be put to the sword." A cloud passed over his young face as he choreographed the story with dramatic gestures, his sword hand flying out from his pyjamas towards the young lord's chest. "So she made the English promise before God and heaven that if they had the castle and all that was within, they would set her son free. And the oath was given."

"I'm delighted to hear it."

"But it was an English oath, Mr Jones."

"Suddenly I feel very close to my Welsh roots," Harry muttered.

"The Lady of Lorne knew she could not trust them. So she begged for a few minutes to say goodbye to all the things that she had loved and held dear, and disappeared from sight, but as the English waited outside, they began to see smoke coming from within the castle. The Lady of Lorne had set it afire, with herself inside. Oh, how the English tried to batter down the door, but it was too strong for them. They could only stand back and watch as the fire took hold and worked its way up. And then, as the very top of the castle was consumed by the flames, they saw the Lady standing on the ramparts, dressed in her finest gown, the one in which she had married her slain Lord. And as the tongues of fire licked at its hem, the English saw her cast herself off from the rooftop towards the rocks below." Nipper's young voice was full of pride and defiance as he recounted lines that had been handed down through generations. "She fell towards the raging brine and the English jeered her fate, but as the foul breath left their bodies they saw our Lady change into a beautiful white seagull and soar away to freedom. So they got their castle, or what was left of it, nothing but smouldering ruins. But they said it was a place of evil and magic, so they ran from here even more quickly than they had arrived, and never came back."

"That's a wonderful tale, Nipper. But the son? Did he survive?" Harry asked.

"Of course, otherwise I wouldn't be here!" Nipper laughed at the naivety of the question. "But the English said that because they hadn't got their castle intact, the Scots wouldn't get their Lord intact. So they gouged out his eyes."

"They can be terrible people, some of them," Harry agreed.

"But it had a fine ending, Harry. The new Lord spent the rest of his life rebuilding this castle in memory of his mother. He laid many of the stones himself."

"But he was blind . . ."

"The seagulls guided him, called out to him, told him where each stone should be put. It was his mother, really."

"This truly is a magical place, Nipper."

"I knew you'd understand, Harry. That's why I want to fly. Like the seagulls."

Damn, he liked this kid, so much it almost hurt. For some reason he couldn't quite define spending time with Nipper had made Harry question who he was, and where his life was heading. He was, or had been, so many things. A brilliant student, a superbly trained soldier, a skilled politician. Yes, he was playing at being a Lothario, too, for the moment, at least, but right now, sitting on the end of Nipper's bed, he realized there was an entirely unexplored part of him that very much wanted to be just an everyday guy reading stories to his kids — kids he hoped would be as full of mischief and character as Nipper. But for that he felt he rather needed a wife, and he was already two strikes down on that score. Life's a bitch — well, Mel most certainly had been. But Julia, his first wife, had been killed in an accident when she was pregnant. A little after that Michael Burnside had crossed his path. He often wondered whether the two deaths had been connected, and how much of himself he'd left back along the way.

"Great story, Nipper."

"And every word of it true."

"Thanks for sharing it with me. Let's hope those wicked English don't come battering on your door again, eh?"

"Impossible! No one will ever destroy Castle Lorne, not while we have the dirk," Nipper replied, with a conviction that only the innocence of youth would bear. The boy scuttled out of his bed to take one final look at his precious heirloom. "It will keep us safe. It's well known in these parts."

"I'm very glad to hear it."

But, of course, it was no more than a myth.

Saturday, 9.43p.m. British Summer Time; 4.43a.m. in the Room of Many Miracles, Shanjing.

So great was their concentration and so compelling their task that Fu Zhang had scarcely noticed they had worked through the night. Now, as dawn broke, the tide of adrenalin that had kept him afloat was beginning to run into the sands. Fu envied the youthful resilience of those who still toiled around him. He rubbed the exhaustion around his eyes. During the night he had grown ever more confused by what was before him, streams of computer code and Western alphabets that danced across the screen and left him giddy, yet he wouldn't weaken, wouldn't admit to his middle age while these young men and women still had the energy to finish their task. Onward! Onward! This was a day of conquest, one that would be marked down and taught to young children many generations in the future. Great-Uncle Fu, they would call him, the man who helped forge the Chinese miracle.

His dreaming was interrupted by the phone on Li Changchun's desk. The director picked it up, nodding as he listened. He turned to Fu.

"It appears a detachment of soldiers has arrived outside, Minister, to secure the facility."

"Excellent! Now we can be certain of no interruptions," Fu warbled. The army sent to support him. It made him feel all the more a warrior. And perhaps they might include the troops who had so brazenly mocked him earlier. Now they would realize who he was. He would take great joy watching them melt in humiliation and fear. Then he would deal with them, every wretched one of them. Today was a day of reckoning, on all sides. For Fu life didn't get any better than this.

Saturday, 10.12 p.m. Castle Lorne.

They sat at the dining table as the three of them talked, and planned, and plotted, in the manner of a great conspiracy, with only candles and shadows for witness. They didn't debate specific military targets, that would be for the planners on their staffs, but they discussed the political targets, the big beasts of the diplomatic jungle who would need to be brought on board — the functionaries of the United Nations, the flunkies in the European Union, the Indians and Japanese, those in Taiwan, and any of the non-aligned nations who might be browbeaten or bribed. It could be done, they felt sure, if they acted quickly. And together.

That was how they would kick their own systems into subservience, they decided. The National Security Council, the Joint Chiefs, the intelligence agencies, the Cabinets, the Congress.

"In hours, not days," D'Arby emphasized.

"On television. National addresses, all three leaders," Washington argued. "In their own capitals yet side by side, not just on screen but in tone and manner and purpose. Swamp the doubters."

"But first the military," Shunin insisted. "Not even in my country will they launch an attack on the say-so of just one man, not any more. I am Shunin, not Stalin. The first hours must be spent with them. They will start by not understanding, and soon they will turn to worrying. But they will come with us, when they see all three of us."

"There must be no gloating," D'Arby instructed. "No claims of victory over the Chinese. We must say we are doing this *for* the Chinese, in their interests as well as ours. Extend the hand of friendship."

"Even after we've broken every one of their fingers," Shunin muttered, but he did not disagree.

It might not prove to be so simple, they all understood that. It might mean a new Cold War, a world divided, white against yellow, but once the dice were thrown they must let them roll.

Shunin appeared to be slumbering over his glass, relaxed now that the decision had been taken. D'Arby allowed himself a final nightcap, in celebration and also in order to anaesthetize himself. It had been bloody work. He was halfway through the glass when Shunin, without otherwise stirring, opened one eye and began to talk. "And we shall stand side by side on all the other matters, of course."

Suddenly D'Arby was alert, his politician's instinct sensing a Russian flanking movement. He wished he'd not had that final whisky. "What matters did you have in mind, Sergei?"

The chin rose slowly from the chest, both eyes now open, as bright as ever, like a ferret's, hungry, avaricious. "The tub of sewage that is Chechnya."

D'Arby couldn't restrain his irritation. He'd thought they'd come to a conclusion, now the bastard seemed intent on still more haggling. "You know we have no intention of interfering in Russian affairs, Sergei."

"But you do!" Shunin protested. "Every time in recent years when I have tried to clean up the Chechens' act for them, your so-called human-rights groups have started whining. Demonstrations, petitions, uttering so many kinds of anti-Russian slanders . . ."

"You know we don't control them, Sergei."

"You could ignore them. Stop pandering to them."

"We don't do that."

"I can name seventy Members of Parliament from your own party who have signed or marched or otherwise incited them."

"In a Parliamentary democracy —"

"They tried to kill me, Mark, even on my way here."

"Are you serious?"

"A car bomb. But I had switched cars. If they had succeeded, everything you have talked about here would have been to no purpose. They are your enemies as well as mine, Mark."

"It's just that —"

Shunin's glass came down on the table with a crack, cutting right across the Prime Minister. His voice, when he spoke, emerged quietly, yet had the force of a gale that had blown a path all the way from Siberia. "We are allies. Or we are not."

There was no mistaking Shunin's demand. He wanted a free hand. D'Arby had only a half-formed idea of where Chechnya was — tucked away somewhere near the Caucasus, wasn't it? A distant land of which he knew little and, in all honesty, cared less. He glanced towards Washington; together their eyes flickered in submission.

"Whatever you do, just try to make it quick and keep it away from the cameras, Sergei."

The Russian raised his glass in salute. "And intelligence, of course. Whatever intelligence you both have on the enemies of Russia, I expect you to share it with us."

"What enemies, Sergei?"

"I shall give you a list."

D'Arby knew the list would be long. They weren't going to get away with simply turning a blind eye. With Shunin, nothing was simple.

And while they made their preparations in the dining room, Harry crept silently from the room at the top of the castle where, at last, Nipper had fallen asleep. Outside he could hear the sound of a rushing wind, and the old windowpanes rattled in their frames. The moon peered between muscling clouds, glancing off waves that had begun to rise and turn the causeway into a deceptive silver highway. It would be one of those nights when the castle would need its thick walls. Memories came back to Harry of a time when he was a boy, younger even than Nipper, looking out of another window on a storm-tossed night, waiting for his father to come home. His parents had had the most heart-tearing of rows and Harry wanted his father to return and put all the pieces back together again. But his father never did come back, no matter how long he waited. Afterwards Harry promised himself that never again would he wait for life to come to him but instead he'd chase it down and kick it until it surrendered. Perhaps that's why he'd spent so much of his life on his own; no one else seemed capable of keeping pace.

A squall threw itself against the window once again, causing tiny rivers of rain to slip down the panes like a flood of tears. Damn, it was one of those nights when he wanted so very much to be home, yet even as the desire came to him he wasn't entirely sure where home was. He wanted that sorted, and soon, but for the moment anywhere would do so long as it was away from this place with its dirty trades and bloody conceits. He wished he'd never come.

The panes rattled in their frames once more. That's when Harry thought, from somewhere behind him, he could hear a door being gently opened.

Saturday, 11.48p.m. Castle Lorne.

The man crept through the house in stockinged feet, the noise of his passing drowned by the wind and the rumble of the heavy sea. Down the stairs, through the hallway, past the dining room, struggling to get his bearings in the dark, until he reached the kitchen.

It took him only moments to locate the oil line, plastic-coated 10mm copper piping, that ran round the skirting board until it ended in a brass elbow joint beside the Aga ovens. He knelt down and wrenched at it, once, twice, three times.

Castle Lorne was large and relatively inaccessible, not the sort of place you wanted to get stuck without fuel, which was why Alan MacDougall had decided to install one of the larger types of oil tank that would provide a safety margin in case of difficulty with supply. It worked with a simple gravity feed, no fancy mechanics, just old Isaac Newton. Ater the third tug at the fuel line, and using nothing more than the power of gravity, thousands of litres of heating oil began spewing out across the stone floor.

The man retreated as the oil advanced. He struck a match, threw it into the spreading pool, a little tumbling arc of flame that flickered through the darkness, but it spluttered and died as soon as it hit the oil. So did the next three matches. Heating oil wasn't explosive like petrol, it needed much more persuasion, but the man had foreseen this, had come prepared. He disappeared from the kitchen, returning two minutes later with a plastic container, which he emptied across

289

the floor. Now the intoxicating smell of petrol began to mix with the sweeter scent of the heating oil.

He stood behind the door when he lit the next match. It was a sensible precaution, because when he threw it into the kitchen the petrol vapour ignited explosively and a fireball flashed straight past him and into the hallway. It was followed in close order by a tide of flame that surged across the kitchen floor, and was soon beyond.

Castle Lorne was burning.

CHAPTER
NINETEEN

Sunday, 12.23 a.m., Castle Lorne.

As Harry had turned in the hallway, he had discovered Blythe by the open door to her bedroom. She stood tall, willowy in her flowing pale silk dressing gown, and vulnerable.

"I hoped it might be you, Harry Jones," she'd said, her voice hesitant.

He'd moved towards her to comfort her and she'd stepped back to lead him inside. Without a word she'd poured two large whiskies and stretched herself out on the bed, her back to the headboard, patting the place beside her. "Here, Harry. I need you right now as my best friend in the world."

Cool, calm, yet in turmoil. So they'd sat on the bed, side by side, like two kids at a sleepover.

"You think we're being hasty?" she asked.

He knew she was testing herself as much as him.

"Mark said something to me, about how we dig our own graves."

"Better that than letting the Chinese dig them for us."

They paused, reflecting, sipping.

"You really sure?" Harry enquired.

"Sure? Hell, no, but . . ."

"But what?"

"We have to come to a decision, and yet . . . the others talk about a new world order. Truth is, I'm not sure there'll be any sort of order, not after this."

"More like the Little Big Horn after the Apaches arrived."

"I think you'll find they were Cheyenne, but we're not talking bows and arrows, Harry. You know Mao is a monster."

"Agreed. But what does that make us if we climb into bed alongside animals such as Sergei Shunin?"

"You mean what does that make *me*. And suddenly I feel like a twenty-bit hooker."

"I didn't mean that."

"Oh yes you did." She sighed. "And maybe you're right. I feel like I've been cornered. I'm so *angry*. And every time I try to get my thoughts in a row, the anger pushes in and kicks them all over the place."

And then they had talked, a little about Arnie, much more about Abigail, and she had cried, and they'd sipped more whisky, and cried some more, and eventually Blythe had fallen asleep on Harry's shoulder. Yet even in her sleep her agitation continued, mumbling, stirring, until she reached out for him and held him tight. She needed someone, something, to hold on to.

Harry didn't disturb her, he let her sleep, her breath falling gently on his chest. Perhaps the greatest service he could perform this weekend was to enable Blythe to sort through her troubles. Not that people would understand if he were discovered here. Damn it, Jones, you've got yourself into some tight spots, but never before into a president's bed.

He was in the process of debating whether he was more likely to be awarded the Congressional Medal of Honor or to get himself shot when, through the jumble of conflicted thoughts, he had some sort of premonition that all was not well. It was a sense more than a sound, but it caused him to unravel himself from her arms and creep back out once more into the hallway. That's when he knew what was wrong — could smell it, scouring out his nostrils. Burning. He bounded down the stairs, and almost immediately he could see the glow of the fire from the ground floor.

What the hell had happened to the fire alarms? he wondered. He had no way of knowing they'd been disarmed, every one. By the time he reached the bottom of the stairs, it was already too late. The hallway was a puddle of fire, the generous wooden panelling beginning to smoke and split, the ancient silk tapestries already streaking with soot, the tide of flame advancing inch by quickening inch, devouring the thick tartan carpet and grabbing at everything in its path. Soon it would reach the stairs, and since it was coming from the direction of the kitchen Harry rightly reckoned that the back stairs were already gone. Fingers of acrid, evil smoke were reaching for his throat. He began to choke, retreating, his eyes stinging. As he stumbled backwards he knocked into the dinner gong. He grabbed it and began beating it with all his strength, shouting for their lives as he hurled himself back up the stairs.

293

Harry threw the gong aside as he crashed into Blythe's room. The metal dish gave a last scream of protest and tumbled into a corner, but she was still no more than stirring, half awake and completely unaware. He scooped her up in his arms and ran into the hallway to discover the tall, gangling figure of Washington tumbling down the stairs from the floor above.

"Thank God!" Harry cried. "Get the others. Then get out!"

He continued his own charge towards the ground floor when Blythe came to her senses. "Put me down! For God's sake, put me down!" she cried.

"You're OK, Blythe. I'll get you out."

"I'm fine, Harry, you idiot. Go get the others!" The fire was already licking up the banister rails at the foot of the stairs. She put her arms around his neck and, for one brief moment, held him. "I'm really fine," she whispered. "Save the rest of them."

He turned to discover that Washington was already behind him, D'Arby at his side, and between them they were struggling to carry Flora. Nipper was dancing in agitation behind them, his eyes wide in alarm. Blood was dripping from the old lady's temple.

"She fell," Washington cried, "but I think she'll be fine." His eyes wandered to the pool of fire that was waiting for them below. "Holy Mother," he groaned, and stumbled on.

"The Russians?" Harry shouted after him.

"The young one's already gone, his door's open," Washington replied. "Shunin's seems to be locked. I couldn't hang around to check . . ."

294

But already Harry was running.

He found the door to the Russian President's room as Washington had reported. Shunin had to be inside, no way would he have locked it behind him on his way out. Harry suspected that he was doused in so much alcohol that only the fires of Hell would ever stir him, and by then it would be far, far too late. He heaved himself at the door, and gave a sharp grunt of pain as he bounced off; like the rest of the castle, the doors were solid and would break almost any shoulder in a straight fight. Smoke was drifting up the stairs, clinging to the ceiling, soon it would thicken and drop, and set about its killing. From below came the sound of glass or something ceramic shattering in the heat.

He tried to force the door with his shoulder once more but he knew it was futile. He cast desperately around him, the glow of the advancing fire growing all too bright, when he caught sight of a pair of antique battleaxes several hundred years old arranged in a display on the wall. He grabbed one, wrenching it from its setting, swinging it for balance before attacking the lock. Two stout swipes and the ancient head came off, flying back across the hallway, but the second axe did better. The door began to shudder, the lock starting to give. Harry forced the blade into the jamb of the door and heaved. It was enough. With a shower of splintering wood, he burst into Shunin's room.

By now Shunin was awake, sitting up in bed, deeply alarmed.

"Get out," Harry shouted. "The place is going up."

Yet Shunin took no heed. He sat staring at Harry from the darkness, his expression lit by the glow of the approaching fire and filled with suspicion. This man trusted no one.

Then understanding dawned. Shunin jumped from his bed, gathering his clothes in his arms, stopping only to push his feet into his shoes. "I wonder, are you here to save me, or to kill me, Mr Jones?"

"I told you, never had a Russian die on me yet, Mr President," Harry replied. It wasn't entirely true, he'd never had a Russian die on him by accident, but this was neither the time nor the place to explore Harry's past. He grabbed the Russian's arm, but even as they started back down, one half of the staircase was already being chewed away by the flames. The tall, upright walls of Castle Lorne were turning into a chimney with the great oak staircase as its fuel.

Harry squeezed past the fire, Shunin one step behind. The flames were grabbing for them, clawing at their clothes, singeing their hair, pummelling at them with fists of heat. And when at last they stumbled, coughing, through the great front door of Castle Lorne, they found the others in varying states of disarray scattered across the forecourt and lawn. Washington was in his tracksuit, pacing back and forth, wringing his hands. Blythe had covered her dressing gown in a jacket that D'Arby had given her. The Prime Minister seemed unreasonably well presented given the circumstances, Harry thought; he'd even found time to put on his socks. Shunin was struggling into the clothes he had managed to salvage, pulling them directly over his pyjamas, while Lavrenti was there, too, in the shadows, keeping himself apart. Blythe was bending over Flora, who was laid out on the grass wrapped in a blanket. Harry kneeled down beside the old lady to see if he could assist, but even as he did so she moaned and began to show signs of recovery.

There was no saving the castle. The front door was gaping wide, like a flue, left open as they had fled, while the gusting wind seemed to seek out the fire and fan it to an ever-greater intensity. Windows were shattering, ceilings collapsing, flames roaring in triumph.

Then, through the sounds of destruction, came a scream of terror. Flora was sitting up, watching her beloved home being consumed by fire, her lips letting forth one agonizing cry that continued until there wasn't an ounce of breath left in her.

The cry was formed of one word.

Nipper.

One moment he'd been with them on the stairs, the next, not. They'd all assumed amidst the confusion of Presidents and Prime Minister that the boy had carried on down, with one of the others, but now they could see him waving and shouting from the window of his room at the very top of the castle. Instantly Harry realised what had happened. Nipper had gone back for his dirk. Now he was alone, trapped.

Some men see life as little more than a journey to their deaths. They string out their time in caution, with every breath and every beat of the heart seen as one more to be struck off an ever-shortening list. Harry Jones wasn't like those men. If life was a race to the death, it was a race in which death was cheated as often as possible so that every day became a victory. It wasn't so much a matter of not knowing fear, as of conquering fear in order to know what it was like simply to be alive. Even Nipper had known that.

They tried to stop him, D'Arby in particular, but Flora's cry spoke louder than all the Prime Minister's spluttering entreaties. Harry grabbed the blanket they had put around Mrs MacDougall, wrapped it around his shoulders and threw himself into the seawater that was chasing waves across the causeway, soaking himself to the skin. Then he covered his head like a shawl, running past the flailing arms of D'Arby straight back into the house.

Harry knew Nipper was still up there, alive, but even now the smoke would be seeping under his bedroom door. It might already be too late. And between Harry and the boy lay a highway of fire, of retching smoke, noxious gases, flaming obstacles, pain. It was a road Harry started on without any rational hope of survival.

The oil had been burning for many minutes and was finding its grip on the things it touched. Furniture. Curtains. Antique silk tapestries that Alan MacDougall had spent a lifetime hunting down. And by the time Harry squeezed through the foul-smelling curtain of flame and smoke that shrouded the entrance, the fire had begun to eat away at the main body of the stairs as well. It didn't surrender easily, but the fuel had seeped into the space beneath and fire was eating the treads from below. The burning point of wood is about two hundred and eighty degrees Celsius, that of skin nearer fifty, and the furnace effect of the wind and fire were already stoking temperatures far beyond these levels. Yet oak is a dense wood, it gives itself up slowly and retains some internal strength even as it burns. Harry hit the stairs praying that they would still be strong enough to carry his passing weight.

He leapt up more by instinct than by sight, the soaking blanket pulled around his eyes to protect them from the heat and filthy smoke, keeping close to the wall where the structure might have more strength, struggling not to panic, but it wasn't easy, the noise and heat jarring at his senses, clouding his mind, cheating his resolve. Even as he started his charge he felt the fourth step collapsing beneath him, but only in the moment that he was past. The fire attacked him more ferociously with every step he took, he could feel it on his feet, his legs, arms, face; the blanket was beginning to smoulder, making it ever more difficult for him to see, the noxious, superheated air attacking his throat, even as every muscle in his body screamed at him to take a deep lungful of air. He knew that if he did it would be his last. From somewhere close at hand came an explosion that sent sparks chasing through the air and clinging to his cheeks like drops of acid snow. The skin on his ankles and calves was beginning to burn. His knuckles felt on fire, searing with pain as he tried to grip the blanket ever more tightly around him for all the meagre protection it gave. His head began to fall, his focus to waver. Even as he turned the stair and started up the second flight, he knew his gamble had failed.

He was forced to take a shallow breath and immediately his lungs began to fill with the caustic, searing smoke; now he was burning from the inside, too. His legs began to buckle, the muscles no longer willing to listen to his commands, paying heed only to their own pain, and Harry began to falter. He was going, falling.

Suddenly Harry felt his arm being grabbed, pulling him on. It was Marcus Washington. "Couldn't have you tripping over again," the American roared above the fire. The man seemed almost to be smirking. And as they stumbled onward, they could see parts of the stair that were not yet afire, where they could tread without their shoes beginning to melt, and by the time they reached the second floor it seemed as though they were through the worst, for the moment, at least. Harry tried to take another breath and screamed inside as his lungs tore themselves apart in the struggle to grab oxygen from the poisoned air. Beside him, Washington slumped against a wall, his tracksuit on fire. Harry smothered it in the blanket, as Washington cried out with the pain.

Harry looked into the eyes of the other man. There was no more sign of smugness, only fear, and Harry knew it was no more than a reflection of his own.

"What the hell you doing here, Mr Washington?" Harry asked, when at last he could.

"Sorry, force of habit," the American spluttered, trying to catch his breath. "Can't trust you Brits to do anything for yourselves nowadays. Thought you might need a little help."

"At least for once you haven't arrived late."

The American nodded, tried to smile, his eyes lifted up the stairs to what lay ahead.

"Got time for that second lap, Mr Washington?" Harry enquired.

"No time like the present, Mr Jones."

So they ran once more. As they reached the third floor they could hear the sound of something substantial falling apart. The back staircase? It had been burning longer. This one would soon follow. But even as they climbed the stairs, believing that for the moment they'd left behind the worst of it, the fire was playing a foul, evil trick. The rear staircase was narrow, enclosed, it acted like a flue, and it had sucked up — convected — the heat to the top of the building, where it built, grew in strength, until it touched a thousand degrees. The very fabric of the building began to burst into flame, from the ceiling down. The tops of curtains, the books piled above the wardrobes, then the wardrobes themselves. Oxygen was sucked from the air, to be replaced by poison. A death trap. And as they climbed higher, they began to lose focus — oh, Christ, carbon monoxide, the silent killer. They weren't heading away from danger but directly into it. Harry fell to his knees, desperately searching for air to breathe, crawling, scrabbling, surrounded by smoke, choking, coughing up his lungs, his face on the floor. It was only Washington dragging him forward once more that enabled him to make the final few yards to

Nipper's door. Harry reached for the handle and gave a gasp of pain; it seemed to sink teeth into his flesh, hot enough to fry eggs. He used the blanket as a fire glove, and burst into the room.

The boy was sitting patiently on his bed, the dirk in its case on his lap, as though waiting to go off to school. "Hello, Harry, Mr Washington. I knew you'd come."

Despite the brave words, Harry could see the fright in Nipper's eyes. The room was already filling with smoke.

"It's all right, Nipper, it's all right," Harry lied, grabbing the boy's face and forcing him to concentrate on his words instead of the fire. "Look at me. Do you have any rope? A fire ladder, perhaps? Anything like that?"

The boy shook his head, his eyes darting back and forth in alarm. From below came the sound of some further collapse, so fundamental that the castle shook.

"You sure, Nipper? Anything?" Harry pleaded.

"Perhaps the roof, Mr Jones," Washington suggested.

"For once, I accept your suggestion," Harry replied. "How, Nipper? How do we get there?"

All three of them were coughing; they didn't have much time. Nipper pointed, indicating a door in the far corner of the room that Harry had assumed to be a cupboard, but the boy tugged at his hand, pulling him forward. The door opened to reveal a short flight of steps leading to a trapdoor. They could smell the fresh air beyond. And a few moments later they could see the sky.

Harry stood still, letting the wind clear his lungs and cool his flesh. He even allowed it to bring back a little hope. As his stinging eyes adjusted to the darkness, he searched around the roof space. It was flat, but lurking in the shadows near the ramparts was a half-obscured object that made his heart leap with excitement as he began to figure out its form. A builder's hoist! One that Alan MacDougall had used to haul all manner of things up — and down — the castle sides.

"Come on, this is the way out!" Harry cried, yet even as he lunged forward, doubts began to smother this new-born hope. As he touched it, flakes of rust scratched at his hands. There was an electrical motor but, as Harry hit every button, no power. There was a manual release for the drum, but even as Harry snatched at it, the damned thing kept jamming.

"What do you suggest we do, Mr Jones?" Washington's question was put softly, not screamed.

"I suggest we should have stayed at home."

"I guess it's Plan B, then."

"Remind me about that one, will you?"

Washington pointed at the hoist. "The old Indian rope trick. We play out the wire by hand."

Even as they began unwinding the wire, they could feel the heat spreading up through the roof.

As carefully as he could in the darkness, Harry fashioned a small noose at the end of the steel rope. "Nipper," he cried, grabbing the boy, "you put your foot in this and hang on. We'll lower you down. You understand?"

Nipper nodded.

"Scared?"

Nipper nodded once more.

"Clever boy. Now don't look down, just hold on tight."

But the boy still had the dirk case under his arm.

"Better give me that for safekeeping, Nipper. Don't want you to drop it."

Nipper looked at Harry cautiously. "You're not English, are you?"

"Jones. It's a Welsh name, Nipper."

"You sure?"

"You can ask anyone."

"OK," Nipper replied reluctantly, handing over the case.

Harry took out the dirk and tucked it in the back of his belt. "I'll give it back to you later. That's a promise."

And as Harry struggled to release the sticking drum, Washington stood on the ramparts, taking the weight of the boy as he lowered him, as smoothly as possible, over the side. Down below the others had seen them and were shouting encouragement. The fabric of the roof was beginning to smoke.

Nipper was still nearly thirty feet from the ground when the drum seized, and no amount of kicking or cursing could persuade it to change its mind.

"You're going to have to jump, Nipper," Harry bellowed above the noise of the fire, looking down over the ramparts.

"I don't want to, Harry," a small voice floated back up.

"You can do it. Like the Lady of Lorne, remember? There's magic in this place — MacDougall magic. You don't have anything to worry about."

Nipper peered down, then looked back up to Harry once more. "You still got her dirk?"

"Safe and sound, Nipper. I'm right behind you!" If only . . .

And Nipper jumped. D'Arby was there, arms outstretched to break the fall, and they both tumbled to the ground. Through the darkness and swirling smoke, Harry thought he could see both of them clambering to their feet.

"You're next," he said, turning to the American. Suddenly, he saw Washington's hands. They were covered in blood, his palms shredded. The steel wire had torn them to pieces, yet he had made no sound of complaint. He stepped gingerly over to the hoist and began attacking it yet again, trying to release the drum. The stench of scorching roof felt was foul. As the American stood over the machine, Harry could see the surface of the roof was melting.

Then the entire frame of the hoist shuddered, slipped sideways a fraction, started to tilt. Washington turned to Harry, who was still clinging to the ramparts. Both of them knew what was about to happen, the horror of it written in the American's eyes. Harry reached out towards Washington, who stretched out his own bloodied hand, but not far enough.

The American didn't cry out, perhaps there was no time, even though what happened next seemed to occupy half of eternity and would be remembered by

Harry for the rest of his life. The hoist shook once more. Then a mouth of flame, filled with jagged teeth, opened up beneath it, and swallowed it whole, taking Marcus Washington down with it.

Harry had no time to dwell on what had happened. As the hoist disappeared, it dragged its steel pipe with it. The wire whipped past Harry's head, snaking out with an evil ripping sound, snatching at him. He looked at the flaming gap, which was pouring cinders into the sky, knowing the rest of the roof couldn't be long in following.

The heat was rising with every heartbeat. Harry put a tentative foot on what seemed like solid roof, but it stuck to his shoe. From far below came cries of alarm. There was no way back down.

As quickly as he could, but with great care, he clambered along the ramparts in search of some unnoticed ladder or fixture, but there was nothing, only a precipitous drop that he knew would kill him. His skin was burning from the heat, he could smell his hair singeing, and instinctively he made his way round to the seaward side of the castle, where the salt wind coming off the water was cooler. Even above the thunder of the fire, Harry could hear the tide as it beat against the footings of the castle. Somewhere below him, three floors, was a library whose books were already burning. The history of the MacDougalls was being lost forever. His mind fixed on the view from the window, of the unforgiving rocks lashed by spray that reached sometimes as high as the windows themselves.

Desperately he tried to recall those ribbons of rocks surrounded by wave and tide, and where one finished and the others began, but no matter how hard he tried to imagine it differently he knew he could never jump far enough to reach the safety of the sea. Only seagulls could survive down there.

He stood on the ramparts, facing out to the ocean, into the wind. Beneath him the castle was groaning. His mind wandered to that arrogant, eccentric, extraordinarily brave man, Marcus Washington, who had just died at his side. How Harry had misjudged him. But Washington had been fortunate, too, his suffering was over. He hadn't been left to roast slowly on the ramparts. An old bullet wound in Harry's back was screaming in insult, it felt as if it were melting, and the rest of his body wasn't far behind. He took a deep breath, tasted the salt, the wind, the ocean, trying to cling to this last moment. He didn't want to die, yet the only thing left to him was to decide the manner of his death. He would jump, of course, anything but the fire. But was it better to go feet first, or some other way? That and a hundred other questions hurtled though his mind but they encountered not a single answer.

And suddenly, sitting on the ramparts nearby, through the swirling smoke he thought he saw Michael Burnside. He was laughing.

Harry was still arguing with himself, standing on the ramparts, when the roof behind him collapsed. The eruption of flame and heat that was thrown up smashed into him harder than anything had ever hit him in his life, and all further decisions were ripped from his hands. He was picked up and sent hurtling through the darkness as, behind him, Castle Lorne finally died.

CHAPTER
TWENTY

Sunday, 1.17 a.m. British Summer Time;
8.17 a.m. Beijing.

Sir Wesley Lake was shaken awake. He forced his eyes open to discover two guards standing over him. God, not another beating, he moaned. He had little idea of the passage of time — they'd given him drugs as well as roughing him up — and he had even less idea of what he might have told them. Anything they wanted, perhaps. Or nothing. He didn't know, but if he had told them anything, they wouldn't still be interrogating him, would they?

Yet, as his senses came into focus, he was surprised to discover that his guards had changed. They were no longer screaming at him but simply telling him to follow them. Breakfast had been set in the room outside, but they allowed him little opportunity to eat it. "You come!" they instructed. And soon he found himself squeezed between two other stiff-faced guards in the back of a car, the horn blaring, speeding through the streets of Beijing. It didn't stop until it was inside the compound of the Ministry of Foreign Affairs.

As he climbed stiffly up the steps, refusing an offer of help from his escort, he couldn't help noticing the size of the military guard, not just at the entrance but inside, too. That wasn't normal, but what was normal any more? His world had lost its shape; this wasn't the China he recognised. He was still trying to find his way through the thicket of his thoughts when, waiting for him in one of the Ministry reception rooms with its huge stuffed armchairs and elaborate Chinese decorations, he was astonished to discover Sammi Shah. The BBC man was looking scarcely better than the ambassador felt.

"Hell!" Lake exclaimed, catching sight of the other man's bruises and cuts. "What happened to you?"

"Guess I got too nosy. You?"

"Must have forgotten to pay a parking ticket. You know how upset the Chinese get about traffic congestion." He couldn't tell him the truth; he didn't know what the truth was. He fell into one of the armchairs. Sammi followed.

"You notice how these armchairs are placed with their backs right up against the wall," the BBC man remarked.

"Your point?"

"I feel like I'm about to face a firing squad."

"You're a cheerful sod this morning."

Yet Sammi wasn't smiling, and when he opened his mouth to talk, Lake noticed he had two teeth missing.

They were interrupted as the richly carved doors to the reception room opened. They were astonished to see the diminutive figure of the Foreign Minister walking towards them, his face set grim. The two Britons didn't bother to struggle to their feet.

"If he offers you a cigarette," Sammi whispered, "remember to duck."

Sunday, 1.32a.m. Castle Lorne.

It was the force of the explosion that saved him. It hurled Harry further away from the walls than he could ever have jumped, far enough to reach one of those coruscating ribbons of sea that had cut their way into the rock, just deep enough at high tide to break his fall. He did it feet first in the end.

He was held under by the current, but it did him a favour, dragging him out to sea and away from the surf that was trying to smash him onto the rocks. He drifted with the sea for a short while, letting the water revive him, before kicking out towards the shore and the gently sloping beach a little along the bay. He had to ride the tide; Harry had reached the point of physical exhaustion that brought a man close to collapse. But he was in no hurry, not any more.

As he dragged himself from the water, Harry looked back towards the castle. It appeared like a candle. The walls still stood strong, for the moment, but every window and aperture glowed in the night, and the roof had been replaced by an outpouring of flame. Everything that Castle Lorne was, and represented, was gone, along with a very brave American. Harry began to stumble his way back, and as he did so, his exhaustion was replaced by overwhelming anger. None of what had happened should have been, and with every step his rage grew. In the end, it was what drove him on, keeping him going, even after his legs began screaming for him to stop.

Outside the castle, the group had recast itself at the edge of the circle of light thrown out by the fire, on the far side of the causeway. For the moment Blythe Edwards had ceased to be President of the United States and was comforting Flora, who sobbed quietly in a confusion of misery and relief as she sat before the ruins of her home, her arms clasped firmly around her grandson as though determined never again to let him go. D'Arby paced up and down in agitation, while Shunin sat on a rock, crossing himself as he gazed silently into the fire, marvelling at its ferocity. Lavrenti was nowhere to be seen. He had disappeared into the night. Lost in their own troubles, no one missed him.

D'Arby was the first to see the figure of Harry stumbling towards them along the beach. He cried out. "Look — they're alive!" Yet as he ran towards Harry, he slowed as he saw there was only one. "Where's Washington?" he asked. Harry pushed him savagely away.

He collapsed onto a group of rocks, his legs numb with fatigue. As D'Arby hovered in uncertainty, Blythe came to his side.

"You OK?"

"Been better."

"Marcus?"

As he looked up Blythe saw that Harry's face was a battlefield. The eyelids were raw, scoured by salt and smoke, he had a cut on his scalp, his forehead was an artist's palette of matted hair, blood and wounds. And if his face were a mess, so too were his emotions.

"Marcus didn't make it. But he's the reason Nipper and I did."

She hid her face, her shoulders slumped in sorrow.

"A terrible, tragic accident," D'Arby offered.

In an instant of anger Harry's face was only inches away from the Prime Minister's, his mood wild, his lips drawn back as he panted with passion. "This was no accident!"

D'Arby stepped back, startled. Harry pursued him. "The castle's gone. Washington with it. The boy nearly died, too!"

"Harry, I'm devastated, but you can't blame me."

"Then who else? I promise you I'm going to nail this on someone, and you're right at the top of my list."

"But this is ridiculous. You're clearly in shock, you need time," the Prime Minister said, anxious to console, turning away from the accusation and kneeling down next to where Nipper and Flora were sitting, trying to deflect the conversation. Yet not everyone was as keen to put the matter to one side. Shunin had wandered over. "What are you implying, Mr Jones?" he asked.

"I'm implying — *stating* — that there's a maggot in our midst. The fire wasn't started by accident and certainly not by the incendiary division of the People's Liberation Army, but by someone here on the inside."

"Who? Why?"

For a moment, Harry didn't answer. He stared at all those around him, testing, accusing. Then he laughed, a dry, unhappy sound. "You know, Mark, for a while there I thought it might have been you."

"I set the fire?" the Prime Minister gasped in alarm, jumping to his feet. "You're quite mad! What the hell made you think that?"

"You set everything else up. You're the only reason any of us is here. And you appear out of the fire immaculately dressed, with everything in place. You even found time to lace up your shoes. It was almost as if you were prepared, waiting for it."

"I'll excuse your ramblings only because you've clearly hit your head," D'Arby responded tetchily. "For God's sake, I couldn't sleep. I heard the commotion. I didn't hang around."

"I can see that now."

"How?"

"Your socks, Mark."

"My bloody socks?"

"You flashed them when you knelt down. They're different colours."

D'Arby hoisted his trousers above his ankles. One black. One grey.

"Guess you dressed in a hurry," Harry said.

"I'll take that as your apology," D'Arby muttered resentfully. "Anyway, as I remember matters, *you* were the first one to discover the fire. I seem to recall you running *up* the stairs. You were the one with the opportunity, perhaps the motivation, too. You obviously have no liking for what we came here to do. You've been getting in our way ever since we arrived, always questioning, casting doubts. Motive enough."

314

Shunin was nodding; even Blythe was looking on quizzically.

"So, since you're kicking allegations about others around so freely, Harry, care to share your alibi with us?" D'Arby demanded.

"I wasn't making allegations, Mark, simply offering ideas."

"Enough with ideas. Let's talk location. Where were you when the fire started?"

"Yes, come on, Mr Jones, what's your alibi?" Shunin joined in, keen to show that hostility and suspicion weren't solely a British preserve. They were all on edge, rattled by their narrow escape.

Harry defied them with his eyes, but he offered no explanation.

"Seems you're better at asking questions than answering them, Mr Jones," Shunin observed.

"I'm his alibi," a voice whispered from the darkness. It was Blythe. "Harry was with me. In my room."

The admission covered them like a bucket of cold water. It took a moment to shake themselves and recover.

"Discussing tactics, I suppose," Shunin said. "So, it seems we have an interesting situation. If it wasn't the Prime Minister, and since both you and the President appear to have an *alibi*" — the word dripped with insinuation — "what are you suggesting, Mr Jones? That it was Mr Washington?"

It was an insidious suggestion that wormed its way into them all. Marcus Washington was a man driven in life by so many insecurities — could he have been driven to his death by guilt? It was an easy suggestion to accept, but Harry would have none of it.

"It wasn't Marcus Washington who ransacked my room, Mr Shunin."

"Your room?"

"You went through everything — drawers, cupboard, luggage, even my wash bag. Would you like to tell us why?"

"No," he replied, softly, his face inscrutable.

"And last night you went for a midnight stroll. Several miles of it, halfway towards Sullapool. You had a rendezvous, met with someone. I'd dearly like to find an innocent explanation for that, but I can't. Can you help us, Mr President?"

The Russian's face stiffened. "You are an inquisitive fool, Mr Jones."

"As you are brutal, Mr Shunin. You came here, accepted Mrs MacDougall's hospitality, then violated it. You beat your own son-in-law senseless. The reason he disappeared isn't because he had an accident but because his face has been mashed to a pulp."

"Is that true, Sergei?" Blythe breathed. "Did you?"

"Are you trying to suggest I locked myself in my own room? This is ridiculous!" The impassive mask cracked and fell away. "I am the President of Russia," he flared, the blood rushing to his cheeks. "I need give no explanations."

"Marcus Washington died," Blythe persisted, "and I'd like to know why."

"You accuse me?"

"No. I simply enquire."

"I don't think you're in much of a position to discuss anything apart from your tactics with Mr Jones," the Russian threw back. "The two of you have the dirtiest hands here."

"You bastard," Blythe spat.

"And what do your nocturnal negotiations make you, Madam President?" he retaliated. "Forgive me, my English isn't so good. What is the word . . .?"

He was reaching for it, about to produce it, when Harry hit him. On the jaw. A straight right. His fist seemed to connect with a sharp, cracking sound, almost like a gunshot, and he felt a stab of pain in his arm. Shunin fell backwards, and Harry fell on top of him. As he did so, he saw that they were both covered in blood.

Someone had shot the President of Russia.

Sunday, 1.40a.m. British Summer Time; 8.40a.m. in the Room of Many Miracles, Shanjing.

Sleeplessness was clogging Fu Zhang's mind. He had long since ceased to have any understanding of the details on the screen, relying entirely on the director to guide him, literally by the hand, until he was told to make the final keystroke. Fu Zhang was making miracles, the glory was his, and it had been enough to get him through the long hours of the night. He had been denied his tea; not even a Minister was permitted to bring drinks into this electronic paradise, yet still his bladder had flooded, with excitement, and he was now wriggling with discomfort. "What are we doing?" he

317

enquired, moving closer as once more the screens shifted their focus and moved on.

As he felt the warmth of the Minister's body, it was Li Changchun's turn to shift uncomfortably in his chair. "Water," he replied. "London will have too much of it, once the flood barriers fail, but Birmingham, the country's second-largest city, will have too little."

"Tell me more," Fu demanded, his lips wriggling in anticipation.

"They add all sorts of chemicals to their water. Chlorine. Fluoride. Many others. Tiny amounts. But we are about to add a whole lot more."

"We will poison them?"

"No, not directly, not unless they drink as much as a horse. The harm will be largely psychological. They will quickly discover the problem, and it will be easily remedied, but there will be a panic. First at the water works and reservoirs, then amongst the British media, and finally amongst the public. Britain's drinking habits will change overnight, dramatically. The editors of the press will encourage the British to think that every cupful of water their children take will shrivel their testicles or grow them an extra head. No one will feel safe."

Fu chuckled as Li continued working away on his keyboard.

"Very shortly, they will be afraid even to turn on their taps," the director said. "No one will die, Minister, but they will come to live in fear."

"A nation at war with itself."

"Our ancestors will applaud you, Minister."

318

"After which I must sleep," he said wearily. "And I shall wake to find a different world is waiting for us, Li Changchun!"

His celebrations were interrupted by new arrivals. A senior PLA officer was at the entrance, accompanied by two armed troopers. When the officer saw Fu Zhang, he marched towards him, the guard in close attendance. He stopped before the Minister and saluted sharply.

"Vice-Minister Fu! General Wang Qishan has asked me to present his compliments, and request that you join him in the outer office," he barked.

"General Wang himself is here?" Fu exclaimed in delight. The general was a most senior army official. And he'd thought it was simply a truckload of callow, disrespectful yobs. "Please thank the General and tell him I shall be with him very shortly. There is something here I must attend to first." He waved at the screen.

But it wasn't simply the patterns on the screen he didn't understand. Instead of retreating in respect, the officer continued to stand in front of him, insistent. Rather insolent, really. And as Fu Zhang's lips danced in bewilderment, he found himself staring down the barrel of the officer's gun.

CHAPTER
TWENTY-ONE

Sunday, 1.43a.m. Castle Lorne.

They had both been shot. The bullet had passed through Harry's upper arm, somehow missing bone and artery, before nicking Shunin's chest, leaving him with a deep flesh wound but nothing that would prove of long-term consequence. Harry's punch had probably saved Shunin's life.

After the angry sound of the bullet had passed into the night, a silence fell, punctuated only by the cries from the dying castle. Harry and the Russian had both slumped to the ground behind the rocks, grateful for the cover. It was at this point that D'Arby decided it was time to make his presence felt once more. He scampered across to the wounded men with the intention of taking control of the situation. Just in time, Harry kicked his legs from beneath him. He was sent sprawling as two more bullets scythed through the air.

"You stand out like a target at a fairground against the flames," Harry panted, still biting back the pain. Someone seemed to have stabbed a serrated kitchen knife into his arm and was twisting it.

"Thank you," D'Arby whispered, lifting a mournful face from the shingle, his eyes bulging with fright.

"Make yourself useful," Harry instructed, scrabbling with his good hand in his pocket and producing a large handkerchief. "Keep that pressed hard over the President's wound. It'll stop the bleeding."

"I, too, seem to owe you my thanks, Mr Jones," Shunin muttered through lips that struggled to hide the pain.

"You owe me an explanation," Harry snapped back.

The Russian President closed his eyes, his defiance seeming to melt into resignation. He whispered only one word. "Lavrenti."

As though on cue, another bullet ricocheted off the rock above their heads.

"Enough, Lavrenti!" Harry cried out. "He's dead."

Eventually a voice answered from the darkness. "How can I believe you?"

"You saw him go down."

"I'm coming to make sure."

"Do that and you'll be the next to get shot," Harry shouted fiercely.

"You're not armed."

"Then you just go ahead and prove me wrong, Lavrenti. I haven't shot a Russian since Afghanistan," he continued, lying, "but I think I can remember how it goes."

Konev fell silent.

Beside Harry, Shunin twisted his lips in a sardonic smile. "I believe that's what they call information warfare, Mr Jones," he whispered.

"I was married once. Became something of an expert."

"What do you reckon? He believed you?" D'Arby demanded.

"Bet your life on it," Harry replied grimly, ripping the sleeve from his shirt and attempting to twist it into a tourniquet for his arm. As he struggled with the makeshift bandage, he slumped back against the rock, his stomach wanting to heave. His body was trying to protect itself, numb his senses rather than feel the pain, but he had to fight it; men died when their wits grew dull. When the wound was bound he turned to Shunin. "So, we appear to have got ourselves wrapped up in a little family business — *your* family business, Mr President. I think you owe us an explanation."

Shunin bit his lip, in reluctance as well as pain. He didn't want to share, but he knew he owed Harry. "Someone inside the Kremlin has been betraying me. Dripping information about my travel plans, where I will be, and when. Making me a target. The car bomb was waiting for me as I drove to the airport, even though I had only made those plans the day before. It had to be someone close. Very close."

"Lavrenti."

"I didn't want to believe it. Anybody else but him. He is my son-in-law, Katya's husband. I had even allowed myself to dream he might be the future of Russia." He groaned as D'Arby changed his dressing, pressing a fresh handkerchief onto the wound. "So I brought him with me, here. To test him. To look for any sign."

"You used us to sort out your own private squabble," Harry snapped.

"You want to hear my story or deliver a sermon?" Shunin's eyes glared defiantly through the haze of pain, but he was wheezing once again, his asthma back and his medication lost in the castle. "You said you saw me disappear last night and followed me. But you were following Lavrenti. I saw you both. Why, you really think I am up to hiking for miles through the hills at night?" He spluttered, and not for effect.

So there had been two of them out there in the dark, Harry realized. It was Lavrenti with the cigarette, leaving Shunin with the midge bites. "He had made an arrangement to meet someone," Harry mused. "Must have been when we went to Sullapool. He disappeared for a while, down to the harbour."

"But why?" D'Arby asked.

"At a guess, to find something incendiary, something with which to start the fire," Harry replied. "This wasn't a spur of the moment thing, after all, not if he had already tried with a car bomb. He told me himself how much he hated you, Mr Shunin."

"He said much the same thing to me. That's why we had our . . . disagreement."

"He said you would end up killing us all."

"I promise, I shall kill only him."

"So why *did* you search my room?" Harry asked.

"Someone had stolen my gun. I thought it might be you. I think we know now who it was."

"You brought a gun?" D'Arby protested. "For God's sake, why?"

"For my security!" Shunin snapped defiantly. "Quite clearly the security you offered has left a lot to be desired."

"And as a result you nearly ended up killing us all!"

Their faces were raw in the lurid light from the fire, yet as they confronted each other another voice cried out from the darkness. It was Lavrenti. "I want — I want political asylum."

Harry saw the alarm rise in Shunin's eyes; if they let him back in from the night and he found Shunin still alive, anything could happen.

"Should have thought about that before you killed your father-in-law," Harry shouted in return.

"I had no choice."

"And neither do I, Lavrenti."

"I want to do a deal."

"Get real, Lavrenti. You only get one type of deal for killing the President of Russia."

"But we are in Britain."

"OK. So I tell you how it works here. We give you two choices. You throw us your gun, then we talk."

"And if I refuse, Mr Jones?"

"It's simple. I see you, I shoot you."

They waited for his response, but none came.

"You're good at your mind games, Mr Jones," Shunin said softly. "A remarkable man, I think. You have saved my life twice already tonight, and still you fight for it."

"There's a prime minister and another president to think of, too, Mr Shunin, not to mention a rather fine Scottish lady and a very special young man."

324

They were interrupted as a huge section of masonry fell from the upper floor of the castle, crashing onto the rocks below with a mighty explosion that sent cinders like wasps of fire sparking high into the sky. From where she was tending Nipper with the help of Blythe, Flora turned and held her hand to her lips, muffling a whimper of despair.

"You think he's still out there?" D'Arby asked, his voice tight with concern.

"No bloody idea. Let's try." And Harry shouted once more for Lavrenti, but all he got back was an empty echo.

"Thank God, he's gone," the Prime Minister exclaimed.

"But where would he go?" Shunin asked.

"Only one place to go," Harry answered. "Sullapool."

No one talked as they all conjured up an image of sleepy, innocent, unaware Sullapool being hit by a desperate Russian with a gun in his hand.

"Oh, bugger," Harry swore, "I suppose I'd better go after him."

"Harry, leave it to others," D'Arby instructed.

"You forget, Mark, this is one of the most isolated parts of the kingdom. There are no others." He took a deep breath. "Anyway, I think I owe this one to Marcus Washington."

"What will you do?" D'Arby asked, his voice full of anxiety.

"Play the Chinaman. Try and find some way of beating the bastard without him firing first. It's a useful technique when you're armed with nothing more than fresh air. What's he got anyway, do you know?" he asked Shunin.

"My Makarov PM."

Nothing too insignificant, then. Harry flexed his arm; it worked, after a fashion, so long as he was willing to ignore the herd of buffalo that trampled across it every time he moved.

Shunin was sitting beside him, his back propped up against the same rock. "I'd like to join your posse, Mr Jones."

"Can't let you do that, Mr President. It could get a little hairy out there."

"But I can help. I have some experience in these matters."

Yes, I bet you do, breathed Harry.

"And, as you say, I am a president, you cannot stop me," the Russian continued. "Anyway, it's my gun, my family, my problem."

Harry looked at him with curiosity. "You pulling rank?"

"If that's what it takes." The Russian turned. "What about you, Prime Minister?"

D'Arby hesitated, but only for a fraction. "I'd better stay here, look after the others — just in case he comes back." It was, of course, the right thing to do, someone had to stay behind, yet Shunin didn't bother to hide the contemptuous curl of his lip.

Harry tugged at his bandage to make sure it would stay in place. "Better get on with it. You ready, Mr Shunin?"

"As ready as I'll ever be."

So they left the protection of the rocks, skirting low, scuttling like crabs in case Lavrenti was still close at hand, until they had some confidence they would no longer be framed against the fire, and then they set out on the road, not side by side but separated, so as not to make too convenient a target. The wind was still blustering and the clouds sailing like ships across the sky. The moon was pale, hiding them, but hiding their quarry, too. Harry's arm complained with every footfall, and he discovered he had a limp — he wasn't too sure whether he'd burnt his leg or bloodied it in the fall — but what bothered him most was the midges. As soon as the two men left the cover of the fire and its protective smoke, the midges descended on them like Visigoths and proceeded to attack every morsel of exposed flesh. Ridiculous. A bullet through his arm and a bloodied leg, yet he was worrying about insect bites. Somehow, Jones, he told himself, your life seems to have lost its perspective.

They made slow progress, Harry dragging his leg, Shunin wheezing hard, until they saw it, up ahead, a brief, wavering light that flickered in the heavy summer darkness. It was a cigarette being lit. Lavrenti's cigarette. Difficult to tell just how far away it was, but no more than a couple of hundred yards. Harry drew alongside Shunin and silently indicated the light. The Russian nodded. It seemed as if the game had taken a turn in their favour.

They pursued him, drawn on by the dancing ember of light and the other cigarettes that followed in continuous order. Harry found it exceptionally hard going, battling not just with the hill but also his exhaustion, yet Lavrenti seemed to be making even poorer progress; they kept him in sight and gradually gained on him as they climbed up the coast road.

It was yet another cigarette that undid them. As Lavrenti paused to light it, he must have glanced back along the road to the castle, which was still burning madly, and seen against its backcloth the silhouettes of the two men as they followed. A shot rang out, wildly, in panic, which hit nothing but the night, yet now he was alerted and all but invisible once he had thrown away his cigarette. In the pale reflection of the moon they saw him dash from the road towards the cover of the gorse that hugged the cliff top. Then he was gone.

Harry and Shunin huddled by the side of the road. "You sure you're up to this?" Harry demanded.

The Russian was wheezing even harder. He didn't speak, merely nodded.

"Look, the gun he's got, the Makarov, it's probably not accurate over more than forty yards, and then only when it's handled correctly. After a hundred yards the bullet's dead and wouldn't do much more than bruise you even if it hit you. I'm betting that Lavrenti's an amateur."

Shunin nodded in agreement.

"He could miss a brick wall at five yards if he's flustered, so we need to distract him. I'm going to try to get up behind him —" Harry indicated with his left arm towards the cliff top — "while you carry on up the road until you're beyond him. All I want you to do then is to make some kind of noise to grab his attention.

He'll be confused, distracted. That will give me my chance."

"For what?"

"For . . . whatever. Hell, I don't know, I'm making this up as I go along."

The cliff tops were formed of a mixture of rock, gorse, heather, and coarse rabbit-cropped grass. It was too dark for Harry to be sure of his footing; he stayed low, moved slowly, trying to avoid the proliferation of holes, gnarled roots, and other pitfalls that lay in wait for the unwary. He kept stopping, listening, his senses alert. As the adrenalin pumped once more through his body, he found he barely noticed the bullet wound or the battered leg, and he had completely forgotten to fret about the flying midges. He estimated that Lavrenti was no more than a hundred yards ahead and since he could detect no sign or sound of movement, Harry reckoned the other man was staying still, waiting. It was several minutes later when, from some distance up ahead, came the sound of what appeared to be a cry, as if someone had fallen. It was soon followed by the noise of a man hobbling along the road, heading away in the direction of Sullapool. Shunin had done his work well. And, as if to confirm the fact, set against the thin milk sky Harry saw the outline of Lavrenti rising to his feet. He was barely twenty yards away. Close enough to use the Makarov, but too far to be taken by surprise. Bugger. *Bugger!*

The sound of Shunin's footsteps had disappeared. Harry was left with only the incomplete cover of darkness. That might not be enough. His heart began to pound, it brought the fire back into his arm, his breathing grew like the sound of trumpets, it must surely give him away. It had become a dance of shadows and silhouettes as Harry made the few extra yards he needed, keeping low, melting into the cliff top. Every footfall seemed to bring cries of complaint from the heather, every rustle of his clothing was like the flapping of a great sail, yet somehow it was all lost amidst the noises of the night and carried away on the stormy breeze from the sea. The Russian appeared lost in thought, or indecision, turning towards the direction of Sullapool, the gun still in his hand, while Harry crouched, and crept, on all fours, balanced, like a sprinter in his blocks, waiting for the moment when distance and adrenalin and plain fortune came together to decide.

It was while the gods were making up their minds that a rabbit got in their way. As Harry placed one final, cautious foot forward, it proved one step too many for the rabbit, who had been skulking in the heather and sulking at all this human intrusion on his patch. With a scurry of alarm he set off, causing Lavrenti to turn, just as the moon squeezed itself between the clouds, leaving Harry looking straight down the barrel of the Makarov. Lavrenti, in alarm, took three or four paces back, too far for Harry to throw himself on him, but still close enough to give the Russian a considerably better than fifty-fifty chance of placing a bullet somewhere between Harry's temples and testicles, no matter how bad a shot he was. Neither alternative gave Harry much comfort.

330

Lavrenti was excited, alert, and to Harry's eyes his gun hand appeared disappointingly steady.

"Ah, Mr Jones, is that you?"

"Hello, Lavrenti, how are you?"

"I am well, thank you, but you, I'm afraid, are — what is that word of yours?"

"Screwed."

"That is it, Mr Jones. You are screwed."

"You don't need to take it out on me, Lavrenti."

"But I see you lied to me. You're not armed. And you pursue me. You are not my friend, I think."

"I tend to take exception when people shoot at me."

"Anyone who stands too near my father-in-law finds themselves in danger."

Lavrenti waved the pistol theatrically — he was holding it in only one hand. Yes, an amateur, Harry concluded. He must have got lucky when he hit Shunin.

"What happened between you and your father-in-law?" Harry asked. Keep talking, Harry, keep him talking, and pray that something might turn up. Otherwise . . .

Yet Lavrenti seemed eager — desperate, even — to talk about his father-in-law, and to describe the horrors of the man in a manner that by comparison made Josef Stalin seem little more than the author of nursery rhymes.

"I had to, Mr Jones. I had no other choice! The beating he gave me — do you know why? Because I had committed a great crime. I told him I disagreed with him. I opposed him. And he said *I had become a*

331

problem. Do you have any idea what that means in Russia? Do you?" Lavrenti demanded, his passion growing.

"Tell me."

"He boasts he is a problem-solver. Bring him a problem, and he will eliminate it — that's what he said at the last election, just after he'd had two of his opponents arrested and charged with corruption. Back in Russia, he promised, I would no longer be his son-in-law, I would never see Katya again. He could do that, you know. And, after a little while, I would disappear, another of his problems solved. I would be a dead man, along with all the others." He was waving his free arm, punctuating his words with violent gestures, but the gun hand remained all too steady. And Harry, still crouching, could feel his legs going numb.

"You could have applied for asylum — before you shot him."

"You think your Mr D'Arby would have listened?" Lavrenti spat. "I think he would have suddenly found himself suffering from a case of diplomatic deafness. Anyhow, what would have been the point? With Papasha still alive, I'd be simply one more Russian exile found dead on the streets of London in strange circumstances." His chest was rising and falling, his breath consumed by his outburst. "And why should I run? Why should I live in the shadows because of one overblown tyrant — a man who is like a plague of rats, who destroys everything in his path? Why, even his own daughter hates him."

Harry was wondering how long he could keep this man going, and how long he might stay alive, when out of the darkness another voice interrupted.

"Don't you dare talk about Katya. I'll wring your neck with my own hands, you ungrateful shit!"

Lavrenti span round, the gun barking in the darkness, and Harry threw himself at him but his muscles were heavy, his legs senseless, it turned into more of a despairing stumble than a life-saving leap and Lavrenti had time to turn yet again. Another bullet passed just inches from Harry's head with a sound as though the air was unzipping, and the pistol smashed into his wounded arm. The pain was overwhelming; he slumped into the heather and lay groaning, defenceless. Lavrenti was back in charge.

Harry fought for focus, swimming against the grey tide of pain that for a few seconds obliterated everything else. When at last he had recovered his senses and was able to take in the scene, he found Lavrenti pointing the gun at the lumbering figure of his father-in-law.

"I'd hoped you were already dead," Lavrenti exclaimed, "but now you're a fool to give me a second chance, Papasha."

"If you say so, Lavrenti. Scum." Shunin spat.

"But this way it is better, more personal." There was no mistaking the genuine hate that welled between them. "What does it feel like to be staring down the barrel of your own gun?"

"In the name of God, are you going to shoot me or bore me to death?" Shunin sounded disinterested, certainly not a man on the edge of fear. A professional, Harry remembered.

"Before you die, Papasha, there's something I want you to know."

"If I must."

Lavrenti gave a small, tight laugh. "It is something I forgot to tell you when I married your daughter. I am a Chechen, Papasha." The words slipped out so softly, yet struck the Russian President full force in the face. His body stiffened, like a dog scenting a bear.

"What is this nonsense? You are Russian, a Konev."

"Only on my father's side. Not through my mother."

"No! I won't hear of this," the older man stormed, clenching his fists.

"Nevertheless . . ."

"You — the son of a Chechen bitch? You deceived us, right from the start."

"No," Lavrenti shook his head, "not everyone. Only you."

Shunin seemed to take several moments to collect his wits. "What are you trying to say?"

"Katya knows. Has always known. She chose me over you. And our child will be a Chechen, too. Oh, but that's right, we haven't told you yet. She is pregnant. You're going to become a grandfather, Papasha. I congratulate you."

And as Lavrenti mocked, an animalistic growl of fury escaped from Shunin. For the first time he seemed to lose his self-control. He took a heavy step forward. Lavrenti sprang back. Then Shunin was hit by a bout of

334

coughing. For a moment he doubled up, spluttering, then slowly fell to his knees.

All the while, as the Makarov waved back and forth, Harry had been calculating the odds. Six rounds gone, and a Makarov usually held eight. But sometimes ten. Either way, enough. A bullet for both of them. And it seemed as if Lavrenti had picked up on these thoughts, for he took three steps backwards, away from any danger. He glanced behind him, making sure of his bearings; the cliff face was close by. Moonlight sparkled off the sea and the rumble of the surf welled up from below. Back along the road Castle Lorne still burned, but not as vehemently. The fire had done its job and it, too, was dying.

And suddenly the gun was pointing only at Harry.

"I am sorry, Mr Jones. I rather liked you. But you have played too many tricks," Lavrenti said. He was calmer now, and had two hands on the gun, not so much the amateur. There was little point in further discussion. Harry was going to die. He could hear the sighing of the breaking sea, the song of the wind and the bicker of complaint from the gulls clinging to the rock face below. In Harry's mind they seemed exquisitely beautiful sounds.

"Would you allow me to get up?" Harry asked. "It's a thing with me, I always wanted to die on my feet, not on my back, or on my knees." That wasn't entirely true. He'd have been happy to die in almost any position with Gabbi but now he wasn't going to get the chance. So many things he would miss.

Yet even as Harry prepared to lever himself onto his feet, he saw Lavrenti's finger squeezing the trigger. Every sound seemed magnified, every moment slowed. The barrel of the pistol looked like a cannon pointing between his eyes, wavering just a little, but not enough, not for Harry. The finger was still tightening. He saw the final movement, the last small jerk of the pistol, and the hammer falling on his life.

CHAPTER
TWENTY-TWO

Sunday, 2.36a.m. British Summer Time; 9.36a.m. China Time, Saturday. Shanjing.

Fu Zhang's mind was awash with bewilderment. He couldn't comprehend how such confusion could have taken place. A Minister frogmarched out of the Room of Many Miracles, brutal hands pinning his arms, the cold stare of the general who seemed to have little idea who Fu Zhang was. "I shall make sure that Mao Yanming hears of this. You insult him by interfering with me," Fu had shouted, but the general hadn't said a word. He had simply nodded to the officer and the guards, who had continued to hustle Fu out of the building and into the car park. Fu's official car was nowhere to be seen, its place taken by military trucks that had disgorged their cargo of hard-eyed troopers. He thought he saw amongst them those who had jeered at him earlier, and he turned to the officer to let him know that when this mistake was sorted out he, Fu Zhang, would make sure that both the officer and his men would be charged with high crimes and insulting the state. The officer responded by tripping Fu Zhang from behind, sending him sprawling to his knees.

When he had recovered from the shock and raised his head, Fu found himself surrounded by a ring of soldiers. Now he was certain they were the same troops he had met on the road, but they were no longer jeering. Instead their faces were stiff, filled with an air of earnestness, and expectation. Then he felt something cold, evil, touch the nape of his neck. The officer's pistol.

What? Now, for the first time, he began to be afraid. He thought his bladder had burst; he could feel the warmth of his own fear spreading down his legs. He screamed at them, to tell them they had made a mistake, he was engaged in an historic attack on the enemies of their country that would bring them all glory, and he personally had launched the attack. But the officer said he knew. And that was why they were going to execute him.

Fu Zhang thought they must be trying to humiliate him, as he himself had done to others during the madness of the Cultural Revolution, reducing them to blubbering, incontinent fools. But then he heard the safety on the pistol being released. They were going to shoot him? Like a common criminal — on his knees, in a car park? He couldn't comprehend the disgrace.

Fu Zhang was still struggling to understand what was happening, and why, when his world turned as white and glistening as the snow on a Himalayan peak, which faded into the biting, blinding crystals of an ice storm, swirling, screaming, before it went entirely blank.

Sunday, 2.42a.m. The cliffs above Castle Lorne.

Harry was astonished to discover that he was still alive. Lavrenti's gun had failed to fire. As Harry clambered unsteadily to his feet the Russian pulled the trigger again, and again, yet there was nothing but the click of a hammer falling on an empty chamber.

Now Shunin was lumbering to his feet, wheezing. "Ah, Lavrenti, you blind fool. You forgot about the two we used at Sheremetyevo." He patted his pocket. "And you never found the extra magazine." He burst into mocking laughter. "Looks like I won after all."

Lavrenti's eyes flooded with confusion and fear. He stepped back, but found he could go no further. He was on the very edge of the cliff. "What are you going to do?" he asked, his voice difficult to make out above the gusting wind.

"You don't imagine we're going to let you walk away from here, do you?" Shunin growled, the fresh magazine was in his hand. "A little hunting accident, I think — don't you, Mr Jones?"

"I can't let you do that, Mr President," Harry replied.

"But I think you cannot stop me. I have complete diplomatic immunity. In any event, I'm not even here, the world thinks I'm a thousand miles away back home." He turned to his son-in-law. "But I am not an unreasonable man. I will do a deal with you, Lavrenti. A fine funeral, I think. Military bands, much wailing and mourning. Laid out, stiff and cold, in the Kremlin.

339

A Russian funeral. No one's going to know you're a stinking Chechen half-breed."

As his father-in-law mocked, Lavrenti fell to the ground his head bowed.

"And I'll take care of Katya's condition. You can trust me on that," Shunin whispered, the words wrapped in menace.

"Papasha, please! Leave her alone, at least . . ."

"Perhaps, Lavrenti. We'll see. Now give me the gun."

Lavrenti sobbed, and his shoulders gave a final heave, weighed down in submission. "Not Katya, Papasha . . ." He held out the gun, the grip towards his father-in-law.

"Mr President, he is on British soil," Harry began to protest.

"Stay out of this, Mr Jones. It's family," Shunin barked, and took a step towards his son-in-law, reaching for the gun.

Yet even as his fingers closed around it, he found his wrist had been seized. Lavrenti's face was up, he was no longer sobbing but smiling, a serene look of triumph glowing in his face. Shunin tried to pull away but he was leaning forward, off balance, out of breath. And now both Lavrenti's hands were on him.

Lavrenti heaved, with all his might, backwards. Shunin had no means of resisting. The younger Russian tumbled off the cliff. And Shunin followed.

Lavrenti didn't let go of his father-in-law's wrist until they were falling. He was content to die with him, but had no desire to die beside him. Shunin was still

340

spluttering in disbelief, even as Lavrenti gave one final, glorious roar of triumph.

There were other lights, apart from the glow of the dying fire, by the time Harry found his way back. The road beyond the causeway was teeming with flashing lights and the commotion of officialdom. The fire had been spotted from the distant Isle of Mull and the emergency services called, but it had proved entirely too late. There was nothing to be done but let the fire burn itself out. There would be questions, of course, but already D'Arby was on the police radio, fixing things.

"Chief Constable, I want to make one point absolutely clear, this situation is to be treated as a tragic fire, nothing more. I appreciate this is a tricky situation for you, but you have any number of anti-terrorist powers to use in order to keep the lid on it. I'll happily explain the circumstances face to face when you come to London — in the very near future, I'm sure. Aren't you due an investiture or some such thing? In the meantime, this is a matter of national security and I will personally rip the balls off anyone who allows this to leak."

D'Arby broke off as he saw Harry. "Where are they?" he asked in alarm, searching around, seeing more than he wanted in Harry's face.

"At the foot of the cliff."

D'Arby gasped, his body slowly twisting in shock. "How in God's name do we explain that?"

"We don't. The Russians do. Shunin himself suggested it. A hunting accident."

"You can't seriously —"

"Either that or they'll have to admit to having their president murdered by a Chechen rebel who also happened to be his son-in-law." Harry shook his head. "Too messy. They'll go for the hunting accident."

D'Arby's mind was spinning. So many loose ends . . . He turned once more to the radio. "Yes, as I was saying, in the very near future, Chief Constable."

Harry wandered away, leaving him to his grubby work, feeling numb. He thought he'd better find someone to look at his arm; soon it would start hurting like hell again. Check on the others first, though. He found Blythe wrapped in a thermal blanket. Nobody seemed to have recognized her, not with rattails of hair wriggling down her normally immaculate face.

"You all right?" she asked.

"I'm badly hurt."

"How?" she asked in alarm.

"You called me an idiot back in there."

She smiled, relieved. "And you are." But her smile faded as quickly as it had appeared. "Poor Marcus," she whispered.

Harry nodded. "You know, I think I could have got to like him, after all."

Yet already she was being distracted as, behind his shoulder, another figure appeared through the confusion of the night. It was Warren Holt. She gasped in surprise. "What are you doing here?"

"I tried to phone. It doesn't work."

"I know."

"Are you OK?" he asked.

"Sure, but . . . I told you only to contact me in case of war."

"Or something similar." He looked uncomprehendingly at Harry, failing to recognise him. It was scarcely surprising, Harry looked like an extra from a cheap horror movie. "Can we go somewhere a little more private, Madam President?"

"Come on, Warren, this is Harry Jones, you don't need to worry about him. We have remarkably few secrets."

"Well . . ." He hesitated, but only for a second. The entire world was going to hear about it soon enough. "It's war of a kind, Madam President. In China."

"What?"

"It seems Mao was planning to take a pop at other countries behind the backs of most of his Politburo and the army. The details are still pretty vague, but it seems Mao was about to launch some sort of cyber attack, very big and hugely controversial. The PLA got wind of it and acted first. Came together with his political opponents inside the Politburo and — well, it seems they walked into Mao's office and kind of kicked him out."

"Got rid of him?" She demanded, her voice rising in excitement. She grabbed Holt's arms, as though trying to shake the answer out of him. "Are you telling me he's gone?"

"Permanently, it seems. They must have been terrified by what he was planning."

"They weren't the only ones!" she cried.

"But what about those who've taken over?" Harry demanded. "What have they said?"

"Very little," Holt replied. "You know the Chinese, all smoke and mirrors. But their Foreign Ministry has called in some of the ambassadors — the British as well as our own — and offered what amounts to a quiet apology and a reassurance that whatever toys Mao was throwing around would all be put back in the box."

"Details?" Blythe demanded.

"Not clear yet, but you're needed back at post, Madam President." He hesitated, then took a step forward. "Jesus H. Christ, I saw the flames from ten damned miles away. You scared the hell out of me, I can't tell you how worried I was — and how wonderful it is to see you." His rebuke faded into overwhelming relief.

"Thanks, Warren. For everything you've done."

"And one other thing while we're at it."

"Yes?"

"I just hate being President."

"You know, sometimes so do I."

And Harry saw a look come over her face, an expression that said she was back in business.

"I don't suppose you have a raincoat in the back of your car, do you, Warren?" she asked. "I'm feeling very slightly underdressed."

He scurried off. The sky was beginning to lighten. It was a new day.

"If I leave now, I can make it back to Balmoral for breakfast," she said.

"As if none of this had happened," Harry added.

"I guess so." She turned to him, wanted to draw close, but presidents had to be tougher than that. "Looks like we got out of this one, Harry."

"For the moment, at least. Mao may have gone, but those toys of his, they're still scattered around the playroom, waiting for someone else to pick them up."

"Seems like I've got a lot of things to sort out in Washington, Harry." She paused, her presidential mask slipping. "Will you promise to come and see me?"

"I may have to go to Manhattan first."

"Someone there?"

"Perhaps."

"That's good to hear." She leaned forward, kissed him. "Good luck, Harry Jones."

Then she was gone, whisked away in Warren Holt's raincoat.

The sky was lifting rapidly, and along with the night had faded so many of its fears, yet still there was Castle Lorne, or what was left of it, a blackened, ugly reminder. Harry saw Nipper and his grandmother in wheelchairs about to be loaded into the back of an ambulance. He hobbled over.

"Are you all right?" He demanded, alarmed.

"In rather better shape than you, Mr Jones, it would seem," Flora replied earnestly. "They're just taking us to the hospital for a few wee checks. Cuts, bruises, but no more than that. You, on the other hand . . ."

"Did you really get shot, Harry?" Nipper demanded with guileless enthusiasm.

"Seems like it."

345

"Now, Nipper," Flora scolded, "you'll be remembering your manners."

The boy's brow clouded. "Yes, of course." He gulped. "Thank you very much for saving me, Harry." Very stiffly, he stretched out his hand.

Harry took it, and squatted down beside him. Nipper wouldn't let him go.

"And I'm so sorry about Mr Washington."

"Wasn't your fault, Nipper. You didn't set the fire."

"Mr Jones," Flora whispered, her voice tight with emotion, "there's something I wish to say about that, if you'll allow me."

"What can I say, Mrs MacDougall? I apologize from the bottom of my heart. I'm afraid we've brought you nothing but pain."

But the old lady was shaking her head. "You don't understand. These are tears of relief. Tears of great celebration, Mr Jones — and thanks to you, for bringing my bairn back. Nothing else on this earth matters as much."

She reached out and took his free hand, squeezing it. A pillar of fire scorched a path up his arm, but from somewhere he managed to find a smile. With his good hand he scrabbled behind his back. It was still there, the dirk, tucked into his belt, the only thing to have survived the fire. He handed it back. "We flew, didn't we, Nipper? Just like the Lady of Lorne. They said it was a myth, but you and me, we know better."

"We sure do!" Nipper exclaimed, his eyes brimming with excitement.

346

"Next time, though, let's try a different approach. Why don't we use a plane, eh?"

As they laughed and Flora continued to weep her tears of gratitude, D'Arby appeared from out of the fading night, at last separated from his radiophone. "I'm so very glad to see you smiling, young man," he said tousling Nipper's hair in a too-familiar fashion.

The boy nodded silently, and Harry thought he noted flecks of grey resentment creep into his grandmother's eyes. Perhaps D'Arby saw them, too, for he turned, awkwardly.

"What can I say to you, Flora? We'll find some way of overcoming this tragedy. We'll rebuild Castle Lorne for you — I don't know how we'll do it, but I'll find a way, some departmental budget, one mechanism or another that will get us there, and if we can't do that we'll raise the money privately. That's my promise. The country owes you a debt of honour."

"Thank you, Mr D'Arby. But it were better you had never come."

Strange, Harry thought, how the Prime Minister was able to start a war on the other side of the world yet was apparently reduced to scratching around to find some means of doing what was right on his home turf. And his words fell well short of the apology that was due to Flora, as if the chaos had been entirely someone else's responsibility.

The two men stayed until the ambulance had drawn away, leaving them alone. Firemen were damping down the ruins, but from a safe distance; the walls were cracked and clearly unstable. At some point soon, the castle would be razed, for safety's sake, and who would have the strength and patience to rebuild it, despite all of D'Arby's assurances? Castle Lorne wasn't just walls, it was an expression of a family's place in the world, and that world had changed. By tomorrow some official would have arrived with a notebook and a set of building regs that would ensure Castle Lorne could never recapture its ancient grandeur. Better it be left to its ghosts.

D'Arby interrupted his thoughts. "If you're up to it, Harry, it's time for us to go. You need some help with that arm of yours but, if you could tolerate the inconvenience, we'd be best putting some distance between us and this place. Before journalists start scratching around and asking their damn-fool questions. I've got a helicopter coming. We'll be back at Chequers in a couple of hours. Tell you what, I'll treat you to lunch."

"I guess I'll live," Harry muttered in reply. It was more than three other men had managed in the past few hours.

Sunday, shortly after first light.
Elsewhere in the World.

They had hoped to finish the task while it was dark, but it wasn't to be. Dawn had already broken by the time the USS *Reuben James* slid from her bed of sand, backwards, hauled out by an ugly, sea-churning tug. She made her way the couple of miles to international

348

waters under her own steam, guarded from the air by any number of US warplanes, and escorted until the very end by dancing Iranian gunboats with their flags fluttering in triumph. It all made excellent news footage, and was soon being shown around the world, much to the Americans' despair.

Yet eventually the frigate made it to safe seas and her crew could breathe a sigh of relief. As could everyone else. There wasn't going to be a war in the Middle East, not today, at least.

It was about the same time, after a night spent balancing on the edge of fear, that the engineers at Sizewell began to see the temperature in the reactor core slowly dropping, although it would be another four days before they could be certain there had been no breach of the reactor vessel and that radiation wasn't seeping into the outside world. There wasn't much judgement involved in this, only luck. A huge amount of it, as it turned out.

And in another time zone seven hours away, Sir Wesley Lake sat down inside the British embassy for a very private lunch with Sammi Shah. Just the two of them. No rules but plenty of beer. They had a lot to talk about. And they were both determined to get just a little bit drunk.

EPILOGUE

Sunday, 8.35a.m., Chequers, Buckinghamshire.

The helicopter trip seemed interminable. Several times Harry found himself on the point of collapsing into sleep, only for the helicopter to give a fresh twitch or judder, with every jolt turning his arm to molten steel. At last the red-tile roofs of the Chequers estate came into view beneath them, set amidst the thousands of acres of sweeping Buckinghamshire parkland. They circled, preparing to land on the expanse of lawn at the end of Victory Drive, only to hit yet another air pocket. The helicopter pitched, sending Harry's stomach reeling and finally ripping his arm from his body. At least, that's how it felt. He fell as much as climbed from the craft, grey and exhausted.

"Need to get you patched up, my friend," the Prime Minister said, taking him by his good arm, offering support as they walked towards the house. "Borrow some of my clothes — a little large around the waist, but they'll do. And I've got a police doctor waiting to take a look at you. He won't ask questions. By tomorrow, this whole thing will be as though it had never happened."

"Sergei Shunin might disagree, Konev and Marcus Washington, too."

350

"Well, they're not in much of a position to cause a fuss, are they?"

They walked through the Rose Garden once more, greeted by a full refreshing sun, towards the house. A steward was holding a door open for them, but Harry lingered. "Let me sit a while out here," he said, "say hello to the world." He fell onto a garden bench. The smell of roses was irresistible, bringing colour and refreshment even with his eyes closed.

"I'll get the medic to patch you up. Afterwards it's breakfast and a bath for you," D'Arby said. "I'll go and make the arrangements."

But Harry stretched out a hand, holding him back. "Why me, Mark? Why did you have to drag me along?"

The Prime Minister turned, then slowly seated himself on the bench. He placed his hand upon Harry's. "As I told you, there was no one else I could trust. And I was right. You've been magnificent, Harry."

"You used me." The eyes were still closed, the voice drained.

"Of course. That's my job, to bring the finest people around me and to make the most of their talents. I'm proud — and grateful — for what you've done." D'Arby's tone was bullish, but his expression was tinged with concern as he examined Harry.

"You wanted my backing, if things got messy," Harry continued, his voice a monotone.

"True enough. I've always been grateful for your support, Harry, you know that."

"And I guess you thought perhaps I might provide some measure of physical security."

"I wasn't far wrong there, either!" Yet despite his jocular tone, D'Arby found that his hand on top of Harry's no longer felt appropriate. Hesitantly, he withdrew it. Harry's eyes opened. They stared, red and rimmed with reproach.

"But most of all you wanted me to work on Blythe. You suspected she'd be reluctant, wary. You needed me to win her over."

There was no doubting it was an accusation. D'Arby's tone became more cautious. "Yes, the American point of view was always going to be crucial. And I'd have been a fool to ignore your persuasive powers in that quarter. In no sense did I wish to embarrass you —"

But Harry cut through him. "You played me for a fool."

"I played you for a giant!" the Prime Minister answered firmly. "Harry, you're the best in the business. Why else did I ask you to join the government? You said it wasn't the right time — well, I think that time has come. Damn it, you've shown how indispensable you are, and you're in a position to ask for any post you want. You can go all the way, Harry, you know that, right to the very top. If you want my job — well, when the time comes, I'll back you every step along the road."

D'Arby made it sound like an act of generosity, but Harry knew he was proposing a deal. He pulled himself up on the seat so that he could turn to face the Prime Minister. "That's very flattering, Mark, but I don't think that's going to be possible."

352

"And why is that?"

"Too soon for me, even if I wanted it."

"Too soon for what?"

"To throw my hat into the ring. When you resign."

"When I *retire*." He clearly preferred the word. "I hope that'll be some time off, Harry. Lots still to do, particularly now, building bridges with the new China and a new Russian president. Christ, we've had a tough weekend, but think of the good that can flow from it." He leaned forward, came closer, wanting to re-establish their intimacy. "Harry, I know up in Scotland we had our misunderstandings, a few short words, in the heat of the battle, but from my point of view the last couple of days have done nothing but increase my already great regard for you. I hope you'll forgive any cross words I might have uttered. I didn't mean them, you know that."

"Sticks and stones, Mark," Harry uttered wearily.

The Prime Minister grew animated, clenching his fists in passion. "We're on the brink of a new world, Harry. And Britain's a player once again. Perhaps it's too much to hope that we'll all be cosy friends, but it'll be a world in which we understand each other very much more closely. That's a better world, a safer world, Harry. And much of that is down to you."

It was what Mark D'Arby had always been so good at, subtle flattery, finding balm for open wounds.

"But this weekend's been mostly down to you, Mark."

"Kind of you to say so," D'Arby smiled.

"No, you don't understand. It was an accusation."

The smile withered. "I beg your pardon?"

"You planned the entire weekend, right down to the breakfast menu. And, God, you played your role magnificently. You exasperated them, stirred them up, pushed them on, all the time. They came for a weekend and almost ended up in a war."

"You know why that was, Harry. Britain's neck was on the line and they wouldn't have lifted a finger to save us. I had to give them ownership, make them feel it was their operation, otherwise they would never have agreed."

"You deceived them."

"All diplomacy requires deception, Harry. Surely you understand that."

"But you could never be certain they'd swallow it all, could you? That's why you had to go the extra mile."

"Cutting off the phones, you mean?"

"It got me thinking, that's all."

"About?"

"What else you might have arranged to make sure you got what you wanted."

A silence hung between them, growing heavier with every breath. A butterfly perched on the back of the bench, wanting to spread its wings in the sun, but quickly flew off again.

"As you said, America — *Blythe* — was crucial," Harry continued.

"Which is why I needed you."

"And why you needed the *Reuben James*."

"What?"

"I kept wondering about your addiction to the news, turning it on, almost as if you were expecting something. And what you got was the *Reuben James*. One hell of a lucky coincidence. Couldn't have gone better if you'd planned it."

"Are you suggesting —"

"What, that you had a word with someone down at GCHQ, whoever's in charge of our own cyber-war capability? Fed them this national-security crap about how you and he had to save the country from damnation — the sort of stuff you gave me? Yes, that's what I think happened. And he did what you asked, gave you another little party piece to add to your drama. Enough to drive Blythe over the top."

"That is total bollocks!"

"Is it? You see, we share so many of our guidance systems with our American allies. We're in a much better position to take a crack at the 5th Fleet's navigational gear than the Chinese."

The Prime Minister sat silent, stunned.

"And you see, Mark, the Chinese didn't fit the picture for me. They're bending over backwards to *avoid* military confrontation, that's why they've chosen the cyber route. Taking on the 5th Fleet would be the last thing I'd consider, if I were them."

"Clearly they lack your exceptionally vivid imagination."

"You're probably right. The Chinese like to stick to form, to a pattern of behaviour — like attacking our utilities, our transport system, our money, our machinery of state." Harry paused, sighed. "And also, we're supposed to believe, one little old lady tucked up in a hospital bed in Massachusetts. But that's the other bit I couldn't swallow."

"What the hell are you implying?" D'Arby was shaking with anger.

Harry chewed on his lip; it had a wound on the inside, swollen and sore, tasting salty, of blood, something he hadn't noticed before. "I don't think the death of Blythe's mother was down to the Chinese at all. I think it was you."

D'Arby stared in astonishment. Harry stared back, searching for the flicker of guilt.

"I think that was another bit of theatre, Mark," he said, "specifically designed to bring Blythe alongside. Yes, those were the words you used — and that phrase of yours. *Whatever it takes.*"

"Good God, you've gone quite mad. How on earth could I persuade anyone to do something like that?"

"You persuaded the most powerful politicians in the world to go to war, Mark. You're a very persuasive man."

D'Arby stiffened, his whole body seemed to tighten in anger. His voice came as though it were the first breath of winter. "You start making allegations like that, Harry my boy, and they'll need an excavator to find what's left of you. I'll pile so many writs and security notices on you that by the time they get to you there'll be nothing left but a shadow."

"Do I take that as a threat?"

"Yes, please."

Harry sucked at his tattered lip once more. "Only one way to stop me, Mark, you know that. And I don't think you've got the balls to kill me, not face to face. I suppose one anonymous little old lady on the far side of the world may barely tickle your conscience, but I don't think you've got it in you to do your own dirty work."

D'Arby stared, speechless for the moment, twisting in turmoil.

"You're no killer, Mark, just a politician in a hurry. Too much of a hurry."

D'Arby gasped, as though he had been slapped. "No one has to know about this, Harry. No one need be any the wiser."

"That's precisely what I'm proposing should happen. When you resign."

"For pity's sake, you know sacrifices sometimes have to be made. It gets tough out there. You get your hands dirty." He was waving an arm, punching the air, his voice rising in indignation. "I was working to save my country this weekend, so don't come snivelling to me about spilt milk."

"Blythe's mother," Harry said softly, "was a little more than spilt milk."

"She was an elderly lady who was going to die soon anyway. Don't you realize that? She was on her way out!"

"And you decided to play God."

"No, I decided to be a leader! Doing what was necessary for my country, even if it was a little messy." His emotion had propelled him to his feet; he was standing over Harry now, looking down on him, contemptuous. "And I thought you'd understand, you of all people. I know enough about you, Harry, to know that you've got blood not just under your fingernails but most of the way up to your armpits. Got yourself a reputation for always cutting corners, you have. So don't you dare go judging me, Harry Jones. Climb down from your pulpit before they drag you out and stone you as a stinking hypocrite."

"Using a hospital ward as a battlefield?" Harry shook his head.

"Everywhere's a battlefield nowadays." D'Arby cast his arms wide, as though appealing to some vast but invisible audience. "War isn't fought with rulebooks any more, the bombers, the terrorists, the Chinese, the Islamists — they're not gentlemen. They don't stop and invite you to tea before they blow your fucking brains out. It's not a world I like, Harry, but it's the one I'm forced to live in and it's the only one we've got."

"Mark, even when you're in the gutter you have the option of looking up at the stars."

"Until someone slits your throat!"

"Or screws around with your insulin pump."

In the distance a steward approached with a tray of tea but D'Arby waved her angrily away. He was breathing heavily with the desperation of his argument, forced to struggle in order to control himself. He knew it was no good trying to bully Harry into submission, he had to find another route.

"What is it you want, Harry? Tell me, for God's sake. You can have anything — *anything*."

358

Harry took his time before replying. "I want you out, Mark. Resigned, retired hurt, rained on, ruined — however you want to put it. But I want it now. Right this minute."

The Prime Minister spun round, turning his back on Harry, struggling to protect himself from the other man's words, trying to hide the alarm that was gouging at his face. "Why, Harry? Pity's sake, why?"

"Because you involved me, and I don't go round making war on innocent old ladies."

A knee buckled and the Prime Minister fell back onto the bench. "Give me a chance, Harry. Please."

"But I am. I'm giving you the chance to walk away with your head high and your reputation intact, rather than being dragged out and thrown to the pack of drooling dogs that's waiting right outside your door."

"Jump or be pushed? What sort of choice is that?"

"About as good as I had last night at the top of the castle."

"Harry, there must be some other way . . ." Yet suddenly D'Arby knew it was useless. His life was over, destroyed by one small mistake and this man he thought was a friend. His face twisted to contempt, and the words were spat out with such force that they sprayed into Harry's face. "You stinking hypocrite! You sit there with your pathetic conscience, moralizing over me, when your entire piss-miserable life should be plagued by ghosts!"

Harry wiped his face, yet he found it more difficult to get rid of the Prime Minister's accusation. There was too much truth in what D'Arby had said. Harry had spent these last few years running from bed to bed, from alibi to excuse, always moving on, never looking back, afraid that his conscience might catch up with him, that if ever he stood still and spent too many nights on his own he might end up with no one apart from Michael Burnside and the others. That's what he'd been afraid of. Yet Burnside had been different from Blythe's dear old mother. He'd deserved it. A court might not come to that conclusion, but justice wasn't only blind, it sometimes lost its sense of smell and couldn't tell a rose from a rotten fish.

It was when he saw the cloud of doubt passing across Harry's face that D'Arby decided it was worth one last try. "Do you believe in redemption, Harry?"

Harry looked up. He could sense another impassioned plea coming on, but he was past playing D'Arby's games. He'd been doing that all weekend and it had got him shot and half burned and nearly killed when he should have been in the arms of a beautiful woman from Manhattan. He'd had enough.

"Do I believe in redemption? I hope so, for my own sake. But I find it easier to believe in things like . . ." He sighed, bone-weary. "Oh, I dunno. Breakfast in bed. It's a much more straightforward concept."

"You bastard," D'Arby hissed, realizing the other man wasn't going to play any more.

"We dig our own graves, Mark, I think that's what you said."

"And I'll spend the rest of my days making sure they bury you in yours."

360

This wasn't getting anywhere. "Go to hell, Mark. Just write your letter first."

Harry was exhausted. He clutched his arm and closed his eyes, his wearied mind stumbling through the thickets of what had happened, and what might have been. Eventually it collided with images of Gabbi. It kept doing that, he realized. He wanted to be with her, and not here, to haul his conscience along with him and see if the three of them could spend time together. In the background he could hear D'Arby's footsteps dragging across the flagstones like an army in retreat. Harry wondered what the time was, whether he could get his arm fixed and clean himself up, give her a call, find a lift back to London. Sleep for a week, preferably in her bed. See how much he might grow to like it. That would have its risks, of course, but for the moment it seemed a marginally less dangerous proposition than many of the others he'd run into during the last couple of days. The sun was trying to prise his lids apart. He opened them, glanced around, searching. Damn, what had he done with his mobile phone?